-One-

In 1902, in the provinces of a quiet and long-forgotten corner of the world called Lithuania, the brief summer was fading. A gentle rain had fallen all night and when it stopped in the early morning, Ada Varnas peered out the window at the gossamer mist covering the fields like a bridal veil.

Lithuania had once been the largest country in Europe, stretching from the Baltic Sea to the Black Sea. With time it had shrunken and disappeared into the Russian Empire in 1795, its name deleted from the world maps, now called the Northwest Provinces. By 1902, though the first steps into the twentieth century had been taken, it was still the age of failing empires and the small countries devoured by them.

At twenty-three, Ada was shy, willowy and as yet not burdened by the tragedies of history. Nevertheless, she had her own worries, as all young girls have about love and marriage, but on this particular Monday, her vague uneasiness about her future was about to become more urgent.

Near the Baltic Sea was Sapnai, a village named after dreams, though few remembered why. In this timeworn village, there were eighteen small farms, each with its own story.

In the misty morning, Ada had barely finished her chores when she found her mother, Elzbieta, a rotund, red-cheeked woman, leaning on the fence, looking furious. Calling Ada over, her mother whispered that she overheard Ona, the village busybody, telling her daughter, Petrike, that Ada was becoming a spinster.

"Me, an old maid?" Ada was simply stunned at such a pronouncement.

Her mother took a deep breath to calm herself. The fog swirled and moved to make way for them as they walked over to the neighbor's wattle fence. Petrike and her mother sat on a bench under a crooked tree peeling apples into a large bowl. "Good morning," Elzbieta called to her neighbor, using all the control she could muster. "Did I hear correctly that you've been calling my Ada a spinster?"

Ona's head jerked up, shocked that her words had reached Elzbieta, whose own tongue was known to do enormous damage if she had a mind to do so. Dropping her apples into the bowl, Ona's hands flew to her burning cheeks. "Oh Elzyte," she said, hoping the diminutive form of her name would placate her neighbor. "I was only repeating what others had said."

"Ada's hardly a spinster," Elzbieta trilled loudly despite her attempts at self-control. "And besides," she said accusingly, "your daughter is the same age as my Ada. Doesn't it make her a spinster as well?" She planted both hands firmly on her ample hips.

To Elzbieta's surprise, Ona nodded, and a smile spread on her thin face as she got up from the bench, her clogs slapping her heels as she came to join the women at the fence. "Well, you'd be right if it wasn't for something that happened yesterday."

Petrike, her long face dotted with three moles on her cheek, came over to join them, her head held high as if she were the tsarina herself. "You must have stayed in town longer yesterday. The matchmaker's cart came down the road, the bells jingling merrily on his horse, announcing his arrival in Sapnai."

She smiled so widely, her large ears seemed to bend backward.

"Really?" Ada was intrigued. "Where did he stop?"

Petrike laughed, unable to contain her joy. "Why here, of course."

Ada's face dropped. "Here?"

"Yes," Ona said proudly. "My girl will be married after the potato harvest. Isn't it wonderful news?" She lifted her apron to wipe a tear. "How I've waited for this day."

Ada had a sinking feeling. She hadn't worried about marriage so long as Petrike, whom everyone regarded as unmarriageable, was still single. But now even Petrike had found a husband. Ada took a brave breath and hugged her across the fence. "Congratulations," she said, trying to sound happy. "And who is the proud husband?"

No one said anything for a long moment as mother and daughter exchanged uncomfortable looks. Finally, Ona mumbled quickly, "It's Gadeikis."

"Gadeikis?" Elzbieta sputtered, picturing the old widower who lived in the last farm in the village, a small place that needed a woman's hand. Gadeikis was twice Petrike's age. Elzbieta stood there blinking. She seemed to have lost her tongue entirely. Finally, when the silence became uncomfortable, she managed to say, "Well then, I wish you the best."

"Thank you," said Petrike, still smiling, but now there was something a bit cold in her eyes when she addressed Ada. "All those years I watched the matchmaker's cart come to your house, I felt so envious of your suitors. Yet, I never imagined I'd be the first to marry and leave you and Elena the last old maids in the village. Life is sometimes surprising, isn't it, Ada?" Petrike's eyebrow lifted imperiously.

Ada tried to swallow, but the lump in her throat wouldn't go down. She nodded, forcing a smile, but was unconvincing. In truth, she felt a sense of doom settle over her. It was true, the matchmaker's cart hadn't come to her house in years. Maybe she was no longer desirable as a wife, and only old men like Gadeikis would consider her for marriage. What kind of life would that be? Suddenly, she felt sorry for Petrike. After all of their girlish dreams of the man they wanted to marry—tall, handsome, smart, with a good tenor voice, to settle for an old widower. Yet life didn't always give you what you wanted. That much she had sorely learned.

But how awful to be left behind, like a lame horse. Her friends were getting married, some with babies already, while she still mourned Henrikas. But now, it seems, she'd turned into an old maid, almost overnight, as though some wicked fairy had put a spell on her.

"Come, Ada," her mother said gruffly, throwing one last glance at Petrike as she muttered her way back home. "Ada, I know you loved Henrikas dearly and have been in mourning, but even so, I never worried about your wedding because everyone said you were the prettiest girl in the village." Elzbieta sighed, remembering the good days, now apparently gone. "But Ada," she continued, clucking her tongue, "I think you'd better find a husband before it's too late."

Ada's sister Dora, already twenty, was waiting to marry her Jurgis, but custom dictated that the eldest daughter marry before the younger daughters could wed. Everyone in the family felt for Ada as the anniversary of her beloved's death approached, but Dora's patience was coming to an end. "Ada, it's been four years since he died." There was a barely hidden frustration in her voice.

"But, Dora…" Ada didn't know what to say. She felt attacked from all sides.

Her sister cut her off. "My Jurgis can't wait forever." Dora resembled their mother, with her wide face and thick waist. But Dora was normally sweet-natured like her father.

"And what about Julija?" Elzbieta shook her finger. "She's already seventeen. Soon all of my daughters will be old maids."

At the mention of her name, Julija, a wisp of a girl, came to see what they were arguing about. The baby of the family, she had dark braids and her head in the clouds dreaming of knights and ladies.

"What about Petras?" asked Ada with rising anger. "He's already twenty-two and no one urges him to marry?"

"You know it's different for a man," her mother admonished her. "I'm going to ask the matchmaker to find you a match." Her mother crossed her arms. "Honestly, Ada, some days you remind me of my sister, Kotryna. Another stubborn old maid."

It dawned on Ada that she had crossed the river, so to speak, from young womanhood into the dreaded old maid's territory, where women like the priest's housekeeper went to live and work in the rectory because they had no husband to keep them. Or they lived with their brother's family, fated never to have one of their own.

Ada sighed. Suddenly everything around her looked different, even her beloved home. She saw it all through new eyes—a spinster's home. Her family's cottage was set back from the road with the last of the season's marigolds still blooming behind the fence. Beyond the green shutters, three birch trees stood by the front gate. Above the covered porch, carved fretwork decorated the gables. There was the kitchen garden behind the cottage and an orchard with beehives. Beyond, lay their fields.

This was her grandfather's land, where he had been born in a two-room house with a tamped dirt floor. His own father, a serf, had been given a small parcel of land when the serfs were emancipated in 1861 and had worked hard growing rye, wheat, oats, and potatoes. By the time Ada's grandfather married and had his daughters, he had increased the land to thirty hectares and enlarged his cottage.

Inside, the rooms were clean and neat, with a wooden clock by the door. Three red geraniums bloomed in pots on the windowsill behind the lace curtains. The house had a kitchen, pantry, parlor,

11

and a room for her grandfather behind the kitchen stove, where it was warmer.

The granary in the farmyard also served as sleeping quarters for the girls and the hired help in good weather. In the winter, the hired help returned home and the girls slept in the kitchen for warmth.

Ada went to the orchard to look for her grandfather, Viktoras Kulys, seventy-four, stout and hearty, with a full head of silver hair. He was carefully tending to his bees, often talking to them while they slowly droned around his head. He lifted the top of the first hive, sending bees flying.

Seeing Ada looking upset, he went to join her at his favorite bench. When a bee landed softly on her finger, Ada flinched and her grandfather warned, "Never harm a bee or a worm. We need them more than they need us. Go back home, little one," he said to the bee, offering his calloused finger. He watched the bee walk to the end of his finger and fly away, back to the hive.

"What is it, my girl?" he asked. "You look as if you've lost everything." He rubbed the gray mustache that covered his thin lips like a roof.

"Grandfather, it seems I've become an old maid." Her chin quivered.

"You, an old maid?" He lit his curved pipe and let out a giant puff of smoke. "Don't be ridiculous," he said, dismissing the notion. "Why do you bother to listen to foolish gossip?"

When Ada told him about Petrike, he scratched his ear, puffed his pipe, and let the aromatic smoke curl around his head. He gave her his best advice, distilled from long years on earth. "Life is unpredictable, Ada, and will bring you what's yours no matter what any of us want for you."

"Mama's threatening to get the matchmaker to find any man in the district who is still single, even if he's the last herring in the barrel. But you can't just pull a husband out of a sleeve like a handkerchief. There has to be some attraction, if not love."

Seeing her sadness, Viktoras tried to reassure her, reminding her she hadn't yet let go of her first love, Henrikas. "Perhaps the time has come."

At the mention of his name, Ada felt a painful stab and had to look away for a few moments. But when she looked back at her grandfather, she realized that one day she hoped to find a husband just like him—strong, intelligent, courageous, and full of love for his family. She had been spoiled by two good men, her even-tempered father and her wise grandfather. They had been her measure of a man.

"My poor Ada," he said, taking her cold hand in his warm one. "This is all my fault. I blame myself entirely. I've abused your good nature by letting you help me with the book smuggling. If I hadn't kept you busy, you might have found a husband by now. You had so little time to dance and flirt because you've been so busy teaching and helping me."

"But I needed something after Henrikas died. I wanted to be useful and I've grown to love the work," she said fervently. "Every bit of it, but especially the teaching. I'm proud of what we've done together."

"Yes, it's important work," he nodded. "Holy work to keep a culture from dying. But Ada, I hereby relieve you of all your duties as a book smuggler, clandestine teacher, and book distributor." He smiled. "You hereby have a new job—to find a proper husband and get married so I can see great grandchildren."

His dog, Margis, came over and Viktoras petted his head. "Ada, don't worry. There are still many good men in the world, and you, of all girls, will find the right one." He put his pipe back in his mouth and puffed away. "I have to admit I hadn't noticed how quickly my favorite granddaughter has grown into a woman. Of course, I knew that I'd lose you once you married and went to your husband's farm, yet I hadn't realized how quickly that time had come." He cleared his throat as if to expel his sadness.

"But before you stop your book smuggling, I have one last favor to ask of you. There is one final job for Father Jurkus tomorrow and then you will be free to scour the countryside for an eligible man to marry." He chuckled into his fist, his eyes full of mischief. "The priest has gotten some new books and journals. Some are for his secret school, but others must be brought here to distribute. If you can use that special skirt you made to hide them and bring them home, I would be very grateful. This will be your last bit of book smuggling. I promise." Her grandfather nodded. "And thank you sincerely, my dear, for all your years of helping me." He squeezed her hand.

"It's been a privilege to do it alongside you," Ada replied earnestly.

"Thank you, my dear," he said with a catch in his throat. "Now, go run to the woods before your mother finds work for you. Run and take some time to read poetry," he said, handing her a small book.

Ada headed for the woods. Crossing the meadow, past the pale birch trees lining the road like sentinels, a mist swirled around her all the way to her favorite clearing. The fog made the woods seem filled with spirits rather than trees. Everything was misted and blurred. She sat down, her back against an old pine and began to read the book her grandfather had given her, *The Forest of Anyksciai* by Baranauskas, a bishop and poet who described the beauty of the pine grove before the Russian Empire had destroyed it by logging.

Lithuania was like that pine grove destroyed by the Russian Empire. The melancholy poem suited Ada's mood. It seemed to her that all the sadnesses had melded today: the sadness of one country oppressed by another, the sadness that those you love will die, and the sadness of becoming an old maid. And the sadness that always threatened tears was Henrikas's death. No one could have predicted such an end for such a strong and handsome young man, one who loved her. And then one day like any other, he drowned

14

while swimming. That was all it took to carry Henrikas out of the world. Ada sighed deeply, the tears rising. All the sadnesses pressed down on her today.

She spoke softly, "I feel like I've been holding my breath since you died, as if that would keep you with me." Tears rolled down her cheeks. Now that she had been declared a spinster, suddenly all her longing for love flooded over her. Picking a fluffy white dandelion globe, she whispered, "Good bye, my love," and blew the fluff away, watching as a chill wind picked it up.

Standing, she suddenly felt cold and pulled her jacket close as she headed back home, feeling troubled that it might indeed be too late for her, that her life may no longer hold any promise for love.

-Two-

The day was cool and windy. Ada wore her jacket, her special wool skirt with the hidden inside pockets, and several skirts over that one to better hide the books. She started for the church with Dora, who wanted to go along to buy some ribbons in town.

Leaving the village, Ada could feel eyes upon her. By now the news of her spinsterhood must have spread from house to house. Petrike must have made sure of that. But it seemed like only yesterday they were girls playing and then flirting. Now they were marrying. Perhaps her grandfather was right that she had been too busy helping him with the smuggled books to notice.

There was a chill in the air as the sisters walked along the muddy path, their boots sinking slightly with each step. The vivid colors of summer were fading, the leaves changing colors. Pointing to the stork's nest on Balys's farmhouse, Ada said, "How sad to see the empty nest."

"We won't see the storks again until next spring," said Dora. Nearby, they could hear Kreivenas sawing wood while his wife sang a sad and plaintive song in the kitchen. The woman abruptly stopped singing when she noticed Ada and Dora pass by.

After walking the two kilometers to Raudonava, the nearest town, the girls headed for the square lined with Jewish merchant shops. At one end was a tailor, bakery, two butchers, and a large synagogue and yeshiva. At the other end stood St. George's Church with its churchyard and rectory. Besides the Lithuanians, Raudonava had a considerable Jewish population along with a mixture of Poles, Belarusians, and the ever-present Russian soldiers and magistrates. Ada parted with Dora, telling her she'd meet her at Rosenberg's shop after a visit with the priest.

When the yellow Baroque church came into view, Ada quickened her step to the rectory that was home to the pastor and Father Jurkus, the latter beloved by all in the neighboring five villages. When she opened the iron gate and stopped at the dark rectory window to look at her reflection, she saw her face looking much the same, with the long blond braids and small eyes. She wondered if others saw something else now, something spinsterish.

When she knocked on the door, Stasia, the thin old maid housekeeper to the priests, opened it. The woman had turned sour with age, her face etched by lines of disappointment at how little life had given her, even though she ruled the rectory like a duchess. The many times Ada had seen Stasia when she came to teach the students in the basement, she had always felt sorry for the woman. But now she seemed like a living cautionary tale. Following the housekeeper inside, Ada greeted the burly priest in his dusty black cassock. "Good day, Father."

"Ada, my dear. Come in, come in," he urged, ushering her inside his study where a green glass oil lamp sat on a gleaming oak table. He turned to the housekeeper. "Stasia, please bring us some tea." The smell of frankincense lingered on the priest's cassock as he went to get a log for the fire.

"It's chilly today; winter's coming, whether we're ready for it or not." She watched him lighting a fire and wondered how such a man decided to become a priest. Strong and hardy,

Father Jurkus resembled a robust farmer rather than a holy man. He helped her grandfather distribute the forbidden Lithuanian books that were printed in East Prussia and smuggled across the border. In addition, he often pitched in to teach history to the older students in his secret school. Sometimes he would turn up at her home to read the latest smuggled Lithuanian newspaper. She greatly admired the tireless priest.

There was a knock on the door, and the housekeeper came in with a tray. "Will there be anything else?"

"That's all, Stasia," said the priest, pouring the tea. When the fire was going strong, the priest seemed to sense something different in Ada and asked her what was troubling her. She told him about recent events, and how her grandfather had relieved her of all her book smuggling duties. "I think I need to find a husband before I'm forced to marry an old man in desperation."

The priest laughed kindly. "Well, then perhaps this is a bit of luck for us," he said teasing her. "Now you can take your vows to become a nun and teach here for the rest of your life!" He was smiling broadly now.

Ada frowned. "You're joking, aren't you? But I don't think it's funny."

"Oh, so you've taken this bit of gossip to heart, have you?"

She shrugged and looked down at her hands.

"Ada, you simply haven't found the right man yet," the priest offered reassuringly. "But I'm sure God has a plan for you. He wouldn't abandon a selfless girl who has done so much for this parish."

She looked up, smiling a bit. "Thank you, Father. I'll continue to help in the school for the time being."

After their tea, Ada and the priest climbed the bell tower to the belfry, where his smuggled books were hidden. There were prayer books, newspapers, novels and pamphlets. Ada was excited to go through each new book and curious to read them all. Father Jurkus handed her a book written by a woman called Žemaite, saying,

"You might enjoy her book." Ada leafed though the pages.

"Many smugglers brought their books to me to distribute, but your grandfather and his friend, Jeronimas, made the trip to Tilsit four times a year. I have to say, they were two of the best. Sometimes they even gave books away if they saw that the person couldn't afford to pay for them."

He put a pile of books to one side. "These will go to Old Grigas, the teacher at Graf Valinskas's manor. The count paid for our schoolbooks and also for those at his school. He dreams of opening a Lithuanian school one day. Recently, he even offered a stipend to the teachers."

"Really?" Ada was pleased.

"Yes," said the priest. "And these will go home to your grandfather."

Ada was happy, craving the distraction of new books this winter. Father Jurkus left the room, giving her the privacy to place each book, pamphlet, and newspaper into the many pockets she had sewn into the inside of her skirt. She had to make sure to balance the heavy books so she wouldn't list to one side. When finished, she went out into the hall, telling the priest she was leaving. He cautioned her to keep her wits about her and be careful of the "mustaches," as they called the gendarmes. "And send my best regards to your grandfather."

Ada's heavy skirt made walking slow and clumsy. Her grandfather had also told her to carry an apronful of apples to divert attention away from the bulky skirt.

Before leaving, she ducked into the church to say a quick prayer. It was dim and cool, with shafts of sunlight streaming through the stained-glass windows depicting Saint George slaying the dragon. Blessing herself, she prayed for protection in her book smuggling. At the end, she added, "St. George, don't let me die an old maid."

When she opened the creaking door of the church, she blessed herself with holy water and headed toward the other end of the market square, to meet Dora at Rosenberg's shop. The square was quiet today compared to market day or Sunday. There were the usual shoppers buying herring or bagels. A group of boys played with a ball near the butcher's shop, while inside the yeshiva, Ada could hear other boys repeating a lesson in Hebrew.

Slowly walking the cobblestones past the Russian school, Ada saw Captain Pyotr Yurevich Malenkov coming around the corner, barrel-chested in his belted uniform. Seeing her, he stopped in front of Zimmerman's tavern and caught her eye.

"Just a moment," he barked.

Ada hesitated, wondering if he was talking to her. Her eyes swept up over his high leather boots, his holstered gun, his belted uniform, all the way up to his curled, waxed mustache. Under his visor cap, his small dark eyes had a slight Asiatic look, definitely not from her Baltic tribe. No, he was Slavic through and through. His black hair, his eyes that bore into her, the eyes of the conqueror. While she was the conquered and therefore must be docile and obedient. Her heart beat faster, but she forced her face into a pleasant mask, hiding her fear, knowing that if he saw it, he would want to know why she was afraid and would take her in for questioning.

"What's your name?" he barked.

"Ada Varnas," she said, speaking slowly to hide her nerves, though her body was humming with tension.

The captain nodded deliberately, studying her as if examining her very soul. She knew enough to look down at the cobblestones, so as not to give her apprehension away. Though she had been helping her grandfather with the smuggled books for the last four years and had sometimes encountered the gendarmes, she had never before been stopped by one of them, so his sudden interest unnerved her completely.

"What have you got there?" he asked in Russian, pointing to her apron.

She froze for a moment, her heart thudding in her chest. Forcing a smile, she faced him, "Apples, sir." A lump of hard fear rose in her throat that she wanted to swallow but dared not. "Would you care for one?" She looked up fleetingly, opening the corners of her crumpled apron, revealing five green apples. She could feel the books weighing her down with their bulk. The penalty for circulating such books was jail or exile to Siberia.

Captain Malenkov refused the apples, but his eyes were still fixed on her. She tried to slow her breathing before bidding him good day, only praying he wouldn't dare ask her to lift her skirts. The books and newspapers made her gait more awkward, but she soldiered on, desperately trying not to be clumsy. One of the books was already beginning to chafe against her knee. There would be bruises.

After she had taken a few steps away, she closed her eyes in relief that he hadn't yet stopped her. She could still feel his eyes on her, so she said a silent prayer, hoping he was thirsty enough to want a drink in the tavern more than he wanted to stop and question her. The wind ruffled her skirts and with the next step, she heard a slight rip. The hair on the back of her neck stood on end as she trudged on, praying a book wouldn't fall on the cobblestones. When she finally reached Rosenberg's shop, it felt like she had just taken the most perilous journey of her life.

Once inside, she let out a tremendous sigh of relief, close to tears. Near the counter, Rosenberg's son Nahum was showing Dora spools of ribbon.

While the population of most towns in Lithuania were fairly Jewish, the rural villages were mainly where Lithuanians lived. The two worlds seldom met except at the market square, each with a different language, making communication difficult, unless they resorted to Russian or Polish in order to be understood. But Nahum had taken the trouble to learn some rudimentary Lithuanian, and his customers appreciated the effort.

Ada stood there a moment to collect herself. The store smelled of soap and the dust from a hundred spools of thread and countless bolts of cloth lined up like religious scrolls. She walked over to her sister. "Come, Dora, get what you came for and let's go," she said, anxious to get out of town.

"What's your hurry?" asked Nahum, giving her an appraising wink and nod. Ada didn't know how to respond to this handsome young Jew flirting with her.

"Dora, please!" Ada's voice rose. "We have to go home."

"Wait. I can't decide," said Dora, irritated by Ada's tone.

"I'm leaving without you," said Ada, heading for the door.

"Oh, all right," said Dora, shaking her head. Turning to Nahum, she smiled, telling him she'd be back soon.

Before Ada went out the door, she looked to make sure the captain wasn't anywhere in sight. She let out the tense breath she had been holding, relieved that he was probably in the tavern. Still stunned that she had escaped such a close call, she headed across the square again, turning every so often to make sure the gendarmes weren't after her.

-Three-

When Captain Malenkov entered the tavern, the keeper greeted him as an important customer. "What are you drinking today, Captain?" asked Jacob Zimmerman, a stout, avuncular Jew wearing a white shirt with a black vest. His bearded face looked oppressed from listening to the endless troubles of his customers. His only solace was to realize their problems were not necessarily his.

"Vodka," barked the captain, looking around to see who was there. The tavern was small, with wooden walls and rustic tables smelling of stale beer and sweat. Two large barrels of beer sat on the bar. The tavern was already filled with regulars, who were drinking, playing cards and telling anecdotes, tobacco smoke curling in circles over the tables. The captain found Modestas Bogdanskis, who descended from a noble but ruined family. The man could never resist a card game. Tall and thin with a curly sparse mustache, Bogdanskis sat at their favorite table, fanning his cards out. Two of the captain's men, Nikolai and Ivan, examined their own cards while talking about women.

"Did you see that pretty girl with dark eyes in the bakery?" asked Nikolai, a squat older man, who smelled of sweat.

"Oh, to get my hands on those wide hips of hers."

"*Chort!* I need a woman," yelled Ivan, a thickset young man, already half drunk.

Nikolai laughed and winked, saying Zimmerman could make the usual arrangements with the "ladies."

"No, I want my Lena!" Ivan pouted.

Nikolai shrugged. "Suit yourself, but she's far away."

"She's sweet like honey," said Ivan, slapping a card down.

"They say a woman is like a bee," said Nikolai, winking. "She has honey, but she also has a sting."

"Kolya," Ivan said thickly, wagging his finger. "Not my angel." He stood unsteadily and raised his fists. "Not another word about my Lena."

Nikolai backed off. "Ivanko, I meant no offense. Relax."

At the bar, Zimmerman was on alert. When Lithuanians got drunk they sang and laughed with their friends, but Russians were quiet drinkers until they got sad and then angry, picking fights to prove their worth once they'd had enough vodka.

"Ah, the eternal topic—women," the captain said, snickering. "Sit down, Ivan, and keep a cool head," he ordered. It was evident Ivan Alexandrovich had too much to drink, staggering a bit until Nikolai settled him back in his chair.

The captain leaned over to ask Bogdanskis to join him outside for a moment. He surprised the tall, haughty young man so that he bent low to peer out one of the small windows to see if there was something unusual there. But he couldn't see anything out of the ordinary, so he followed the captain out the door.

"Do you know that girl there?" the captain asked, pointing to the two girls slowly crossing the square. "The thin one with the blond braids."

"Well, I've never been introduced, but I've heard someone mention she's from Sapnai."

The captain nodded. "I have it on good intelligence there are book smugglers in that village."

"Those girls?" Bogdanskis almost laughed.

"The book smugglers are sly foxes with their books from Prussia, but we'll hunt them like rats." The captain had been pursuing them for years, but they had proved to be wily adversaries. He had jailed smugglers in the district and had sent others to Siberia.

Scanning the square, the captain watched the girls walking slowly. "I want to know what's going on in that village. There's a nest of smugglers near Sapnai and I want to find it, you hear me?" Captain Malenkov didn't mention that the tsar's secret police had threatened to reassign him to a dusty outpost if he didn't root out the book smugglers in the district.

"But why are you telling me?" asked Bogdanskis in a bored, indolent voice, shrugging his shoulders.

"Because I think you could be of help to me." The captain gave him a direct look.

"Me? I don't get involved in that sort of business, Captain," he said with polite condescension. Frowning, he opened his cigarette case and offered one. "*Papirosi?*"

The captain took a cigarette, and Modestas lit it with a match. Blowing the smoke up, the captain smiled and took the silver cigarette case, admiring the workmanship. "Tell me, Bogdanskis, how much money do you owe me by now?" The captain smiled when he saw the rumpled nobleman flinch. The gentry never discussed money. The captain continued undeterred. "What is it... close to nine hundred rubles by now?" His smile widened.

"No, it can't be that much?" Modestas's eyes were suddenly wary.

"I won back a hundred and eighty rubles last week," he whispered, looking around nervously.

"Don't forget, I have your signed notes." The captain wagged his finger, taking evident pleasure in having the upper hand. "Could you honor them, if I was forced to call them in?"

Modestas blanched, shocked that these innocent evenings at cards had come to this. He had no way to repay the captain.

"Here, Captain, take my silver cigarette case in partial payment," he said, handing it to him with trembling fingers.

"Keep your case, Bogdanskis," said the captain with a mocking smile, watching the haughty man squirm. Modestas continued to fidget for a few uncomfortable moments, then throwing his cigarette down, he stamped it underfoot.

Captain Malenkov smiled. "But perhaps we could work something out between us as gentlemen."

"Yes?" Modestas nodded hopefully.

"Listen carefully. I have an offer to make you."

"An offer?" Modestas was sweating.

"Let's make a final wager. But if you lose, I'll get your home, and if you win I'll tear up your notes and give you a hundred rubles, enough to get some decent clothes and take your mother and sister for a visit to the city like the old days, eh?"

"But how?" Modestas was confused.

The captain tilted his head to consider. "I want you to woo that girl we saw, the blond one from Sapnai. Get yourself invited to their farm. Find out what those book smugglers are up to."

"Woo that village milkmaid?" Modestas protested. "That *muzhik* family! It's unthinkable! I'm a Bogdanskis. We are from the gentry!" He turned alarmingly red but controlled his anger. He had an innate pride formed by a privileged childhood, but since his family's fall from grace, his arrogance was a mask he used to fend off any belittling.

"Your family, your family," the captain muttered, disgusted with the whole Bogdanskis charade. "The truth is your family is on the verge of total ruin!" yelled the captain. "Penniless paupers still living a dream that died when your father lost his manor house at the gaming tables. It must have hastened his death and your swift decline." The captain shouted his tirade all at once. "It's true you have manners and education, but what's left of your estate, eh? Your family was forced to sell the manor house and move to your country home and sell whatever you could."

To look at Bogdanskis, the captain thought he saw something troubled in his eyes, even when he smiled. Perhaps it was shame that Bogdanskis couldn't stop himself from following his father's path to self-destruction.

Modestas frowned, resentful of the insult to his family honor. He turned away from the captain with a bitter twist to his mouth and spoke quietly. "But our name, Captain, is still a fine one, respected by all in this district."

"Your fine old name won't save your home. I could make it very difficult for you unless you make good on your notes. Otherwise, you and your mother and sister will be asking the Varnas family for a job as hired hands on their farm." Captain Malenkov burst into a staccato laugh.

Bogdanskis's eyes seemed to narrow with wounded pride and wariness. It was true, he was without means. His meager income came from the three tenant farmers who rented parcels on his land. All that was left of their estate was the summer house, a cow, some chickens, two horses, and a kitchen garden. All cared for by one hired Polish girl.

Modestas rubbed his brow, his face a mask of worry, and for a few long moments he was without words. "I'm sorry, Captain," he said softly, "but I just can't do it. It would kill my mother."

The captain could see he had deeply offended the man. "Listen, I'm not asking you to marry her. I only want you to woo her, to get into the good graces of the family."

"And how long will this farce last?" A nervous smile played over Modestas's face.

"Hmmm," the captain considered a moment, looking down at his polished boots to give the nobleman more time to sweat. "If you find something useful, then we'll both be off the hook."

"What will happen to my reputation if word gets out?" His frown deepened.

"What are you complaining about? Why that girl is one of the prettiest in this forsaken backwater. Look at that flaxen hair," Captain Malenkov said, pointing out the window. "Look how it shines like the sun. I don't think it would be a hardship for you to spend some time with a beauty like that." He watched Bogdanskis struggle with his decision.

There was a long pause before he finally relented. "I-I- don't know what to say," Modestas stuttered, utterly defeated.

"I tell you what. I'll sweeten the deal," said the captain. "We can make another wager here. If you manage to seduce the girl, then I'll add another hundred rubles. It will make a good story."

"Seduce her?" Bogdanskis was shocked by the crudeness of the offer.

"Yes. That's not a bad bargain, is it?" Captain Malenkov laughed loudly. "You've probably seduced a number of girls in the district who thought you were wooing them for marriage."

Modestas looked cornered. "But how would I prove it?"

Inside the tavern, they heard an argument heating up as voices rose. Zimmerman could be heard trying to calm them.

The captain smiled. "Don't worry, I'll be able to see it on her face. She's not the type to take such things lightly, especially if you fail to marry her. I want you to begin immediately. I'm getting hounded for information, so I want them off my back. And if I can send a few more book smugglers off to Siberia, so much the better. Then I'll be able to breathe again." He pointed a finger at Bogdanskis. "As will you, my friend, if you cooperate," he said with an air of triumph. Taking the defeated man by the arm and leading him back to their table, Captain Malenkov ordered a bottle of vodka for the table. "And who knows, I may even get promoted." His explosive laugh echoed in the tavern.

-Four-

When Ada reached home, she was still very troubled. Hurrying to her room, she lifted her skirts and saw she had two large bruises where the books had banged against her legs. She rubbed the painful places and then hid her precious books and newspapers under her bed for the time being.

Outside, her mother was hanging laundry. Ada asked her, "Where's Grandfather?"

"Sowing winter rye in the fields with Papa and your brother." Ada ran to the field's edge, calling to her grandfather, anxious to tell him about her run-in with Captain Malenkov.

He stopped and turned to her, annoyed to have his work interrupted, but he trudged over nevertheless, already frowning. "What is it that couldn't wait until I was finished?"

She leaned over to whisper, "Captain Malenkov stopped me in town."

The old man blanched. "What in heaven's name did he want?"

"He only asked my name, but it really frightened me when he looked me over. For a moment, I thought one of the books had fallen out from under my skirts and was left behind on the cobblestones. I was terrified." Her hands still trembled from the encounter.

Shaking his head, Viktoras berated himself for sending her on such a dangerous errand.

Soon her father and Petras came to join them, their bags of seed over their shoulders. "What is it, Ada?" asked her father, still a bullock at forty-nine. "I saw how upset you were. What's happened?"

When she told him, he too was shaken by the close call. "Did he say anything to you?" her grandfather asked.

Ada nodded. "He asked what was in my apron. I had the apples you told me to put in my apron to take attention away from my skirts, so I offered him one, but he didn't take it."

Viktoras stood lost in thought for a few moments, while Stasys, normally easygoing, now looked very upset. Turning to his father-in-law, he said harshly, "Why send Ada on such perilous errands? What if they had stopped and searched her? What if the books had been found and they arrested her? She'd be in Siberia before we knew it." He turned to Ada. "I know you wanted to help your grandfather after Henrikas died. I felt sorry for you, so I agreed, thinking it would get your mind off the tragedy of his death. But now I say this must stop immediately," he said, with anger rising. "I won't let you put yourself in harm's way!"

Viktoras nodded, chastened and troubled. "You're absolutely right. I am so sorry, Ada. I never dreamed the captain would question you. I should never have let you get those books from the priest."

"But this isn't the first time I've done this," said Ada. "You know it's easier for me to get past the gendarmes with the books hidden under my skirts. A man would get stopped immediately and thoroughly searched."

"That may be true, but I couldn't bear the thought of something happening to you," said her father.

"He's never stopped me before," Ada replied, coming to her grandfather's defense.

Stasys stepped up and hugged his daughter. "Ada, my Ada, how could I have let this go on so long? I'm angry with myself for being so blind to the dangers. But no more, my dear." Turning to his father-in-law, he added, "Hear me, Viktoras," he declared with rare fervor. "I respect you like my own father, but I won't let you risk my daughter any longer."

Even her brother cautioned her. "Ada, it's foolhardy. We're nothing but tiny ants going against the giant Russian Empire."

"Don't worry," Ada reassured them. "Grandfather already said this was my last attempt at book smuggling. It was already decided we would stop after this."

"Thank God," said her father, visibly relieved.

Viktoras nodded. "Come, let's hide the books immediately before the gendarmes come searching. I'll tell the villagers not to come by for books until we give them word. Something's just not right. I can feel it in my bones. Something's happened to make the Russians more vigilant."

Generally, Viktoras was more stoic and reserved, like many Samogitians in the northwest. Stubborn and proud of their dialect and character, they were different from the Highlanders to the east.

Stasys and Petras returned to the fields to finish sowing. Ada and her grandfather hid the books, pamphlets, and newspapers in a specially built beehive Viktoras had devised, one of many such hiding places on the farm. Once he was finished, he went to tell his neighbors but was uneasy the rest of the day, often flinching and looking over his shoulder at any noise down the road. By nightfall, he had decided to go to St. George's Church the next day to warn the priest.

At night, when sleep wouldn't come, Viktoras went over his many years as a smuggler, starting with the uprising of 1863 against the Tsar. He recalled that the Russian governor-general, had afterward initiated a brutal Russification policy, banning all Lithuanian books and replacing the Latin alphabet with the Cyrillic one, which Lithuanians couldn't read. Russian was to be spoken in all public places and all Lithuanian schools were closed, forcing students to attend the Russian schools. Lithuanian mothers began to teach their children to read their language at home. Some sent them to the illegal secret schools, to be taught by priests or laymen in barns, manors, or church basements. The books Viktoras and others smuggled were the seeds that would sow literacy in the next generation. Father Jurkus often said if it weren't for the stubbornness of simple farmers, their ancient language would have surely become extinct.

The Russians despised the Catholics, trying to convert them to Orthodoxy. But Russification only enraged Lithuanians, stimulating patriotism for their besieged country. Priests joined the struggle to keep the language alive. Prayer books in Lithuanian were some of the first books to be printed in Prussia and then smuggled across the border. Both Viktoras and Father Jurkus had been book smugglers in their younger days. Now they left that dangerous work to younger men while still helping with the distribution.

Viktoras's thoughts and fears wouldn't let him sleep. Though he had been faithfully smuggling the forbidden books for nearly forty years, tonight he felt exhausted and discouraged by his long battle. Growing up near the German border, he knew every section of it—where it was safe to cross, which border guards he could bribe, and what time of the night to cross. He'd had many close calls with the border police, but they had never caught him.

He wondered how many books he had brought across the border. Too many to count. It was so good to read in one's own language. All those books ran through his head along with the brave men he had worked with, ordinary, illiterate farmers. But after the ban on the language, it became a matter of honor for Lithuanians to oppose it by learning to read in their own language.

According to Father Jurkus, most of the farms in the district had those precious books hidden.

Though he had been a good book smuggler, tonight Viktoras felt disheartened that the press ban had not yet been overturned. He never thought the struggle would go on this long. Some of his fellow book smugglers had been arrested, some deported to Siberia, others shot at the border. His good friend and fellow smuggler, Jeronimas, had long ago given it up and returned to his farm in Kelmai.

Though he was nearing the end of his fight, Viktoras often wondered who would take his place once he was gone. Who would remember his sacrifices? His one regret was he didn't have sons to carry on his work. His two daughters were all he had, and, sadly, his favorite one had fled to Smolensk. He had so much knowledge to impart to someone—the best routes, hiding places, rest stops. His grandson, Petras, a year younger than Ada, didn't want to risk his hide for books, even though he benefited by reading them. To his dismay, it seemed as if this new generation had forgotten the struggles of the last one. They had other interests, other worries; their lives headed in other directions. Only his Ada, God bless her, had helped him, but that had to stop.

Viktoras felt it would be such a shame to lose such an ancient language like Lithuanian, one of the last two Baltic languages left on this earth, the other being Latvian. There was once another Baltic language—Old Prussian, but it had died out in the seventeenth century, due to wars and plague. Prussia was no longer Baltic; now the Germans had it. He thought of how poor Ireland, Scotland, and Wales spoke the English conqueror's tongue. Now Russia was doing the same thing, trying to excise the very thing that made them Lithuanian—their language. No, he couldn't let them do it.

"Bah, the devil knows what the captain wanted with Ada," he hissed under his breath.

These thoughts weighed him down lately as winter neared. Somtimes at night, Viktoras felt like he was the last book smuggler left in Lithuania. Finally, exhausted by worry, he fell asleep.

-Five-

In the last two weeks, whenever Ada came to town, whether for the market or for church, she seemed to find Modestas Bogdanskis. Wherever she turned, there he was circling around, finding excuses to walk with her, or simply offering one of his sly, worldly smiles that made her wonder what he was thinking.

From Lithuanian nobility, Modestas had Polish pretensions and courtliness, but to Ada, he seemed quite old at thirty-five. And the fact that he was from another class made her uncomfortable. While she didn't know what to make of his sudden attention, it was nonetheless flattering to find that someone still flirted with her, despite her having recently been declared a spinster.

"Good morning, Ada, nice day, isn't it?" Modestas asked, tipping his cap.

Feeling shy and awkward, she reddened, keeping her eyes lowered, not knowing what to say to a man she hardly knew. She had seen him in town but never at the village fairs or weddings where young people from the surrounding villages gathered. Raising her eyes, she nodded and then walked on.

"Can I help carry your basket?"

"No, thank you," she said too quickly. "I can manage."

She hastened her step, grateful not to be carrying books under her skirt today, but Modestas took such large strides with his long legs that she wasn't able to scurry away. While she admired him for his education, even though it was in Russian and Polish, she couldn't understand why he took a sudden interest in her. There were girls in town more worldly, with prettier dresses and livelier conversations. It was certainly puzzling.

When they reached the square, Ada informed Modestas that the priest was expecting her. She skittered to the church, leaving him standing near the tailor's shop looking perplexed. What she hadn't told him was that she was about to teach at the priest's secret school in the rectory basement, where nine of her students, six boys and three girls, waited for her and the books Father Jurkus had recently obtained from the exile presses in Germany. She taught the youngest students reading, writing and arithmetic, while Mr. Kuprys taught the older students.

Each student brought a small blackboard, hidden under their homespun shirts and jackets. One student stood guard by the door, another by the church as a lookout for the police. Ada's former teacher, Old Grigas, had taught her to keep a large bag of feathers nearby in order to hide their books, while the children pretended they were pulling feathers off their quills for down.

As she gathered the books and pamphlets, Ada remembered the captain's look that day on the square and it gave her a shiver. She prayed he would never find the secret schools that dotted the countryside. Sometimes in the winter, when the work slowed, some of the parents came to her class to learn to read and write. The upper classes preferred Polish and regarded Lithuanian as a peasant's language. Not many self-respecting Lithuanians went to the state Russian schools, at least not until they had learned to read and write in Lithuanian first.

"Never tell anyone that you are going to a secret school," Ada reminded her students. "If anyone stops you, say you are going to confession. And always walk alone, so it wouldn't create suspicion."

Ada read a poem by Maironis about the ruins of the ancient castle of Trakai. Her students wrote, memorized, recited and finally erased the poem from their small chalkboards. It was a long afternoon of looking at maps, with Ada explaining the history of Lithuania and the significance of the castle in Trakai. "It belonged to the Grand Duke Vytautas, one of our greatest rulers. And one day, God willing, we'll be free of the Russians."

"Oh, I hope so," said the youngest student, Ignas, who earlier told her the pages were finally talking to him.

In the first week of September, the autumn rain had let up. Ada woke in a strange mood, as restless as a flea jumping from one task to another, never entirely happy anywhere. While preparing to leave for town, Dora came bounding into the kitchen. "Are you going to the market?"

"Yes, with Elena to sell our mushrooms and berries."

"I want to buy those ribbons I was admiring at Rosenberg's."

"Not so fast," scolded her mother. "Finish your chores first."

"But it's market day," Dora pouted, not wanting to be left behind.

Ada told her to meet them at the market after she finished. Hearing this, Julija wanted to join her sisters.

"No, no, my little magpie!" Elzbieta protested that she needed her. "Come to think of it, Ada," said her mother, absent-mindedly, "I may have some things for you to do before you go."

"Don't be hard on the girls, Elzbieta," said Viktoras. Padding over to Ada at the door, he whispered, "run, run and flirt with the young men before you're called to duty with the others. I'll tell your mother I sent you to town on an errand." His smile crinkled the corners of his eyes. "Run along, my little sparrow."

Ada met her neighbor, Elena Kreivenas, and together they walked under the dripping fir trees, consoling each other over the sad fate of becoming old maids. What was to be done?

Elena confessed that she hoped to find Zigmas Bartkus in town. "But what about Modestas?" She teased Ada. "He's been buzzing around you like a bee to honey. You won't stay an old maid long."

"Don't exaggerate," Ada frowned, but then she whispered, "You really think so? Why would someone from the gentry be interested in me?"

"You're pretty," said Elena.

Ada squirmed a bit, embarrassed. Shy and bookish, she valued sincerity and learning over looks. Elena, a plump girl with a flat face, was a bit cheeky, always eager to laugh, which often made up for her lack of beauty.

Each hoped to sell a basket of mushrooms and a bucket of berries at the market. Elena wanted to buy ribbons, while Ada was saving for the book by Žemaite, the writer the priest had admired. Tuesday's market served the five villages in the area. The square smelled of damp straw and horse manure, full of wagons with villagers selling chickens, eggs, cheese, baskets, hand-carved rakes, pitchforks, and surplus from the harvest.

The market square was where the young folk gathered, eager to have some fun. Elena's lively company suited Ada, the two girls trading gossip with their friends and watching the young men and women walk by, shyly flirting and teasing. Across the square, Ada spotted Modestas with two young Russian gendarmes, all laughing so hard that one of the gendarmes doubled over. How had they become such friends, she wondered? It struck Ada as strange that he seemed at home with the Russians, while she feared them.

Once the girls had sold their mushrooms to the townsfolk, they went to Rosenberg's and found his son Nahum leaning on the counter with his elbows. "Hello, girls, what's new out there?" He gazed out to the square with longing.

"The girls all said they missed you," teased Elena, looking through ribbons until she found the color she liked.

"How do I look?" she asked Nahum.

He looked her over. "Like a countess." He laughed, winking. After they left the shop, Dora ran up to greet them.

"I've been looking for you everywhere," she gasped, winded from her run. "Oh, your new ribbons look pretty," she said to Elena, raising her hand to her own braids, the disappointment evident on her face.

Ada laughed and pulled two lavender ribbons from her pocket, handing them to Dora. "Were these the ones you wanted?"

"Thank you, Ada." She put them in her hair and checked her reflection in the shop window. "I hope Jurgis likes them."

When the three girls entered Goldwasser's teahouse, the warmth and smells of baked goods enveloped them. It was a small room with six tables and a big samovar in the corner with its gleaming brass belly bubbling happily. Apple cake and raisin buns sat on the counter along with poppy seed rolls. The girls were examining the sweet buns when the bell at the door tinkled and Modestas Bogdanskis walked into the tearoom, wearing his usual long black jacket over his white shirt, his slim volume of Pushkin partly tucked into his pocket.

"*Bonjour, mademoiselles*," he said, bowing in their direction, saving his best smile for Ada. "I saw you from across the square and I wondered if you would allow me to treat you ladies to tea?"

All three girls looked at each other, a bit embarrassed by his offer. "Oh no," said Ada, a blush blooming. "Thank you, it's very kind, but we couldn't accept." It seemed strange to have him be familiar with them. The girls were acutely aware of the class difference between them.

"Ah, but I insist," he said, not waiting for any further protests. Walking over to the owner, he whispered something and pointed to a table. Goldwasser was surprised to see him keeping company with village girls. Modestas turned and ushered them over to a table away from the window, making sure the townsfolk wouldn't see him with this gaggle of farm girls.

Before long, Goldwasser brought tea and sweet buns on a tray held over his large stomach and placed it on the table. "Here you are, ladies." He raised his eyebrows. "Lucky man in the company of all these beauties." Elena and Dora tried to stifle giggles.

When Ada introduced her friends, Modestas bowed his head to each, saying he was delighted to meet them.

To look at him, one could hardly believe he came from nobility. With his ragged-collared coat, dusty from walking the country road, his vaguely troubled air, and his scuffed boots, he might have been taken for a poor clerk. Yet, his posture demanded a show of respect, an acknowledgment of his family's former status.

The girls ate their sweet buns, reluctant to say something lest they embarrass themselves by sounding uneducated. Modestas took the reins of the conversation and began to tell a bit of his family history. "This morning I woke from a dream of my childhood home in the city. I still really miss it." Sighing deeply, he looked out the window toward the tavern. What the girls didn't see was the rolling of his eyes when he spotted Captain Malenkov wading through the crowd at the market, heading for the tavern.

Ada felt a stab of pity for Modestas. "It must be hard for you."

"I really shouldn't complain," he said, putting his teacup down. "When I was a child, I used to look forward to my summers here. In fact, I used to count the days."

Ada was charmed by the idea of him as an eager boy.

"My father loved horses and occasionally he'd take me riding." Modestas lit a cigarette, picking a sliver of tobacco from his tongue. "In the fall, we'd return to the manor house." He sat with his legs crossed, lifting his teacup with long fingers, cigarette smoke swirling around his head, causing his eyes to water. When a woman from the Valinskas manor came into the shop,

Modestas turned away, mortified to be seen with this rustic crowd.

Ada sat back in her chair, observing him. She liked him, yet she was cautious, having seen an entirely different side of him earlier. "I saw you with some Russian soldiers in the square," said Ada. "Talking and laughing like old friends."

Modestas shrugged, biting his curly dark mustache. "One of them told a joke."

Suddenly, from outside, the Bartkus brothers knocked on the window, looking confused to see the girls sitting in the corner with Bogdanskis. They came inside. "So, this is where you've been hiding," said Jurgis, nodding to Dora.

Elena nudged Dora and stifled a nervous laugh. She always said Jurgis was as handsome as the devil but as stupid as a log, while Dora always countered saying his brother, Zigmas, was as clever as the devil but as ugly as a toad.

"Oh, it's hard to believe you'd be selfish," teased Zigmas, jutting his chin out to Modestas as if insulted.

"Selfish?" Modestas smiled politely, but his irritation at the intrusion was evident.

"Tell me, how did you manage to keep all these young ladies to yourself?" Zigmas asked, winking at the girls. "It's not fair to the rest of the competition."

Modestas coughed and smiled weakly while both men pulled up a chair and introductions were made. Modestas offered each of them a Russian *papirosi*. Ada could see that her friends were a bit uneasy around him, and he with them. Compared to the Bartkus brothers who worked the fields, Modestas looked pale, as if he never left the house or saw the sun. It seemed unnatural the way the upper classes prized their idle lives, soft hands, and pale skin. Though not considered handsome, Modestas had a worldliness about him that intrigued her.

When they were finished, Modestas walked with Ada, leaving Elena and Dora to walk home with the Bartkus brothers. Now it was her turn to talk as Modestas peppered her with questions about her family, especially about her grandfather, Viktoras. "Does he ever go abroad?"

"Abroad?" Ada repeated. The very idea was absurd. No one in the village went abroad. "Where would he go?"

"Oh, let's say to Konigsberg or Tilsit," Modestas said lightly. "It's just over the German border."

Ada shook her head, but his question seemed odd. When Modestas walked through town with her, she could feel the stares of the parishioners, their heads turning to follow them. Ada felt they must wonder why he was walking with a village girl. She noticed the envious looks of more sophisticated and fashionable girls from town, probably wondering what he wanted with her. And to tell the truth, she felt self-conscious walking alongside him.

Soon all the young people began returning to their villages along the sandy paths that led there, some still shyly flirting, others talking or singing. Modestas walked with Ada for a time, and they parted company at the crossroads, long before Sapnai.

When Dora and Elena saw Ada was alone again, they left the Bartkus brothers and ran to join her. Elena wanted to know everything. "It's a bit of a thrill to see you two together. He's very courteous, a real gentleman. It's like a fairy tale and you've won the heart of the prince," she swooned.

"Ah, exaggerating again, Elena," said Ada, laughing, though she secretly felt pleased and relieved that someone was still showing an interest.

-Six-

The evening had turned cool and windy, but inside the warm kitchen Ada was busy helping her mother prepare supper. Elzbieta was bustling around, red-cheeked from the hot stove, adding sour cream to the borscht. Ada wiped her hands on her apron and brought the soup to the supper table. Viktoras came into the kitchen and sat down with the others. "By God, it smells good."

At the stove over a sizzling pan, Dora was frying potatoes, which she soon brought to the table, looking as if she was nearly bursting to say something. She managed to keep quiet during grace, but the minute the family said "amen," Dora spilled her news, "You'll never guess what happened!" Her small eyes sparkled and her moon-shaped eyebrows rose with excitement.

Everyone looked at Dora expectantly.

"Guess who treated us at Goldwasseris's today, with his eyes never leaving Ada?" Dora's smile was mischievous.

Ada waved away her sister's teasing. "He was just being friendly."

"Friendly?" Dora's eyes widened. "He walked you halfway home, smiling like a true suitor! Soon we'll be listening for

the matchmaker's bells coming down the road." She laughed merrily.

"What's this?" asked her mother, licking her butter-glistened lips. "Well, spit it out, Dora. Who was it?"

Ada shook her head. "Mama, don't listen to her. She's making too much of it."

"I'm not," Dora protested. "All of Raudonava was talking."

Her mother was exasperated. "Tell me at once!"

Dora paused, looking around the table, relishing her news. "Modestas Bogdanskis."

"Bogdanskis?" Her father stopped eating and glanced anxiously at his wife.

"Is it true?" Her mother raised her eyebrows, looking at Ada with new respect.

Ada shrugged. "He treated us to tea and sweet buns."

"Oh," said her mother. "I always dreamed my daughters would marry well. Modestas Bogdanskis would be quite a catch." She shook her head and laughed. "It turns out our Ada may not end up an old maid after all," she teased. "In fact, she may make the best marriage in the whole village!"

Stasys looked worried. "But what sort of dowry would such a man require? And would we be able to provide it?"

Ada's mother sighed. "I don't know."

Dora smiled slyly. "Modestas is an odd one. Though he's Lithuanian, he quotes Russian poetry everywhere he goes from that Pushkin book in his pocket."

Julija added, "Not odd. It makes him seem very romantic."

"Modestas taught me how to say hello in French. *Bonjour*," Ada chirped self-consciously.

"Oh, teach me, please," Julija begged. "Now, there's a real nobleman," she said, her brown eyes darting around like a squirrel's. "Ada, just imagine being married to someone from the gentry." Her eyes were dreamily looking at such a future. "How your life would change! You'd be respected rather than pitied as an old maid, and live in a large summer home much bigger than our village homes, and not work like a farmer's wife. Ada, you'd be free to read to your heart's content or learn to play the piano like a real lady or mingle with the gentry in Valinskas's manor, wearing nice dresses." All this sounded like a fairy tale to Julija. "Ada, I'm so envious of you," she said plaintively.

Ada looked at her sister and realized that perhaps her sister was a bit infatuated with Modestas.

Like Julija, her mother was beside herself with excitement. "I pray it's true. Imagine what it will mean to have the Bogdanskis name associated with ours. You know, I think I should ask him over next Sunday after church. Then we'll see what he's up to."

"Oh Mama, I'm sure it wasn't serious," Ada protested. "He'd never marry me. Besides I don't think I could ever love him."

"Love?" Her mother puffed out her cheeks. "Love is one thing and marriage is another. Love is a luxury few can afford. You're lucky we haven't forced you into an arranged marriage."

"I don't think Bogdanskis is for me," Ada said. "He has no life in him."

"Well then, if not Bogdanskis then tell me, please, who is for you?" Elzbieta was becoming heated. "How much longer can you wait?" She shook her finger. "You've already been called an old maid. People are talking."

Ada bristled at the injustice of such a verdict. Without thinking, she blurted out, "Old maid, old maid, that's all I hear anymore! Teta Kotryna is the only old maid in this family, not me!" When Ada realized what she had said, her hand flew to her mouth, too late to muffle her words.

At the mention of his other daughter, Viktoras looked up, surprised. No one said a word, looking down at their hands, only glancing surreptitiously at their grandfather as he sat at the head of the table drinking his tea.

No one in the family had breathed a word about Kotryna

47

since the day she had left home eight years ago. It was strictly forbidden to spare him heartache.

"Forgive me, Grandfather," Ada said quietly. "It slipped out. I'm sorry."

Viktoras frowned under his bushy eyebrows but kept quiet, making her feel even worse.

Ada had never given her aunt's fate much thought, but now she saw how bitter the life of a spinster must be for Kotryna.

Everyone was quiet for a few uncomfortable moments until Elzbieta tried to change the subject. "Well, I think Ada would be the luckiest girl in Sapnai if Bogdanskis asked for her hand." She glanced at her father who had been as quiet as a tomb all this time, and chirped, "Wouldn't she?"

Viktoras replied with a curt, "No!"

"But why?" Elzbieta whined.

"What does he want with our Ada?" he burst out angrily. All discussion stopped at once. He rolled his watery blue eyes in exasperation. "Ada, if only I were younger, I'd find you a proper husband."

Elzbieta's head shot up, surprised. "And what's wrong with Bogdanskis?"

Viktoras said nothing, but Ada saw how hard he worked to regain control of himself. "What is it?" she asked.

"Forget I said anything," he said, his jaw muscles working.

Ada watched the various emotions flicker over his face. "You don't like him, do you? I can see it on your face."

"Don't listen to my grumbling. I'd probably find fault with any of your suitors."

Ada frowned. "Tell me."

"Ach, it's nothing." He looked at her sideways. "So what if they say Bogdanskis drinks and gambles the way his father used to." He shrugged. "People say all sorts of things. We don't need to believe such gossip, do we?" He took another sip of milk and wiped his mustache with the back of his hand. "Even if his father did drink his way to an early grave. What of it? It doesn't mean the son has to follow in his footsteps, does it?"

"Papa, why say such unflattering things?" complained Elzbieta.

"I fear Modestas would break her heart. Ada's right—he's not the husband for her." His eyes flashed. Viktoras had always suspected Modestas's father had cooperated with the tsar's secret police, the Okhrana, a traitor to his own people.

"Maybe he's in love with her," said Elzbieta.

"No matter how much he's in love, I guarantee Bogdanskis's mother would never allow such a marriage. I know that family from the days of serfdom. The elder Bogdanskis was a harsh master who beat his serfs the same as he beat his animals."

Stasys didn't like what he was hearing about Modestas. "Did his father really gamble away his fortune?"

"Yes, and the apple doesn't fall far from the tree," said Viktoras. "You can't really change someone—a hunchback is a hunchback to the grave."

Elzbieta clucked her tongue dismissively. "Papa, it's just gossip."

Viktoras thought his daughter was as blind as a turnip.

"Imagine our family linked to such a name," said Elzbieta.

This was too much for Viktoras. "His name is all he has left. A nobleman with patches on his trousers. He's neither a gentleman nor a farmer. He doesn't know how to work the land, nor can he afford to be part of the leisure class. I tell you he's probably bankrupt."

Elzbieta bristled. "But Papa, Modestas is the best catch in five villages. And if he marries Ada, she'll be the envy of every girl in Sapnai." Turning to her daughters, she asked. "Won't she, girls?"

"With that long, thin face and nose like a boat rudder?" Dora said and burst out laughing.

As always, Julija agreed with her mother. "Modestas isn't handsome, but he's aristocratic and educated," she said with a serious expression to make herself seem older than Dora.

"He's too old," Dora retorted. Her eyes had a mischievous glint. "I wouldn't want those long bony fingers touching me." A peal of giddy laughter followed.

"Really, Dora, that's enough." Her mother frowned.

Ada's laconic father was getting worked up by all this talk of marriage. He didn't like Bogdanskis any more than Viktoras did, but he was not prepared to fight with his headstrong wife just yet. Frowning, he cleared his throat and scratched behind his ear. "We're putting the cart before the horse," he said.

"Exactly," said Viktoras. The two men always saw eye to eye. Stasys stood up and thanked his wife for supper. "There's been too much talk this evening. Petras and I had better go check the stable." Father and son went outside while Ada and Julija cleared the table and washed dishes.

Ada couldn't get her grandfather's words out of her head. But if not Modestas, then who else would have her? She dried her hands and stood at the window, her emotions tangled. What was she to do? She had lost her Henrikas but at least Modestas still wanted her company. And certainly her mother thought he was a prince among men. Was this her last chance to be a wife? But her grandfather was unhappy now. Oh, it was all too confusing. When she was younger, everything seemed possible and she had all the time in the world to make life's decisions. But now time had run out and only one candidate remained. Except she didn't love him. He wasn't brave or handsome or funny like her sweet Henrikas. But he was from the gentry, apparently well-read, with fine manners and intelligence, even if he was without means.

Putting her woolen shawl around her shoulders, Ada sought her grandfather in his usual spot in the orchard, smoking a long curved pipe.

"Grandfather, tell me truthfully why you object to Modestas."

"Simply put, I don't trust him. You should look for a decent, hard-working man to be your husband."

Ada sighed. "But he's the only suitor I have."

Viktoras took a puff of his pipe. "I didn't like Modestas's father, but if you like his son, then let's have him over to see what he's made of. But I warn you, not a word about book smuggling to that man, do you hear? We've been very careful since that encounter with Captain Malenkov, and thankfully nothing came of it, but we must be vigilant."

Suddenly, she remembered Modestas's raucous laughter with the Russian gendarmes and wondered if she should mention it.

Viktoras blew out a puff of smoke. "On an evening when he's had too much to drink, Bogdanskis might let something slip, and I don't have to tell you the consequences."

"I promise, Grandfather."

"I only want your happiness," Viktoras said gently. "You know I loved your grandmother very dearly until the day she died. I'd like you to feel that way about your husband. A good marriage is a balm on life's wounds, but a bad marriage is a hell all its own. I know that a good man will come along who will win your heart, and you will love and respect him, sharing both the good and the bad that life will throw your way." Kissing her forehead, he added. "And he will love you almost as much as I do."

He pointed up at the crescent moon. "Some people call this the sickle moon, but I call it the smiling moon. Whenever I see it, I think that no matter what's wrong here on earth, nor how many Russians abuse our country, the moon still waxes and wanes, just like all else. Everything changes with time. Yet every month the moon smiles down at me, and long after I'm gone, it will continue to smile at you. I gaze at that moon observing our daily lives, having a good laugh at our troubles, both big and small, and I smile back." He chuckled, patting her hand.

Sitting beside her grandfather, Ada pulled the shawl around her shoulders. Looking up at the smiling moon, she wondered what life would bring her way.

-Seven-

The following Saturday, the north wind whistled through the cracks in the buildings of the Varnas farm, making the cows uneasy in their shed. The dog curled up in a ball and the white geese huddled together behind the well. It rattled the window in Viktoras's bedroom, causing him to turn over and moan in his sleep.

In the village of Sapnai, it was generally said that the northern people were a hardy stock, with a great respect for the four winds, but that night, when the north wind blew with such a mournful howl from the marshes into Sapnai, it unsettled even the bravest of souls. Some villagers said the demons, banished by the priests and witches, had returned. Others claimed it was the lonely moaning of the last of Napoleon's soldiers, whose spirits still wandered the wetlands searching for the way home to France. Still others heard the cries of Northern Crusaders reenacting the bloody baptism of Lithuania, the last country in Europe to become Christian. Or perhaps the ghosts of the Golden Horde were thundering in from Mongolia on their small horses.

As the north wind forced its way through the loose boards of the cottage, Viktoras half-woke with a shudder, rubbing his eyes, hooded by a slight Mongolian fold, a genetic remnant of that horde. He had been dreaming he was dancing with his late wife, Emilija. His friend Balys played the concertina while he kicked up some dust with her in the warm sunlight of the farmyard. His wife whispered in his ear, a stinging plea to bring his estranged daughter back home.

He heard the wind whistle and trembled, feeling something cold brush against his cheek. "Come, Viktoras," a voice whispered so soft and inviting, calling his name pleasantly, yet with such insistence. "Come," she repeated, implying something mysterious and hard to resist. When he realized it wasn't his wife, he pulled the eiderdown over his head and squeezed his eyes shut, hardly breathing, the hair on the back of his neck standing on end.

It was the raven hour just before dawn when Death came trailing her tattered white dress like a faceless bride. The hour when she plucked souls like withered flowers hanging loosely on their stems, gathering them for their last journey. All they had to do was answer her seductive call.

Was this the end of his long life? Viktoras wondered. Was he to die alone in his bed tonight? He kept his eyes shut tightly, not wanting to see her terrible, eyeless face. In truth, he had been expecting her long before she showed up at his bedside. For many nights, he had felt her drawing near, listening for the rustling of her dress and dreading the feel of her cold breath on his cheek.

He lay very still, stubbornly refusing to answer death's call. Even though he had lived a long life, outliving two wives, he wasn't ready. There were things left undone, important things. He would resist with all that was in him until they were done. He couldn't die before his daughter Kotryna forgave him. Steeling himself, he waited, barely breathing.

Outside his window, the wind howled through the bare linden tree while Viktoras muttered silent prayers to God, Mary, and the tribe of saints in heaven to protect him until this night was over so he could be delivered safely into the hands of dawn. The wind moaned and the marshes seemed to be calling, summoning him, as if the whole unseen world was agitated. The dead were visiting the living while demons howled in harmony with the wind. He prayed to see his Kotryna once more. It squeezed his heart, remembering her as a young girl—the way she would run with all her might like the wind, or hug him around the neck fiercely.

In the other room, he could hear his son-in-law snuffling and snoring, while his daughter let out a whimper. This wind was agitating them all, their sleep disturbed, their dreams troubled. His family was away in the land of sleep while he waited for the cocks to crow. If he lived to see the light break the darkness, he vowed he would send his daughter a letter this very day.

The lonely night seemed endless, yet he held on until Death finally seemed to fade away with the darkness, though he knew she would return again. Raising himself on one elbow, he parted the muslin curtain to look outside as the stars paled. He sat up, quietly waiting, resolving not to sleep, waiting with only a sliver of a moon to keep him company.

When the cock finally crowed, he felt reborn. Suddenly he felt like crying when he saw that first light pierce the darkness. The night had been brutal, but when the sky lightened to a soft gray, the four winds dispersed to other parts of the world to do their mischief.

The old patriarch rubbed the stubble on his face as if to prove he was still there. Sniffing loudly, he wiped a drop from the end of his nose with the back of his hand, relieved that Death had only played with him the way a cat will sometimes scare a mouse, holding it for a while, only to let it go again.

When the light sifted down, solidifying the vague dark shapes outside his window into the familiar landscape of his farm, he heard someone rustling inside the house. A door closed and the cows softly lowed, waiting patiently with their full udders. Outside his window, he could see Ada, her face still puffy from sleep, her thick blond braids to her waist, as her clogs crunched through the farmyard. He only hoped when the time came for Ada to marry, she would choose a better man than Bogdanskis. Perhaps this was only a slight flirtation that would pass like a faint breeze.

He watched Ada stop for a moment with her milk buckets to look out over the melancholy orchard. The trees were bare, the kitchen garden harvested, and the farther fields lay quietly, resting until awakened again in spring. After the blustery night, the mysterious stillness of the land and the ancient pine forest beyond felt like a reverent prayer.

The horizon brightened, glowing in pinks and gold as the sun rose in all of its splendor. Viktoras stood at the window to greet the sunrise. Though his joints ached and he felt stiff and creaky, he was grateful to have survived the night. It seemed grand to be alive, watching Ada go about her ordinary chores, slipping into the cowshed, disturbing the doves, which began to murmur, lifting their wings and preening their feathers. Outside the window stood the maple tree he planted when Ada was born, and next to that, the birch tree he planted when Kotryna was born. His two favorite women—one absent.

His breath left a cloud on the cold window. A thin mist was rising in the empty fields. Would he live long enough to see the pale green buds unfurl in the spring or see the storks return to their nests, or taste the wild strawberries of next summer? The same earth that fed him would soon embrace his bones.

Now he could hear the others tending to their chores, so he dressed and went into the kitchen to light the stove. Then he sat at the table, staring at his hands, wide as paddles, thinking about the things left undone and the little time left to do them.

Soon Ada came through the back door, kicking off her clogs and placing the milk buckets down, her sleep-softened face reminding him of his late wife. "Praised be," she said gaily.

"Forever and ever," he answered.

"What is it, Grandfather? Is something wrong? Did you not sleep well?" She seemed to read his mood in an instant.

He turned his hands over and examined them. "Look at how old these hands are, but how well they've served me all my life."

Ada looked at his face, "Are you feeling well?"

He shrugged dismissively. "Ach, I'm like that old oak tree outside. We both creak in the wind."

His face was lined and weathered like the old wooden planks of the barn. He had once stood tall and stout but had shrunken now and only stood a head taller than his granddaughter, though he still prided himself on his full head of silver hair.

"Were you able to sleep with that wind howling?" he asked.

"It was a terrible night," she burst out, "as if all the devils in the world were loose." She looked wide-eyed. "But this morning I had such a vivid dream about you. You were young and dancing with Grandmother in the sunlight while Balys played his concertina."

He studied her, wondering at the coincidence. "That's curious. I had the same dream. Your grandmother, may she rest in peace, must be trying to tell us something."

"Really? But what?" She frowned, putting a kettle on the stove. "What do dreams mean? And why is our village named after dreams?"

The old man scratched his ear. "I remember a widow, the last of her family who had the gift of divination by dreams. Once, many had it, but the church forbade such pagan ideas. I say if you scratch a Lithuanian, you'll find a deeply reverent pagan who watches the earth, the animals, and his dreams for signs."

Ada leaned over to kiss his wrinkled cheek, and the genial fire in his eyes slowly returned.

"Perhaps the dream is about your Teta Kotryna," he said softly, a catch in his throat at the mere mention of her name.

"Teta Kotryna?" Ada was shocked to hear him speak her aunt's name aloud. The whole family tiptoed around the subject.

Though she had brought it up recently, Ada still trod carefully into this forbidden territory. "Mama said Teta lives in Smolensk."

He looked out the window. "Kotryna became a domestic servant for a Jewish family. They took her along when they moved." He cleared his throat. "It was my fault," he said in a hoarse whisper. "I'm a stubborn old man." He coughed.

"Ada, I want you to write her. My writing has become too shaky." He raked his hair with his fingers.

Ada was surprised, but said nothing.

He seemed lost in thought for a moment. "She was like you, Ada. Balys used to say she was pretty and had so many matchmakers that our old dog went hoarse barking." He shook his head and smiled sadly. "But she only wanted Aleksas Simaitis." His eyes began to smart. "I have to write to him also. In America."

"But where? It's such a big country."

He took a folded piece of paper from his shirt pocket and handed it to her. "Father Jurkus said Simaitis works in the coal mines in Shenandoah, Pennsylvania, and had raised money to send shipments of Lithuanian books to St. George's."

Ada repeated, "Shenandoah" like a magical incantation while she went to bring paper to the table and prepared to write.

My Dearest Kotryna,

We have not seen each other for eight long years. The time has come for you to come home. I want to see you once more. Your mother often appears in my dreams, asking me to remedy this hardheaded mistake of mine. Forgive your old father and please come quickly.

Once Ada finished the letter, the old man signed his name with his shaky, spidery signature. Then he sealed the letter and began at once to dictate a letter to Aleksas Simaitis, apologizing for having wronged his daughter's suitor. "Ada, I want you to post these letters in town."

"Can I tell the family?"

He frowned. "Don't say anything just yet." He picked up an empty bucket. "I'd better fetch some water," he said, going out to the well. When Viktoras pulled the well sweep, it screeched, scaring a gray mouse out. Seeing a nearby crow, he whispered, "run, run." The crow swooped down after the mouse, which barely escaped by darting to a shed. Viktoras smiled, whispering to the hidden mouse that they had both eluded death this morning.

Later that evening, Viktoras stood at the foot of his bed, afraid to lie down, afraid to shut his eyes, afraid of Death. He stood frozen by his own cowardice and fear until weariness forced him to sit on his bed. Keeping an uneasy watch for Death, he realized this would be the hardest struggle of his battle-scarred life. How long could he forestall the inevitable? Fear clutched at him as he sat, trying to console himself with the fact that two letters had gone out into the world today. One might bring his daughter home, and one that might reach the far shores of America to soften the heart of Simaitis, making him return to Lithuania. Who knew what miracles those letters might cause? Viktoras smiled bravely and finally put his head on his goose down pillow, in the exact spot that was indented from the previous night.

He let out a small sigh. But, then again, he thought, what if Kotryna was still angry and ignored his letter, or what if she had married someone in Smolensk? And what of Simaitis? He might have married a cowgirl in the New World. He may have died in the coal mines. Viktoras shook his head. Life was full danger and worry. Maybe it was good that his life was coming to an end. He was getting too old to worry about everyone. With a head full of apprehension, he fought off sleep as long as he could, but at long last he succumbed to fatigue.

In the raven hour before dawn, Viktoras was dreaming of Kotryna calling him to help her bring in the cows from the meadow. "Papa," he heard her call and turned to see his daughter chasing a runaway cow. "Papa," he heard her again, only this time he was half-awake when he suddenly realized it was not Kotryna calling, but Death, her breath dank and cold like the grave. His heart quickened and he held his breath, once again refusing to answer her. "Your letters are written. Come," she urged firmly but invitingly.

No, he couldn't die yet. What would happen to Ada? What did his sweet granddaughter know about men like Bogdanskis? Viktoras distrusted the man completely and was determined to protect her. He gritted his teeth and steeled his will, all the while praying for the blessed morning light to splinter the darkness.

-Eight-

The world was sunk in a milky fog. Upon waking, Viktoras looked out his window, wondering if he had died already and was now resting in the clouds of Purgatory. He blinked twice to clear his vision, but the blur remained. Outside, his dog was barking, announcing visitors, so he must still be alive. He blessed himself, relieved to be given another day.

How far had his letter gone into the world, the one that would hopefully bring his daughter home? Had it reached her yet? Though he knew it was impossible, Viktoras quickly dressed and went outside to see if by some miracle Kotryna was arriving. But when he looked into the milky distance, he couldn't see a thing. He realized he had uncharacteristically slept through breakfast and that his family had already gone to church.

On the next farm, he heard Kreivenas yelling to his daughter, Elena, to bring in kindling. The fog made everything sound much louder and closer than it really was, as the farms were not close to one another. Viktoras's dog Margis barked again, not knowing what to make of the unaccustomed noise.

Before long, he saw his family returning from church. Ada, her face flush with excitement, came at once to tell him Modestas was coming today. He didn't like that bit of news but for her sake he tried hard not to show it.

Elzbieta, glowing with anticipation, said, "Papa, I invited the Bogdanskis family but the mother and daughter had other plans. But Modestas is coming. Won't the villagers be surprised when they see one of the gentry visiting us?" She smiled proudly.

It was too much for Viktoras. "You're pushing Ada right into his arms, aren't you?" he said angrily.

"You say that as if I'm about to send her to prison. Would it be terrible if she married at long last? And especially to such a distinguished man?"

"The man is merely playing with her for his amusement, or God knows why."

"Oh Papa, he's an interested suitor, that's all." Elzbieta went to ready things for Modestas, who had promised to follow soon.

After finishing preparations, Ada came out into the thick fog to see why the dog was barking and almost bumped into her grandfather. She jumped, startled to find him there.

"You're as skittish as a cornered cat, Ada."

Ada laughed softly. "By now Elena must have told the whole village Modestas was coming, and they're all probably peering curiously to catch a glimpse of him." Ada was suffering from a case of nerves, worried about this visit, wondering how a man of the world would look at her humble cottage. How would her family compare to his?

Julija was always reminding her she was lucky, and her mother was so excited by this visit that it was contagious, yet Ada was thrown by the seed of doubt planted by her grandfather.

By afternoon, the sun had melted the fog, and the lingering mists had cleared. Modestas finally negotiated the boggy road to Sapnai. He arrived at the farm gate in his horse-drawn cart, finding the Varnas family waiting. Elzbieta's face shone with anticipation when she met him, as if waiting for the magic words that would make her daughter a member of his vaunted family.

"It's such an honor to have you in our home," she said, ushering him in.

The tall and imperious suitor's discomfort seemed to have entered the room with him, making everyone a bit uneasy.

"Bonjour, Madame," he said, clicking his heels and bowing to kiss Elzbieta's hand, making her blush and giggle as if she were the one being wooed rather than her daughter. And when he straightened again, for a brief moment it seemed as if he was ready to run out. Instead, he handed her a small bag of hard candy and Elzbieta thanked him, dismayed to notice his frayed cuffs.

Ada, wearing her best blue skirt and homespun white linen blouse, reddened greeting him shyly. Every time she saw him, it seemed her usual carefree nature simply evaporated. When he bowed to kiss her hand, she could feel the tickle of his curly mustache and smell the violet pomade in his hair.

"Welcome to our home," her mother trilled, ushering him inside. The parlor was large with a long, narrow wooden table covered with a hand-loomed linen tablecloth and long benches along the sides, and her grandfather's favorite armchair at the head. A carved cupboard filled with pottery stood nearby. At the other end of the room sat a large bed for Elzbieta and her husband, Stasys, covered with a hand-woven bedspread and a picture of the Sacred Heart over the bed to watch over them all.

Moving deliberately, Modestas greeted the rest of the family, examining the small but neat cottage, scanning the cramped rooms and the rustic, simple furniture, alert for any evidence of smuggling. The table was set with poppy seed cake, raisin buns, cucumbers with honey, and farmer's cheese.

Petras was already seated at the table with Viktoras, who greeted Modestas tepidly. "Good day to you, young Bogdanskis. I knew your father in the old days," he said with a direct look to let Modestas know that his opinion of his father wasn't favorable.

Modestas cleared his throat, looking a bit on guard, a defense against his diminished circumstances.

"Never mind the old days," said Stasys, trying to rescue an uncomfortable moment by opening the vodka bottle. "Let's have something a little stronger than tea for the men." Raising his glass, he said, "To your health." Modestas, relieved by the break in the tension, raised his glass.

Julija prodded her brother to get out of his seat and let Modestas sit next to Ada. "Dora, bring the tea," Julija commanded. *"Bonjour,"* she said shyly, practicing her French while trying to rein in her self-satisfied grin.

"Bonjour," Modestas replied, smiling at the fuss Julija was making. *"Merci beaucoup, mademoiselle* Julija," he said, glancing around to see its effect on the family.

The effect on Viktoras was immediate. Such posturing only made him want to take the young man down a peg or two for his pretentiousness. The Polish gentry were often disliked for just this reason, as were the Polonized Lithuanians like Modestas. "Tell me, Bogdanskis," he asked, "do you read and write?"

He watched as his barb caused the young man to flinch. "Of course," Modestas said with a dismissive sniff. "I'm an educated man. I can read and write in Polish and Russian and have a bit of French from my mother."

"Not in Lithuanian?" asked Viktoras, glancing at Ada.

Modestas immediately took an interest, looking at the grandfather for any confirmation that he had Lithuanian contraband books in the home. "I would love to read in Lithuanian, but where would I find such a book?" Modestas fussed with his collar, now captivated by the grandfather's every word. "And, if I may presume to ask, does this family know where to get a Lithuanian book?"

Viktoras grunted in reply, ignoring his question. "Ada has such a beautiful hand. She recently wrote some letters for me."

Elzbieta's head whipped around. "What letters?"

"Later, my dear," her father said dismissively.

"Did you go to the Russian school?" Modestas asked Ada.

"No," she said. Seeing his discomfort, she wondered how to make him more at ease. He might be a bit down-at-heel, but he had a fine old name and a pride that didn't like trampling. There were still a few old people who bowed to him, remembering his grandfather's estate, where they had worked as serfs.

"Don't mind Grandfather," she said, trying to placate his wounded pride. "He's afraid we'll lose our language and end up speaking nothing but Russian."

"Exactly," sputtered Viktoras. "The conqueror's language. Or even worse, Polish." He made a face.

Across the table, Elzbieta stared at her father in mute reproach.

Modestas continued his line of questioning. "Ada, if you didn't go to the Russian school, then how is it that you learned to write?"

Ada shrugged, careful not to talk about the secret schools or the smuggled books. "Here and there," she said, looking down at her hands. "I love to read."

"What authors?"

Ada didn't want to name the Lithuanian authors, so she said Adomas Mickevicius, a poet claimed by both the Lithuanians and the Poles.

Modestas brightened. "Mickiewicz, a wonderful poet."

Ada smiled, grateful she had said the right thing.

"And Pushkin, have you read him as well?"

"No," she said, hoping he would stop this line of questioning.

Her father poured another round of vodka, while Modestas once again scanned the room hoping to find some books. Not seeing any, he squirmed in his seat, not knowing where else to take the conversation.

No one said anything for a few awkward moments. Then Elzbieta cleared her throat. "Let's have some poppy seed cake," she said, nervously cutting thick slices. Julija put the hard candies in a dish and offered them around the table.

"How is your family?" asked Elzbieta, hovering over him.

"As well as can be expected, thank you," Modestas said, sipping his tea and glancing at the old man as if expecting a blow. "These days they mostly stay at home," he added, taking a small bite of the cake.

Ada's family rarely saw the sickly old maid sister or the cold and regal mother, except at church. Both women were recluses, bitter at their fallen fortunes. Word in the village was that Modestas's mother was desperate for him to marry someone with money, prestige, or land—anything to better their situation.

Modestas fished through his pockets and pulled out a box of Russian *papirosi,* offering it to the men. Stasys took a cigarette and lit it, taking a long pull.

Ada could see she wasn't the only one who felt uneasy around Modestas. Everyone looked a bit uncomfortable. She hoped that their conversation would knit together soon, making him feel less of an outsider.

"I've decided to try my hand at a bit of farming," said Modestas, almost smiling at his lie. "It will do me good to get my nose out of books and get some fresh air." He turned to Ada's father, who had taken special pains this morning to trim his whiskers carefully. "With your permission, I'd like to ask Ada if she wouldn't mind showing me around your farm."

Stasys blew out a puff of smoke. "Of course, of course." His broad, bald forehead shone above his thick eyebrows.

Viktoras stopped him. "Before you go, let me offer you some advice about your future farming plans." He adopted a serious look, but the thought of Modestas trying his hand at farming tickled the old man. "When the moon is young, a new moon, you must sow cereal crops, especially spring crops and flowers. It's also a good time to cut hair, shear sheep, trim horsetails, and cut clover and hay, but definitely not a good time for threshing grain, picking cabbage or storing crops, for they will end up worm-ridden. Those things should be done during the waning moon." He knew it would sound laughable to Modestas's ears, though, in fact, this advice had always served him well. He smiled when he saw the puzzled look on the young man's face—a look that indicated his opinion of such medieval advice.

Feeling self-conscious about their humble farm, Ada took Modestas around, showing him the granary, barn, cowsheds, the kitchen garden and the orchard. All the while, he scoured every inch looking for anything suspicious but was extremely disappointed to find nothing out of the ordinary.

When they reached the bench in the orchard, he asked if they could sit for a while by themselves. Sitting down next to her, he tentatively put his arm around her shoulder and Ada jerked away in surprise.

"Ada, I'm sorry. It's just that you make me feel so at ease with you." She reddened but didn't say anything. "I'm very interested in your books to see if we are reading the same authors. Where do you keep them?"

Immediately alert, she answered cautiously. "We keep no books here. I had only borrowed a friend's book." She didn't like his question.

"Oh? Which friend?" He smiled to reassure her.

Ada frowned. "I can't remember." She reddened and looked down at her hands.

Sensing her tension, he took out his Pushkin to read a few choice lines:

> *A magic moment I remember:*
> *I raised my eyes and you were there,*
> *A fleeting vision, the quintessence*
> *Of all that's beautiful and rare...*

Then, hoping the poetry had softened her, he asked, "My dear, may I kiss you?"

Ada froze, not knowing what to say. It seemed too soon for kisses, but she didn't think it was polite to refuse him. "Yes," her voice trembled and Modestas smiled in spite of himself. When he leaned in, she turned her cheek to him. He stopped momentarily and then kissed it. "Very sweet," he whispered, close to her ear, coming in for another kiss, but she stopped him. She wasn't keen on kissing him, and that in itself seemed to say something important about how she felt about him.

Surprised by her reaction, he shook his head and gave her an apologetic smile as they walked back to join the others. His patrician face had changed a bit, looking a little colder.

Once Modestas left, Elena burst through the kitchen door. "I sat at my window until I saw him leaving." She took Ada's hand. "Tell me every detail."

One by one, various neighbors from the village dropped by to ask for news. "Would there be a wedding soon?" They pestered her with questions, and soon everyone was speculating how long it would be before Modestas returned with a matchmaker.

Ada objected to this speculation, but no one bothered to listen.

"You might be the next lady of the manor, so to speak," said Elena. It would continue to be a source of endless gossip for the villagers. It was delightful gossip for everyone but Viktoras. The thought of his granddaughter marrying Modestas troubled him. Was it fitting to give a lamb to the wolf? Why was Elzbieta so taken with him? A crow is black its whole life; it doesn't suddenly turn white.

Viktoras went out to his domain in the orchard, now bare of fruit and leaves, to sit alone and sulk. This was where he carefully cultivated his fruit trees, made cherry wine and pear brandy from the surplus fruit, and tended his faithful beehives. Taking out his large handkerchief, he blew his nose.

It was said that ancestor spirits lived in orchards, therefore he would never cut down the trees they had planted long ago.

It soothed the old man to sit among his ancestors pondering the turns his life had taken. It felt significant to him, yet most of the young villagers knew nothing about his long and eventful life. It seemed a shame not to tell them.

Perhaps it was time for another letter. This time he would ask Ada to write a friend from his book smuggling days. It would be a joy to see him and relive their old days together.

After supper, he went into the parlor to find Ada sitting by an oil lamp embroidering a pillowcase. After she finished and bit off the thread, he took her into the kitchen, away from the rest of the family.

"Ada, my little sparrow," he said, his pipe never leaving his teeth. "Could you write one more letter?"

"Yes, if you like."

"To my old friend, Jeronimas Balandis in Kelmai. I want to invite him and his family for a visit."

Once the letter was written and sealed, Viktoras smoked his evening pipe, watching the gathering darkness with a sense of dread. It was a race they were having—he and Death. Did he have enough time to accomplish his last wishes, or would Death come for him before his work was done?

On the way to Raudonava, Modestas had to navigate the muddy roads. When he finally reached Zimmerman's tavern, he found the captain and requested a word outside. "Captain, I simply can't continue this idiotic charade."

"What charade?" The captain eyed him warily.

"Wooing that naive Varnas girl. It's impossible to keep up this ruse. These damned peasants are thick-headed, without a grain of sophistication. I hardly know what to say in their presence, and they don't seem comfortable with me either, especially the grandfather, who seems to dislike me. I'm not used to being among these simple-minded villagers. I prefer those of my own class." He was biting his mustache from nerves.

"I beg you, Captain. Please release me from our agreement."

"They've already gotten the better of you, have they?" Malenkov snickered, but when he turned, his smile faded. "What have you been able to find out?" he demanded.

"Next to nothing. The grandfather asked me if I read in Lithuanian. It's obvious they do, but when I question them as to how they learned it or what books they were reading, I only got evasions. The girl even took me on a tour of their farm, but I saw no evidence of contraband books."

The captain's sagging eyes glared at him as if Bogdanskis were solely responsible for his dreary and dull station at this provincial garrison. "Of course, if you want to quit now, you can simply pay me my money and we'll part on good terms."

"You know very well I don't have the money!" Modestas exclaimed.

"Well then, give me some evidence," the captain demanded.

"There was none to be found." Modestas squirmed.

Captain Malenkov cleared his throat. "Then give me some smugglers to send to Siberia." When he grabbed Modestas by his coat lapel, his face contorted. "You better try harder, my friend. Or you'll lose what little your family has left. Do I make myself clear?"

Modestas anxiously nodded his assent.

-Nine-

E lzbieta sat knitting while practicing the new French word she had learned. *"Bonjour,"* she said, haltingly, but no matter how she turned her tongue, she couldn't make it sound right and would ask Julija to repeat it. All of this was so annoying to Viktoras that he finally told them he'd have no more French in his house. No one said anything for a few moments. Viktoras put down his pipe, and looking around the table, announced he wanted the village coffin maker to make his coffin.

Ada blanched. "Your coffin!"

Elzbieta looked at her father, unsure what to make of this. "Is this a joke?" She asked, with a half-smile.

"No," said Viktoras, his face grim.

Spitting three times to ward off bad luck, Elzbieta added, "Papa, whoever heard of such a thing? To have your coffin made ahead of time." She looked alarmed. "Are you ill?"

"Just call it a premonition." Viktoras looked at his hands. "Life moves ahead like a swift current and we move with it, whether we want to or not."

Ada thought he must be ill and simply not telling them to spare their feelings. She went to her grandfather and pressed her cheek to his. "Oh, Grandfather, I pray your premonition is wrong."

He was touched by her reaction. "There, there," he said patting her cheek. "We'll all go out like candles one day." He cleared his throat to mask his rising emotion.

"I'm sure you've got many years ahead of you," Ada said, gripping her grandfather's hand, as if to push this idea of death away. It was a well-known fact that when some old people decided it was time to die, they simply sat down in a chair and willed themselves to do it. Such stories were told in the village.

"You used to let me climb onto your lap and would listen to me, defend and advise me. What would I do without you?" Ada asked, tears rising. For a few moments, no one spoke.

As Viktoras looked at her, a smile rose, bringing him out of his sadness. He wiped his eye with his calloused finger, too moved to say anything.

Taking a breath, he added, "I'm not afraid of death. It seems like the night that comes after a long summer's day, a time to rest and to join your grandmother. My generation has all died except for a few lonely survivors like Balys. Sometimes I feel as if they've all gone off to some celebration and forgotten me." He tried to smile. "But don't worry, my dear. I'm not eager to join them just yet. I still have a few things left to do."

Three days later, the coffin maker arrived to take the old man's measurements. Baffled and uncomfortable, he stammered, "I've never done this for a man still living rather than a corpse," He looked at Stasys and then Elzbieta. "It doesn't seem right."

They shrugged and nodded in agreement.

Viktoras smiled. "If you live long enough, you get to see all sorts of unaccustomed things."

Before the man was finished with his measurements, neighbors were already knocking at the door, wanting to know

72

who had died. When they saw the coffin-maker measuring a man still living, tongues began to cluck. This was unheard of. Poor Viktoras must be at death's door, they whispered to one another. That, or he was losing his good sense.

On Friday, Father Jurkus came for a visit. Ada greeted him at the door and led him to the parlor, where her grandfather was sitting alone, keeping a dark hour, looking back on his life's failings and missteps.

"What's this I hear about you having your coffin made?" Father Jurkus said bracingly. "I thought I'd better come by to see for myself if you were in need of last rites," he said, half-joking.

Viktoras smiled sheepishly, inviting the priest to sit.

"I can see something is sitting heavily on you. What is it, my friend?" A silence fell between them.

After a few uncomfortable moments, Viktoras unburdened himself. "Father, you'll think this a bit peculiar, but on some nights Death comes to call me," he confided. "It seems my days are numbered, so give me your blessing, and when my time comes, you'll say a word at my funeral."

Father Jurkus studied him for any hints of illness or instability, but his old friend looked the same. "Ah well, we aren't as young as we used to be in our book smuggling days, but you look fine to me." The priest was decades younger, but his paunch was growing and his hair was graying.

The priest told him that soon he would be crossing the border to East Prussia, the region they called Lithuania Minor, where many Lithuanians still lived. There he would meet with the Lithuanian exiles, who printed the banned books, newspapers, and pamphlets urging resistance to the Russian Empire.

Taking out a bottle of his plum brandy, Viktoras proposed a toast. "To our book smuggling days. I wish I was still vigorous enough to cross the border with you."

"I usually leave this to the younger men," he said, "but I want to meet with some of our exiled patriots. They're urging an end to the ban on Lithuanian press and language, and autonomy for Lithuania. Their voices are calling for freedom."

Viktoras lit up at the news. "You've just added ten years to my life! I swear by my stubborn Samogitian ancestors, I'll live to see that day come."

The following Tuesday, the wagon carrying the pine coffin came down the rutted road, listing this way and that, almost dropping its load several times before it arrived.

Viktoras propped it on a long bench in the farmyard and lit his long clay pipe. The coffin smelled of fresh-cut wood. A heavy sadness flooded over him at the thought of being buried in this humble coffin. Soon Margis curled up next to him on the granary porch as he sat plowing through his long life. It was a melancholy meditation, as memories came flooding back of his mother singing lullabies, of his father teaching him how to harrow a field, of his many brothers and sisters, all dead and buried. There were so few alive who shared his history.

Looking back over his life, Viktoras felt regret that the press ban had not been lifted in his lifetime. He thought of his book smuggling days, his radical youth, his yearning for an independent Lithuania, the one his father and grandfather had always talked about. If only he could live to see these dreams come true. But he knew that Death sat in the shadows of his room, waiting to pluck his soul. His life suddenly felt like a long, fevered dream, yet it was sad to leave it behind. What was life, he wondered, looking at his coffin. Why do we live? What is the reason for such strife and heartache, such grief and loss?

Nearby, on the granary porch, Ada had been painting her green dowry chest with birds and flowers. Now she came to see what her grandfather was contemplating so seriously. "Doesn't it feel strange to be looking at your own coffin?"

Sucking on his pipe with a quiet dignity, Viktoras considered the question. Cloudlets of smoke hovered overhead. "I want to paint my coffin the way that you painted your dowry chest."

"Paint your coffin?" Ada was astonished into silence. To paint a dowry chest was perfectly acceptable, but to paint a coffin was altogether odd.

"Yes, with scenes from my long life like a story. And in between the scenes, I want you to paint your flowers."

Elzbieta came into the farmyard, having overheard their conversation. "Oh, God help us! It's not enough to have your coffin made, but now you're going to paint it! What will people say?"

Her father bristled. "To the devil with them if they don't like it!" He enjoyed painting. In the parlor, there were several landscapes he had painted long ago, but he had no will to paint these last years without his wife's encouragement. He stood, wincing due to his bad knee, and went into the house to find his paints.

All afternoon Viktoras sat considering the relentless hammer of time. Every so often, one or another member of the family came out to sit with him. He remembered his tiny sister, Maryte, who was born blind and lame and died before her fifth birthday. What did the blind dream of if they had never seen a flower or a bird? He had not thought of her in decades, but now she seemed so dear to him that he started to paint her portrait.

The next day was sunny, and everyone wanted to be outside. Though Viktoras's fingers were the size of sausages with yellowed fingernails like thick horn, he was still able to make the brushes do his bidding.

Viktoras spoke to Ada while he painted. "Across the turbulent Baltic Sea is Sweden, but at Lithuania's back is Russia with its yoke. The tsar is called 'little father' by his people, but I, like most Lithuanians, spit whenever his name is mentioned, in the same spirit in which I spit at the mention of the devil. And Russia,

God help us, with its gendarmes and its magistrates, still clings to the land like an epidemic." He spat and wiped his nose.

He finished one story and went on to the next. "Why was Catherine called the Great when she murdered her husband, the tsar, and later ordered the partition of the Polish-Lithuanian Commonwealth in 1795?" He told Ada it meant the end of sovereignty for each country, and therefore he would never paint the German-born tsarina. "Lithuania was given to the Russians, and it began a long dark night in our country. That night is still upon us, and dawn seems far away, but I won't live to see that dawn. I only hope you get to see it, my dear."

He began to weave another tale while painting Napoleon's *Grande Armée* as they advanced across Lithuania: French soldiers, dressed in blue and red uniforms, marching in cadence into Vilnius. Lithuanians joined his troops because Napoleon had promised to defeat the Russian Empire and restore freedom to Lithuania.

Viktoras despaired, realizing more than a hundred years had passed since Lithuania had been absorbed into the Russian Empire. He had not yet been born when Napoleon, the great liberator, marched into Lithuania, but elders had told the story of his march through Vilnius often, and it had fired his imagination ensuring he would remember it always. He could still picture those soldiers vividly, as though he had been there himself, so he never hesitated to tell it over a glass of beer.

Ada watched him paint, listening to his stories, though she had heard them many times before. She loved his enthusiasm, his love of life's unexpected surprises, and his colorful, old-fashioned language.

The bitter October cold returned the next day and lasted through the week, making it difficult for Viktoras to stay at his painting long. Rubbing his hand absent-mindedly over his brown wool pants, he welcomed a break when Stasys brought in the winter cabbage, perfect for making sauerkraut. The two men sat, cutting the cabbage into the large barrel, adding apples, caraway seeds and carrots and plenty of salt for the cabbage to ferment. It would have to last the winter.

A week later, the weather warmed a bit, so Viktoras continued his work on the other side of the coffin. Ada went about her daily chores of feeding the cackling chickens and honking geese. From time to time, she would stop to check on his progress. He had just finished painting his wedding to his beloved Emilija. Ada recalled how he had mourned for months after her death, sitting as if lost, his eyes wet with uncried tears. Nothing would cheer him up that year or the next.

When Ada asked about his first wife, he told her about how she had died in childbirth, as did the son she had borne. He said Jadze was now the palest shadow of a memory, while his Emilija still seemed to be in the next room, or milking the cows—just out of sight momentarily. Sometimes he woke thinking she was still sleeping beside him. His timeworn features softened with remembered love. "She was the best wife a man could have. How could she die before me when she was fifteen years younger? It was unfair." He had always worried about leaving her a widow.

From time to time he got lost in his memories, slipping briefly away from the conversation with the gaze of an old man. When Ada brought him some tea, he looked up as if awakening from a near doze. She wondered why was it hard to believe that the old had once been young, strong, and in love?

Viktoras put down his paintbrush and took out his handkerchief to wipe his nose. "I married your grandmother late in life, and she gave me two daughters. And now I have you, my dear." He patted her hand and smiled, his eyes crinkling in the corners. "And, of course, your brother and your two silly sisters too." He laughed as he took out his pipe and lit it.

Elzbieta came out with her shawl wrapped around her head and shoulders to see what her father was painting. When she saw the image of a bride, she gasped.

"That's mama, isn't it?" She quietly studied the image.

"It is." Viktoras nodded and turned to his daughter, putting his brushes down. "She was a beauty just like our Ada."

"Let's go inside before we all get the grippe," said Elzbieta. As they warmed up by the stove, Elzbieta turned to her father. "Papa, the other day, you told Modestas about some letters Ada had written for you. To whom?"

"Didn't I tell you?" When he saw his daughter's perplexed look, he wheezed his characteristic laugh into his fist, enjoying her confusion. "To your sister. I've asked Kotryna to come home."

Elzbieta shook her head in disbelief. She looked from Ada to her father, whose bushy eyebrows rose and fell with each suck on his pipe. "To Kotryna, after all these years of total silence?"

Her father frowned. "I was wrong. I finally see it."

By the end of the week, when the weather cleared, Viktoras put on his sheepskin jacket and went outside to finish painting. He sat down with a weary sigh. The sky was cobalt blue and brilliantly sunny but with a cold wind blowing from the north, making his rheumatic knee worse. He clenched his teeth and grumbled, "To the devil with these hot pains."

Margis trotted over, wagging his tail and licking the old man's hand in sympathy. Viktoras smiled and petted his faithful guardian. Before long the cold wind was biting, so he asked his grandson to move his coffin to the barn. In the gloom of the drafty old barn, he decided to paint the freeing of the serfs in 1861 by Tsar Alexander II.

Soon Ada came to keep him company. While painting, he told her how it had been a true wonder to finally be free from serfdom. He had thought he would never live to see the day. Now he was on his own land, and his family was no longer enslaved to the manor.

While painting the foot of his coffin, he told her about the revolt of 1863 against the Russian Empire. Once Lithuania was forced into the Russian Empire, he said, there followed many attempts at restoring independence, but he couldn't forget the terrible revolt of 1863. All of his young hopes for freedom were invested in that uprising, yet it failed. Russia crushed the rebellion by deporting thousands to Siberia, while others were hanged or imprisoned. Viktoras bitterly related how Muravyov the Hangman had said, "What the Russian bayonet didn't accomplish, the Russian school will." Even singing the national anthem was a criminal act. Centers of resistance sprung up in Tilsit and America. Viktoras lost many friends in the uprising.

That was when he had joined the book smugglers.

"This part of my history is still too dangerous to put on my coffin," he explained. "I'll just paint a book here and there."

At breakfast the next day, while Viktoras ate, he started a story and Ada listened spellbound. He had seen both Tilsit and Konigsberg aboil with revolutionaries: Socialists, Marxists, and the radical Nihilists, each plotting against the tsar.

"Death had stalked Tsar Alexander II for a number of years," Viktoras said. "In the late 1860s, a mine was laid in front of the tsar's train, but he escaped unharmed. Five shots were fired at him in 1873 but missed. In 1880, a revolutionary set off a bomb in the Winter Palace, while the tsar waited for his dinner. Again, Alexander escaped. In 1881, a revolutionary hurled a bomb at the tsar's carriage. The tsar thanked God he wasn't injured. A second assassin said it was too early to thank God and threw a second bomb. Death finally caught up to the tsar." Viktoras yawned and stretched.

"His son, Alexander III, reversed the liberal reforms of his father and restored repressions, imposing severe Russification. He demanded that Governor-General Mikhail Muravyov 'make a Lithuania with nothing Lithuanian in it.' But the tsar had underestimated the stubbornness of the farmers."

Viktoras carried on. "In 1894, Nicholas II became the tsar, but he never had the stomach for it. Like his grandfather, Nicholas had the uneasy feeling that Death sat on his nose counting his days." Viktoras sighed, knowing Death was also counting his days. He gazed into the distance for a few moments. "What is sadder than a dying language? If our language dies, then who do we become? Russians?"

"Language is what makes us Lithuanians," said Ada, watching her grandfather paint with a quiet appreciation. His hand wasn't steady and his vision was weak, but the scenes jumped to life. After each scene was finished, he'd blow on his stiffened fingers to warm them, laughing that if he lived any longer, there'd be no room left on his coffin. He seemed in good health, so neither Ada nor anyone else believed death was near.

Having his life laid out before him put Viktoras in a philosophical mood. Life, he mused, was filled with good and evil, poverty and grief, joy and sorrow. And yet, eventually, everyone died. And time erased everything. "When you look at the path your life has taken, you see there was no other possible direction." He looked at his granddaughter, who had so much life ahead of her. "Ada, I've finished. Now, come paint your beautiful flowers."

"What kind of flowers would you like, Grandfather?"

"Oh, make me a whole field of wildflowers, those delicate purple ones we see in spring, my dear, and some blue forget-me-nots with those yellow eyes in the center."

Viktoras stood watching Ada paint her flowers, marveling at how the tiny blossoms bloomed from under her brush. Her flowers looked so real that it seemed the dew still clung to them. Ada had painted Dora's dowry chest with daisies and Julija's with violets. Those chests were the envy of every girl in the village.

"What's ahead for me, Grandfather? Will I ever find love?" asked Ada plaintively.

"Oh Ada." He sighed deeply. "I guarantee love will find you."

Later, after supper, Viktoras's thoughts returned to Kotryna. Where was she? Why hadn't he heard anything from her? Had she received his letter? Why hadn't she written him? She must still be angry with him. What if she had taken ill and died during those eight years? Wouldn't someone have written him?

Oh, he drove himself mad with all the things he imagined. All the things he had willed himself not to think about for eight years now came flooding in like water through a broken dam.

That night, when he looked outside, the night was clear and filled with innumerable stars. Where was heaven, he wondered? Somewhere beyond those stars? It seemed far away. When sleep wouldn't come, he numbered his dead. Where were the souls of his departed parents, wives, or his stillborn son, may they rest in peace? He tossed and turned, wrestling with his thoughts long into the night, while remorse hid in the shadows and regret pressed down on his chest like a coffin lid.

-Ten-

When he finished painting his coffin, Viktoras stood looking over his fields, filled with an intense love for the land where he was born, and where his father and grandfather had died. He walked through his fields, taking strength from the land. Every path, every tree felt like an old friend, every sheaf of rye had fed his family. Soon, he would have to leave this all behind like a misty dream.

For a long time, he stood lost in thought, but when the cold and damp finally penetrated his bones, he went inside to ask his grandson to invite the neighbors to bless his coffin the next day. Stasys and Petras carried the painted coffin into the parlor and placed it on chairs. They wondered how the neighbors would react to such a strange request.

The next morning, a cold wind hissed across the farmyards, slamming the door shut just as Ada was about to leave. Viktoras nodded sagely. "Such a wind is carrying something new your way." In his opinion, everything could be foretold if only you watched the signs. Everything seemed to speak to him—the weather, animals, crops, even birds.

The neighbors managed to come despite the weather, wondering if it would be the last time they would see the old man alive. This was a weighty event in Sapnai, for Viktoras Kulys was one of their most honored patriarchs. Word had spread that Viktoras had painted his coffin, raising everyone's curiosity.

"How is he?" asked Kreivenas, a round, balding man.

Stasys shrugged. "Still breathing."

In the parlor, they huddled around the coffin, ears red, noses running, listening as Viktoras explained the various scenes on his coffin. At first, they were bewildered, never having seen such a coffin, but before long they began to admire the art, commenting on the various historical scenes he had painted. "I've never seen a such a beautiful coffin,' said Gadeikis, truly impressed.

Even Modestas Bogdanskis managed to come in his cart, covered in bedraggled furs. He saw this as an excuse to take another look around the farmhouse. Hopefully someone might say something about smuggled books so that this visit might yield something more fruitful than the last. Sauntering into the parlor, he gave the old man a brief bow of respect, which galled him as he remembered how his father never would have bowed to these peasants. They should be bowing to him instead, yet another reminder of how far he had fallen in one generation.

When Ada brought in some cheese, Modestas greeted her. "Ah, *Bonjour*, Ada," he whispered.

For the first time, she felt a tinge of annoyance at the French. Why couldn't he just say things plainly? "What do you think of grandfather's painted coffin?"

Modestas smiled indulgently. "Very unusual," he said. "Is this a custom in this village?" He rubbed his hands together for warmth, his eyes darting over the coffin's images.

"No," answered Ada. "Grandfather simply got it into his head to paint his coffin with scenes from his life."

Overhearing Ada's remark, Viktoras added, "We'll all need a coffin someday, but I thought I'd make mine more interesting."

84

When Modestas looked around at the assembled villagers, he tried to hide his distaste for the rustic crowd. He forced a smile and wandered the room, examining every detail of the coffin, until he noticed a few books painted in random places. He eased closer to search for any Lithuanian writing on the covers and turned to ask Viktoras about them.

The old man shrugged. "They're just books." But he didn't like this question.

"Why put them on your coffin?"

"No reason. I didn't see Napoleon march through Vilnius, yet I still painted it."

"Then why is Napoleon on your coffin?"

Viktoras tried to think of a good answer when Margis began barking incessantly, followed by the sound of horses in the farmyard. A loud knock at the front door startled him. Dora ran to answer the door, and was shocked to find Captain Malenkov with several uniformed men behind him.

"Come in," said Dora, stepping back in fear.

When the captain entered, he examined the gathered group. "There have been disturbances in our province," he said. "We heard reports of a meeting, so we came to investigate." Stepping back out to the farmyard, he ordered, "Men, search the farm."

Elzbieta went to the window, anxiously watching the gendarmes fan out to the granary, stable, and barn, poking their rifles into the hay, moving trunks and examining barrels. The gathered neighbors stiffened in fear as they heard the noise of furniture overturned in the granary.

"What is the nature of this meeting?" The captain asked in Russian.

The neighbors looked around nervously, but no one dared say a word. Finally, Viktoras spoke up, in his rudimentary Russian. "I've invited my neighbors to bless my coffin," he said quietly, but inside he was seething with anger.

Captain Malenkov looked confused until he saw the painted coffin. "What is this?"

"My coffin, Captain," he said. "I painted it myself."

"I've never heard of such a thing," he snapped. He examined the coffin closely, noting Napoleon with his tri-cornered hat, then he spotted the old tsar, but couldn't make out the rest. "Why is everyone gathered here if it's not for a funeral?"

After a string of curses came from the barn, Elzbieta ran to the window in time to see chickens flying up to the roof of the outhouse. Captain Malenkov scanned the neighbors, who looked uneasy, as if regretting having come to the coffin blessing. When he saw Modestas, he nodded. "*Pan* Bogdanskis," he said with a hint of sarcasm.

"Captain," Modestas bowed slightly, looking oppressed.

The captain opened the coffin lid to make sure it wasn't a vehicle for contraband. "Where is the body?"

"I told you," said Viktoras. "This is *my* coffin."

The captain eyed him warily, then went into the kitchen and searched the other rooms. Everyone waited silently, fear making their stomachs turn.

Soon, one of the gendarmes came into the parlor. Saluting, Ivan said, "We found nothing suspicious, Captain."

The captain addressed the gathering. "There's been trouble at the border and there's a fugitive on the run. Therefore, we're checking every village." With that, the captain told his men to mount up, and they thundered out of the yard.

Viktoras walked over to shut the door. "Good riddance," he said quietly, letting out a deep breath. He glanced back at Modestas. That the captain had acknowledged him bothered the old man, but he was more worried about the trouble at the border.

Stasys and Elzbieta went to check on the animals, while Viktoras poured drinks all around to soothe frayed nerves. Raising his glass, he asked the forgiveness of neighbors for any wrongs he might have done them. They drained their glasses, relieved the ordeal was over. And then, one by one, it was their turn to ask for Viktoras's forgiveness.

First came Duda, a decent man except when he drank. He brought two hand-woven sashes wrapped around the saw he had forgotten to return. His two daughters were hired hands, and if it weren't for the son, who worked the land, there'd be no food on the table. Viktoras always made sure to hire his daughter, Nele, and since she never had time to go to the secret schools, Ada had taught her how to read and write during whatever time the two had together, quietly taking her to the barn with a blackboard.

"I'm sorry," Duda shrugged, handing the saw to Viktoras, who nodded, shaking Duda's hand. He asked Ada to bring him a jar of gooseberry preserves. "We need sweetness to make up for the curses I uttered the many days I looked for my old saw and couldn't find it. To your health!" Both men lifted their glasses.

Kreivenas brought over a sack of beets. "You know the pear tree at the end of your orchard? I could never resist picking them whenever I walked by." Kreivenas laid the sack on the table. "There, now we are even." Then he whispered in Viktoras's ear that he wanted the latest newspaper from the exiled press.

Viktoras whispered back, "Now is not the time. Besides, what are you going to do with all those newspapers? Wrap herring with them? Your wife recently told me you couldn't read a word."

Kreivenas bristled. "I can still support the good men in their cause. Besides, my son reads them to me."

Viktoras smiled. "You'll have to wait until next week." Across the room, Modestas leaned in, hoping to hear them.

Povilaitis, the best-known god-carver in the area, came with his old maid sister, Vanda, a vinegary spinster who wore such a large scarf that only her sharp nose was visible. Neither of them had married, caring for their farm together, though most of the work fell to Vanda. Povilaitis was a gifted sculptor of angels, saints, and the wayside shrines often seen on the country roads. His hardened older sister earned a bit of extra money as a midwife and also by washing the dead and preparing them for a wake.

Vanda eyed Viktoras's coffin and looked the old man over, assessing how much longer before she would be called. It gave him a chill to see that cold, appraising eye of hers. Her softer, more artistic brother brought one of his famous wooden statues of Jesus the Worrier, sitting with his head resting in one hand, concerned about the state of the world. Povilaitis apologized for not being able to repay an old debt. It was part of the Lithuanian character not to owe anyone. A man who didn't owe his neighbor considered himself wealthy.

"Ah, thank you for the little Worrier," said Viktoras, examining the wooden statue. "Let him worry about the rest of you when I'm gone." He filled the man's glass. "We'll call the debt paid if you build my Jesus a little roof so that he can watch over me when I'm in my grave."

"That will be a sad day, old friend," said Povilaitis.

In the afternoon, Father Jurkus arrived to join the gathering. "So, it's my friend's coffin we're blessing."

Viktoras nodded and poured the priest a drink. "Tell the truth. Have you ever seen a more beautiful coffin?"

Father Jurkus laughed heartily and raised his glass. "To the most beautiful coffin made by the best man in these or any other parts of this old nation. May you live to be a hundred, for we won't find another as brave as you." Everyone raised their glasses to Viktoras, who nodded his thanks through watery eyes.

The priest pointed to the coffin, "May this carry you like a ship up to the gates of heaven, and may you sit at the right hand of God and tell him of our troubles here in Sapnai so that he doesn't overlook us." The priest paused and cleared his throat. "I'm sorry to be late but I had something to attend to." He looked around the room, and when he saw Modestas sitting with Ada, he said, "I'll tell you later."

Modestas took note of how the priest censored himself.

Father Jurkus continued. "Now let's have a toast to Petrike

and Gadeikis, who will be getting married this Saturday."

They raised their glasses to the odd couple sitting together. Gadeikis had put on his best shirt for the occasion. He kept smiling shyly at Petrike, who self-consciously blushed.

The unusual ceremony went on all afternoon—toasting, apologizing, the bringing of gifts large and small, the shedding of tears, and, later singing, much drunken hugging, and telling old stories. It wore Modestas out until he couldn't bear another moment. Saying his goodbyes, he left quickly.

Once the priest was sure Modestas was gone, he glanced around the room to be sure it was safe, then pulled a folded newspaper from his boot. "Would anyone be interested in the news from Tilsit?" Near the border, Tilsit was the center for publishing the contraband books. It was bustling with book smugglers alongside other contrabandists smuggling cigars, alcohol, and tea. They all had to cross the border, the tsar's police buzzing thick as flies.

Everyone came alive despite the drinking and brought their chairs around the priest. Viktoras motioned for Petras to sit next to him. Ada also came, as hungry for the news as everyone else.

Father Jurkus put on his eyeglasses, mended on one side with string. "I wanted to read this by Kudirka:

> 'The purpose of the Press ban was to bring Lithuanian peasantry into closer relations with Russia and Russian culture. In fact, by arousing their specifically Lithuanian national feelings and inspiring them to effective resistance against Russification, it managed to achieve the exact opposite result.'"

Father Jurkus removed his glasses. "Our oppressors have taken away our language, our schools, and our very freedom. But we are proud and stubborn, so we'll fight with our books."

Viktoras stood up, his cheeks blazing. "By God, we were born Lithuanians and we'll die Lithuanians." He pounded the table, and the men in the room murmured their agreement.

After reading the newspaper, he folded it and slipped it back into his boot."I couldn't say anything earlier, but there's some bad news, I'm afraid. The reason I was late was because I was trying to find out who was arrested at the border. I think it was Norkus. He may have been injured. They say the gendarmes appropriated his horse and wagon along with the books he was carrying."

"Norkus?" Petras was shocked. "I just saw him two weeks ago. We were laughing at the Bartkus brothers because they had had too much to drink." His anger began to smolder. "It can't be."

Viktoras bristled at the news. "Damn the Russians for making criminals out of simple men who read their own language. Captain Malenkov came earlier and mentioned trouble at the border."

"He's already hunting for more smugglers he can send to Siberia," said the priest.

"These Russians won't leave Lithuania!" Viktoras bellowed. "God save us from war, famine, plague, and the Muscovites! We've been fighting our enemies all the way back to the Crusades when they came to baptize us with a sword. All of Europe bowed, but we resisted. We stubbornly endured. It's our best quality. They've taken away our land, our language and even erased the name of Lithuania from the map, but we will persist."

"Well said!" exclaimed Petras. He turned to the priest. "Father, I'd like to help, if I could."

"No!" Elzbieta was aghast. "Look what happened to Norkus."

"We'll see," said Viktoras. Smuggling was too dangerous to try to talk someone into it. It required courage, belief, and training. Still, Viktoras closed his eyes in silent thanks for answered prayers.

Across the room, Ada listened with a mixture of fear and envy. It felt as if her brother was now taking her place as a book smuggler.

-Eleven-

Ever since the day of the coffin blessing, the whole village had been furtively watching Viktoras for any sign of his imminent demise. But after a few weeks, when All Souls' Day rolled around in November when by tradition, all work in the fields and gardens must be finished, the neighbors were surprised and, if truth be told, a bit puzzled to see Viktoras still puttering around his farm. After all of that lamentation and leave-taking, after all the righting of past wrongs, after all of that worry, weeping, and hand-wringing at his coming death, they thought Viktoras could at least have the decency to make good on his promise.

Whenever the villagers saw him, humming and tinkering, they scratched their foreheads and hitched up their pants, half embarrassed for the old man that his predictions were not materializing, and half feeling foolish, as if he had played an elaborate hoax on them.

Elzbieta's nerves were also fraying. Each day she carefully watched her father for any hint of illness, fretting over every cough, holding back tears at every groan. But there he was, sitting next to the painted coffin in the parlor, humming happily while he sharpened his favorite whittling knife on the whetstone, testing the blade by slicing through an apple like it was jelly. Satisfied, he looked up and smiled.

"Papa, I've had enough of that coffin," she snapped. "Take it out to the yard. It's only inviting trouble."

By Thursday all thoughts of Viktoras's coffin were set aside in preparation for Petrike's wedding. Gadeikis had bathed in the village sauna and beaten himself with birch branches. He asked his neighbor to cut his hair, and then he took a bit of butter to keep his cowlicks in place. Wearing a brown suit that had served him well since his last marriage, he put a freshly washed handkerchief in his pocket.

Petrike, wearing a white dress that her mother had sewn, couldn't stop smiling when they met in church to say their vows. Gadeikis wiped his tears with his clean handkerchief. Elena and Ada sat sighing over another friend entering married life while they still waited, their hopes slowly seeping away.

Petrike and Gadeikis's wedding was celebrated with two days of food, drink, and revelry. Everyone congregated in Petrike's parlor, where the table groaned from the plentiful food. As people ate heartily, toasts were given and kisses exchanged by the new couple. Ada and Elena were amazed to see how Petrike seemed to take it all in stride. They had expected tears and lamentation at leaving home, but instead, the young bride seemed to enjoy the company of the quiet and shy Gadeikis.

Later, the tables and chairs were pushed to the walls and a small band of musicians played while everyone danced until the floor shook, raising dust. To Petrike's surprise, Gadeikis loved to dance, his face getting redder with each polka, until he finally took his jacket off to twirl his new wife around the parlor.

Outside, a small group of neighbors left the overheated room and huddled on the granary porch discussing Viktoras. "He's been acting strange lately," said Balys. "I don't know what to think. Can you imagine that after all these years, he wrote a letter to his daughter asking her to return home from Smolensk?"

"No! What could he be up to?" Ona asked, narrowing her eyes. "He's not breathed a word about her in years, and now this. He's only holding on until she arrives, don't you think?"

As if the neighbors didn't have enough to talk about, what with the wedding, the painted coffin, and the recent border trouble, now the tasty nugget about the old man's letter to Kotryna began to reach the ears of the rest of the villagers. Men began placing bets on whether or not Kotryna would return to Sapnai after her years in Smolensk.

"Do you really think she'll come home?" asked Kreivenas. Balys thought she might have forgotten how to speak Lithuanian.

"Even worse," said Ona. "She'll come back with a horrible Russian accent. We won't be able to bear it."

"She'll be used to city ways now," said Vanda, nodding deliberately. "She'll be no use on the farm anymore."

Povilaitis, the god-carver, smiled, "Do you remember how she was the prettiest girl in the village? She broke a few hearts before she left with the Feinstein family."

"She hauls water for Jews now, as if she couldn't find a place among her own kind," said Vanda, clucking her tongue in disapproval. "Pretty or not, she'll never find a husband now."

Oh, there was nothing like a bit of juicy gossip to liven up a party. They dredged up Kotryna's sad history with Aleksas Simaitis, everyone wondering what became of him in America. As yet, no one knew about the other letter their esteemed neighbor Viktoras had sent to that same Simaitis.

A week after Petrike's wedding, Father Jurkus returned for another visit with Viktoras, relieved to find him still in this world rather than the next.

"How are you, my friend? Still healthy, thank God. I was very happy not to have to say any masses for the repose of your soul," said the priest with a teasing smile.

Viktoras laughed softly. "Thank you."

"I wanted to tell you we've just received two more boxes of books from Simaitis in America."

"Really? That's wonderful news!"

"But I also have some bad news," Father Jurkus said solemnly. "I learned that Norkus was not only arrested but seriously injured. They shot him in the leg while he was crossing the border."

Viktoras nodded, hardly able to speak, burning with anger at the injustice. "What happened to the other man?"

"Tomas Kontautas, one of our best men, wasn't caught. Somehow, he made it across the border. I don't think they saw him, but we're not sure, so we've sent word for him to go into hiding. But I've heard that gendarmes have begun searching houses for contraband, so pass the word on to the villagers."

Viktoras frowned. "Yes, of course. I'll tell them."

The priest coughed into his fist. "I'll need Petras's help soon, but I'll need another man to replace Norkus, if you know of someone."

The old man nodded. "Perhaps."

After the priest left, Viktoras sat thinking of his own book running days. All that work, all those arrested, all those books confiscated by the Russians, and still nothing had changed. It sat heavily on him.

In Sapnai, it was a week of talk about poor Norkus. Prayers were said for him, masses were offered for his release. Father Jurkus tried to intervene, but there was little he could do since Catholic priests carried no influence with the Orthodox Russians.

Many years ago, Father Jurkus had been caught with smuggled books, but rather than imprison him or send him to Siberia, the Russians had confined him to the monastery in Kretinga for two years. There he met other priests who were punished for their work on behalf of Lithuanian freedom. Since the convent was near the Prussian border, the priests spent their time writing books and articles, which were smuggled across the border to the Tilsit presses, and then smuggled back to the convent as books or pamphlets to be distributed.

The neighboring villagers hid their contraband books, and secret schools were curtailed while the villagers went about their daily tasks. But something in the stomach felt sour, and sleep was troubled. Everyone worked, keeping their heads down until this Russian storm passed and dissipated without any more arrests.

-Twelve-

The winter twilight came a little earlier each day. November brought a cold spell, signaling the change in seasons. As the dead leaves crunched under Viktoras's boots, he realized the weather bothered him more than it used to. Now it seemed to go right through his bones, making them ache. The light had changed to a dusky color, and the sky hung lower as the short days rolled by.

All around the village, smoke rose from the chimneys and work was slowing. The growing season was over, and the earth would sleep through the winter, patiently waiting to be reawakened.

It was not like Viktoras to complain, but lately he had begun to grumble. He was cold no matter how many sweaters he wore or how many blankets he put over his legs.

When Elzbieta felt his forehead, she found it a little warm, so she made him tea and checked on him throughout the day. The next day Viktoras had a fever and took to bed with the grippe. Everyone in the family worried that if he contracted pneumonia or, even worse, consumption, it would indeed be very serious. Every village had lost someone to those dreaded illnesses, so they thought that the poor man's time had coming at last.

At night, he tossed and turned violently, and when the raven hour came, Death blew into his room like a wisp of smoke. "Viktoras," she called gently. "Your coffin is ready." Her tone was sympathetic, like that of a mother prodding her slow son.

Still half asleep and feverish, he moaned and pushed his eiderdown away.

"Come, I'm waiting for you," she whispered.

When he finally heard that voice from the other world, his heart drummed furiously. He wanted to tell her to leave him alone; that he was still waiting for his daughter. Instead, Viktoras pulled the covers over his head and said every prayer he knew.

Another feverish day finally dawned. He was very weak, barely able to whisper. When Elzbieta sat at his bedside, mopping his burning brow, he kept mumbling to her as if she were Kotryna already arrived to forgive him.

All week long, the family kept a vigil at his bedside, praying, nursing, and waiting for the inevitable. Ada even wrote a second letter to her aunt telling her to hurry.

"Where on earth could Kotryna be?" Elzbieta fretted. "Not one word from her. You'd think the earth had swallowed her."

Ada sat by her grandfather's bed, only leaving his side to sleep. She held his hand, read to him and put cold compresses on his fevered brow as he grew weaker day by day, his eyes unfocused and heavy with fever.

One morning, two weeks before Christmas, the sky opened and dropped enough snow to bury Sapnai. Ada sat by her sleeping grandfather, staring out the ice-glazed window, watching the thin wisps of white smoke rise from the Kreivenas's chimney down the road. A sleepy silence lay over the village, still and hushed after the snowstorm. This was one of those days in winter when the world turns completely white, fresh snow covering everything like an eiderdown, its softness rounding every corner.

As Ada gazed out the window, she thought that from afar, the neighbors' cottages looked like snow-covered mushrooms. Everything was still, as if the world was holding its breath. Behind the poplar tree, she could see a tiny bird's track like a seam. Grandfather's snow-covered beehives looked like mere bumps, the bees inside, slumbering contentedly. Ada stood up stiffly and stretched. Her grandfather still slept, breathing softly.

Outside, she could see her mother tending to the animals. A small cloud of vapor escaped Elzbieta's mouth as she left the cowshed, trudging through the snow in her felt boots. Chilled, Ada hurried to the kitchen and found Julija already making porridge.

Soon Petras came in with an armload of wood.

"Shut the door quickly before we freeze to death," yelled Julija, shuddering.

"You see my arms are full. You could help instead of yelling." Her brother put the wood near the stove. "Julija, God help your poor husband, if you ever manage to trap one," he said, wiping his hands on the seat of his pants.

Julija frowned but put her chin up proudly. "I won't have a lout like you for a husband. "I'll marry a cultured man like Modestas."

This was more of Julija's romantic nonsense, thought Petras, chuckling as he threw some wood into the stove. "Tell me, why does a farmer need culture? New ideas, machines, progress, that's what we need."

"You and your progress!"

At the kitchen door, Elzbieta stomped the snow from her boots and came in carrying a milk bucket. "I covered the animals with blankets." She shuddered and took off her sheepskin coat and boots. "It's so cold out there, it takes your breath away."

Down the road came the sound of sleigh bells, breaking the wintry silence. When Ada ran to the window to see who could be traveling in this weather, she was surprised to see it stop in front of their farmyard. Who could this be?

Stasys trudged through the drifts to see who had arrived. After the sleigh pulled into the yard, he saw a woman swaddled in wool scarves up to her eyes. He helped her take the fur covers from her lap, caked with snow and stiff from the cold. Ada and Petras came outside.

For a few seconds, the woman couldn't talk, her mouth still frozen. But when she saw the strangely painted coffin, leaning against the barn with a blanket of fresh snow, she stood up stunned, then broke down in tears. "Have I come too late? Has he gone?" A sob escaped. "I'll never see his gentle eyes again."

"Ada, you better get your mother," Stasys said sharply while the woman tottered over to the door. Shaking the snow from her coat, she stamped her boots at the door and stepped inside. "I'm too late." With trembling fingers, she unbuttoned her coat, still weeping.

Ada did as she was told, then returned to help the woman, who was shocked, hardly taking note of Ada. "Those eyes are closed to me forever," she whispered. It was only when she unwound the many wool shawls covering her face and neck that Ada recognized her Teta Kotryna and greeted her almost like a stranger for she hadn't seen her for many years. Helping her aunt pull off her near-frozen overcoat, she hung it near the stove to dry.

Elzbieta came stumbling into the room, wiping her hands on her apron and blinking as if looking at an apparition. "Kotre, is it really you? Thank God, you've come at last! I thought you'd never arrive." She hugged her sister.

"Elzyte, I'm frozen to the bone," she whimpered, using the diminutive form of Elzbieta. "I'm afraid I have frostbite. My fingers are blue." Her nose and cheeks were crimson, and she complained they stung from the cold.

"Come warm yourself by the stove." Elzbieta rubbed her sister's stiff, cold hands. "Why were you traveling in such a snowstorm? You could have frozen to death."

"My train was delayed. You can't imagine the hardship I've endured traveling these roads. I had to pay that man double his price, and even then, he was reluctant to take me. At first, it was only snowing lightly, but then the storm almost buried us."

The driver came inside, dragging the first of two large trunks. He wore a long fur coat and had wrapped a blanket around his shoulders and a scarf around his neck that covered most of his face. The mangy fur looked like rabbit that was about a hundred years old. Stasys went out to help the driver stable and feed his horse and then invited him inside, while Elzbieta made breakfast. The driver bowed. "I'm very grateful, for it's brutal outside."

Kotryna walked stiffly and sat down at the table, asking softly, "I saw the coffin in the yard." Her lower lip quivered as she looked around the room. "Am I'm too late then? Will I only see him lifeless in his coffin?"

For once Elzbieta was speechless.

"What illness finally got him?" Kotryna held her sister's hand and tried to read what was in her eyes. She glanced around anxiously, her eyes darting from person to person. "Will no one tell me?" Folding her hands in prayer, she looked up. "Papa, I've been away from you too long. Oh, Papa, we've had so much anger between us, and now it's too late." With this string of words, Kotryna crumpled in her chair with long wailing sobs.

Stasys nervously played with his whiskers and looked down at his callused hands, red as ham hocks. "Kotryna, calm down," he said gruffly. "Your father is not dead, but he's been very ill. We fear the end may be near."

Kotryna's head shot up. "Not dead?" she asked, blinking back her tears. "Papa is alive?" She wiped her face with her sleeve, her chest still rising in hiccoughs from crying.

Elzbieta twisted the corner of her apron. "He's been very sick, but I know he's anxiously waiting for you." The sisters went to knock on their father's door. When no one answered, they peeked inside and saw he was still asleep, so they went to his bed.

Kotryna leaned over and touched her father's shoulder. "Papa, it's me, Kotryna. I've come just like you asked in the letter. I came as fast as I could, but the weather and the roads were terrible." She listened to his soft breathing. "Papa," she repeated, shaking his shoulder a bit. When he didn't wake, she touched his hot forehead.

Viktoras adjusted his position, not yet opening his eyes, for he thought it was that ultimate trickster, Death, come again, this time pretending to be his daughter to fool him into answering her call. He wouldn't fall for this ruse. No, he'd turn over and go back to sleep. Let Death take herself to someone else's door. With that thought, he snuffled a bit and drifted back to sleep.

Standing over him, Kotryna was shocked to see how her father had aged in the eight years she had been away. He had shriveled and his cheeks had hollowed. Tears fell as she watched him sleep. "Will he live?" Kotryna asked.

"God knows." Elzbieta said. "We've done all we can."

"Let him sleep a bit and we'll try to wake him later," said Kotryna, the relief evident on her face.

Though weary from her travels, Kotryna examined her childhood home, relieved her father was still alive. Sighing, she looked around, astonished to see how much the children had changed in eight years. "My dear ones, let me look at all of you! Dora has grown into quite a woman. And good Lord, can this be Julija? When I left, you were a long-legged stork. And Petras! A grown man and so handsome." She tilted her head appraisingly at Ada. "Such a beauty and still not married?"

Ada bristled at her aunt's assessment. "I've become an old maid." She wanted to add *just like you* but held her tongue.

"You, an old maid? I can't believe it." Waving the idea away, Kotryna turned to her sister. "Elzyte," she said, "You look happy and well fed." She smiled wistfully at Stasys. "You've taken good care of your family."

Elzbieta eyed her stylish sister with a hint of envy. "*Nu*, and you, my dear, are very thin. Didn't they feed you anything in Russia?"

Kotryna wore a dark brown jacket over a white high-collared blouse and a brown wool skirt—a fancy city outfit in the family's eyes.

"Oh, I ate well enough."

Ada admired her aunt's elegant boots with their buttons and small heels, while Julija was simply mesmerized by this beautiful lady.

When Kotryna rubbed her hands together for warmth, Ada noticed they weren't rough and weathered like her mother's hands. Her aunt's hands were soft like white yeast rolls, and she wore a small garnet ring. Ada inspected the way she had twisted her hair into a chignon, held in place with tortoise shell combs. When she hung her aunt's coat, she could smell summer roses. How was it possible this worldly woman was her aunt? It was said Kotryna had been a beauty, and to Ada, she was still beautiful at thirty-seven.

"My goodness, look at all my nieces, almost ready for marriage." Kotryna's chin quivered. "While I'm a hopeless spinster."

She blinked away tears. "Elzyte, you can't believe how surprised I was to get a letter from Papa after all these years. How I waited for that letter every day. When it finally came, I cried myself sick. I quit my job and decided to come home."

Stasys turned to his wife. "Elzbieta, look how our Ada resembles her aunt. They're so similar except one is blond, while the other is dark."

Elzbieta nodded, comparing them. She looked at her younger sister with mixed emotions. While happy to have Kotryna home, she had some reservations because her sister was always so headstrong and nervous. Elzbieta could only hope that Ada wouldn't be influenced by her flighty sister.

After breakfast, the driver took his leave despite the snow, which had started again. Large snowflakes drifted down slowly and thickly, as if suspended in the air. Kotryna stood at the window, watching the driver struggle through the snow until she heard a raspy coughing from her father's room. Knocking softly on his door, she listened but didn't hear any noise.

"Papa, it's Kotryna. I've come home," she whispered, opening the door a crack and then entering.

At first Viktoras refused to open his eyes, but after she called him again, he opened one eye. When he saw his daughter, he rubbed his sleep-encrusted eyes as if mistrusting the vision. "Is it really you, my dear Kotryna, or am I still dreaming?"

She bent over to kiss his cheek. "It's me, Papa. I've come home." Tears fell like peas when she hugged him. "I'm so happy to see you again."

"You've come at last," he rasped, choked with emotion. For a long time neither could speak. Finally reunited, father and daughter held each other for a long time until Kotryna's shuddering sobs quieted. Then wiping their tears, they smiled. And it didn't take long for recriminations to follow.

"Why did you leave home like that? Without a word," he demanded weakly, as if the heartbreak were still fresh.

Shocked, Kotryna replied with her own accusation. "Why were you forcing me to marry Pocius, when you knew I loved Aleksas?"

"Why am I stirring up old mud?" He shook his head. "Forgive me, my dear." He took her hands in his.

"It's you who must forgive me for running away, for not obeying you." She hiccoughed.

"Don't cry, dearest," he said.

"Papa, I was so happy to get your letter after all those years."

"Why did you take so long to come home, my dear?"

"Mrs. Feinstein wouldn't pay me until she found a suitable replacement. Finally, a few days ago, my nerves gave out during a tea party. I walked into her parlor filled with guests and told her I was leaving in the morning. She finally paid me that day. I was already packed and ready to leave. I couldn't wait a moment longer to see you, despite the snowstorm."

Kotryna sighed deeply. "But Papa, what a fright I had when I pulled into the farmyard and saw a coffin. I thought it was too late."

Viktoras listened to his beloved daughter, all the while smiling but too choked with emotion to interrupt her. He was relieved he hadn't died before seeing her again and thankful she was no longer angry with him. "Forgive me, child," he begged earnestly squeezing her hand. "Forgive me," he echoed his plea, holding her hand tightly the whole time until he began to cough.

Kotryna ran out to make him some tea. When she returned, he wouldn't let her go for a minute. They sat together the whole day, each happy to be in the other's company. From time to time, her father would nod off still clutching his daughter's hand, as if afraid she'd run away again to some foreign land.

That night, Viktoras's fever finally broke. Though he was over the worst of the grippe, he felt as frail as a newborn lamb, only able briefly to sit up in bed and to have a bit of soup. But by the end of the week, he could sit at his usual place at the supper table.

Elzbieta declared that her sister's return was like a tonic for the old man. Each day he seemed to be getting stronger, willing himself to live and make things right again. Kotryna's homecoming made him feel reborn, healing his troubled heart, letting it stop its eight-year battle with itself. Kotryna's return even chased Death away, banishing her from his bedside.

He thanked Ada again for writing the letter that returned his daughter, but he didn't tell Kotryna about the letter to Aleksas Simaitis. He would wait for a response from America. No use getting Kotryna's hopes up if they were only to be dashed again. At dinner, Viktoras brought out the cherry wine he had made last summer and raised his glass. "To my daughter, finally back at her hearth after so many years among strangers."

The following Sunday, the entire village came to welcome Kotryna home and were surprised to see Viktoras on his feet again. "The man rose from his deathbed," said Kreivenas, shrugging.

"Like Lazarus from the grave," said Balys. "It's a miracle."

Later in the afternoon, the Bartkus brothers arrived, bringing a visitor. "Look who we brought with us from town." Zigmas laughed while Modestas followed him in the door.

Elena smiled when she saw them enter. "The Bartkus brothers always bring some fun." She winked at Zigmas and nudged Dora. "We told him the news about your aunt's return from Russia, and he wanted to meet her," said Jurgis Bartkus.

"We're lucky to find so many beautiful women in one room, eh?" teased Zigmas, winking at the Varnas sisters.

"Indeed," said Modestas, smiling politely.

"This is a nice surprise," said Ada. "I want you to meet my aunt." Her pride in this worldly aunt was evident.

Bowing, Modestas kissed Kotryna's hand, admiring this well- dressed aunt from Smolensk with her city dress and garnet ring.

"Good day," she said, her attention drawn to his threadbare coat. This was not how she remembered the Bogdanskis family. They had always dressed well and never mingled with villagers.

"*Bonjour, mademoiselle.*"

"Pleased to meet you, *pan* Bogdanskis," she said, nodding slightly, still a bit awed to see him in their home.

He asked about Smolensk and how she had liked Russia, sprinkling a few more French phrases into his conversation. But soon he lost interest, tired of the pretense. When Kotryna offered him something to drink, he gladly accepted, sitting next to Ada.

"Isn't my aunt wonderful?" Ada whispered.

"Yes, but what was she doing in Smolensk?"

"Taking care of children for a Jewish family."

106

"I see," he said, lighting a cigarette. Holding it between his yellow-stained fingers, he languidly surveyed those around him. "I have some news," he said, leaning over. "My family will also have some visitors soon. My mother is thrilled that her friend, Neda Ciginskas, has accepted her invitation to stay with us this summer. She's bringing her poor daughter, Magdalena, already a widow at the age of thirty-two. Her husband died of the grippe recently. She's also bringing her ailing son, hoping the country air and rest will do him some good."

"Thirty-two and already a widow," said Ada. "Poor woman."

"Not so poor," said Modestas, raising one eyebrow, with a slight smile. "Her husband left her quite well off."

"Why is it we never see your sister?"

"I sometimes think Helena's problem is a broken heart."

"Oh?" Ada found it romantic to be hopelessly in love.

Blowing a string of smoke up, Modestas added, "I can't bear to retell that whole sad story. Let's just say my mother didn't approve of the match." He smiled at Ada as if he had heartburn. "My diminutive mother is as unmovable as a mountain on certain things," he added, picking a bit of tobacco from his tongue.

Overhearing their conversation, Kotryna turned to Modestas and added dramatically, "I have great sympathy for Helena. I know what it's like when someone disapproves of the one you love, even if you love him more than your own life." Her voice trembled a bit. "What is love if not a fever like the grippe?"

Across the room, Stasys turned to look at his son and arched a brow. Petras smothered his laugh.

In the evening, after all the visitors had gone, Viktoras took Kotryna aside to ask what she thought of Modestas. Leaning over so Ada couldn't hear, she whispered into her father's ear. "He looks as though someone's tied a millstone around his neck. Is he always like that?"

Her father nodded. "I'm afraid so."

"And he's dressed poorly, yet he puts on such airs," said Kotryna.

He smiled. "Yes, it makes you laugh up your sleeve at this moth-eaten nobleman with his Polish pretensions and his bit of French." He chuckled. "And I hear he's whistled away whatever little was left of his father's money."

"What a shame," said Kotryna. "And he asks questions like a nosy old woman."

"Is that so?" He wondered what questions had been asked this evening.

"Do you really think he has his sights set on our Ada?"

"Not if I have anything to say about it," Viktoras retorted, frowning. "Elzbieta is blinded by the Bogdanskis name, but he's not the man for our Ada."

Kotryna looked at her father for a long moment. "Be careful, Papa," she said, arching a brow. "This meddling in matters of love has a familiar ring to it." She smiled ruefully, for this was still a sore spot between them.

-Thirteen-

Three weeks later, on an afternoon full of light snow flurries, another of Viktoras's letters finally bore fruit. His old friend, Jeronimas Balandis from Kelmai, dressed in his Sunday best under a warm sheepskin jacket, came to visit his fellow book smuggler and brought along his only son, Jonas.

At sixty-two, Jeronimas was strong and big-shouldered but listed a bit like a ship on a rolling sea, the result of a childhood injury that had never healed properly. Jonas was twenty-six with nut-brown hair that fell in his eyes and a wide smile with teeth like garlic cloves. He resembled his father with his warm amber eyes. They were as alike as two drops of water, except the father was a full head shorter than his strapping son and had gray hair.

"Well, well, the 'Fox' is here at last. How are you, my old friend?" asked Viktoras.

"Fine, fine," answered Jeronimas. "How has my friend, the 'Owl' been?" The former book smugglers greeted each other warmly using their secret names, glad to have a chance to reminisce about the old days.

Jeronimas introduced Jonas, who greeted each member of the family, but when his eyes met Ada's, he hesitated, searching her pale blue gaze. Something stirred in her as she felt his look burrow into her. His eyes were calm and trusting, and she sensed Jonas was quiet, a bit shy and reserved like she was. But also beneath his reserve she could sense a hidden sensitivity, a quality that intrigued her. His smile, his face, red-cheeked from the November wind, all left her feeling the oddest sensation in her throat.

Nearby, Viktoras watched, taking great delight. He hoped something might bloom in this encounter. He clapped Jonas on the back, urging him to sit, for it was time to celebrate.

Jonas smiled. "My father has always told such wonderful stories about his daring and heroic friend, Viktoras Kulys," he said. "It's such an honor to finally meet you. He said you smuggled enough books and newspapers and pamphlets from Prussia to fill all of St. George's Church, and that you risked your life many a time to keep the Lithuanian language alive."

The young man's words touched Viktoras, making him momentarily at a loss. "Ah, you give me too much credit." He mumbled his thanks, embarrassed and secretly delighted by the praise.

"We went to Prussia several times a year for books. Sometimes the border crossing was very dangerous, but other times it was easy, when the Lithuanians, who lived in the part of Prussia we call Lithuania Minor, would throw packages of books across the ditch at the border at a specified place. We'd get them and hide them in a hay loft or a wood pile until it was safe to bring them home." He smiled, remembering good times.

Viktoras looked at Jeronimas. "But where's your wife?"

"I left Domicele at home to tend to the animals and the farm.

"She sends her greetings to the entire family."

Food was brought to the table. After a hearty meal of barley soup, followed by ham and potatoes with clabbered milk, Viktoras and Jeronimas resumed their stories of their old days, when they crossed the border, occasionally bribing the border guards with rubles. Viktoras asked Jeronimas if he remembered the time they saw those hellish tongues of flame over the marshes at night.

"When I told Father Jurkus about them, he called them *ignis fatuus*. They were probably caused by the escaping gas in the marshes. But the locals had other ideas, believing the tiny flames were lost souls or imps."

Jeronimas slapped his thigh and chuckled. "We saw them once as we ran with the border guards in hot pursuit."

"Oh ho! What a day that was! Did you bring the book I asked for in my letter?"

"No," Jeronimas said, "I left it at home. How could I have forgotten it? That book has such a story." He turned to Elzbieta. "Why, that book saved your father. I'll never forget that day with bullets flying past us while we ran for our lives."

"I've never heard that before," she said, turning to her father with new respect.

Stasys perked up. "Oh, now this sounds like a good story," he said, rubbing his hands together.

Sitting back in his chair, Jeronimas began. "This happened years ago, when we still went by our secret names." He looked at Viktoras and laughed quietly, shaking his head. "I remember it was a bad year—a drought year in which the redemption payment for the farm land would be impossible to make, so I joined Viktoras in his book running. We crossed the border, bringing Lithuanian books and some contraband to sell to help with our payments. We were crossing at night when we heard the border patrol yelling for us to stop. When they fired the first warning shot, we bolted, racing through bushes, our faces scratched, jumping over logs as if we were still young." Jeronimas laughed.

Viktoras picked up the story. "We ran for the woods, trying to reach our usual hiding places. When the gendarmes saw we weren't stopping, they began to shoot in earnest, bullets zinging by our ears. I thought we were done for." He shook his head.

"Viktoras is something rare, I tell you," said Jeronimas. "I've never met anyone with such fire in his eyes. I dived into a thicket while he ran, bullets ricocheting against the trees. I hid in a hundred-year oak tree like an owl. I didn't move all night."

"A bullet zinged right past my left ear," Viktoras added. "Another bullet hit me in the back. Fortunately, that's where I had the books in my sack. I dropped my sack into the brush and ran to the dreaded marshes where no sane man dared go. When I finally stopped, I shook like a leaf for the rest of the night, thinking Jeronimas had been shot or apprehended. What an awful night."

Excited, Jeronimas pounded the table with his fist. "I escaped, but I thought it was you who had died that night. When I returned home the next day, I went straight to bed, so upset I couldn't utter a word. Domicele kept watching me and wondering what was wrong, but I was as quiet as a dog that swallowed soap. And then what do you think happened?" Jeronimas paused.

"Like some revenant, Viktoras showed up at the farm the next day—alive, unhurt except for his bruised back." Jeronimas smiled broadly. "And he had the money in his hand. He had waited until the border police left and then retrieved his book sack, delivering his books as promised, keeping only one book—the one that stopped the bullet meant for his back. Oh, I tell you, we got so drunk that night." Jeronimas hooted.

Laughing, Viktoras added, "I always said books were more powerful than bullets, but by God, I left that book at your house and have never laid eyes on it again."

The two men had continued their smuggling for years until Viktoras felt his age had slowed him, making him a danger not only to himself but also to others. Jeronimas continued for a while but soon gave up altogether. It just wasn't the same without Viktoras. The two men had gotten along well, their natures complementary, laughing easily, talking of life and farming, their political beliefs. Now only Viktoras distributed the books.

Across the room, Jonas smiled as he took note of Ada's admiration for her grandfather's heroism.

Viktoras told his friend of Norkus and how he had been shot recently.

Jeronimas's face contorted with the effort to keep from cursing in good company. He shook his head, asking if there was anything he could do to help the poor man.

"Father Jurkus has already tried. I heard they burned the confiscated books in the square as a warning to others who are smuggling them."

"Burned them?" Ada asked. "We could have used those books for our schools."

Viktoras told them that Ada taught at the priest's secret school.

"Really?" said Jonas with obvious admiration.

Ada smiled, feeling the blush blooming on her cheeks.

Viktoras watched them both. "The priest told me he's looking for a new man. Our Petras has volunteered, but the priest needs another." Viktoras searched Jonas's face for any spark of interest. Father and son exchanged a glance and Jeronimas nodded. Viktoras decided to say no more for the moment. A seed had been planted.

"Sing that wonderful song of yours about the three brothers who went off to war," Viktoras encouraged Jeronimas. "In truth, I liked your gypsy song better, but there are young girls here." He chuckled and winked at his granddaughters. "And send Jonas back soon with my book."

"Done!" Jeronimas, who had had one too many glasses of the home brew, clapped Viktoras on the back and began his song. Before long, Jonas joined his father with his deep baritone voice, a voice so sonorous and melodious that Ada and the other women turned to him in admiration because a man with a good voice was worth his weight in gold.

"Lithuania is a singing country," said Jeronimas. We have a song for every occasion and sometimes just for the simple pleasure of singing."

Viktoras agreed and started another song. Soon the rest of the family joined in harmony, and even Petras was permitted to sing, though he had no ear and generally irritated those who sang alongside him.

Ada could see this was like a tonic for her grandfather. He appeared younger as the evening wore on.

When it was time to leave, Jeronimas thanked his hosts warmly. Viktoras made him promise to come again and to bring his wife next time, while Jonas promised to bring the legendary book. As he was leaving, Jonas reserved his warmest smile for Ada, telling her how much he enjoyed himself, and what a great man her grandfather was. When he said this, he looked deeply into her eyes as she slowly reddened right up to her ears. A lightning current seemed to run through her whenever he glanced her way.

When Jeronimas went out into the farmyard, he noticed the painted coffin, which he had missed in all the excitement of his visit. He walked around it and turned to ask Viktoras about it. "I've never seen a painted coffin before," he said. "Who is it for?"

"It's for me," Viktoras replied." I painted it myself. Well, that's not entirely true. My granddaughter Ada helped me. I painted the scenes from my life, and she painted all the flowers in between."

Jonas smiled at Ada. "You have quite a gift."

Pushing back her braids, Ada stammered her self-conscious thanks. She frowned, embarrassed by her awkwardness. What was wrong with her? She excused herself, not even looking into those eager eyes of his that would cause her cheeks to heat up all over again. She knew it was rude, but she couldn't stay another second.

Jonas frowned as he watched her walk away.

After examining the coffin, Jeronimas turned to his friend.

114

"Why have you prepared such a beautiful coffin when it's obvious you are healthy?"

Viktoras didn't want to tell him Death was visiting, or of his feeling that his life was like a thread that had come to the end of its spool. He coughed into his fist to give himself time to think. Then he looked up at Jeronimas and smiled. "This coffin reminds me life is short and I better do those things I've been promising myself I'd finish before I died. I come out here and I think, oh ho, I better hurry."

"In that case, I should start to paint my own coffin," Jeronimas said, laughing. "It would be the perfect cure for my laziness." Viktoras laughed too, relieved not to be asked any more questions.

Jeronimas climbed into his cart and looked for his son, who was watching Ada walk to the orchard. His father called to him. "Let's get going and leave these good people to their work."

Jonas ran to the cart and jumped in, bidding everyone a fond goodbye. When they drove out of the farmyard, Jonas craned his neck to get a glimpse of Ada. He saw her turn toward the road to watch them leave. He waved to her as the horses kicked up dirt and watched her wave back.

As they disappeared from view, Ada sat down on an old tree stump, covering her burning face with her hands and feeling like a complete idiot.

-Fourteen-

The December days were pitifully short, while the nights were endless and frigid on the snow-muffled landscape. Viktoras glanced out the window at the thick roof of snow on his painted coffin. It looked so lonesome and forlorn that he asked Petras to help him move it to the barn before it warped.

Afterward, he spent the morning talking to Kotryna, as he often did now that she was back home, peppering her with questions about her time in Smolensk. He wanted to know about the Feinstein family and whether she had a suitor there. "Did you make any friends?"

"Well, of course," she said in a peevish voice. "There were other servants who became my friends once I learned to speak decent Russian." What Kotryna didn't say was how disappointing her home seemed after all of her years away in the grand Feinstein house. How everything in Sapnai looked shabbier and smaller than she remembered, and how her beloved village now seemed so sheltered from the larger world, unlike the worldly family she worked for in Smolensk. But she didn't mention it to her father, for it would needlessly hurt him.

Kotryna took her father's hand. "Papa, I've come back to start my life again, if I may stay here."

"Of course, you'll stay here." He shrugged. "This is your home. You're my daughter, not some Gypsy off the road. It was my fondest wish that you come home." He kissed her on the forehead. "Now it's time for me take a little nap." Kotryna watched her father walk, his age more visible in his stooped back.

In the parlor, Ada worked the whirring spindle, while nearby, the rhythmic clacking of the loom sounded as Dora wove a bedspread for her sizable dowry. Petras studied a pamphlet about the Socialist future that a stranger had been handing out at the market. It talked about the brotherhood of men, equality, and the end of empire, words that filled Petras with hope for the future.

Sitting at the window, Kotryna stared at the endless white snow, remembering her youthful love, Aleksas Simaitis. It seemed so long ago and yet like yesterday. She wondered what he was doing in America. It pierced her heart to think of him, to remember her girlish dreams and hopes for love, left behind when she fled to Smolensk. Had he found someone else to love? As she sat feeling the sadness of what might have been, she heard her sister singing in the kitchen. Suddenly, Kotryna felt out of place in her own home, as if she were an extra appendage. Bored and restless, she moved into the kitchen to see what her sister was up to.

Elzbieta had tried repeatedly to get her sister to help with the borscht, or to make cheese or butter, with no success. Today, she finally lost patience with Kotryna's lassitude and coaxed her into helping prepare the sourdough rye. Petras fired up the clay bread oven.

In a long wooden trough used only for the bread, they mixed the flour with the sourdough starter that had been passed from mother to daughter for countless generations. Each family made their own starter, which lent a distinct taste to the black bread. Elzbieta would pass it on to each of her daughters when they married, another way of knitting the generations together.

After kneading in the caraway seeds, each sister covered their loaves with linen towels.

"Let's get lunch ready while we wait for the dough to rise," said Elzbieta. When she began to prepare lunch, the shelves in the pantry began to rattle and Kotryna jumped.

"You've become very nervous since you returned, my dear. I don't remember you quaking at every noise."

"It reminded me of Smolensk," said Kotryna.

"What happened with the Feinstein family?"

Kotryna frowned. "Life was very different there."

"Was it the Jews? You hear about all sorts of strange practices—unfamiliar holy days, hats, and rituals." Elzbieta felt a shiver run up her spine.

Kotryna interrupted her. "No, no. I liked the Feinstein family. They were a little different, and it took time to get used to them, but they always treated me well, especially the mistress. She even gave me the clothes she no longer wanted. That woman always had her nose in a book. *Madame Bovary* was her favorite. She read it many times and told me how Emma had fallen in love with a scoundrel. Sometimes I'd find her crying and ask her if it was that scoundrel again and she'd nod and say love was a curse. I always agreed because, you know, I also had a sad love story. When I told her about Aleksas, the mistress felt sorry for me and gave me this ring." She held it up for her sister to see.

Elzbieta admired the small garnet ring on Kotryna's white hands, but she had the feeling her sister was hiding something. "Is there something you're not telling me?"

"There is, but I don't want to speak of it yet."

She eyed her sister suspiciously. It was not like Kotryna to hold back.

When Kotryna caught her sister's look, she sniffed and turned away. "Don't look at me that way. I've missed my family so much. Fate has dealt me some cruel blows. What do I have in life? Nothing. No husband, no children, no home of my own."

"Teta," said Ada. "You have us and we're glad you're back."

"Yes," added Elzbieta. "We'll find you a husband."

"But I'm thirty-seven already. Who wants such an old maid?"

"Well, there's Balys. He's a widower now, or Povilaitis the god-carver."

"Those old men?" Kotryna wrinkled her nose.

Ada brightened. "What about Morkunas? They say he's got a bit of money put away."

"He's too shy. I think he's afraid of women. Besides, he has a nose like a potato."

"Well, that leaves Faustas," Elzbieta said.

"That drunken matchmaker! I'd go back to Smolensk first." A ripple of laughter rolled through the young women.

Elzbieta bristled. "You haven't changed a bit except to become pickier. Why, Papa had chosen Pocius for you, a fine, decent man with a good farm. True, he had a pockmarked face, but he was a hard worker and his farm had prospered. But you only wanted Aleksas Simaitis."

"Don't be angry," Kotryna pleaded. "You know I've always been guided by my heart. My life would have been very different if Papa had let me marry Aleksas."

"You would have lived a beggar's life." Elzbieta saw she had angered her sister, so she said no more.

Ada helped her mother make dumplings when something thumped loudly in the pantry. "What the devil was that?" snapped Elzbieta. "Is someone hiding in there?"

Dora whispered, "Maybe it's a Gypsy."

Julija added, "Or a gendarme."

Ada said, "No, it sounded more like a potato hit the door."

Elzbieta frowned. "And who threw that potato?"

Sitting at the table, pale and mute, Kotryna kept her head down.

Two more thumps, and Margis whimpered, leaving the kitchen.

"There it is again," said Elzbieta. "Look, even the dog is frightened. Go get your father, Ada."

Stasys and Petras both ran to grab some pitchforks and returned to the kitchen, followed by Viktoras, who had heard the commotion. "Who could it be?"

"I think it's an animal," said Petras. The three men stood by the pantry door. Stasys motioned to Petras. "When I open the door, be ready to chase it outside."

Petras slowly opened the creaking pantry door. When nothing came out, Stasys went inside. "There's nothing here. I think you women are imagining things."

"We heard it as clearly as I'm hearing you," Elzbieta insisted.

"Well, come see for yourself," he offered.

Kotryna trembled and held her sister back. "Don't go in there, please." There was a note of hysteria in her voice.

"Why not?" asked Elzbieta, as she peeked inside the pantry. "Say what you like, I heard those thumps and something had to make them."

Ada blessed herself while Dora and Julija hid behind their mother.

Viktoras went inside to look for himself. He was about to leave when a jar of applesauce fell, breaking on the floor in front of him. The women screamed.

"What the deuce?" Viktoras's eyebrows shot up. Looking around, he found nothing out of the ordinary.

"He's followed me." Kotryna wailed.

"Who's followed you?" asked her alarmed father. "Is someone after you? A Russian?"

"It was supposed to stay there."

"Get a hold of yourself," said Viktoras.

"It's the *domovoi*," moaned Kotryna. "I thought I left it behind in Smolensk. I should have known they only follow old maids."

The whole family gaped in awe.

"What's a *domovoi*?" asked Dora.

"A house imp," sniffed Kotryna.

Stasys looked back inside the pantry. "An imp?" He searched the room and then turned back to Kotryna. "You can't be serious?"

"A ghost?" asked Julija, eyes nervously darting around.

"God forbid, is it a demon?" asked Elzbieta.

"Lord, I'm sick to death of his tricks," said Kotryna, dabbing her eyes with her apron. "In Russia, they say a *domovoi* is an old household imp with a hairy body and a tail. It's full of pranks. In the Feinstein house, it made the wife snore loudly, or hid the master's boots, or curdled fresh milk. We don't have these things in Lithuania, but oh my dears, you have no idea how frightened I've been these last eight years. Russia is filled with demons. It's terrible how many different kinds of imps live there." She began to tremble.

"There's a *Huldra,* a beautiful young girl who makes men fall in love, following her deep into the forests until they are hopelessly lost. And forest *Leshii* with bluish skin, protruding eyes."

Stasys scratched his head, looking at his sister-in-law as if she had lost all reason. "Is this a joke?" Petras rolled his eyes and added, "Oh come now, we don't live in the middle ages anymore."

Viktoras was shocked. "My poor dear, I had no idea you had to live under such horrible conditions. Why didn't you let us know?" he asked, his guilt rising. "I would have brought you home."

Kotryna continued her catalog of imps. "Oh, dear ones, there are many more. There's a *dvorovoi*, a demon who lives in the yard like a dog, and the *vodyanoi,* old and ugly with a green beard."

"Enough, please!" Elzbieta sucked in her breath. "We'll all have nightmares. What a horrible place Russia must be. No wonder they took over our country. They probably need to get away from those terrible demons." Elzbieta had forgotten how chaos and trouble seemed to follow her sister.

Suddenly, the shelves in the pantry began to rattle again.

Ada yelped in fright, and Julija ran to her father. "Papa, do something." Stasys closed the door.

"I need some vodka, please," said Kotryna, standing shakily. "For my nerves."

Viktoras went to get a bottle and noticed his heart was pounding, so he poured himself a drink as well.

"For the love of God, how do we get rid of this horrible thing?" asked Elzbieta.

"I don't know," Kotryna replied and downed the vodka in one gulp. "In Smolensk, they tried everything, but nothing worked."

Viktoras clucked his tongue. "It's bad enough that the Russians have taken over our country. I refuse to let Russian demons take up residence in my home!"

Petras waved his hand in dismissal. "I don't believe a word of this. It sounds like something out of an old folk tale." He went outside with his father to tend to the animals.

Ada wasn't so sure. Each time she went by the pantry door, she would bless herself and spit three times. Even so, her skin prickled and the hair on her neck stood up. She wanted to get the priest, but her mother didn't allow it, saying it would bring shame.

The long winter nights stretched out endlessly, while the frosty days flew by swiftly. Sometimes, the pantry was quiet for days on end, and other times the wind blew through it like a storm from the Russian steppes.

One day, when they were housebound, their *domovoi* was particularly full of pranks and deviltry. Elzbieta would drop a spoon and then pick it up, only to have it drop again. Petras carved a ladle and found he'd cut a hole in the bottom, making it useless. Julija was mending a shirt when she realized she'd sewn the sleeve onto her skirt. Ada was surprised to see that the tulip pattern on the sweater she was knitting was beginning to look more like a row of toads. While knitting gloves for her father, Kotryna cursed under her breath when she found she had knitted two thumbs on one hand of the glove.

Many oaths were muttered when Viktoras couldn't find his boots. Murmuring curses, he finally looked in the pantry and found them in a basket. Later in the day, the leg of a bench collapsed when Stasys sat down.

When the chickens simply stopped laying eggs for a week, the family began to resent Kotryna and her imp.

"Don't be so hard on me," she begged. "I've been so lonely while living in Smolensk without my family."

"Saints preserve us," said Elzbieta. "Other people bring wonderful things from foreign places—chocolates from Prussia, dolls from Poland, money from America. But what does my sister bring back as a souvenir from Russia? A *domovoi*, as if anyone here needed any more bad luck."

-Fifteen-

In midwinter, the long winter nights pressed down heavily on Viktoras. Looking at the night sky, he felt insignificant, the darkness of the season seeping into his very soul. What does it all amount to? he wondered as he often did these long nights. We are born, we love, have children, work, grow old and die—our lives a fleeting spark in the darkness. Once Zimmerman, the Jewish tavern keeper, told him that God created us because he loves the stories. These were the thoughts Viktoras pondered until exhaustion finally allowed him to sleep.

Just before dawn, a cold draft wafted into the cottage, and it seemed as if a white specter blew by his ear and settled at the end of his bed. Death had returned with her tattered white dress, waiting patiently to pluck his soul—a late harvest.

Hovering at the foot of his bed, she called to him, but though it still startled him, he was beginning to get used to his visitor. They were getting to know each other. Tonight, when he heard her approach, he started a silent litany to the saints and before he was finished, he fell back asleep.

In the morning, it comforted him to remember how Father Jurkus always reminded his parishioners that life had an order.

Morning sun always broke through the black night. Winter, though often harsh, always gave way to spring, which woke the land, the warmth bringing abundant food. In spring, Viktoras felt as if he could live forever. The priest was right. There was an order to life that he had learned to trust.

Yet even in the long and frigid winter night, Viktoras loved how the stars sparkled in the coal black night, and how, in Sapnai, the darkness was lit by candles in windows that made the bluish snow outside glow.

On Christmas Eve, Viktoras's family gathered for the most magical time of the year. It was said that when the nights got long between All Souls' Day and New Year's, the veil that hid the living from the dead became permeable.

Magic was in the air. At midnight, the animals talked in human voices and the water in the wells turned to wine. On that night, many things could be foretold by omens, divination, and augury. Luck, illness, or bad harvest could all be foreseen by pouring melted wax into water and reading your future in the shapes made when the wax cooled. On Christmas Eve everything was watched for omens of good or ill fortune.

After the evening meal, Ada and her sisters went into the darkened back room to look into the mirror, for on this night, a girl could see the face of her intended in the mirror. Dora was the first to try, impatient to see if Jurgis would ever be her husband.

"Why do you always have to be first?" complained Julija. Teta Kotryna came into the room. "Your mother and I did this when we were young. Every year I swore I saw Aleksas's face in the mirror." She blew her cheeks out and shook her head. "You can see how that turned out."

When Dora looked in the mirror, she was confused to see a face that looked like Zigmas's rather than that of his brother, Jurgis. Blowing on the mirror until it misted up, she wiped it with her apron, but when she looked again, the same face appeared.

"Well, who was it?" Julija asked, grabbing the mirror. "Jurgis," lied Dora, but her worried face betrayed her.

When Julija looked in the mirror, she was mystified to see no one but she told them she saw a prince on a white horse. Giving the mirror to Ada, she said, "You're the only one with a real suitor. I'm sure you'll see Modestas."

Dora was annoyed. "I have a suitor too."

"That hayseed!" cried Julija dismissively. "At least Ada is going to marry someone from the gentry."

Ada wasn't eager to play the game, but she took the mirror and closed her eyes. When she opened them, she saw a man's face with amber eyes. The vision faded in an instant.

"Was it Modestas?" asked Julija eagerly.

Ada shook her head, feeling the oddest sensation. Those eyes seemed familiar.

"Who was it, then?" Julija demanded.

"I'm not sure." Ada sat staring at the mirror in her lap as if it would tell her its secrets.

Finally, Julija took the mirror and handed it to her aunt. "It's your turn," she urged.

"Me?" Kotryna shrugged. "I think my time has passed."

"Oh, just for fun," coaxed Julija.

"All right. For you, Julija, I'll look." Kotryna picked up the mirror, but when she looked into it, she screamed.

"What is it?" asked Ada, frightened.

"I saw something ugly and hairy," Kotryna croaked.

"No," said Julija. "It couldn't be that horrible thing in the pantry, could it?"

All three girls ran to tell their mother who refused to have anything ruin their Christmas Eve. She made the sign of the cross over each girl and told them to set the table.

Viktoras said a prayer, then, taking the first of the Christmas wafers, he offered it to Elzbieta and Stasys. "I wish you both good health," he said solemnly. He went to each member of the family letting them break off a piece of the wafer.

"These are my wishes for the coming year. A husband for Ada, courage for Petras, patience for Dora, and good cheer for Julija." When he got to Kotryna, he said, "I wish you release from the *domovoi*."

"Some peace for all of us, God willing," said Stasys from across the table.

The family ate the customary twelve dishes, one for each of the twelve apostles on the last day of the Advent fast. There were several kinds of herring, pea and bean porridge and pike. Afterward, they left the dishes on the table because the ancestors would return after midnight for their own dinner once the family was asleep.

On Christmas morning, the sun glinted blazingly off the snow and ice as Ada took her shawl and went outside, her heart soaring at the brilliant beauty. Everything sparkled as if covered with diamonds. Squinting in the bright sunlight, she admired the glistening icicles that decorated the eaves of every building.

In the afternoon, Elzbieta came into the parlor with a ham for the Christmas table. After the meal, Kotryna announced, "I have presents for each of you." She left the room to rummage in one of her trunks and came back to present her father with a new pipe, two combs for Dora's hair, a lace-trimmed handkerchief for Julija, a fancy nutcracker for Stasys, a penknife in the shape of a tree branch for Petras, and a soft blue woolen shawl for Ada.

Kotryna saved the last present for her sister, a navy dress with a lace bodice, much finer than any they had seen. Elzbieta's eyes widened with longing. She had once been slim and beautiful like Kotryna, but with each pregnancy, she had to let out her dresses a bit more. She hadn't given it much thought until she saw her sister's fancy clothes. It wasn't fair. Kotryna had never cared about such things when they were little, while Elzbieta had been the one who liked to dress up and play the lady.

"Oh, this is beautiful. But where would I wear such a dress?"

"Wherever you like," answered Kotryna, pleased with her sister's reaction.

"Everyone will think I'm from the manor." Elzbieta smiled coquettishly.

Kotryna laughed. "Try it on. It may be a little snug. Mrs. Feinstein gave me three dresses and this one was the largest."

Elzbieta took the dress to the other room to try on, but Kotryna couldn't button the back.

"Maybe if you wore a corset?" said Kotryna.

"Me, a corset? I couldn't breathe in one of those." Elzbieta held her breath while her sister pulled the back of the dress together and finally buttoned the first two buttons. But when Elzbieta exhaled, the second button popped off and flew across the room. Ada stifled a giggle, watching her mother squeeze into a dress meant for a woman half her size.

"It's no use, you'll only tear it," Kotryna said unbuttoning it, muffling her own laugher at the comic sight of her sister sucking in her stomach until she turned purple.

"What's so funny?" Elzbieta sat on the bed, deflated and breathless from holding her stomach in. The dress ballooned around her.

Kotryna tried to control herself, but one look at her sister's disapproving face and she erupted into laughter.

"You did this on purpose, giving me a dress that's too small," Elzbieta sulked.

Her sister looked up at her but the more she tried to stop, the more she laughed until tears ran down her cheeks. Soon Ada and Julija caught the contagion, helplessly laughing along.

"That's right, laugh, Kotryna." Elzbieta was deeply offended. "Go ahead and laugh at this simple farmer's wife who has never had such a beautiful dress. Laugh, that I hoped it fit, so for once I could go to church looking like a lady." Elzbieta pouted.

All the laughter stopped at once. "I'm sorry, Elzyte," said a contrite Kotryna.

"What kind of present leaves you feeling badly? You did this on purpose."

"No! I swear I didn't mean to hurt you," Kotryna protested.

"You always think only of yourself."

"I do not," Kotryna said, frowning. "You were the one who always lorded over me."

Elzbieta threw the dress across the room. "Keep it! I don't want it."

Kotryna could see that her sister was on the verge of tears. "Listen, Elzyte, is there someone who might alter the dress?"

Elzbieta brightened at the prospect. "There's a good tailor in Raudonava named Glauberman. But how much would it cost?"

"I've saved some money," said Kotryna, smiling and taking her sister's hand.

A week later, the tailor, Yakub Glauberman, managed to come by sleigh from Raudonava. The stooped man stood at the door, his hat and coat dusted with snow. A cold draft blew in with him while he stood in the entrance hall.

"Please shut the door quickly," said Elzbieta. Yakub dutifully obeyed and then, slipping off his coat, he shook the snow off and hung it on a hook by the door. He did the same with his fur hat but left his boots by the front door, padding into the parlor in his thick woolen socks.

A tall man with thin dark hair and a furrowed brow, he stood in the doorway as if trouble weighed down his shoulders. First, he measured Elzbieta, and then he measured the dress and whistled through his teeth. "Missus, I may have to add a panel of material on each side to make it fit you." His whole face contorted with the effort of making these unaccustomed Lithuanian sounds.

He continued. "I heard there's been some trouble in the next district. My uncle Perskis is a peddler who comes to stay with me in the winter. He said that two weeks ago four men were arrested for handing out pamphlets."

"Were they book smugglers?" asked Elzbieta.

"I don't think so. I think he said they were urging revolution against the tsar."

"That's even more dangerous," Elzbieta said, suddenly remembering just such a pamphlet that Petras had shown her.

Glauberman nodded. "Indeed, very dangerous."

Julija and Dora had to stifle giggles, because Glauberman's singsong Jewish accent was made worse by a stuffed nose. The tailor spoke Russian, Polish and Yiddish perfectly, but barely enough Lithuanian to get by.

The sisters always found market day entertaining, listening to one Jewish merchant talk to another in Yiddish, their voices melodically rising and falling, hands moving dramatically to punctuate their emotions. By nature, Lithuanians were more reserved and shy so the girls marveled at such lively and effusive people.

The tailor measured Elzbieta again, then examined the dress and scribbled a few notes in an old copybook using the nub of a pencil that he licked between each scribble. At the next measurement, the measuring tape dropped out of his hands and each time he tried to pick it up, it eluded him. "What the devil?" He looked around suspiciously until his eye landed on Kotryna.

Kotryna frowned and looked away ashamed, as if she had an unfortunate deformity that he was rude enough to mention. No one said anything, but the tailor could sense the discomfort in the air.

Elzbieta rubbed her eyes while her sister went to the window to hide her embarrassment.

Suddenly they heard a rattling in the kitchen.

Ada looked up, wondering if this was the *domovoi* or

something else. She went to find Viktoras standing at the door, shaking his fist. "Be quiet, you scoundrel!"

Yakub raised his eyebrows. "Missus, what is one to make of this?"

Elzbieta covered her mouth with her handkerchief. "Something has gotten into the pantry." She couldn't look Glauberman in the eye.

"An animal?" asked the tailor.

"Not exactly," said Elzbieta, uncomfortably.

The tailor looked around the room, but no one would meet his eyes.

Finally, Viktoras blurted out. "If you must know, it's a *domovoi.*"

The tailor smiled uneasily. "Oh, come now. These are modern times, after all."

"Suit yourself," said Viktoras and went back to his room. The tailor looked helplessly at Kotryna. "He's joking, right?"

Kotryna looked away, leaving the tailor frowning and not saying anything for a few moments. Then she brought over a glass of tea with a spoonful of jam and offered it to him. He eyed her with a touch of fear and suspicion, stirring the jam at the bottom of the glass and blowing the hot tea. He turned to Elzbieta. "Don't worry, I'll make you look like a lady."

Elzbieta smiled slightly, holding her chin a bit higher. It was almost enough to forgive her sister for the disgrace of bringing home a *domovoi.* Almost, but not quite.

-Sixteen-

Zimmerman's tavern was crowded after the holidays, the windows fogged from the many customers. For a few kopeks, a Gypsy violinist would play a tune or two. When the music stopped, Duda, ruddy-cheeked and bent by life's disappointments, called Zimmerman, "Uncle, another drink."

"I think you've had enough, Duda," said Zimmerman.

When Captain Malenkov entered, he was annoyed to see that the benches at each table were full. The captain tossed a coin to Zimmerman who quickly made room for him by asking Duda and his friend to move to the bar.

"Why do I have to move?" Duda asked indignantly. Cursed with a keen sense of smell, Zimmerman had to turn away from the man's ripe odor. Duda staggered to his feet and tripped over a stool, mumbling oaths until he saw the captain waiting for his table. He scuttled away at once. The Gypsy violinist began another lively tune, and Duda clapped along. "Play 'Golden Earrings!'" he begged the Gypsy. "I love the sad songs best."

When Modestas Bogdanskis, who had been playing cards, looked up and saw the captain, his stomach turned. He drained the vodka he had been nursing and prayed the captain had business with someone other than him. He had been desperate to find some evidence of book smuggling in that backwater village but had failed miserably. Modestas bent down, trying to keep out of sight, hoping the crowd would shield him from the captain.

Ignoring everyone but Bogdanskis, Captain Malenkov sat down and called him over. Modestas felt as if the sword of Damocles was hanging over his head by the thinnest of threads. Walking across the room, he tried to fabricate some shred of evidence to present to the captain, but his mind was a complete blank. He didn't know if it was a bad case of nerves or too much vodka. He sat with the captain but could barely look at him.

"Your time is up, Bogdanskis," the captain said brusquely. "Do you have anything for me, or are you ready to pay up?"

"Well, perhaps, I…" Modestas began, squirming in his seat.

"You have nothing?" The captain's eyes bore into him.

Modestas called for drinks. "Well, something caught my eye," he said, desperately searching his memory for any scrap of news to report. "I found something very odd the last time I went to Sapnai." Zimmerman brought a tray with vodka and glasses to the table.

"Oh?" The captain picked up his glass. "What was it?"

"Do you remember the coffin Viktoras Kulys had painted?"

"Yes, what of it?" the captain asked with more than a hint of contempt.

"I think he means to fill it with smuggled books."

"The coffin is all you have for me?" The captain's thunderous face leaned across the table over Modestas. "You must think I'm a complete fool," he boomed, froth and spit spewing with his words. He hoisted Modestas by his jacket lapels, ready to punch him, but Modestas shielded his face with his arms.

"No, Captain. I have great respect for you," Modestas pleaded, cowering. "I'm sure the coffin is filled with illegal books. Viktoras Kulys is still alive and well, but now they've taken the trouble to hide his coffin in the barn."

The captain released him. "I've had it with you, Bogdanskis. This is all you've found?" The captain looked murderous. The thought of tramping through the snow to investigate a coffin filled him with a silent rage. "I'll investigate when the Orthodox Christmas is over. And for your sake, it better be filled with illegal books!" he jeered, loudly pounding the table with his fist. Duda jumped in fright, and the Gypsy stopped playing his violin.

A week after the Orthodox Christmas, Captain Malenkov and his men rode to Sapnai to see the painted coffin. Tethering their horses to the fence, they entered the farmyard and knocked on the door, stamping the snow from their boots.

"Please come in," said Stasys stepping aside warily. "Is there a problem?" When Elzbieta came into the room, she gasped to see the captain. Stasys quietly asked his wife to make tea. Elzbieta could see the fear in her husband's eyes.

"No, don't bother. We won't be here long," said the captain. "I came to speak to Viktoras Kulys."

Overhearing the conversation, Viktoras came into the parlor, followed by Ada and her aunt.

The captain and Viktoras looked each other over as adversaries. "I came to take a look at your painted coffin."

"But you've already seen it," said Viktoras.

Looking looked around the parlor, the captain's eyes stopped when he noticed Kotryna.

"This is my younger daughter, Kotryna," said Viktoras.

The captain turned to her. "Do you live here?"

"I just returned from Smolensk," she answered in Russian.

"Smolensk?" He was curious. "Why were you there?"

"Caring for my mistress's children," replied Kotryna, warily.

The captain nodded, but soon lost interest and turned back to address Viktoras. "I'd like to see your coffin?"

"I'll just get my jacket." While the old man went to his room, the pantry door shook violently and the Varnas family flinched.

"What in heaven's name was that?" The captain pulled his revolver out.

"It's just a strong wind," Stasys assured him, but Captain Malenkov could see how everyone stiffened. He could sense something was not right and went to the pantry while his two men stood by.

The door rattled again. "Oh no," Kotryna whispered.

"Open the door at once," demanded the captain, sure that there was a smuggler inside.

"I'm afraid," whimpered Kotryna.

The captain tried the door but couldn't open it. He asked Stasys, "Why is this locked? Open it at once."

"It's not locked," Stasys replied

"Ivan, open the door." Ivan did so, carefully peeking inside. "There's no one here," he announced.

The captain stepped inside behind Ivan to inspect the room. No sooner had he entered than a jar of pickles smashed onto the floor in front of him, covering the captain's boots in pickle juice.

"*Chort!*" he snarled, running out of the pantry and ordering his men to investigate. Nikolai, the boot licker, entered, and suddenly the door slammed, shutting him inside.

"Let me out," he yelled, banging on the door. But when the captain tried to open the door, he couldn't budge it.

Viktoras came back with his jacket on. "I see you've met our visitor from Smolensk," he said, smirking. He opened the pantry door easily and saw the gendarme and the broken jar.

"What visitor?" Captain Malenkov looked at him as if he were a half-wit.

"The *domovoi*, of course."

"That's ridiculous!" The captain looked like he had heartburn. "Stop wasting my time and let's go examine the coffin." He followed the old man to the barn where the painted

136

coffin stood leaning against the wall. Nikolai and Ivan removed the lid and were not surprised to find it empty. The captain was so angry he kicked the coffin, knocking it to the ground.

Viktoras stepped back.

"I'll tear this whole farm apart if I have to!" the captain shouted and ordered his men to search the rest of the barn. His men couldn't find anything, so they searched the house. Finally defeated, they left the farm and went straight back to the tavern.

"God save us from evil spirits." Ivan crossed himself.

Captain Malenkov searched the tavern for Modestas but found no sign of him. "I don't want to hear another word about it, you hear?" His mood had soured considerably.

Zimmerman brought them a tray of drinks. "Why does it smell like pickles?"

The captain said nothing about his boots. Clearing his throat with a low-pitched growl, he drank his vodka down in one swallow. "God save me from these primitive backwaters," he mumbled. He cursed the witless Bogdanskis under his breath and drank another shot, longing for his Mother Russia.

-Seventeen-

By Shrove Tuesday, the villagers of Sapnai were restless and ready to chase winter away with a carnival in February. Celebrated with music, food, and costumes, it was the last bit of revelry before Lent. The next day was Ash Wednesday and the fast was severe—no meat, milk, or fat. Yet it was not as harsh as when laughter or sex were forbidden by the church. Lent came just when the larders were almost empty and stored food from the last harvest was becoming depleted. The old potatoes and beets in the root cellar were wrinkled and shriveled.

Ada spent the day frying dozens of the traditional thin pancakes, symbols of the returning sun, while her mother made sausages. Since meat was forbidden throughout Lent, plenty of it was eaten on Shrove Tuesday. The pastor had said that the word "carnival" came from the Latin meaning farewell to meat.

Petras was about to try one of the pancakes when the dog barked, followed by a knock at the door. During carnival, young people dressed in costumes and masks went from house to house acting in silly skits, playing tricks, and eating their fill. Ada was about to answer it when she stopped herself. "Shh, wait," she whispered. "It must be the troupe we heard next door at the

Kreivenas farm. That noisy band is trying to sneak up quietly. You can be sure they're up to no good, playing some prank again."

"Hah! We'll show them something," said Petras. "Remember last year, when the Bartkus brothers came to the door yelling, 'Winter's freeze, leave us please.' When I opened the door to come outside, they threw a pail of ash on me. Well, this time, I'm going to give them a taste of their own medicine. Get me that bucket of water, Julija, and when Ada opens the door, I'll let them have it." He could hardly contain his glee.

Ada waited until Petras was ready. When another knock came, she flung the door open while her brother drenched a solitary man.

"Jesus and Mary!" yelled the astonished young man, blinking in utter surprise. He was definitely not wearing a carnival costume. "Is this any way to greet a guest?" he sputtered angrily, dripping from head to toe.

While he shook the water from his arms, Ada held her crimson face in shame. It was Jonas Balandis, dressed in a brown padded jacket and a woolen cap, holding a package. Unable to utter a word in her defense, she turned to her brother who apologized.

"Oh no, I'm terribly sorry!" Petras gasped. We thought our friends were at the door with pranks for the carnival. I'm such an idiot. Come in, come in and dry off by the stove." Petras led the dripping man inside and brought a chair over to the stove. "Please take your jacket and hat off, we'll dry them here." Jonas took off his wet garments while Ada brought some towels.

His shirt collar was a bit damp, but thankfully his shirt was dry. To everyone's relief, Jonas began to chuckle, rubbing the water from his hair and face. Julija began to giggle helplessly.

"Well," Jonas said with a smile. "I must say I've pulled many pranks myself on Shrove Tuesday, and many have been tried on me, but this is the first time I've been so startled." He shook his head. "I hope you all remember me," he joked and his smile brightened when he glanced Ada's way.

And with that glance, her face flushed anew.

"Of course we remember you!" Viktoras said heartily. He'd come out of his room to see about the commotion. "How could we forget you?" He smiled widely. "And you won't soon forget that welcome Petras gave you." He laughed. "But where is the rest of your family?"

"My father would have come, but he has a terrible grippe, so he sent me instead to bring that legendary book you asked for."

"The grippe seems to be hitting us all," said Viktoras. "May your father's health return quickly, and then, we'll look forward to another visit."

"Thank you. It's always a pleasure to visit here." He looked at Ada as he said this. "Only next time I'll stand aside when I knock on your door." Jonas's hearty laugh won over the hearts of the whole family.

"Please forgive us, you're always welcome in this house." Stasys poured a shot of plum brandy and handed it to Jonas. "To warm you up until we eat. The women have made pancakes. You'll stay the night, of course."

"Thank you kindly, but I don't want to bother you."

"You have no choice," laughed Petras. "Your jacket is wet."

"In that case, I humbly accept your offer." Jonas lifted his glass. "To your health." He swallowed it in one gulp and Stasys refilled it, lifting his own glass. "To our damp guest from Kelmai."

Ada sighed. How mysterious Jonas Balandis was. How curious that when he smoothed his mustache and looked up at her, something in his eyes and in his bearing left her feeling breathless.

"I think it's about time this came back to you," Jonas said, handing a damp package to Viktoras. The old man carefully untied the parcel, unwrapping the moist paper. Inside was the book by Donelaitis with a bullet still stuck inside.

Petras whistled. "What a history this book has, eh?"

"It saved my life," Viktoras said, nodding, as he appraised it.

141

"Your father told the story the last time he was here. It's a wonder we're still alive. Though I haven't smuggled books across the border for years, I still cross that border every night in my dreams with the border police at my heels." He examined the book and touched the bullet lodged inside. A sheet of paper with Bishop Valancius's image fell out. Viktoras picked it up.

"Now here was a great man," he said. "Imagine, it was a Samogitian bishop who went against the mighty Russian Empire and started an illegal press across the border, organizing men to smuggle the illegal books back into the country. Oh, I only wish I could have met the man to thank him. He's a hero like Bielinis, the king of book smugglers."

Suddenly, they heard the sound of young people laughing and singing ditties in the farmyard. Petras went to the window. "Ah, here they come at last." He turned to Jonas and smiled. "Well, I think we've had enough pranks, eh?"

Ada looked out the window and saw a troupe of young people. They soon knocked on the door and Ada answered it. They were wearing the traditional wooden masks and costumes of beggars, Death, devils, matchmakers, Gypsies and Jews. They were followed by others dressed like horses, goats, and cranes. The masks were long wooden caricatures with horsehair hanging in miserable strands, silly grins, lolling tongues, and bugged-out eyes. Death was dressed in her long tattered white gown. Her white mask had long strings of flax for hair.

The entire group stood at the door ready to perform the usual skits. The Gypsy was accused of stealing the horse, while Death fought the devil for the Gypsy's soul, the beggar staggered while drinking from an empty vodka bottle, the Jew bargained to buy the horse, while the matchmaker went searching the cottage for any old maids.

The revelers pulled a reluctant Kotryna into their merrymaking, and there was nothing else for her but to go along with the skit, while the sly matchmaker proposed a match with the drunken beggar. Ada watched her aunt get pulled into the skit and was thankful they hadn't yet chosen her for the old maid. At first Kotryna resisted, but then she saw it was futile. "If you marry this poor beggar, at least you won't die an old maid," said the matchmaker. "And you'll be assured of a seat in heaven for helping the poor." The beggar kissed Kotryna's hand and winked, pulling her toward the bed in the corner. Everyone erupted into laughter.

"Oh, thank you, kind beggar, for your offer of marriage." Kotryna forced a smile and played along, but Ada could see it irked her.

When they finished, Elzbieta invited them to eat and drink. "You're lucky you didn't arrive a few minutes earlier or you'd all be wet." Elzbieta told them what happened to Jonas. She admired the masks, telling the horse how funny it was. "I love the way your eyes cross and your tongue hangs out."

"Why, it's me!" Zigmas Bartkus took off his horse mask.

"Oh, dear," said Elzbieta. "You fooled me completely."

Giggling, Julija whispered into Ada's ear, "His mask looks just like his face."

The Jew came up to Dora and swept the mask from his face. "At your service," said Jurgis, delighting the girl.

In the back of the room, Viktoras retreated when Death entered the parlor. Though he knew this was merely a costume, part of the usual carnival antics, it still unnerved him. When Death took off its ghastly mask and the ordinary, wide, smiling face of Elena Kreivenas emerged, it was a relief.

Standing in the corner of the kitchen, Ada glanced at Jonas, who caught her look and smiled. He approached her. "Your family is wonderful, Ada. They make me feel at home."

"I'm glad," she said. "You fit right in." She remembered how Modestas seemed out of his element whenever he came to visit, feeling so ill at ease that it made everyone else feel awkward

143

around him. But with Jonas, everything felt natural, as if they had all grown up together.

"Ada," interrupted Kotryna. "Help me pour the beer."

"Yes, of course." Ada ran to get another pitcher, glancing back at Jonas, whose eyes followed her every move. She poured the beer, trying to collect her wits. The rest of the troupe was busy laughing and talking until they heard the loud rattling in the pantry. Several people stopped to bless themselves. "What in heaven's name is that?" asked Zigmas.

"It's nothing, probably the wind rattling the door," Elzbieta replied, almost apoplectic but trying to hide her nerves with forced hospitality. She began to sing a rather hysterical version of an comic song as a diversion. The young people reluctantly joined in, when suddenly the door swung open and a cold wind blew through the house. Then, just as quickly, it slammed shut.

"There it is again." Jurgis's eyes opened wide.

Dora tried to reassure him, but he quickly finished his beer and stood to leave. The rest of the guests put their masks on, excusing themselves. They had other farms to visit. They thanked the hostess and were leaving when Viktoras tried to intervene.

"Listen, don't be alarmed. It's nothing," he said to wave off their worries, but the group still couldn't leave fast enough.

Elzbieta stood at the door, wringing her hands while several men lit torches outside.

Seeing how uneasy the Varnas family was, Jonas tried to ease the situation. "What a wonderful troupe," he said cheerfully, deliberately ignoring the strange events. He turned to Ada. "Perhaps we could join them?"

She was so grateful he hadn't bolted out the door with the others that she wanted to cry from sheer relief. Instead, she addressed a more practical matter, in the hopes of getting her emotions under control. "But I'm afraid your jacket is still wet."

"You can borrow mine," offered Petras. "It's the least I could do after soaking you earlier. Here, take my sheepskin."

144

Jonas tried it on and was relieved to find that it fit. "Will you accompany me?" he asked Ada.

"Yes, I'll go," she said, grabbing her jacket.

Jonas shouted for the group outside to wait. They stopped but eyed Ada with a hint of suspicion. He could see they didn't know what to make of the strange events.

"Wait, I'm coming too," yelled Dora, running after her sister.

Julija, not wanting to be left behind, also grabbed her jacket, but her mother stopped her at the door.

"You are still too young to rattle around with the others," she insisted. Julija protested indignantly that she was no longer a child but her protests fell on deaf ears. Elzbieta was not in a conciliatory mood.

Julija stood at the door like an orphan, sadly watching the vivid flock of masqueraded youth walk down the road, holding torches against the darkening sky. Petras came to join her at the door, and together they watched until the torch-lit group was nearly out of sight. From a distance, they looked like fireflies in the snow.

Twilight was falling across the slate-blue sky and the fields were silent and windless. When Ada slipped on the snow, Jonas offered his arm to steady her, and she took it.

"Tell me, Jonas, if you're from our district, how is it I've not seen you before you came to visit?"

"My family goes to St. Casimir's church in Rudnosiai. I'm an only child, so I'm always working on the farm. It doesn't leave me much time to come this way. But now that I've met such wonderful people here, I hope to come more often." His smile brought a slight giggle from Ada, and she was ashamed to think she was starting to act like Julija.

Jonas asked, "What was happening back there in the pantry?"

Ada sighed, not knowing how to tell him. "Nothing really,"

145

she said uneasily, hoping he wouldn't hear the discomfort she felt talking about the *domovoi*.

But he did hear it and decided to say no more. Changing the subject, he said, "You're lucky to have such a wonderful brother and sisters. It's sometimes lonely being an only child."

"Oh, you'd think twice if you had a sister like Julija," said Ada, grateful to talk about other things.

"Poor girl, she really wanted to come along," Jonas remarked. The bright moon was rising, casting purple shadows of the trees on the bluish snow, while Jonas and Ada companionably walked together, trailing the others.

"I like Zigmas's horse mask," said Jonas. "I wish I had thought to bring my peddler's mask with a horsehair beard and hardly a tooth in his mouth. It's comical, but not nearly as good as Zigmas's horse."

Ada listened, thinking here was a good man, not given to self-praise.

"Don't forget the bonfire, my friends," Zigmas called out, reminding the group they would end the evening at the Bartkus farm. There they would light a huge bonfire and burn More, the female demon who had dominion over winter. Her death allowed the return of the sun. The bonfire would last until the church bells rang, reminding everyone to be home by midnight, the start of Lent.

Ada smiled, grateful that the *domovoi* seemed to be forgotten for the moment. The stars began to tremble above the troupe as they left the village and were on their way to town.

"Ada," yelled Jurgis. "Look where we've ended up."

She felt so inexplicably happy tonight that she didn't care where they were going.

"To Modestas's house," said Zigmas, laughing.

"Oh no!" Ada cried in sudden panic. "Let's not go there."

"Why not? We'll play some good tricks on his old maid sister."

Ada wanted to run and hide. Why, of all places, did they have to stop here? This could be so awkward. She felt pulled in two, not wanting to upset Modestas by coming in with Jonas, yet not wanting to discourage Jonas either.

"Not a likely place for pranks," Jurgis said dryly.

"How do you know?" said Zigmas. "We've never been there before. Don't worry, I'll show them some fun." He took off his horse mask and handed it to Ada.

"Here, put on my mask so Modestas doesn't recognize you." She gladly agreed hoping it would hide her. Before she donned the large wooden mask, she turned to Jonas, wanting to tell him about Modestas but faltered, not knowing quite what to say. "I don't want you to misunderstand...I mean...this might be awkward..." She stopped, unsure how to put it in words.

Jonas looked puzzled. He could see through her stuttered beginnings that she was trying to tell him something important, but he didn't push her.

The cheerful band arrived at the Bogdanskis home, singing, dancing, banging pots, and demanding that all old maids come to the door. Modestas opened it and smiled to see such a rowdy troupe. Ada saw something haughty in his face.

"Please come inside where it's warmer." He ushered them into the parlor, where his mother stood at the table, smiling patiently, wearing a white blouse with a high lace collar.

Ada, in her horse mask, noted that the parlor was much larger than any in her village, but everything looked a little sad and tired. Her eye wandered over the age-yellowed lace curtains and the stained and patched damask tablecloth. The room smelled of mildew and melancholy.

Modestas told his guests that this was their former summer home. Though Lithuanian nobility, these days he played the gentleman farmer, barely managing with the rent from his tenant farmers. Modestas smiled at the assembled group, looking a bit

147

lost. Jonas stood next to him amiably talking with some of the masked villagers, laughing at some joke.

Ada compared the two men, noticing how easily Jonas laughed, while Modestas was more self-conscious, his smile forced. She now saw the more evident cracks in his veneer.

"Maman," Modestas asked his mother. "Aren't these masks clever?"

"Bien sur," said Natalija Bogdanskis with a wan smile. "How nice of you all to stop by, wasn't it, Helenka?" The widow motioned to her daughter. She had Polonized their names, mimicking the upper classes who aspired to be like the Polish nobility. Helenka pulled her shawl around her shoulders, then walked over to her brother and took his arm. Modestas could see that for his mother and sister, this merrymaking was to be borne rather than enjoyed.

"Zosinka, bring those sweet buns you made this afternoon," Natalija said, her old-fashioned notions of politeness never failing her. The Polish girl curtseyed and went to the kitchen.

"Good evening," said Helenka. "My, what a cheerful group we have here."

"Good evening," Zigmas echoed. "Perhaps we could persuade you to come along tonight for carnival."

"My daughter is not well, I'm afraid," said the widow. "She couldn't possibly go out on a February evening."

Everyone in the village knew a bit of Helenka's history. How harrowing it was for a young woman not allowed to marry her true love. Some women recover while others waste away. For Helenka, it was as if the very lifeblood were drained from her; her life force weakened. Her steely mother, unmoved by her daughter's wishes, continued the search for a wealthy suitor. If one of her children didn't marry into money soon, the family would be completely ruined.

"We have found a match for you," Zigmas said to Helenka, winking as he brought over the Jewish peddler with his perennial

148

sack. "This is a man who knows how to save his kopeks."
The peddler shook a bag of coins and beckoned Helenka to come
with him. She smiled demurely but refused his offer.

"Well, in that case, we will find a match for the young man
of the house," said Zigmas, playing the deceitful matchmaker.
"Bogdanskis, I tell you, your intended has teeth like none you've
seen. She's strong, has good ears and a sweet disposition and will
be helpful to you on the farm, seldom complaining. What say you
to such a match?" Zigmas grinned.

Modestas smiled and tried to act the part. "But is she pretty?"
"Pretty?"

Zigmas scratched his head. "Well, there are some who think
so." He winked and pulled the reluctant Ada over in her horse
mask. Ada's stomach dropped. This was what she was dreading.

"What do you think of this mare?"

"So that's how it is. You want me to marry her, do you?"
Modestas's attempt to play along was perfunctory rather than
heartfelt.

"And what's wrong with her?"

"I'm afraid I don't fancy your mare." He turned to the horse
to explain. "Please don't be offended." He looked down at her
blue skirt and boots, which looked familiar. For a moment, he
wondered if this could be Ada. "But you are a very sympathetic-
looking horse." Modestas patted the horse's nose. I'm sure you'll
find a handsome mate."

Ada nodded her head, and the horse's tongue bobbed. How
she longed to run away. Fretting behind the mask, Ada glanced
from Modestas to Jonas, who was laughing good-naturedly.

Dora, who had been watching this little skit, could no longer
contain her amusement. "So now you no longer care for her?" She
couldn't stop giggling when she ran over, trying to remove Ada's
horse mask.

"Oh, please don't!" Ada drew back, holding the mask to her
face with both hands. She was desperate not to be unmasked, but

149

Dora wouldn't give up. "Stop," Ada hissed, trying to hide, but the mask came off.

Modestas laughed along with the others. "Ha! You're the little mare behind the droll mask." He stepped up to Ada and chuckled, putting a proprietary arm around her.

Ada smiled weakly and turned to look at Jonas. Flustered, she saw he was paying more attention than she wanted him to. He studied her face, looking confused. Completely rattled, Ada didn't know what to do. She stepped away from Modestas, only to have him pull her back. Jonas seemed to shrink away, while the others shrieked with laughter at Ada's unmasking.

This was too much for Natalija. She suffered from nerves so that everyday things grated on them—the scraping of chairs, the screeching of birds, the coarseness of farmers and merchants. She watched this little play with bile rising, taking the measure of the pretty peasant girl who played the mare. She turned and retreated quietly to her room.

Once Natalija left, Zigmas sidled up to Modestas. "We need to celebrate this match with something...ahem," he cleared his throat, "a little stronger."

Modestas went to the cupboard and brought out a bottle of vodka, pouring drinks all around. "To our beautiful mare and to our being matched this evening." He drank his shot.

"Come, Ada," said Modestas. "Try one of Zosinka's wonderful sweet buns." He handed her a plate and she took one of the sugar-dusted buns but could hardly take a bite. This was all far too confusing and upsetting. Looking around the room for Jonas, she couldn't find him anywhere.

"Dora," she whispered to her sister, "do you know where Jonas went?"

Her sister shook her head. Ada went to the door and opened it, peering down the road. In the silvery moonlight, she saw Jonas walking back down the same road without a glance back in her direction. A cloud curled around the moon, yet the brightness of the veiled moon was reflected in the soft snow, giving it a bluish-silver glow.

The pull of this man was so magnetic that she wanted to run down the road after him.

"Ada, for heaven's sake, close the door," Modestas said with restrained annoyance. "That draft will be the death of Helenka."

This was a night of sighs. Ada sighed as she had all evening and took one last look at Jonas Balandis of Kelmai, the night enfolding him in its dark embrace, before she reluctantly turned away and shut the door.

-Eighteen-

In the moonlight, Jonas walked down the snow-covered road back to Sapnai, his emotions in turmoil. The trees shivered slightly and the snow seemed to glow, but Jonas saw none of this. In his mind's eye, he kept replaying the sight of Bogdanskis putting his arm around Ada. He thought the man seemed very familiar with her, and she seemed to go along as if accustomed to it. It upset him, though, in truth, he had no right to feel this way. He hardly knew her, but he wanted her, God help him.

But how could Ada fall for such a man? This Bogdanskis seemed arrogant and full of his own importance. Jonas tortured himself all the way down the dark road. Perhaps she wanted to marry someone from the gentry.

His strong-willed mother had tried in vain to arrange several matches for him, but he had never found a woman to spend his life with. She favored the Mockus girl, who was mild- mannered and dull, almost invisible in any group. She was a plump blond with cheeks like ripe apples and relentless good cheer that generally got on his nerves. He had flirted with some of the girls in Kelmai, had danced with them, felt infatuated when he walked them home through the meadow, but none of these encounters had ever bloomed into love. But Ada Varnas was a different matter. Jonas wasn't sure when it happened. Maybe in November when he first looked into her blue eyes, or maybe it bloomed today when she walked with him. It didn't matter. All he knew was that he wanted to be with her.

And how unlucky to finally find her, only to see that another man already seemed to have a claim to her. He had hardly been able to breathe when he saw Modestas put his arm around Ada, as if the man might already be courting her.

Jonas mumbled curses at his own foolishness. What right did he have to be upset? Still, he stopped to consider, and this was what confused him the most—he was sure that earlier in the evening, Ada had looked at him with a spark of interest and warmth in her eyes. He waved his hand and continued walking. Maybe he was imagining it; perhaps his head had been spinning when he looked into her blue eyes. He had never seen eyes such a clear blue. Even now, alone and trembling with cold, his heart raced at the memory of those eyes.

When he reached the Varnas farm gate, he was relieved to see the house was dark, everyone apparently gone to sleep. Perhaps he could get his horse and quietly harness it to his sleigh without waking anyone. He didn't want to answer questions about why he was back without Ada and Dora. It was best to leave quietly, for he didn't want to see anyone in this frame of mind.

Jonas opened the creaking stable door and poked his head inside, patting his snorting horse and talking to it in a quiet, reassuring manner. When he led it out of the stable it whinnied, and a dog barked somewhere.

"Who goes there?" Stasys demanded, coming out the door with Petras behind him, still pulling his trousers on.

"Don't be alarmed, Mr. Varnas. It's Jonas Balandis. I'm just getting my horse."

"Oh, it's you? You gave me a fright." Stasys laughed and clapped him on the shoulder. "I thought we had horse thieves."

154

"But where did you leave my sisters?" asked Petras.

"They stayed with the rest of the group. I decided to go home." Jonas looked down at his hands, feeling foolish.

"On such a cold night?" Stasys said. "I won't hear of it. There's nothing on your farm that can't wait until morning. Come inside by the stove, I insist." Stasys escorted him back inside. "My wife has already made up a bed for you in the warm corner by the stove. Have a good night's sleep and we'll send you off in the morning."

"I'm afraid I can't stay," Jonas protested. "Thank you for your hospitality, but I really must go."

Petras came over to finger Jonas's jacket sleeve. "Do you plan to go home with my sheepskin?" he teased. "Or have you forgotten that yours is still drying by the stove?"

Jonas had not given a thought to his coat. "I'm sorry. I completely forgot."

"Must have been quite an evening," said Petras, snickering.

Jonas felt like a complete idiot. He wished them good night and went to lie down on the straw mattress they had placed on the wide bench by the large brick stove. But he couldn't sleep, tossing and turning, listening to every noise, every creak of the house. Oh, what he'd give to be in his own bed this night, away from this house with all of its unsettling emotions. He tossed his covers off, remembering Ada's flaxen braids, her laugh ringing like a tinkling silver bell. It seemed as if hours went by. He could hear Petras snoring peacefully nearby, while he stared out the window at the snowball moon frozen in the winter sky.

Later, he heard the church bells ring from afar. The coming of Lent was announced.

When he heard voices outside, he raised himself on one elbow, recognizing Ada and Dora's soft voices. Several men, perhaps the Bartkus brothers, were escorting them home. He lay back down and listened for Bogdanskis's voice, but thankfully he didn't hear it. The girls quietly wished their escorts good night.

The front door creaked opened and then he heard them as they removed their boots.

Turning away, he pretended to sleep when they peeked into the kitchen.

"Is he still here?' Ada whispered to Dora. He wanted to leap up and go to her, but what could he say about leaving the Bogdanksis home so rudely without a word to anyone? He heard them preparing for bed.

He spent a restless night tossing and turning until he was almost feverish. When he could stand it no more, he looked out the window at the night. He decided he would leave at the first light. No wind blew, nothing moved, as if the whole world slept, resting in the darkness—everyone but him. Staring out into the night, he felt like the loneliest soul in the world, as if God had forgotten to create anyone else and he was doomed to walk this earth alone. Lost in his reverie, he stared at the window for a long time.

In her bed, Ada listened to the soft breathing of her sisters. As she went over the evening's events, her restlessness increased. Each time she remembered Jonas's face when Modestas put his arm around her waist, she winced and tugged her eiderdown over her head. Why did they have to go to that house? Why hadn't she refused to go? Why was she interested in this man from Kelmai? Why did the mere sight of Jonas make her giddy? Her thoughts spun in circles, while she waited anxiously for the morning.

Before the first light, she could bear it no longer. The night seemed to last an eternity. If she had to stay in bed one more minute she would scream. Emerging from her tangled eiderdown, she quickly dressed, brushed her long blond hair and braided it with nimble fingers. She hoped to catch a glimpse of Jonas's sleeping face before she went to milk the cows. What she didn't admit to herself was how she hoped he'd be up. She was startled to find Jonas fully dressed and standing at the kitchen window. Something welled up inside her with a force and a will of its own that she couldn't tamp down.

"I'm sorry," she whispered, "I didn't mean to disturb you."

"Oh, Ada," he whispered, startled out of his reverie. "You're not disturbing me. I can't seem to sleep."

"Nor can I," she said softly. "I was going to milk the cows, but first I'd like a drink of water. Would you like a drink?"

"Well, yes, but won't we wake the others?"

"We will have to be very quiet," she whispered.

Ada dared not talk about what was nettling her heart. She opened the wooden cupboard and wondered why it seemed as if all of life had changed this night. What a turmoil of emotions battled in her! She took two cups and walked over to the pitcher of water on the table.

Shyly fiddling with the pitcher, Ada filled the cups, and when she looked up and saw Jonas smile at her, she almost dropped one. Her heart beat and her hands trembled as she handed it to him and watched as his large hands took the cup from her. She took a quick breath, wanting to touch them—such strong hands, callused from work. These were hands to admire, not like those long thin fingers of Modestas.

When she realized she was staring at his hands, she looked away embarrassed, as if he could read her thoughts. "Are you well?" she asked in a whisper. The courage to talk about what happened at Modestas's house eluded her completely. She sat down with her cup, trying to collect herself.

Jonas hesitated. "Fine." He watched her perform these simple tasks as if they had never been done before, as if it were miraculous that such a lovely creature could perform such everyday things with such grace as to make him want to touch those slender hands.

She didn't know what else to say and raised her eyes to meet his. "Perhaps I should go milk the cows?"

"Oh, don't go yet." Jonas's warm hand took hers. "Stay a moment longer."

"All right." A tingle coursed from his hand to hers, and it felt thrilling. Ada smiled and her heart swelled as she pushed a wisp of hair from her face.

"Good," he said hesitantly.

Outside, the sky was turning a soft gray. Soon the cocks would crow and the family would begin their day with chores and breakfast. Already she could hear the lowing of the cows waiting to be milked, and in the other room she could hear her grandfather coughing. Ada smiled at Jonas and drank her water. He smiled back and drank his. And over those simple cups of water something mysterious was woven between them without another word being spoken.

Viktoras woke, dressed and was about to go into the kitchen, when he spotted Ada sitting with Jonas. At once he sensed that something had changed during the night. He read it in their expressions and decided not to disturb them, to let them have their time alone lest he break the spell. Retreating to his room, he sat down on the bed, a broad grin spreading on his face.

A few minutes later, Elzbieta sleepily entered the kitchen, rubbing her eyes.

"Good morning. Have the two of you been up all night?"

Both Ada and Jonas shifted uncomfortably. "We woke not long ago," stammered Ada.

"Let me make some porridge for Ash Wednesday." Elzbieta began to bang pots and pans around the kitchen, sniffing loudly, as she began to prepare a simple breakfast of tea and porridge for the first day of Lent. After breakfast, the family would go to church for Ash Wednesday. The priest would rub ash on their foreheads saying, "Ashes to ashes, dust to dust," reminding each parishioner of their ultimate fate.

"Where did you go last night?" Elzbieta asked. "To the Bogdanskis house," said Ada quietly.

Her mother turned, pleased to hear this. "Really?" She smiled. "Will Modestas be coming to visit soon? I loved the candy he brought when he came to see you, my dear." Ada winced as her mother glanced at Jonas.

The words had hit home. Jonas stiffened just as Viktoras came in and sat down next to him. "Good morning to you all. Good to see you this morning, Jonas."

"Good morning." Jonas's words sounded strangled, his throat tight. He couldn't look at Viktoras without a pang of guilt, as if he had betrayed the good man by falling in love with his granddaughter who, it seemed, might already be promised to another.

Ada wanted to explain to Jonas that she felt differently about Modestas now, but she didn't dare with her mother and grandfather in the room. Instead, she turned to her grandfather. "Good morning. I'll get the bread for our breakfast." She stood up but glanced back at Jonas, her eyes drinking him in. But Jonas was looking down at the tablecloth, his hands folded.

Ada saw his discomfort and sensed the change in him. Her heart sank when he wouldn't meet her eyes. Taking a deep breath, she tried to rein in her feelings.

When the porridge was done, she woke the rest of the family and then sat down at the table. No longer hungry, she told herself not to stare at Jonas, but she stole a glance or two, and once she caught him doing the same. They both swiftly looked away.

Jonas ate quickly. "It's time to get back to Kelmai," he said. "Thank you again for your hospitality." It seemed as though he couldn't get out of that house fast enough.

Viktoras made him promise to return to Sapnai soon.

Jonas nodded and they parted hesitantly as he took one last glance at Ada. Then he was out the door, leaving her stricken.

Ada watched through the window as Petras helped Jonas harness his horse to the sleigh. Urging his horse on, Jonas left the farmyard, the sled runners squeaking over the snow, his horse's nostrils steaming until the sled rounded the bend. Even after it was out of sight, Ada could still hear the sleigh bells—the saddest sound she had ever heard.

Viktoras felt for his heartsick granddaughter. He had seen her emotions shift like changing weather. Something had gone wrong, but he wouldn't press her.

His thoughts turned to last night, another night of wrestling with Death. Everything had seemed dire, especially just before dawn. Relief had come only with the morning light, when he had seen the two young ones in the kitchen whispering, quietly wrapping their words around one another like the unseen roots of mighty oaks mingling underground.

-Nineteen-

A da listened to the staccato rain beat down on the overturned washbasin outside her window, absently tapping her finger against the window glass. Heavy rain pelted the windows in gusts but later settled into a lonely gray drizzle that turned the roads into bogs. You couldn't force a dog out on such a day, she thought, dismally. The dreary April weather helped curdle the mood of the villagers as they sat, confined in their cottages through three days of solid rain.

Ada's glum mood was perfectly suited to the wretched weather as she stared out the window, her thoughts fluttering around Jonas in silent conversations with him. Each time she repeated his name she felt a leap in her stomach. At night, in her dreams, she saw his eager eyes again. How she lingered in these dreams, drunk with longing. Jonas pulled at her like a tide she felt in her body.

But it was April, and Jonas hadn't returned to Sapnai, nor had she heard a word from him since he left in February. It was obvious that he didn't feel the same way about her. He had probably forgotten about her once he left Sapnai and was already wooing some other girl. Everything between them rested on a few moments together. Nothing had been declared, not even a small kiss had been attempted. What did it amount to, really? A slight flirtation? Or was there more? How was she to know?

Ada mooned around the house, sighing and staring out windows until her mother couldn't bear it any longer. Elzbieta bustled around, humming folk tunes and keeping busy. When she found her sad daughter gazing out the windows, she snapped, "Ada, it's unnatural. Go do something. Take Dora's example and go embroider a towel or pillowcase for your dowry."

Ada picked up the pillowcase and crocheted a line or two and then stopped, lost in thought again.

When her grandfather found her later, asking what was ailing her, Ada hesitated to tell him about Jonas. "Dear Grandfather, what does life have in store for me?"

It was obvious to Viktoras that his granddaughter was in love. Never before had he seen her look this way, especially not with Bogdanskis. "Ada," he replied. "Life has some surprises in store for you. Sometimes you think that you're meant to take one path, but find yourself on another." He chuckled and kissed her forehead. "I think everything will turn out the way it's meant to."

Kotryna came in, feeling restless and sour. Though the *domovoi* had been quiet for days, today it was full of devilry, bumping around in the pantry, rattling things in tune with the rain outside on the washbasin. It had so wrecked Kotryna's nerves that she simply had to get out of the house.

"Ada," Kotryna pleaded, "come with me to town to get your mother's dress from the tailor. The rain is letting up and this *domovoi* is driving me mad."

Ada grabbed her coat and shawl and joined her aunt at the door, but Viktoras stopped them. "If you're going to town, then you can save me a trip. Take the bottle of plum brandy I promised to Father Jurkus." He took a bottle from the cupboard. "Also, I heard a new shop is opening not far from the tailor. I'd like you both to look it over and tell me when it's to open."

He pulled up his trousers, a hint of amusement on his face. "What kind of shop?" Kotryna asked, wondering why her father looked so pleased with himself.

"Wait and see," he said. "You might find it very interesting, my dear." He smiled mysteriously.

After they left, Elzbieta asked her father, "Papa, what do you make of Ada? She's not herself lately. To look at her, you'd think she'd lost her whole family."

Viktoras waved his hand in dismissal. "Ach, don't think anything of it. Youth is like a great storm that blows through your life. We're only lucky to survive those turbulent days." When he saw Elzbieta looking at him blankly, he chuckled. "Don't worry, Ada will be just fine." He didn't add that it was Kotryna he was worried about.

The branches of the birch trees were full of green buds about to burst into life. Ada and Kotryna put their shawls over their heads and walked arm in arm to keep from slipping on the muddy road. Ada begged her aunt for advice about Jonas. "I'm so confused about Jonas and don't know what to do. Should I write him a letter? Mama wants me to choose Modestas, but Grandfather doesn't like him."

"Ada, dearest," Kotryna said sadly. "I'm the last person in the world to ask about this. Love has been my curse. Now I'm condemned to be an old maid with no husband to provide for me, no children to take care of me when I get old."

"Don't worry, aunt. I'll take care of you."

Kotryna smiled wanly. "Thank you, Ada. You have a good heart. As for love, don't make the same mistake I did. Your Jonas, for all we know, may have just been flirting with you. You know how men are when they see a pretty woman. He's obviously forgotten about it already or he would have returned by now. Just be grateful you have Modestas, so you'll escape my fate.

"After all, Ada, love isn't just some old potato you carelessly throw out a window."

Ada sighed and said no more.

The whole market square was aboil with activity, filled with farmers who had brought their calves, chicks, or newborn lambs to sell, along with the rakes, baskets, and ladles they had spent all winter making. Most of the young people who wanted to find work as hired hands on the farms came to the spring market looking for work for the coming season.

On one side of the square were stores, while the other side had wooden houses painted in shades of ochre, red and green, with window boxes. Ada and her aunt walked past the bakery to the tailor shop where Yakub Glauberman worked.

"Good day to you," Kotryna greeted him. "I've come for my sister's dress."

"Hello," Glauberman croaked, holding his head. "Oy, oy, I've been ill with the grippe. I don't know what I'm doing out of bed." His nose was red and swollen and his eyes looked rheumy.

"I'm sorry to hear it," said Kotryna.

"I'll live, God willing, but I'm afraid I've been too ill to finish her dress." He sneezed and excused himself to go to the back room for his handkerchief while Kotryna looked around the shop full of clothes, ribbons, and spools of thread. Unhappy about the delay, she didn't want to disappoint her sister.

The tailor returned, wiping his nose. Seeing the displeasure on Kotryna's face, he relented. "Oh, all right. I tell you what. If you have a bit of time, I'll do my best to finish it in an hour."

"Are you sure? You're not too ill?"

"Ach, I'll do it," he waved away her concern. "I'll do it because I told you it would be done today," he said, tapping his finger on a calendar with a photograph of an exotic city.

Ada inspected the photo. "What city is that?"

"Jerusalem," he said proudly. "The Holy Land. We Zionists, hope the Jews will return to Palestine someday."

"Return? When did the Jews come to Lithuania?" Ada had never thought about this before. She imagined the Jews had always lived in Lithuania.

Glauberman wiped his nose. "It's our curse to wander this earth, never feeling at home, always hoping that next year we'll return to Jerusalem. Jews have traveled from one end of the earth to the other. I don't know where there isn't a Jew. Maybe in the jungle somewhere or with the Eskimos." He snuffled a laugh into his handkerchief and shrugged. When he saw her baffled look, he continued, "Look, they have a pogrom in one country, we move to another. We probably came to Lithuania about the same time the Christians came."

"Really? That can't be?" It didn't seem right to Ada.

"When did the Crusaders attack Lithuania? I'm sure the Jews were one step ahead or one step behind them. It was a terrible time for those who weren't Christian."

Ada nodded, but she knew nothing of Jewish history.

"It was a terrible time for Lithuanians as well," Glauberman continued. "Your people didn't get baptized in the Christian waters willingly, you know. They fought fiercely to keep their ancient religion. In fact, Lithuania won the battle against the famed Teutonic Order." He sneezed loudly and his wife called to him from the other room. "Is that you, Yakub?"

"Who else should it be?" the tailor answered.

"Get back to bed or it'll be the death of you."

The tailor shrugged. "She's right." He suddenly shivered. "Why am I talking to you with this draft blowing in. I'll finish the dress if you'll excuse me." He sneezed again, his face gray. "Come back in one hour."

Walking by Goldwasseris's teashop, Ada glanced inside, thankful not to see Modestas. They continued to St. George's rectory, where Stasia, the housekeeper, let them in. Giving Kotryna a once-over, she told both women to leave their muddy boots on the mat. "I heard you came home, Miss Kotryna." Stasia emphasized the "Miss."

"Yes," answered Kotryna, thanking God she was spared this kind of spinster's work.

"We're here to see Father Jurkus," Ada said.

They followed the tiny, sanctimonious mouse of a woman, who craned her neck to take another look at Kotryna's city clothes and then pointed to the door. "The pastor is in, but I'm not sure about the priest."

"Should I knock?" asked Ada.

The housekeeper shook her head and straightened her scarf. "Oh, no. We can't disturb the pastor."

"We'll wait," said Kotryna, irritated by the woman's manner.

The housekeeper went back to work, wiping a table with an old rag, turning from time to time to keep a suspicious eye on Kotryna, as if she might walk away with the rectory silverware. Stasia's hands and feet were tiny, almost like a child's, yet her face was wrinkled and sunken like a baked apple.

Soon Kotryna lost patience and knocked on the pastor's door. She heard him say, "Come in." Father Kazlauskas stood, his shirtsleeves rolled up and a pair of *pince-nez* stuck onto his pug nose. His red ears and pink face made him look slightly porcine, though no one dared to mention it.

"We're here to see Father Jurkus," said Ada. "Excuse us if we interrupted something."

The pastor seemed relieved that they weren't waiting for him. "Fine, fine, have a seat. Father Jurkus will be back soon." He opened the glass doors of a bookcase. "I need to find a book," he said as if talking to himself. "Let me see." He pulled a book out of the bookcase and flipped through it.

"It must be nice to have such a large library," Ada said admiringly. She wondered if any of them were Lithuanian. More likely they were official publications in Russian.

"Yes, yes, nice," he said distractedly. He put that book back

166

and looked through another. Lace doilies decorated the tables under the candlesticks and newspapers sat on the table. The pastor stopped to examine Ada's flaxen-colored braids. "Tell me, why do you have blond hair?"

"Perhaps it's from my father who was also born with light hair," she replied.

"Probably. This is a field of science called genetics. It's complicated." The pastor had a new theory brewing, tracing the origin of blond hair. Recently he had fallen under the thrall of genetics and evolution. He marveled that in the wide world filled with dark hair, only a small tribe of northern Europeans were blond. His theory was that it had something to do with living in caves during a long ice age. He had read about albino worms and pale insects that live under rocks and dark places. Yet it was a conundrum to the pastor to imagine people living for many years in a dark cave and emerging with hair the color of the sun? Like all true mysteries, it remained unsolved. Yet the pastor hoped to publish his theory in Warsaw.

Ada wondered why this pastor of theirs lived in a world of his own. She remembered how he loved to go on, his sermons an endless labyrinth. Sometimes people simply lost patience and left before he was finished. Though Lithuanian, he often said sermons in Polish, which were never as popular as Father Jurkus's Lithuanian sermons.

Suddenly Father Jurkus came bounding into the room with Stasia slipping in behind him, too curious to be left out. "What a surprise!" said the priest. "What brings you both here?"

"We came on an errand for my grandfather," said Ada. "But first I have a burning question for you. We just came from the tailor, who said the Christians came to Lithuania at the same time the Jews did. Can that be true?"

Father Jurkus often padded his sermons with bits of history. Though the question had been put to the priest, the pastor seized the chance to hold forth. "Well, yes and no," he said, rubbing his chin. "The Teutonic Knights were sent by the Pope to convert the Baltic pagans who worshiped *Zemyna*, mother earth, and *Perkunas*, the god of thunder. Vestal virgins tended the holy fire day and night in sacred oak groves. The pagans defeated the Crusaders, an unheard-of feat. When Lithuanians finally became Christian, they stubbornly brought their pagan beliefs with them. This was not exactly the time the Jews were invited here by the Grand Duke Vytautas and given protection, but close enough. So many came that eventually Vilnius became known as the Jerusalem of the North with the famous miracle rabbis."

"Miracle rabbis?" Stasia eyed the pastor suspiciously, as if wondering how he knew so much about Jews.

Ignoring the housekeeper, Father Kazlauskas went on. "The Lithuanians had been the last country in Europe to become Christian, a mere five hundred years ago. Up until then, they were heathens!" He barked out a laugh.

Father Jurkus objected. "Not heathens, just ordinary people who didn't want to give up the old ways." The priest had grown up in one of the villages in the area. He had an honest farmer's heart with a love for the land and the simple people who tilled it year after year, hoping the land would feed them. His sermons were always sprinkled with good advice about farming practices like rotating the crops. The priest before him, who came from Polonized gentry, told his parishioners to pray in Polish because God didn't understand Lithuanian.

Ada thanked the talkative pastor, as Father Jurkus escorted them into another room. Pulling the bottle of plum brandy from her bag, she presented it to him. "It's a gift from Grandfather."

"Oh-ho!" he said, his face lighting up. "Now there's a good man who knows how to banish the cold in this drafty rectory. Give him my hearty thanks."

Standing by the tavern, Modestas spotted Ada and her dotty

aunt coming out of the rectory arm in arm, no doubt gossiping like pigeons happily cooing. He wondered if either of them knew how closely they were being watched by the gendarmes. When Captain Malenkov noticed the two women, he remarked, "It seems to me the Varnas girl goes to visit the priest too often."

Modestas shrugged. "Does she? I hadn't noticed."

"Have you noticed anything at all, Bogdanskis?" the captain asked, gruffly.

"I've tried my best." Modestas seemed to shrink inside himself. "But it's difficult for me. A ragged group of villagers thought nothing of coming to my house on Shrove Tuesday. It was so annoying."

"Enough!" boomed Malenkov. "You're chattering like an old woman, but I need evidence. Haven't you asked the girl about contraband books? Tell her you'd like to obtain some books in Lithuanian. She must trust you by now."

"I've t-tried, Captain," stuttered Modestas nervously.

"So far, you've been a miserable failure, you hear me?" The captain snarled."

"I've had no luck. Just give me a little more time and I'll find something. I give you my word."

"You've tried my patience long enough."

"I'm doing all I can, Captain. You have no idea how much I've lowered myself to get into that family's good graces. It's humiliating." Modestas shook his head. "Give me one last chance and I promise to find those book smugglers," he pleaded.

Captain Melenkov stood there, scowling. "All right, Bogdanskis. You have until Midsummer's Night when young people are cavorting in the woods. If ever there was a night to seduce a girl, that's it." He smirked. "If not, I'll collect my debt the following day. And that, I guarantee you, is a firm promise."

Modestas nodded, relieved but feeling demeaned to be groveling at the captain's feet. "I won't let you down." He turned to see Ada and her aunt crossing the square. "I think we should go

169

into the tavern before they see us. It will only make my questions seem more suspicious to them."

"Right you are." The two men entered the small tavern, squeezing past Duda, already drunk and singing a lewd song about how all women were either unfaithful or ugly. When Duda saw the men, he offered to share his table with them.

"Bogdanskis, I hear you're courting Ada Varnas, you lucky man." Duda stood up and pushed his chair back, but could barely stand. He lurched toward Modestas, tripping over his own feet. Grabbing the man's sleeve to right himself, Duda heard a rip. Modestas fingered the open seam of his coat.

"Oh, sorry, sorry," slurred Duda, listing toward Modestas again, pushing his florid face close. "Why couldn't you court one of my daughters; take them off my hands?"

Modestas seethed, his jaw muscles working furiously. First, he had to endure threats from the captain and now this drunk ruined his jacket. "Get away from me." He pushed the man back into his chair saying, "You're a menace."

The captain called to the barkeep. "Zimmerman! Take care of this drunk!" Zimmerman promptly came over, guiding Duda out the door and putting him in his cart. With a slap, he sent the horse home.

An hour later, when Ada and her aunt returned to the tailor's shop, Kotryna inspected every seam of the dress and pronounced it well made. She paid the tailor who wrapped the dress and sneezed. Kotryna stood to leave. "I hope you recover soon."

"Thank you." He sneezed again and after wiping his nose with great flourish, he walked them to the door.

Kotryna paused there to ask him if he knew about a new shop opening nearby.

"Yes," said the tailor. "There's a sign posted a few doors down on the right. It seems a man from America is coming to open

170

a photography studio. My family is planning to get their photo taken the day of the Pentecost fair. I only hope he doesn't charge too much."

Ada and Kotryna peeked into each shop until they found a door with a small white cardboard sign written by hand. The ink had smeared with the recent rain, and the corners were beginning to curl from the damp. Kotryna leaned over, gasping when she read it. "Simaitis's Photography Studio will open on Pentecost Sunday."

"What's wrong, Teta?" asked Ada, seeing her pale face.

"Oh, Ada, this can't be." Kotryna stared at the sign as if it had some hidden message. "It couldn't be him," she whispered, white with shock. "It's only a coincidence. We would have heard something, wouldn't we have?" Kotryna was almost whispering. When she looked though the shop windows, the place looked newly painted and readied, but without shelves and only a counter at the front with some chairs. "When is Pentecost?"

"In a few weeks," answered Ada.

Kotryna's lip began to quiver. "If only it were true. Could my Aleksas be returning home from America?"

Ada was both surprised and moved. "Dear Teta, do you still love him?"

"He's the only one I've ever loved," Kotryna declared.

Though it was hard, Ada said nothing about the letter she had written to Aleksas Simaitis in America, because she had promised her grandfather to keep it a secret. Could it really be her aunt's old love was returning because of the letter? This was indeed a mystery. Could love really cause such turmoil? She bit her lip, knowing the answer to this from experience. Ada watched her aunt, realizing love was truly one of God's favorite mysteries.

-Twenty-

The lace curtain billowed, bringing in the fragrant breeze of lilacs though the open window. It was a glorious day and everyone was excited that spring had finally arrived. The life-giving sun was softening the earth, warming and waking the seeds in the fields, pierced by new shoots of life.

Outside, Petras was cutting birch branches to decorate the farm gate and the doors as was the custom on Pentecost, which marked the end of the sowing season and the beginning of summer's work. Ada and her sisters sat on the bench outside, weaving flower wreaths to decorate the cows and sheep. When Viktoras saw them, he pronounced his farm a true Garden of Eden.

Kotryna sat puzzling over the mysterious sign in town. Could this Simaitis at the photography studio really be her old love? Would this miracle happen or should she brace herself for disappointment?

By the time the rest of the family sat down to breakfast, Kotryna had already cinched herself into a corset brought from Smolensk, hoping to have a more girlish figure in the mauve dress Mrs. Feinstein had given her.

While the family was preparing for church, Viktoras came

over and squeezed Kotryna's hand. It stabbed his heart to see the tremulous hope in her eyes. "I have some fatherly advice for you—try not to be anxious, my dear. Try to relax and enjoy yourself today." Viktoras would let his family go to town, while he waited at home. In case matters didn't turn out as he hoped, he couldn't bear to witness it.

As he watched their cart disappear down the road, Viktoras mumbled a prayer, "Lord, life is short and difficult enough. Let my poor Kotryna finally have what she's always wanted."

By the time the cart reached Raudonava, Kotryna was almost swooning, though it was hard to tell if it was a bad case of nerves or whether the corset was cutting off the blood to her head. Elzbieta had to help her off the cart and hold her steady.

Stasys simply shook his head and whispered to his son, "What on earth is to be done with this skittish woman? If she were a horse, someone would have to shoot her."

Outside the churchyard, they saw the usual assortment of tables selling candy and gingerbread, others with holy cards and scapulars, and under the table, hidden prayer books in Lithuanian. When the family got closer to the church gate, they passed a gantlet of beggars—blind, crippled, deaf—each pleading for alms. Ada put a few kopeks in hands and hats, while Kotryna walked by the whole flock of beggars so full of thoughts of Simaitis that she was blind to all else.

After Mass, the parishioners gathered in the churchyard to exchange news and greet friends and neighbors. Men asked about the livestock and the sowing, while women traded bits of gossip, and young men stole furtive glances at the young girls who were blooming into women. But Kotryna had no time for small talk, hardly able to speak for she was on the brink of hysteria.

Modestas was ready to take his mother and sister home, but before leaving, he found Ada to tell her he'd return later for the fair. "I have a gift for you." Ada nodded politely, hardly able to look into his eyes. He had come to see her recently, pulling her into an embrace, but she had pulled away, angry at his advances. He had not returned since, but now he was back with a promised gift. She had not yet talked to him about Jonas because she wasn't sure what to say, since Jonas had not been seen since Shrove Tuesday. Perhaps today she would find the courage to tell Modestas her heart was elsewhere.

Kotryna's heels pounded a staccato rhythm as she came running to Ada. "Come quickly," she said, impatienty, pulling her out of the churchyard. "You promised to come with me to the photography studio." Kotryna quickly ran to the town square. Standing in front of the shop, she breathlessly turned to ask Ada how she looked. "I'm suddenly afraid to go in."

"You look beautiful. Now peek inside the window to see if it's really him." Ada gently pushed her aunt. When Kotryna looked inside the dim room, she could see a man with his back to her. He wore brown trousers and a white shirt with his sleeves rolled up.

"Is it him?" asked Ada, impatiently.

"I can't see clearly. He looks heavier and shorter than I remember. I don't think so," answered Kotryna, straining to get a better look. Ada couldn't wait another moment and pulled her nervous aunt into the studio. Kotryna stopped at the oval mirror by the door to sneak a peek at herself, lest some stray hair ruin her entrance.

It wasn't long before Dora and Julija found them in the studio, with Elzbieta rushing to join them. They could see the photographer bowed under the hood attached to his camera. When Elzbieta saw her sister, she was alarmed at how flushed and nervous she looked. "Oh, dear, will you be all right?" Hives were already visibly jumping out on Kotryna's neck, and she could hardly speak. Her throat had closed, and that was good because her heart was threatening to jump out of it.

Wide-eyed, Kotryna watched the photographer move a little behind the camera. A family was getting their portrait taken in front of a screen with a bucolic painting of a birch woods behind a small lake. An older couple sat formally in chairs while a young man stood behind them with his hand on his mother's shoulder. Kotryna held her breath, watching and waiting to see if her beloved would pop out from under the hood. Ada was busy tending to her aunt and watching the photographer, and at first, she didn't notice the family posing for their portrait. When she finally turned her attention to them, her eyes went to Jonas Balandis, who was posing stiffly with his arm on his mother's shoulder. It was like a blow to the stomach that left Ada weak. She couldn't take her eyes off him, her heart fluttering like a bird trying to escape a cage. She was alarmed by the intensity of her emotions.

Jonas hadn't noticed her yet because he was intent on standing completely still for the photo, his eyes on the camera. Ada studied him and then his parents. Father and son looked alike, but the mother was small and wiry. Ada could see that years of hard work and determination had hardened the woman's expression.

When Jonas finally caught sight of Ada, he smiled, his eyes following her, causing her to blush.

"Please stand still, young man," hectored the photographer. "Look here, please, and don't smile. You'll ruin the photograph." The photographer emerged from under his hood to see who had walked into his studio. When he spied Kotryna, his eyes locked onto hers. "Can it really be you?" he asked in a grave voice as if he were seeing an apparition.

"Yes, Aleksas, it's me," she trilled like a bird, eyes brimming. They stared at each other, wide-eyed and full of emotion.

"Time has been very good to you, Kotryna." His eyes washed over her for a few warm moments. Aleksas was visibly shaken but tried to contain his emotions.

"You as well." Kotryna walked over to him, blinking back the tears that threatened. She studied his face, his brown hair that tended to curl, his high forehead and mushroom-colored eyes, his mustache, waxed and turned up at the ends. "You look wonderful," she said, brightly.

Aleksas smiled and took her hand. "Have I changed? Do I look like an American?"

"I've never seen an American before. You're the first." She tried to sound cheerful, but there was an edge of resentment in her voice, as if one wrong word might send him back to such a wilderness, far out of her reach.

Aleksas pulled her closer. "How lovely you look. It's been so long. Much too long." He looked into her eyes and held her hand, not letting go.

"Much too long." She repeated, helplessly.

Then a loud cough came from behind. "Ahem," Jonas's mother, Domicele, cleared her throat. The Balandis family still stood, stiffly posed. "Could you finish our portrait before you tell your life story?" Domicele looked annoyed, impatiently waiting for this stranger to finish his tender reunion with Kotryna Kulys, all gussied up in her city clothes.

The photographer felt chasened. "Oh, of course, I'm very sorry." Aleksas turned back to Kotryna and squeezed her hand. Please excuse me while I finish this portrait. When Aleksas returned to posing the Balandis family, Jonas kept glancing at Ada, drinking her in. The photographer ducked back under the hood and told everyone not to move just as a giant flash exploded over his head.

The flash of light scared Domicele half to death. She fanned herself with her hand. "Felt like my soul jumped right out of my body when that machine exploded. I thought the Day of Judgment had come."

"I'm sorry, I should have warned you," said Aleksas, bringing her a glass of water.

Domicele blinked. "I can't see anything but spots. Have I gone blind?"

"No, you'll be fine in a minute." Aleksas smiled in spite of himself.

"Here, try some of this American chewing gum," he said, trying to make up for her fright. "I brought it from Pennsylvania." He turned to the Varnas family. "In fact, you must all try it," he said, passing out sticks of foil-wrapped gum.

Jonas kept his eyes on Ada. His burning glance made her face flame, but neither said a word.

"What is this?" asked Stasys, opening the paper and examining the powdery gray rectangle.

"Chewing gum made in Chicago by a man named Wrigley," Aleksas explained.

"Is it candy?" asked Ada.

"Not exactly. You just chew it." Aleksas put one in his mouth to demonstrate.

Petras, who loved progress and everything American, was the first to try it. "It's good," he pronounced.

"Just don't swallow it," warned Aleksas.

"You don't swallow it?" Elzbieta, asked puzzled.

"No, you just chew it until you've tired of it and then you spit it out."

Everyone looked at him with suspicion. What was the point of chewing something if you didn't swallow it?

"Oh, let's try it," said Kotryna seeing the skepticism on her sister's face. "He's brought it all the way from America."

"It's sweet," declared Elzbieta, wondering what kind of country this America was that had to sweeten something that felt like a soft worm in her mouth once she chewed it. Watching everyone's jaws working away like cows with their cud, she was disgusted by the idea of endlessly chewing. Discreetly, she covered her mouth as if to clear her throat, then spit the gum into her palm and looked around to see where she could throw it away.

"How good it is to see you all after all these years," said Aleksas shaking everyone's hand.

Elzbieta tried to transfer the gum to her other hand behind her back, but when she opened her fist, she realized the gum had stuck

178

to her fingers and palms. When she tried to dislodge it, she only managed to get the other hand stuck as well. Aleksas was coming closer so she rubbed her hands together hoping the dreaded stuff would simply fall off. He put his hand out to her, but she kept her hands behind her. Aleksas looked hurt when she didn't offer her hand.

Elzbieta turned a moist red, desperately trying to rid herself of the gum, but the more she tried, the messier it got. Finally, in a burst of desperate vexation, she blurted out, "What is this hellish sweet? It must be the devil's own, for it grabs everything it touches and won't let go." Elzbieta unglued her hands and showed them to Aleksas, who tried but failed to control his mirth. It came out as a cough but his shoulders shook from the suppressed laughter.

Elzbieta shot him an angry look. "Spit your gum into *your* palm and see how funny it is." The rest of the room chewed uneasily, worried about what to do with the infernal stuff.

"I'm sorry." Aleksas got a basin of water and some brown soap, and Elzbieta tried to wash the sticky globs from her hands.

Stasys rolled his eyes. "Can we have our portrait taken before we miss the fair? I'm getting mighty thirsty for a beer."

"Of course." Aleksas apologized. Kotryna chewed her American gum and asked, "Tell me about America. What did you do there?" She took a deep breath, trying to control her rising emotions.

Aleksas sighed. "Oh, the trip to America was frightening. So many days on the open sea, storms raging. I couldn't sleep at night, thinking the waves would swallow our boat and I would sink to the bottom of the sea." He shook his head, as if to rid himself of the image. "And now, when I remember America, I smell the coal dust of the Pennsylvania mines. I went to America to become rich, a fool's dream." His face fell. "I worked hard and managed to save a little, but it took so many years. I thought I'd never see home again. And then his letter came," he said slowly.

"I was surprised. What old wounds it opened." He looked at her with haunted eyes.

Kotryna wondered what this letter could be.

"After that letter, I had to get home."

She wanted to hold him tightly so that no one could ever come between them again, and to tell him she loved him, only him, never another. But she didn't dare. Instead, she held her breath waiting for words of reassurance. "You did well for yourself," she beamed. "I can see that."

Aleksas looked into her eyes. "Are you alone?"

"No, I'm with my family."

"You're married then?" Looking at her garnet ring, he smiled wistfully.

"No, not married." She nudged him playfully. "I was talking about my family here." Smiling her crooked smile, she asked, "And you?" Her voice failed.

"Quite alone."

"I see," she said, eyes bright with love. "Have you no sweetheart back in America?" Such a bold question it took her breath away. Where had she gotten the courage to ask such quetions?

Aleksas smiled shyly. "No sweetheart." Now his cheeks were hot and he tried to change the subject. "Your dress is very beautiful, Kotryna."

"Thank you. A present from the woman I worked for in Smolensk."

"Oh, of course, Smolensk." He looked down at his hands and for a few moments, was speechless. Smolensk was still a sore spot between them. "It does look Russian, now that you mention it."

Stasys cleared his throat. "Our portrait, please before we die of thirst."

"Oh, I'm sorry," he said, nervously. "Seeing Kotryna again has undone me." Aleksas went back to his equipment.

Kotryna wished her father had come to see how Aleksas had made his way in the wide world. Her eyes fluttered closed, remembering how earnest Aleksas was as a young man, always striving to learn, to better his situation. She recalled his shame at being poor, without land, forced to work as a hired hand, knowing her father would never let her marry someone without land or prospects. Now he had lived in America while she had lived in Smolensk. Oh, those wasted years they could have been together, when they could have loved each other and raised children. Those sad years were gone, but there were still years ahead that they might have together, God willing. She didn't dare dream, yet when she looked at his face, she simply couldn't keep from hoping.

-Twenty-one-

Another flash of light and the photographer was done with the portrait of the Varnas family. Everyone in the studio blinked, trying to restore their vision. Ada rubbed her eyes, and when she opened them, she found her brother examining a photo of a Victrola with its large brass horn, and next to it, a McCormick reaper and Ford's first car. Petras examined the photos with the complete fascination of one impatient for progress. He pulled Ada over to look at a stereograph he picked up from the counter with twin photos of Chicago.

"Look, Ada. There's a new world coming. It will be a world of big cities, factories and automobiles."

Ada saw his eagerness for all that was new. "You're such a dreamer, dear brother," she said teasingly. The photo of a bustling Chicago street seemed so real she could almost touch it. When she looked up, she saw Jonas walking toward her. Suddenly she couldn't catch her breath.

"Hello again," he said softly.

Feeling an upheaval of tangled emotions, Ada mumbled, "It's been a while since I last saw you."

Jonas nodded. "That's right. Two months, one week and four

days." He scratched his forehead, slightly embarrassed.

He had counted the days. It thrilled her.

From across the room, Elzbieta spotted Ada talking to Jonas and immediately came over, dragging her husband along like a hostage. "Perhaps you'll introduce us to your mother."

While Jonas went to get his parents, Elzbieta examined the mother. "She looks like a tough old chicken," she whispered to Stasys.

A short, stringy woman with small dark eyes, Domicele looked at everything with a hint of suspicion. She seemed to cast a pall over the meeting.

Introductions were made but no pleasantries exchanged as the two wives looked each other over as if evaluating fish at the market.

For her part, Domicele examined the foreign dresses, especially the dress of the thin, nervous woman who was circling the photographer, and Elzbieta who was like a helpless child with that gum stuck to her hands. Finally, she cast a glance at the girl who seemed to have enchanted her son. Not a word escaped her tight mouth. Instead, it widened into a string bean smile. "My husband has often mentioned the Varnas family," she said tepidly.

Stasys greeted Jeronimas warmly. "I've often looked at that book that your son brought."

"Oh, I'll always remember the day the bullet hit that book," Jeronimas replied. "It was so good to see Viktoras after all those years. Didn't he come with you today?" Jeronimas looked around the room and wondered where he could spit the awful gum. After what happened to Elzbieta, he didn't dare take it out of his mouth. His tongue herded it into his cheek, behind his last molar.

Stasys shook his head. "No, but he would have if he had known you were coming."

"I was looking forward to seeing him again. Jonas has been urging us to come this way again, so we decided to go to the fair hoping to see your family."

Stasys offered to buy him a beer at the festival, wanting to hear more about his contraband adventures, thinking this was a grand way to spend a Sunday. Jeronimas agreed immediately, telling his wife and son that he'd meet them later. The moment the two men went out the door, they spat out their gum.

"What vile things these Americans chew," said Jeronimas as they strolled away.

The photography studio was filling up with customers. At the head of the line stood Yakub Glauberman with his entire family. The tailor, now recovered from the grippe, wore a finely tailored brown pinstriped suit. He greeted Ada and her family, watching in wonder as they chewed, their mouths working without cease. It was enough to make a man queasy.

Seeing his customers awaiting him, Aleksas excused himself.

Kotryna took a brave breath and stopped him. "Would you like to come to lunch next Sunday?" she asked, nervously.

"That would be nice," he said, "but I'm afraid I will be busy."

Kotryna wondered if he was looking for an excuse. "Come on Wednesday, then," she added in desperation.

He bowed his head slightly. "Very well. But now I really must get back to work."

Kotryna let out the breath she had been holding. "Well, it's settled then." She watched him hurry to prepare for the next family's portrait. Satisfied, she went to join Ada who was talking to Domicele and Jonas. "Won't you join us at the fair?"

"Of course," said Jonas before his mother could protest. He gently pushed her to walk with the Varnas clan toward the town square where the festivities had begun. He walked beside Ada in a companionable silence behind the group.

Elzbieta kept stopping to check her shoe to see what was sticking to the bottom of it. Finally, she stopped Kotryna and held onto her shoulder to examine the sole. "It's that infernal gum again! Is there no way to get rid of it?"

185

"Someone must have spit theirs out," Jonas suggested.

Taking a twig to scrape it from her shoe, Elzbieta muttered curses at the man who invented this sticky torment.

Everyone was beginning to gather in the square for the festivities. A band was playing lively tunes as couples paired up to dance. Nearby, a large swing was strung up under a two-hundred-year-old oak tree where girls were taking turns being pushed by their suitors. The Bartkus brothers waved for Dora and Julija to join them on the swing. The girls ran over to wait their turns. They watched Zigmas push the squealing Elena up high, her skirt billowing and her legs flying high into the air.

Ada and Jonas joined the dancers at the far end of the square.

When Kotryna nudged her sister, pointing to the couple, Elzbieta frowned and whispered her complaint so that Domicele wouldn't hear. "That Jonas sticks to Ada like a pancake to the pan. What if Modestas sees them together?"

Jonas pulled Ada into the circle of folk dancers, and soon they were whirling to the music. She held on tightly, laughing as they looped around. Afterward, heated and breathless, she laughed, telling him how much she enjoyed it. When the music started again, Jonas asked her for a polka. He held her by the waist and her arms encircled his neck. Looking into his eyes, she felt like this was where she belonged. Circling and twirling, they danced three polkas, rotating round the other dancers, giddy with delight.

"Can we stop to rest and catch our breath?" she asked, flushed.

"I'll do anything you like for as long as you like," said Jonas bowing. They sat on the grass under an old apple tree, away from the others. For a while, they simply watched the dancers. When Jonas hesitantly leaned closer, her heart raced, feeling the warmth of his body. "I'm so glad you came," she said breaking into a grin and then suddenly feeling shy. Jonas struck her as being steady and sure like a rock, while Modestas was mere fog.

A young dog came over and nuzzled Jonas. "Ah, look who loves me—dogs and horses."

"And the young ladies?" she teased.

Jonas reddened. "I've never been a ladies' man."

"Perhaps we should get back to the dance?" she asked, still unsure of herself.

"Wait, not yet," he said. "I want to keep you for myself just a little while longer."

Ada's heart leaped. He wanted to keep her for himself. A slight breeze rose and white apple blossoms fell around them like snow. She caught the falling petals in her palm. She could see that something weighed on him. He looked as if he was keeping his emotions in check. Laying her hand on his arm, Ada asked, "Is something wrong?" She searched his face. In his eyes, she could see his struggle.

"Ada," he said pleadingly. The sound of her name hung in the air. He put his moist hand on hers and then pulled it away, smoothing it on the cloth of his pants. Finally, he asked the question that had been needling him. "I need to know something. It's a bit delicate so I hope you won't be angry."

Now Ada frowned, suddenly frightened by his hesitant words. "What is it?" she asked quietly.

"About Shrove Tuesday," he stopped and looked away. "Modestas Bogdanskis."

"Yes?" she could barely breathe. Here was the conversation she had dreaded.

"I saw how he put his arm around you."

Ada gulped, feeling a bit ill. She had to be truthful, but without scaring Jonas away. How to say this, she wondered, nervously playing with the folds of her skirt.

"What does Modestas mean to you?"

"Well," she hesitated. "At first, I was flattered by his attention, but after I met you, it all changed..." She stopped, seeing Jonas wince as he looked across the square. Suddenly he pulled away. When she turned in the direction of Jonas's gaze, she saw a tall figure silhouetted against the sun coming toward them. Her stomach dropped when she realized it was Modestas. Without a word, she scrambled to her feet, wanting nothing more than to run away. But she was caught in this web, turning from Jonas to Modestas and back again, completely at a loss what to do.

"There you are, Ada, I was looking everywhere for you," Modestas said dryly. "May I join you?" He frowned, seeing Jonas.

"Please," said Jonas, stiffening. He stood and introduced himself. "We met briefly on Shrove Tuesday."

"Yes, I remember. Shall we sit back down?" asked Modestas, casually waving his hand toward the grass. Then taking off his black jacket, he folded it carefully before sitting next to Ada.

Ada glanced at Jonas who seemed to have turned to stone. So many unspoken feelings hung in the air.

"Have I interrupted something?" asked Modestas, picking an apple blossom from Ada's hair.

Ada looked down at her hands, unsure how to proceed in this awkward situation.

Jonas remained standing. "Excuse me, I must be going. Good day to you both." His look stabbed her as he turned to walk away.

"Wait a minute," she pleaded. Jonas turned briefly as Ada stood up. "Please stay." She tried to smile reassuringly, seeing the anger and hurt on Jonas's face. She took a few steps to join Jonas, but Modestas took her arm, pulling her back.

"Ada, did you forget I told you that I have a little surprise for you today?" He took a small box from his pocket and handed it to her.

Ignoring Modestas, she turned back to Jonas, "Wait for me." She could hardly look at Modestas, her head beginning to pound.

"Open it," said Modestas, forcing a smile.

Ada could see Jonas wanted to say more, but the words stuck in his throat, choking him. He shook his head and turned away.

"Oh, don't go," she begged, feeling her heart sink as she

watched him quickly walk away. "Let go of me," she told Modestas, angrily.

"Wait, open my gift." Annoyed, Modestas opened the box for her. It held an amber brooch in the shape of a leaf. "Let me pin it on your blouse?" He fastened it to her collar, while she stood impatiently fuming.

"Is something wrong, Ada?" Modestas's voice was cold.

"I'm sorry, but I have to go," she said, angrily, her throat tightening. She hurried off without a glance back. Scanning the market square, she searched for Jonas, but he had simply vanished in the crowd. She was so frustrated and upset that she wanted to kick herself. How could she have let him slip away?

The festival continued. The band played on. Filled with regret, Ada went from one group to another searching for him. In the distance, she could hear Dora squeal in delight when Jurgis pushed her swing into the treetops.

Nearby, young people were gathered in a circle for another folk dance. The music started and the circle whirled round until the dancers broke into couples. Zigmas danced with Elena, while his brother twirled Dora. Ada's eyes scoured the fair for Jonas, but there was no sign of him anywhere.

Looking back at the lonely old apple tree covered in blossoms, she saw Modestas heading for the tavern.

It was spring and all around young men were vying for the prettiest girls, courting them. The girls were flirting with the most handsome men or coyly teasing their admirers. Laughter, dancing and riddles were what the day called for.

Like a stone, Ada watched it all as if it were another curious photograph Aleksas Simaitis had brought back from America. As if this spring full of love, longing, and dance was nothing more than another lively scene on a stereograph postcard—one not meant for her.

-Twenty-two-

A fter Kotryna returned from the fair, she found her father checking the grafts on his pear trees. "Papa, you won't believe it!" she said, clapping her hands. "It's a miracle, I tell you."

Viktoras chuckled at her girlish excitement. "Really?"

"Aleksas Simaitis has returned home after all these years in America. Isn't it a coincidence? So soon after I came home?" She shook her head, not quite believing it. "And Papa, you should see his photography shop. Soon the whole town will be lined up for photographs. I tell you, he's a changed man with his own business."

"Is that so? I'm glad to hear it." Viktoras smiled, pleased by his daughter's excitement.

"Are you really?" Kotryna studied his face, not entirely sure if he meant it. "But Papa, how did you know about the shop? You sent me to find it before any of us knew it was there."

"I have my ways, don't worry."

"And Papa," she said, her smile widening. "He was happy to see me, and can you believe he's not married? That is certainly a miracle," she proclaimed with glee.

"Yes, I guess it is," he said, laughing quietly at her enthusiasm.

"You don't still hate him, do you? I was so eager to see him again after all these years that I've invited him for lunch. Do you mind terribly?" She blinked, expecting the worst.

"No, I never hated him." Viktoras shrugged, frowning at the idea. "I only thought that since he had no land or prospects, you both would have to work as farmhands your whole life. I didn't want that kind of life for my daughter. I wanted you to marry Pocius who had a large farm and would have taken good care of you. But when you shocked me by running off to Smolensk, and then Aleksas left for America, it made me very angry. Daughters should listen to their fathers."

Kotryna listened, steaming with anger. "But it never bothered you that I didn't love Pocius, did it?" her voice rose. "It never broke your heart that I'd run away to Russia rather than hurt Aleksas that way, did it?"

Viktoras was shocked by the huge well of anger his daughter still held. He cleared his throat, adjusted his cap, and smoothed his mustache. "Forgive me, my dear. Time has worked on me, and I saw how stubborn I had been and how it hurt you. I'm truly sorry, and I'm glad he's back, my dear. Truly." He took her hands and held them, but never mentioned his nightly battle with Death, his motivation for rectifying his mistakes. "We'll give him a proper homecoming when he comes."

"Thank you, Papa," she said, still uncertain if he was wholly sincere. After all this time, she was bewildered by this sudden turn of events.

On Wednesday morning, Kotryna began her preparations for Aleksas's visit. Everything had to be just right. Rolling the dough for the delicate mushroom-filled dumplings that she remembered Aleksas liking, she hoped he'd feel at home again after his years in that barbarous wilderness of Pennsylvania, wanting to taste things he hadn't eaten since he left home. But most of all, she wanted him to remember how they had once loved each other and to rekindle the warm promise of that love.

Rising early, she baked a plum cake and made cold borscht. What a pleasure it was to cook for someone you loved! Humming long-forgotten love songs, she cut circles into the dough using an inverted drinking glass, filling each circle with fried onions and mushrooms. She hoped it would be a meal he would remember.

"Ayy!" she yelped, jumping back from the table, gooseflesh rising on her arms. Something had brushed by her leg. It felt like a dog, but she had the uneasy feeling that the *domovoi* was under the table. When she stooped to look, she saw nothing. Her nerves must have been playing tricks on her. This was very upsetting and made her even more jittery. She must remember to keep Aleksas away from the pantry.

When the dumplings were finished, she wiped her hands on her apron and went out to the garden to pick dill for the cold borscht. Nearby, Ada sat on a bench leaning against the blossoming cherry tree, looking as if she had lost her best friend. Kotryna sat down beside her. "Ada, you've worn that long face for days now. What is it?" She put her hand on her niece's shoulder.

Crossing her legs, Ada jiggled her slipper against her heel, seemingly holding her breath until she finally blurted out, "Oh Teta, I don't know what to do! I want to tell Modestas to go away, but what would Mama say? She thinks the sun rises with him and his family." She covered her face, gulping down her rising tears. "I just don't have the courage."

"Oh, poor Ada. I've danced in your shoes. And there's nothing else to do but to tell your mother right now." Kotryna took Ada's hand and led her to the parlor. "Go on," she prodded. "Tell her."

Elzbieta, who was smoothing a tablecloth, turned when her daughter approached her. Ada's chin began to quiver as she told her mother, "Mama, I don't want Modestas for a suitor."

"Modestas? But why not?" Elzbieta was stunned. "What happened? He gave you such a beautiful amber brooch at the fair.

Ada, be sensible. You're not getting any younger."

"Teta, help me," Ada pleaded.

Kotryna added earnestly, "Elzbieta, when I look at her, I see myself at that age."

It was completely the wrong tack to take with her sister, and it annoyed Elzbieta beyond words. In her opinion, Kotryna was a wild card in the family, and now she was influencing her impressionable daughter. "Ada, listen well," her mother said harshly. "You are almost twenty-four years old. Do you want to marry or not?"

Ada glanced at her mother. "But I think there might be someone else for me, Mama." She wanted to tell her mother how her soul awoke with pure happiness when she was with Jonas.

"Who?" Her mother towered over her delicate daughter. "You don't mean that Balandis boy, do you?" Her eyes blazed dangerously. "I saw you walking together at the fair and I didn't like it. What will people say? First, they see you being wooed by one man, then another. No, we'll have none of that."

Kotryna put her arm around Ada. "I have great sympathy for you, Ada. I cried so when Papa wouldn't let me marry Aleksas. Do you remember, Elzbieta?"

"I remember," said her sister sharply. "But this is different."

"Is it?" asked Kotryna sarcastically.

Elzbieta looked at her daughter with a jaundiced eye. The girl had the same high cheekbones and pointed chin as Kotryna. "Ada," she said crossly, "girls have wonderful dreams in their heads about marriage, but life is different. Believe me, a mother knows what's best for her daughter. Now forget this Jonas Balandis and let's get ready."

Too upset to eat, Ada asked to be excused and went for a walk in the woods, wanting to be alone with her disappointment.

Kotryna peered under the kitchen table. "I could swear there is something under this table."

Elzbieta spit three times to ward off bad luck. "God forbid," she said. It seemed to her that whenever Kotryna's nerves were strained, it seemed to aggravate the *domovoi*. "That's all we need today."

"I keep seeing that imp out of the corner of my eye, but when I turn, it's gone. Is it real or my imagination?" Kotryna asked uneasily.

"Just calm down," Elzbieta said anxiously. Her sister's bad nerves were contagious.

Kotryna rubbed her forehead. A headache was blooming from the tension of this visit. "I must be jumpy about Aleksas coming." She added fresh dill to the cold borscht. "Nothing must go wrong today," she said, blessing herself and putting a sprig of rue in her hair, the symbol for virginity and protection.

Later that afternoon, the soft wind was tickling the cherry blossoms and ruffling the feathers of the speckled chickens as they pecked at nothing in particular, when Aleksas Simaitis arrived wearing his best brown suit from Shenandoah. To mark the occasion, he wore his bowler hat from Pittsburgh. Tipping his hat, he bowed and greeted Kotryna, dressed in her good skirt from Smolensk with a white high-collared blouse with lace trim.

Leading him into the house, she murmured, "How wonderful it is to see you again. You look the same as you did eight years ago, Aleksas."

"Ah Kotryna, no one is the same after eight years in America. I'm looking forward to a quieter life," he replied, sincerely.

Stasys, who was just walking in the door, stopped when he saw Aleksas's bowler hat. After a swift glance, he promptly turned around and went back outside where he stifled his laugh. He hadn't seen anything as comical as that hat in a long time. All he needed was some more of that awful chewing gum from

America and that would have been comedy enough for weeks of stories in the village. There would be caricature masks made of him for the next Shrove Tuesday carnival—cheeks fat with gum and a black bowl of a hat on his head, like an overturned chamber pot. Skits would be created of Aleksas courting the old maid possessed by a Russian demon. Perhaps he would carve the mask himself.

Kotryna hung Aleksas's hat on a hook and turned, examining the room, feeling skittish and uneasy about the imp in the pantry. When Viktoras came into the parlor, he welcomed Aleksas warmly and took the first opportunity to apologize for his past mistakes. "I caused you both so much anguish and forced you both to leave home."

"It's true I was angry for many years as I set out for America," said Aleksas. "There were hard years where I wondered if I'd ever see home again."

Viktoras nodded. "I humbly apologize to you both for being so hard-headed. I now see it was wrong."

"Thank you," said Aleksas, examining the old man's weathered face. "It warms my heart to hear you say this."

Kotryna kissed her father's cheek and went to bring both men a glass of beer, and they drank a toast to the homecoming. Aleksas grinned, happy to see everyone. "This farm is still so familiar, so little has changed."

Soon Elzbieta brought food to the table. They started with the cold soup and when Kotryna served her mushroom dumplings, Aleksas closed his eyes. "This the most wonderful thing I've tasted in years." Kotryna was delighted to hear it and brought more. While ladling the dumplings onto his plate, she yelped sharply, and Aleksas jumped in surprise.

"What is it?" he asked in concern.

"Something tickled me." Kotryna lifted the tablecloth and looked under the table.

"Has the dog gotten in here?" asked Viktoras. He stood up to open the door. "I'll chase him out if he has, the little beggar."

Craning his neck out the door, he saw his dog lying curled up under the cherry tree. "Why, he's out there, sleeping."

Kotryna looked under the table again and thought she saw something scrambling away. She wanted to hide, to scream that it wasn't fair. This *domovoi* was going to ruin her second chance with Aleksas. The imp obviously wanted to prevent her from falling in love again and marrying because they only stuck to old maids. Determined not to let the *domovoi* ruin things, she hurried the meal along so they could all go outside.

"What is it Kotryna?" asked Aleksas. "You've gone pale. Are you ill?"

She swallowed hard and forced a smile. "No, no, I'm fine, thank you, just fine. Would you care for some more dumplings?"

"No thank you, I've had enough. They were wonderful, even better than I remembered." Aleksas leaned back in his chair, looking contented.

Desperate to get out of the house, Kotryna hurriedly served the plum cake. "Perhaps we could eat this in the garden. It's such a lovely day today."

"Splendid idea," Aleksas proclaimed. "I always love eating outside in good weather." He stood to help carry things outside, while Stasys and Petras went to get a table from the barn. They put it under the cherry tree, and Dora and Julija brought the benches. While Elzbieta covered the table with a cloth, Kotryna went back inside to get the pitcher of beer. She was about to go outside when she lunged, dropping the earthenware pitcher. Her sister ran in to see what happened.

"The filthy thing tripped me," Kotryna whispered, rubbing her sore knee and looking up pleadingly at her sister.

"The *domovoi*?" Elzbieta blessed herself. "Oh my God, what will we do now?"

"Just don't let Aleksas know," whimpered Kotryna, picking up the shards of pottery. "He'll run out the door and never return."

"Help me, please," she said, desperation haunting her eyes.

"Go out to Aleksas," said Elzbieta, wiping up the beer. "I'll get another pitcher."

"Thank you." Kotryna took a long gulp of vodka straight from the bottle. Then she cast one last frightened glance at the table as though they were under siege.

A shiver ran down Elzbieta's back. "Will this never end?"

Outside, Kotryna quickly ate the plum cake, hoping to get Aleksas away before that horrid *domovoi* did anything more. Seeing her anxious face, Viktoras suggested they take a walk by the creek. Kotryna nodded gratefully and took Aleksas's arm.

Once they were walking, Kotryna blurted out her old resentments, the hurt still fresh. "Why didn't you write to me from America?"

Aleksas smiled ruefully. "I was angry at you for running away to Smolensk instead of going to America with me."

"But I didn't know you were planning to go to America." Kotryna's eyes stung. "I was only running away from the marriage arranged by my father. It was hard to leave, but I had no choice."

"It was hard for both of us to leave. I felt like a condemned man when I took the train to Bremen and then the boat to America to join my uncle in Pennsylvania. Once I saw the coal mines of Shenandoah, I thought I had reached Hell itself. Going into those holes in the earth full of coal dust, men with blackened faces, I saw children working the mines like adults."

Nearby, the water gurgled over rocks in the creek. "Tell me more about America," she pestered him. She wanted to know every detail of his life.

"In America, the Lithuanians live next to the Poles, Irish, Italians, Germans, even Chinamen with long, thin braids down their backs. Now that I'm back home, it seems to me that everyone looks the same. In America, there are so many different religions and languages, it's like the Tower of Babel."

What a man of the world her Aleksas had become. "Did you see Indians?"

"Yes, of course," he said, jokingly. "Whole tribes circled my boarding house in Pennsylvania doing a war dance."

Kotryna smiled, unsure if it was true.

"I've talked enough about myself. Tell me about Smolensk."

Kotryna told him about the Feinstein family and the children she took care of. "Life was very different there."

"Yes, I can imagine. You know, I must confess that Sapnai looks much smaller than I remember."

Kotryna hoped he wasn't disappointed in her. Did he think she had aged much?

Walking along the creek, Aleksas took her hand. "You know, I raised money at church for boxes of Lithuanian books we shipped to Father Jurkus. Each time, I hoped the priest would see my name and address and somehow send it to you."

"Really?" Kotryna was surprised and pleased. With this man by her side, she could face anything, even demons. "I wish he had," she whispered. For many years she had cried tears of loneliness. Now her heart leapt in hope for love's return.

"We have eight long years apart to talk about," he said.

Nodding, she knew that he was right, of course. His eight years of coal mines, cowboys and Indians and her eight years of Russian demons.

"And now you have your own successful business." said Kotryna, forcing a smile.

Aleksas suddenly looked deflated. "I only wish it were true."

"Isn't it?" She was perplexed, recalling the line of people in his studio waiting for their portraits.

"It's true I had many customers during the fair, but so few came to the photo shop afterward. I don't know what to do," he said, frowning. "All my life I've been so poor and it didn't get any

199

better in the coal mines. And then I met a prosperous old man who was Lithuanian and had a photo studio so I begged him for a job.

At first, I just cleaned his studio, and ran errands, but later he taught me all he knew. I worked hard and saved my money, bought a camera, thinking I'd make it in America as a photographer. But people here don't have the money that people in America have. Now the customers have stopped coming." He shook his head, not able to look her in the eye. "If this keeps up I'll be poor again. I might even have to work as a hired hand."

"Oh no," Kotryna whispered. It broke her heart to see him so deflated. She wondered what he might do to get more business.

As they slowly walked back to the farmhouse, they stopped to look at the crows squabbling and at a hare running swiftly across a field. "The cities in America were crowded with tall buildings," Aleksas complained. "I saw no woods or fields in the city, no animals except the poor overworked horses that pulled the carriages. I've missed the countryside. The air here makes me feel light-headed."

When they returned to the farm, they found Stasys standing at the kitchen door holding a pitchfork, while Petras held a rake. Both men looked frightened. Elzbieta and the girls huddled together across the farmyard.

"What happened?" asked Aleksas teasingly. "A fox got one of the chickens?"

Kotryna paled, incapable of saying anything. He saw her anxious look and flashed a nervous smile. "What is it?"

"I'm afraid to tell you," she whimpered, unable to look at him, her lips quivering until her confession came in a rush. "A *domovoi* has followed me home from Russia."

His eyebrows lifted. "*Domovoi*, is it?" He smiled briefly, expecting a joke. When no one laughed, he added, "You're kidding, aren't you?" Kotryna was mortified. On the brink of tears, she glanced up at him, her eyes pleading for understanding.

He continued, "My mother used to say the landscape was alive with meaning. An old oak tree was venerated, a spring was holy, an owl could foretell death, a magpie flying in the wrong direction could spell disaster. You just had to know the signs. But in America, an oak tree was simply an oak tree, a crow was simply a crow, and an owl foretold nothing in the coal mines of Pennsylvania. No one talks about imps and omens in America. They simply don't exist." He glanced behind him. "You say one has followed you from Russia?" He waved his hand. "I don't believe it."

Kotryna listened with alarm, hoping he wouldn't bolt back to Pennsylvania.

Suddenly, the back door banged loudly, rattling the windows. Then the door to the pantry slammed, shaking the shelves.

Aleksas jumped. "What was that?" He looked around warily. Stasys nodded sheepishly. "It's what you think. It's been raising hell, scaring the animals so that the cows probably won't have milk tonight and God knows when we'll see an egg again. The chickens have flown into the trees."

Viktoras approached and tried to smooth things over. "Don't worry. It's nothing, really." He patted Aleksas on the shoulder. "These imps only bother spinsters. Once she marries, it'll find another spinster to bother."

Aleksas smiled weakly. A little hot under his starched collar, he felt uneasy and anxious, as if couldn't wait to get away. Looking at Kotryna as if she was cursed, he forced a smile, thanking the family for their hospitality.

"And Kotryna, thank you for making my favorite dumplings." Forgetting his bowler hat completely, he beat a quick retreat home.

Standing in the yard with her family, Kotryna was stunned as she watched him go, wondering if she'd ever see him again after such an afternoon. She almost called to him, wanting to be reassured, but she was sure he was finished with her. "Aleksas will never return. He wants nothing to do with me."

Inside, they heard the rumbling of shelves and a whistling noise. Finally, fed up with the imp's pranks, Elzbieta kicked the door, yelling for the *domovoi* to get out of her pantry.

"I've had enough!" she shouted. "This is my pantry, you little devil. You better leave. Wait until I get my hands on you. When I'm done, you'll think the marshes were heaven compared to our pantry." She shook her fist at the door.

Viktoras turned to see his daughter's thunderous expression and was certain she meant every word.

-Twenty-three-

Elzbieta spent several long nights planning her line of attack on the *domovoi*, though she didn't breathe a word of it to anyone, not wanting any interference. Not only did she want her pantry and kitchen back, but she was also afraid that Aleksas might never marry her demon-afflicted sister. And, God forbid, if word got out about the *domovoi*, her daughters would never find suitors. It was enough that the imp frightened the young people on Shrove Tuesday. Now hardly any of the neighbors stopped by anymore.

On Sunday, while the family prepared for church, Elzbieta told Stasys she was not feeling well and was staying home. Surprised, he looked her over before going to harness the horses.

Elzbieta stood at the gate waving to her family, but inside,she was trembling. Once they were out of sight, she rolled up her sleeves and prepared to wage war. Opening her old dowry chest, she organized her arsenal—a cross, rosary, holy water, and some magic roots from a rowan tree that had been struck by lightning. For protection, she armed herself with rue, the magic herb reputed to cure ninety-nine ailments. A cold shudder of fear ran down her spine as she opened the pantry and demanded that the *domovoi* leave the house at once to join the demons living in the marshes.

In defense, the provoked *domovoi* shook the shelves.

Undaunted, Elzbieta crossed herself three times and stuck her head inside the pantry. "Where are you, you little devil? Come show yourself." Suddenly, a nut came zinging across the room and bounced off her forehead.

"Out, you little demon! I'll teach you to pester my sister. You'll wish you were back in Smolensk when I'm through with you." She lashed the air in all directions with her rowan roots. A basket of dried mushrooms flew to the ground.

Switching to her rosary, Elzbieta attacked the shelves, chanting prayers and flailing her arms. "Go find some other old maid to bother." She felt her kerchief slipping from her head and tried to hold it when suddenly a low growl frightened her. She raked the air until she caught something curved like a horn and suddenly found herself being pulled and tugged right out the front door, yanked outside into the farmyard as if a large goat was pulling her. Digging her heels into the earth, she pulled back, cursing while it bucked and kicked. "You toad's rear, you snake's tooth, you lizard-faced devil. I'll show you a hell right here."

On the road outside the farm gate, their neighbor, Balys, was walking by the farm when he heard Elzbieta's oaths and looked over to see her jumping around the farmyard. The old widower took off his cap to scratch his head and mumbled, "Until the day I die I'll never understand women."

The *domovoi* continued bucking around the yard and back into the house, where, quick as lightning, it jumped back to its familiar lair in the pantry. Elzbieta heard a strange whimpering and scampering, like a cornered animal. "Lord have mercy," she whispered, a shiver of fear running through her.

She took a deep breath. "I've had enough of your antics." Shutting herself inside, she blessed herself. Struggling with all her might, she came to blows with the unseen imp, the pantry pitching and the shelves shaking as if in a storm. "I'll teach you to scare our guests. I'll cover you with tar and roll you in stable manure so that I'll not only see you but I'll smell you coming. Then I'll cut you up for cording and burn you bit by bit. You hear me? Get out now, or you'll regret it! My daughters will never get married with you rattling around my house."

Finally, she brought out her ultimate weapon. Opening the bottle of holy water, she flicked it at all four corners until she heard the hiss of steam. With her last bit of strength, Elzbieta poured holy water on the demon—worse than boiling pitch for such an imp—and banished it. "Run to the marshes where all of your kind live."

Cornered, the *domovoi* pushed her away, causing her to knock her head on a shelf and fall into a heap on the floor. When the small hurricane finally subsided, a high-pitched whine started slowly and grew. The last thing she heard was a hissing whistle that flew out of the room and away from the farm. The neighbors in Sapnai stopped what they were doing to listen to the unholy sound. When Balys looked up to see his storks leaving the nest on his roof, he shuddered and blessed himself.

In town, Modestas found Ada in the churchyard to tell her the Ciginskas widow and her family had arrived. "It's been like a tonic for my mother to have her friend with us for the summer. And I'm afraid I won't have a chance to see you very much while they're visiting because Mother is eager to entertain them."

"I have something I need to talk to you about," she said, intending to tell him about her feelings for Jonas.

Modestas seemed to hardly hear her as he looked around for his family. "Later, my dear. I must go, but I'll certainly look for you at the Midsummer's celebration. *Au revoir, ma chère.*"

Ada took a breath, hugely relieved that Modestas would be taken up with his visitors.

Across the churchyard, Father Jurkus called Viktoras, Stasys, and Petras over, away from the others. "The time has come for Petras to cross the border," he said.

Viktoras protested."But Petras knows nothing of smuggling." The priest assured him that Tomas Kontautas would train both Petras and Jonas. "They'll be following in your footsteps."

"But isn't it still dangerous since the arrest of Norkus?" Viktoras asked. "Shouldn't we wait until things calm down?"

"Once Norkus was sentenced to two years in Siberia, things did calm down," answered the priest. "But you know better than I that this is dangerous work." Father Jurkus turned to Petras. "Are you sure you want to join this band?"

"Yes, Father, I want to go with Jonas. I've been waiting for this chance since I heard about Norkus." He turned to Stasys. "Give me your blessing."

"Of course, my boy," his father assured him. "Only let me be the one to tell your mother. And before you go, let Grandfather teach you all he's learned in his years of smuggling." Viktoras nodded gravely.

On their way home, Stasys heard a whistling noise overhead and stopped the nervous horses to see where it was coming from. Seeing nothing unusual, he continued home.

When he turned into the farmyard, he saw Margis was whimpering under the bench, his tail tucked between his legs. Once the whistling stopped, the farm seemed unnaturally quiet. Not a quack or a cluck could be heard. Viktoras listened intently and realized that the crickets had stopped chirping, the birds had stopped singing, even the cicadas were quiet. The wind had died down and not a leaf moved. He looked up at the blue unconcerned heavens, and it seemed the clouds were standing still and the Sun had stopped its orbit—as if all of nature held its breath.

Then, just as suddenly, Margis came bounding into view, his tail wagging. Soon the crickets began their music, the chorus of birds sang like on no other day, the wind playfully began to tickle the leaves again, and the Sun resumed its daily dance around the heavens. Viktoras scratched his head in wonder.

While Stasys unharnessed the horses, Kotryna went to look for her sister. When she called to her and no one answered, she thought it strange. She searched the house and then the farm buildings calling her name.

Only when Ada returned with the girls, did she think to check the pantry. There she found her mother looking more dead than alive on the floor, her skirt up over her knees. "Mama, oh no, Mama." She burst into tears. The pantry was a mess of overturned shelves and broken crockery. Ada fixed her mother's skirt before she ran to get her father.

"What in heaven's name?" Stasys was shocked to see his stricken wife on the floor. He bent to listen to her heart and check her breathing. "Thank God, she's alive." Dora and Julija ran over and stood behind their father, tears and gooseflesh rising. When Viktoras saw the disarray, the rosary, cross, and rue, he knew at once that Elzbieta had banished Kotryna's *domovoi*. Stasys carried her to their bed, while Kotryna brought a cold compress.

The first words out of Elzbieta's mouth when she recovered were directed at her sister. "It was your demon that did this to me," she said weakly. "I banished him to the marshes, but I thought it was the end of me."

"Elzbieta, how dangerous!" Kotryna had a headache the size of the marshes.

Ada fanned her mother's flushed face and looked around, wondering if the imp was really gone.

"Be a good girl and get me some water." After Elzbieta's bout with the *domovoi*, she was as tired as a newborn lamb. She stayed in bed for the rest of the day, which was unheard of. But she was simply worn out from her battle.

From time to time, Stasys peeked in. "How are you feeling?" he asked timidly.

"I'll live." She felt limp like an empty sack.

But it was Kotryna who insisted on tenderly nursing her sister like a child, feeding her rich broth, repeating how grateful she was to have such a brave sister who feared nothing in this world or the next. "Elzyte, you've saved me. How will I ever repay you?" Kotryna took her garnet ring off and slipped it on her sister's little finger.

"Thank you, my dear, brave sister."

Elzbieta smiled weakly and held up her hand to admire it.

Worn out and wearied, Elzbieta needed to be quiet, to rest and recover. Never in her life had she felt as tired and wrung out like an old rag. Staring out the window in the direction of the marshes, her stomach churned thinking of that marsh filled with demons.

Out the window, the sun descended like a red goat's eye, leaving behind banks of clouds on the horizon lit in lurid colors. The evening seemed demon-filled and portentous as Elzbieta gazed at the crimson sky, feeling uneasy.

-Twenty-four-

On Monday, Elzbieta haltingly tottered out to join her family and overheard Petras asking his grandfather about the routes to Tilsit. "What's this about Tilsit?" Elzbieta demanded, her attention suddenly fastened to their conversation.

Viktoras sighed heavily. This was definitely not the time to tell her about book smuggling. He took her hand. "Calm yourself. Father Jurkus has asked Petras and Jonas to smuggle some books."

Elzbieta protested, feebly, still weak. "What if he gets captured like Norkus? Or shot at like you did? My boy is trying to follow in your footsteps, Papa. He's listened to your stories and now they've infected him."

Viktoras put his hand on her trembling shoulder. "He's no longer a boy, my dear. He's a young man doing what he thinks is right. Like we all did. And you can be sure I'll give him the benefit of my own experience, as will Father Jurkus and Tomas."

Petras took his mother's hand to plead his case. "Mama, it's valuable work and I'm proud to be stepping into Grandfather's shoes." Elzbieta listened and had to resign herself.

Listening from across the room, Ada feared for her brother and was even more shocked when she heard that Jonas was going with them. It was such a blow. She had to see this man again. It was becoming unbearable. She would wait until he returned and then confess her feelings, unburdening her heart even if nothing came of it. Ada closed her eyes and mumbled to herself. "Come home safely, Jonas, come back to me."

The next morning, Ada was the first to notice the house was quiet and woke her aunt. Still anxious, Kotryna kept an ear cocked for that eerie rattling in their pantry. But all she heard was the gentle soughing of the wind through the tender branches of the fir trees. Walking from room to room, she experienced a lightness of spirit. Though still a bit wary, she was so relieved to be rid of the pesky *domovoi* that she danced a jig with Ada. For the first time in eight years, she was free.

Elzbieta woke, complaining, "My dreams were troubled, my digestion is bad, and my nerves are frayed." She looked out the window with a new respect for things unseen.

A week later, in the early hours of the morning, Petras woke and dressed quickly, preparing to meet Jonas and Tomas, the more seasoned smuggler who would guide them into Prussia—their initiation into the world of contraband books. Petras was about to slip out when Viktoras heard him and ran to give him some final bits of advice for crossing the border. "It's best to cross during a storm or on a moonless night." Then he stopped his grandson again at the door. "But why are you leaving without saying goodbye to your parents? It's not right."

Petras frowned. "You know how Mama is. She's been through enough. If she starts to cry, I'll feel terrible. It's better this way. You tell them you've seen me off."

Viktoras didn't like it. "Do you know when you'll return?"

"Father Jurkus said about a week. Don't worry I'll be back before the haying." Petras couldn't hide the pride he felt.

"Take care of yourself." Viktoras blessed him. Swallowing his fear, he forced himself to smile. Petras was out the gate by the time his father appeared. Stasys ran to bless him and hugged him warmly. "May God go with you."

The horizon was just beginning to glow with rosy light when Elzbieta came out, startled to see her husband and father at the farm gate. "Why are you both standing there?" Hesitantly, her husband told her the news.

"Will he be all right?" She searched her father's eyes.

"Of course, he will," said Viktoras. "He's clever, and now he gets to prove himself. He'll come back changed—a mature man."

Elzbieta wrung her hands, looking downcast. "So long as he comes back to me. That's all I ask."

Viktoras felt the need to be alone with his own thoughts. Slowly, he paced the perimeter of his farm, inspecting his fields and going over every piece of advice he had shared with his grandson, making sure nothing had been left out. Father Jurkus had assured him this would be an easy trip in a specially designed wagon with a false bottom, covered with hay. They were to cross the border on foot and then they would be met at a certain point by a wagon. Once they delivered the underground books, and newspapers to a distributor's home, they would return home.

Though Viktoras had spent many years running books across the border, he never remembered being as nervous as he was today. Pacing back and forth, he wrung his hands, realizing he wouldn't get a good night's sleep until Petras and Jonas returned safely. When he went back to his room, he took out his father's prayer book, printed long before the ban on Lithuanian books, to recite a litany to the Blessed Virgin for their safe return. His father had recited the litany so often that the corners of the pages were darker where he had thumbed them. When Viktoras was done, he hid it again, since this little book was one of his greatest treasures.

-Twenty-five-

Wednesday Ada found her aunt gathering eggs, looking lost and dejected, the heartache evident on her face. "Could it be Aleksas regrets coming home?" Kotryna asked Ada, as the rust-colored chicken nervously pecked at her clogs. "I haven't heard from him since that dreadful *domovoi* sent him scooting home. Perhaps I shouldn't expect love at my age. It was all foolish."

"I'm sure you're mistaken," said Ada.

"He no longer wants me after the *domovoi* frightened him." Chicken feathers clung to her hair.

Ada plucked one off. "He'll change his mind after you tell him that Mama banished it to the marshes."

Kotryna considered her advice. "You think so?"

"Yes," Ada assured her. "Besides, he left his bowler hat here. I'm sure he'd like it returned."

"Oh, that's a good excuse to visit."

That afternoon, Kotryna tried to summon her courage to visit Aleksas. Walking down the dusty road, the larks were swooping loops through the warm breeze, while somewhere in the village, she heard two girls singing a love song in harmony.

It made Kotryna sad as she slowly walked to Raudonava, past the familiar wooden shrines that bristled on the road. There was a colorful shrine to St. Isadore, the patron saint of farmers pushing a plow, and a weather-beaten shrine to St. Rita, patroness of unhappy marriages. She picked a bouquet of field flowers from the side of the road. What must Aleksas think of her?

When Kotryna finally reached the town, she went straight to the photography studio, but it was closed, so she walked around to the back where Aleksas lived in two tiny rooms. The door was slightly open. Knocking timidly, she found him with his mother, sitting at a small table, eating herring and boiled potatoes. Suddenly speechless, she stood there until Aleksas invited her to join them. Kotryna could smell the onions on his breath, but her stomach was too jittery to touch any food.

She greeted his mother, who was wearing an old dress, washed so often that the pattern of flowers was barely visible. Though stooped by years of hard work as a hired hand in the neighboring village, her eyes were still young.

"It's good to see you, Kotryna," she said. "Dear God, you and Aleksas have gone to the ends of the earth and back these last years. I'm just happy that you've both returned to Sapnai. My prayers have been answered." Kotryna smiled, relieved to hear his mother had been praying for their return.

Kotryna handed the small bouquet of wild flowers to his mother and then returned the hat Aleksas had left behind.

He thanked her and then proudly showed her what his mother had done to fix up the two rooms behind the studio. "She made new curtains," he said, pointing to the windows covered with flowered cotton.

"It's nothing, really," his mother smiled, shyly hiding behind her hand. "The tailor had some remnants and I sewed them up and strung them on some twine and tied them to a nail." Kotryna could see how proud they were of their first home, no matter how humble.

Aleksas added, "And I painted the walls and even the floor for mama. She'll be moving in after the harvest." He turned to his mother and said proudly, "She'll never be a hired hand again." Looking at her son, his mother beamed with pride.

Casting an eye at the dark, cramped rooms, Kotryna despaired. "You'll be living with your mother then?" The kitchen was tiny with an old knife-nicked table. There was a bed in the other room with a small chest. Though she could see that Aleksas had tried his best, it still looked dreary with cracked walls and a black spot on the ceiling from the kerosene lamp.

Kotryna had always dreamed of having her own farm. The idea of living in town was distasteful enough, but this cramped place was even worse than she imagined. There was hardly room for two and certainly no room for her. She smiled bravely, swallowing her disappointment.

As if he could read her thoughts, Aleksas asked, "It's not much, is it? Perhaps with time we'll be able to afford something better."

"My son is a landowner." His mother smiled at him warmly. "He sent me money from America to buy five hectares of land at the edge of Sapnai behind Gadeikis, hoping someday to build a house for us."

Kotryna heard the emphasis on "us" and realized it didn't include her. "Yes, meanwhile it's very handy to live where you work." Kotryna tried to sound encouraging, but her unhappiness was evident.

"Well, it's better than working for others." His mother seemed to read Kotryna's state of mind. She scratched her headscarf, looking away.

Kotryna blinked back tears. She sighed deeply and turned to Aleksas. "I've been thinking about what you said the other day about not having enough business." She smiled, unsure of herself. "People usually love to look at photographs."

He nodded. "That's true."

"So, I thought perhaps if you photographed some weddings and funerals and then showed your photos in the front window, it might bring in business. People are curious."

Aleksas thought for a moment and then nodded slightly, considering her idea. "I'll try it, but I doubt it'll work."

"Well, it might," said Kotryna, smiling hopefully.

His mother sipped her tea and slid her eyes to Kotryna. "What's this news Aleksas told me about some demon you've brought back from Russia?" Her tone was sarcastic.

Shame washed over Kotryna but she tried to compose herself. Quietly, she said, "I came by to tell you that my sister has banished the *domovoi*. It was quite a battle, but she managed to get rid of it. Now the house is quiet again." She glanced to see how Aleksas was taking the news.

"Really?" His lip curled in a half smile.

Kotryna could see the doubt in his eyes. "I don't know how she dared. I was so grateful I even gave Elzbieta my garnet ring as a token of appreciation." She would have given her brave sister anything for it meant liberation from that demon-haunted world.

"How did she manage that?" asked the mother with a mocking voice.

Kotryna told them the story of Elzbieta's battle with the imp. "When we returned from church that Sunday, it was gone."

"Hmm…" His mother, nodded, unconvinced.

Kotryna took a breath for courage and turned to Aleksas. "Perhaps you'd like to come and see for yourself."

"Thank you for the invitation," he said.

She could still see his reticence. Crushed by disappointment, Kotryna left. When she reached home, she lamented to her father, "Aleksas hasn't forgiven me."

"For what, in heaven's name?" Viktoras was baffled.

"I'm not sure. Maybe for running away to Smolensk or for coming home with an imp." She bit her lip. "It breaks my heart."

It pained Viktoras to see Kotryna so sad. It was bad enough

216

to see Ada mooning around the house, sighing and looking out windows as though waiting for someone. It was obvious to him that she was taken with Jonas Balandis, but somehow, whenever the two met, something or someone had gotten in the way of their courtship—most likely Bogdanskis was the obstacle. And as if one love-sick woman in the house wasn't enough, now his daughter's *domovoi* had shocked Aleksas, leaving Kotryna reliving the loss, unable to think of anything else. It broke his heart to see his two favorite women so discouraged. He wracked his brain wondering how to help, but it was June, the very busiest time of the year— plowing, manuring the fields, planting, and haying.

There was just too much to do, but once his farm tasks were finished, he would put his mind to solving these matters of the heart. After all, he didn't go to the trouble of reuniting his daughter with Aleksas, all the way from America, in order to give up now, nor did he find a proper suitor for Ada to let someone like Modestas interfere. No, he refused to accept defeat. Very few things in life were insurmountable—death was the main one. Everything else was worth fighting for. He would put his mind to it while working the fields.

After all, his time was running out.

-Twenty-six-

Ada went about her chores lost in a fog of love and longing. Where was Jonas? Was he safe? Did he care for her? She had told her pillow of her love, she had told the sickle moon the same, the flat stones in the creek knew of it, the bee hives buzzed with it, the white lilies by the fence heard it daily. Everything knew of Ada's love but Jonas. She had to remedy this, but how?

Elzbieta, came out looking for Ada and found her mooning around in a cloud of dreams as she often did these days. She sent her daughter to town to buy some salt, sugar and soap. Perhaps it would clear the poor girl's head to take a long walk.

As Ada was leaving that afternoon, Viktoras pointed to the pale moon still hanging in the sky. "It's not going to be a good day," he warned. Ada looked up at the anemic orb as he related the story of the Moon, who always pursued his wife, the Sun around the heavens. "One day, the Moon, tired of chasing the Sun, began to flirt with the young Morning Star instead. The Sun's father, Perkunas, furious with the fickle Moon, cut it in half with his sword. As a result, whenever you see the jealous Sun and the fickle Moon together in the sky, you know it will be a bad day."

Ada frowned thinking of Petras and Jonas in Prussia. Gazing at the faint moon, she sighed, wondering what ill might be coming their way. When she looked at her grandfather, she saw he was also troubled, but neither one had the heart to mention it.

As she walked down the road, the sun finally came out illuminating a garden fence ablaze with red and yellow nasturtiums. On the other side of the road, sat a wayside shrine of Jesus the Worrier. To Ada, it resembled her grandfather worrying over the fate of his grandchildren. She leaned her forehead on the shrine and closed her eyes, whispering a prayer for the safe return of Jonas and Petras. The wooden statue had been kissed and lovingly touched so often that it was worn in places. Her grandfather was inordinately fond of the Worrier statue that his friend made for him, which now sat in the corner of his room.

When Ada reached the market, she bought the required items and then went from stall to stall. First, she went to the stall selling gingerbread, then, she stopped to look at scarves. When she looked up, her heart sank to see Modestas rushing toward her. He was the last person she wanted to meet. She wanted to kick herself for lingering at the market.

"Ada," he said in greeting. "I was sitting at the teahouse with our guests, the Ciginskas widow and her family. I told you about them, remember?" He looked like a new man, wearing a new beige coat and crisp white shirt, and he had taken special care to pomade his hair.

"Yes, your mother's childhood friend with her children."

"We were sitting at a table by the window when I saw you walking through the market. Mama insisted I invite you to join them for tea." He smiled.

With a sinking feeling, she looked over at the teahouse. "No, I couldn't."

"Why ever not?" Modestas was surprised.

"I don't even know them." Ada closed her eyes, hoping they'd all disappear.

"Naturally, that's why they want to meet you," he said exasperated. "Come along. It's not polite to keep them waiting."

Turning toward the teahouse, she saw the fashionably dressed young widow waving to them. When Modestas scooted her toward the group, she suddenly felt like running away.

Entering the teashop, she quietly greeted his mother and Helenka, both women wearing fancy new frocks. When he introduced the older widow, Neda Ciginskas, Ada murmured a polite hello, admiring the stylishly dressed widow in her chestnut-colored dress. Her daughter, Magdalena, whom they called Mimi, still wore widow's weeds, for the customary year of mourning had not yet elapsed. Her clothes, though black, were embellished with discreet ruffles and lace. Her face was long and narrow and her eyes too close together like her mother's, but she was one of those women who knew how to play up her good features. Her shiny dark hair was held up with stylish combs, and her smiling dark eyes and dimpled cheeks gave her face a cheerful liveliness. Mimi had been married for the last ten years to an older man who had given her no children but had left her a substantial estate.

Despite her recent bereavement, Mimi seemed to have enough life in her for several women. She looked Ada over without ever stopping her childish and slightly petulant banter. Ada felt shy and self-conscious in front of such well-dressed ladies, ashamed of her own humble blue woolen skirt and white homespun linen blouse. Though ordinary by comparison, these were her good clothes that she wore to town and to church on Sunday. Only the pale blue woolen shawl from her aunt made her look a bit more stylish.

Ada met the ailing son, Vincentas, who sat next to Helenka— both pale contrasts to the vivid widows. Helenka sat quietly, her hands folded on her lap, her hair pushed back into a bun at the nape of her neck, her eyes set like a pudding, the sparks of life already gone. Even though she wore a striking plum dress, her spirit was dulled by illness or heartbreak, which made her but a shadow next to the other women. Beside her, Vincentas looked ashen and drawn from his bout with the grippe. The widows thought Sapnai would be a rest cure for Vincentas's weak lungs. From time to time the quiet young man lifted his handkerchief for a persistent cough that seemed to exhaust him.

Modestas's mother, who now wished to be called Nina, radiated good cheer. It seemed her childhood friend had brought vitality and energy back to the widow. Ada noted that both mothers greeted her with a cold appraising eye.

"We are like characters from an opera." Mimi laughed with forced gaiety. "If only we could sing." She glanced at Modestas smoking his long cigarette and smiled. He watched the young widow with amusement.

Ada suddenly realized that Mimi was flirting with Modestas. The thought amused her and she hoped the young widow would win his affection. That would be a gift from heaven.

When Mimi laughed, Ada noticed that a couple of her teeth were slightly crooked. "Mama adores Verdi and Bizet. I'm lucky she didn't call me Camille." She petted Fifi on her lap and the dog yapped a shrill bark.

Ada thought all three widows looked like exotic tropical birds. She listened but didn't know what they were talking about. What could she add to this conversation? It made her feel imprisoned.

To Ada's surprise, Helenka asked her about Kotryna. "I heard she returned from Russia."

While she sipped her tea, Ada told them of Kotryna's recent homecoming and how her old love had come back from America. Helenka seemed to be the only one interested. "Is it the new photographer?" she asked quietly. "Do you think they'll marry?"

Ada shrugged, unsure of what to say.

Mimi turned her attention to Ada. "We heard the most delicious story about your aunt bringing some sort of imp back from Russia." Mimi smiled indulgently. "You simply must tell us all about it. I adore these primitive folktales, don't you, Modestas?" She winked at him.

Shocked, Ada glanced angrily at Modestas. Seeing her uneasiness, he urged an end to the topic. "My dear guests, we don't want to bring that nonsense up again." He cleared his throat to punctuate his words. Ada hoped that would be the end of it.

"But, of course, we do!" Mimi pouted. "Nonsense is my favorite topic of conversation. If we can't laugh, then what's the point of life? Ada, my dear, you must tell us every detail. Did you see it?"

When Ada saw all eyes on her, she felt cornered. "No," she muttered in anger.

"Well, then how did you know it was there?" asked Mimi.

Ada resented Mimi's questions but guessed the woman wouldn't let go of the subject. "It shook the shelves in our pantry," she said reluctantly and decided to say no more.

"*Mon Dieu*, how awful." Mimi made a face of mock horror.

Ada looked down at her clasped hands, her knuckles white with tension. She was beginning to dislike this woman.

Seeing Ada's discomfort, Modestas asked, "More tea?"

The constantly bubbling samovar made the air in the room steamy. Feeling trapped, Ada found herself studying the pattern of blue and white on the teacups, slowly tracing the pattern with her finger. "No, I must get home," said Ada, frowning at Modestas.

Neda bent over to whisper in her daughter's ear. Mimi squealed, "Oh, of course, *maman*." She emptied the purse of her mirror, comb, and handkerchief. "Mama said I was impolite and might have offended you by teasing you about the imp. I behaved badly and I'm to give you this little gift to remedy my bad manners." Mimi handed the purse to Ada. "Please accept this as my apology, dear."

"No, I couldn't possibly take your purse," Ada gasped, taken aback by the generosity of these strangers.

"But you must take it, my dear, to make up for my rudeness.

I refuse to take it back now," Mimi pouted. "I'll have to give it to the beggars by the church if you don't accept my gift." Mimi shrugged and smiled.

"Thank you." Ada looked at the purse with a silver filigree clasp at the top. Putting it on her arm, she felt awkward as though she were trying to impersonate a lady of the manor. "Very kind of you," she squeezed out.

Nina fingered the cameo brooch at the neckline of her dress. "Well, it suits you," she said, arching an eyebrow.

"Yes, my dear," said Neda. "We'll make you part of our opera yet." She chuckled. "What shall we call her?"

Mimi examined Ada. "Let me think. She's definitely not Manon. I know, let's call her Carmen." Mimi declared. "And you'll join the troupe."

Ada looked around and wondered how she ended up among people she neither understood nor wanted to understand. She felt they were deliberately rude to speak of things like opera, which she had never seen nor heard.

Mimi turned and winked at her mother. "We'll have an opera yet, *maman!*"

"I always said that all of life is an opera." Neda twirled the jet ring on her finger, smiling at her childhood friend, the powder on her face settling into the creases along her mouth.

All at once, Ada had had enough of the three widows. Suddenly she had to get away. She stood and picking up her shawl, she said she really needed to go home and headed for the door.

"*Adieu,* Carmen," Ada heard Mimi calling to her, but she didn't turn around.

Modestas ran after her. "Are you angry?"

"Yes. I felt foolish not knowing what they were chattering about or what to say to them."

"They were only having a bit of fun."

Her anger seized her. "Well, it wasn't fun for me." she said heatedly, realizing it was the first time she had told Modestas exactly what was on her mind.

Suddenly the group inside was laughing. When Fifi started to bark at the loud noise, Mimi came to the door. "Ada, we're going to go back to the house to play *Preferansas*. Won't you join us?"

"No thank you," Ada said a bit too forcefully.

"Well then, how about you, Modestas?"

"Yes, yes, I'll be there in a minute," he nodded.

"I won't keep you," Ada said, her face hot with anger. She wanted to add that this encounter had been enough to last a lifetime, but she held her tongue and turned to walk through the market, scarcely recognizing where she was going. She now saw very clearly how different she was from Modestas and his family and friends. Their way of life was a foreign country she no longer wished to visit, nor did she want to learn its language or customs. Suddenly her simple home looked dearer than any other, and Jonas more beloved than ever.

As Ada walked home alone, the sun was on the tree tops, though, in June, it never got completely dark. One thing seemed crystal clear—there was another man who had won her heart completely. There was something that drew her to Jonas the moment she had looked into his eyes. She was beginning to need him like she needed breath.

Ada looked up at the pale crescent moon that her grandfather called the smiling moon. The old Moon wandered the sky in search of his wife, the Sun. Her grandfather had been right. The Moon and Sun together had brought a bad day, and this evening the crescent moon looked far more like a pair of horns than a smile.

-Twenty-seven-

The lavender twilight was gathering, making the forest mysterious and enchanted as Ada walked home, filled with the emotions stirred up by the day. The fir trees were gently bending in the breeze, as if whispering great secrets to one another, their roots knitting together. There was always something magical about the forest at twilight. Walking on the road between the tall trees, she felt that familiar reverent hush that made it feel eternal and unchanging.

A little farther under a nearby oak, she spotted some boletus, the king of mushrooms. Her grandfather adored mushroom stew with potatoes. It would be a shame not to pick them, but she had no basket. Spreading out her blue shawl, she placed the satin black purse there and gathered the mushrooms in her skirt. Spilling them onto her shawl, she tied it in a bundle.

From behind, she heard the clomp, clomp of horses and the rattling of a hay wagon approaching, so she moved aside to let it pass. Only when a bay horse with a white star on its forehead was almost upon her did she look up and recognize the driver. It went through her like a bolt.

"Jonas?" she asked with a tremulous voice. It was as if she had summoned him here in the woods like an apparition.

"Ada?" he answered, equally surprised. He stopped the horses.

"It *is* you," she said shaken. "You're alive!" She said this with such emotion that she astonished both herself and Jonas.

"Of course, I'm alive." Jonas laughed, breaking the tension. "Ada, you look like an angel in the twilight."

She lowered her eyes. "Thank you," she said shyly. Ever since she heard that he had joined the book smugglers, she had been imagining scenes of his arrest and deportation at the hands of the border guards. Yet here he was.

"But where is my brother?" She looked toward the back of the wagon to see if he was sleeping in the hay.

"He's not there, Ada, but don't worry, he's quite safe."

"Can you stay with me a little?" she asked.

"Ada, I'd like nothing better, but I can't." Jonas looked around to see if anyone was coming down the road. "It's not safe," he whispered.

"Oh." Suddenly she was frightened for him again. "If you can't stop, then can I ride with you?" She couldn't let him slip through her fingers again without telling him her feelings.

"No, I'm afraid not. I must hurry."

She wanted to unburden her heart, yet he was so eager to go. "There's something I've been wanting to tell you. Can I go with you until the crossroads?"

"Ada, that's not wise." The horses neighed and tugged at the reins. "Besides, Father Jurkus would have my hide."

"Please?"

Jonas bent over and whispered cautiously: "You know the penalties if I get caught." He looked around nervously.

"Oh, be careful," she fretted. "I'm just so glad to see you. I've been so worried."

228

"You've worried about me?" His reserve seemed to melt. "Ada, I joined the contrabandists because I saw the look in your eyes when your grandfather talked about his days as a book smuggler. I saw how proud you were and how brave he was in your eyes. I wanted you to look at me that way."

"Oh, I do, I admire your courage," she said dreamily. "Why some nights I could hardly sleep thinking about those stories my grandfather told."

"I didn't think you cared whether I lived or died," he teased.

"Not care! How wrong you are."

"Really?" Jonas was grinning from ear to ear.

"Oh please, just to the crossroads?" she begged him.

Jonas sighed and looked over his shoulder again, throwing all caution to the wind. "All right, climb in, but only to the crossroads."

Clambering up into the hay wagon, she carefully tucked the bundle of mushrooms by her feet. The crossroads was not far. She swallowed hard and began at once. "Jonas, do you remember how you asked me about Modestas?" She flamed red at her own boldness.

He winced. "Please don't remind me. I've kicked myself over and over. I shouldn't have said anything."

Ada felt her heart beat faster. "I'm glad you did. I wanted to tell you how much I enjoyed being with you, how much it meant to see you again."

Stopping the horses, he looked searchingly into her eyes. "Ada, is it really true?" He took her hand in his, stroking it.

She nodded, looking at his gentle eyes, thinking here was a man like a real flint. Not like Modestas and his pretentious visitors, endlessly babbling about operas.

Coming up the road, they heard the clip of hooves. Jonas turned suddenly at the sound of horses approaching and froze. He quickly took the reins but there was nowhere to flee.

To his horror, he saw six Russian gendarmes riding toward them. It was too late to do anything as four men approached the wagon.

Ada's heart thudded when they came into sight, and she recognized Captain Malenkov.

"*Stoj, kuda ty?*" he yelled for them to stop, studying them both with eyes like steel balls. "Where are you going?" he demanded. The other men dismounted and faced them, rifles at the ready.

"This must be one of the men, Captain," said one of the gendarmes. "We were told they might be on this road."

Ada kept repeating to herself to stay calm and not show her fear. This was life or death for Jonas. Terrified they would shoot him on the spot, she had to think of something quickly. If only she didn't feel so pale and bloodless. The trembling in her body wouldn't stop.

Putting her arm around Jonas's neck, she pecked him on the cheek and forced herself to smile. "Captain, why bother two lovers on an evening ride?"

Jonas gulped hard, astonished by her quick thinking, but he immediately got into the act. "You see I'm taking my sweetheart home, sir." Jonas put his arm around her and she could feel his trembling.

"So, it's you again," said the captain, eyeing Ada suspiciously.

Ada nodded and smiled.

"They didn't say anything about a girl," the gendarme whispered.

"What are you carrying in that wagon?" yelled the captain.

"Hay, sir, as you can see," Jonas replied.

"I can see the hay, but what else is in the hay?" He turned to the gendarmes. "Men, search the wagon."

"Nothing else is in the hay, sir." Jonas tried to sound calm.

"Then you won't mind stepping down while we search it." The captain was growing more agitated. "Careful, men, there might be others hiding in the hay."

Ivan pulled Ada off the haywagon, while Nikolai stood, pointing his rifle at Jonas.

"I like girls who are friendly like you, snickered Ivan, poking her in the ribs with his rifle. "They're usually frisky like young colts."

Jonas got down from the wagon, his fury evident. He glanced at Ada, who tried to reassure him with her eyes. "Leave her alone," he said fiercely.

"I wouldn't get so hot with a rifle pointed at you," said Ivan, smirking.

Jonas glared at Ivan, while the other men poked and prodded the hay with their bayonets, flinging much of the hay on the side of the road.

"Oh, be careful with that bundle," said Ada loudly, trying to divert them from their search. She could feel the captain tense next to her and could sense Jonas's rising anger. She prayed he wouldn't do something heroic or dangerous that could get him killed or arrested.

"What have you got there?" asked Captain Malenkov. One of the men brought the bundle to him. He fingered the cloth. "Fine wool. It looks foreign. What's inside?"

"It's nothing," said Ada.

"We'll see," snapped the captain, unwrapping it. He turned to Ada. "Mushrooms?" He spilled them on the side of the road, onto the pine needles and leaves. The black purse fell out last like a giant spider. "Here's something." He picked up the delicate purse. "Why were you hiding this purse? Is this contraband?"

"No," said Ada. "It was a gift."

Holding the small black purse, the captain approached Ada. "Tell me, why were you hiding the purse in the mushrooms?" He opened the purse and found it empty.

"I wasn't hiding it," answered Ada. "I didn't have a basket for the mushrooms, so I put them in my shawl along with the purse." The captain studied her face, to see if she was telling the truth. "Look underneath the wagon, men. The last time we found radical newspapers underneath." The captain turned to Jonas.

"God help you if you're contrabandists or anarchists. I hate the whole sorry lot!" He studied Jonas to get the measure of the man.

Three of the gendarmes poked and prodded underneath the hay wagon. "Nothing here."

"I guess contrabandists don't bring women on their dangerous little journeys, do they?" the captain sneered. "Especially such pretty ones, eh?" The captain tipped his cap to Ada. The other gendarmes snickered.

"Now, go home. We have criminals to catch. If I find those smugglers, the books will be burned, the cigars and brandy will go to my men, and the smugglers will go to Siberia." The captain mounted his horse. "The roads are being searched thoroughly this evening. Nikolai and Ivan, put the hay back and catch up with us. Men, let's get on with it."

Once the captain was out of sight, Nikolai spat and cursed, picking up the hay. "Let them smuggle their books to the devil." He leaned over to Ivan. "Why is the captain driving us so hard? I'm tired of it."

Ivan joined him picking up the hay. "He's pushing us like dogs."

When finished, they mounted their horses and rode away without a word to Jonas and Ada, who stood there frozen in fear. When the men were out of sight, Jonas stood, shaken to the core. "God in heaven," he muttered, taking Ada's hand. He pulled her to him and held her tightly. "I'm so sorry, Ada. What a fool I am to put you in such danger."

She felt his heart pounding. "It was entirely my fault for interfering."

"I'll never forgive myself." He closed his eyes and shook his head. "I can't bear to think of what might have happened to you. I owe you my life. The only reason they didn't arrest me was because you were so brave and clever. If you hadn't been sitting beside me, God knows where I'd be. But Ada, for the love of God, go quickly."

"Wait," she said. "Please, there's so much I need to say to you." She looked into his eyes. "Jonas, you ran away from me at the fair before I could tell you how much I cared for you."

"But what about Modestas?" Jonas jumped down.

"He's not my intended," she shook her head ruefully, trying to rid herself of the idea. "He will never be my intended."

Jonas was hanging on her every word. "But I saw how he seemed to care for you and he brought you a present at the fair. It seemed clear that you were a couple."

"It's true that he was courting me, but that's finished. It's too much to tell now, but I will tell you that my heart lights up whenever I see you. My heart never spoke to me with Modestas."

"Truly?" Jonas lifted her chin so he could see her eyes. Finally, he poured his heart out to her. "Ada, I have such strong feelings for you. Whenever I look into your eyes, my heart melts. No, don't say a word. Just know how much I care for you and that seeing you makes me a happy man."

Flustered, Ada blurted, "Jonas, I have tried to put you out of my mind, but I simply can't."

"That's wonderful!" he burst out, his face beaming. "Oh, if I had only known this. You don't know how I've suffered." He shook his head.

"As have I," she said.

"Oh, dearest," Jonas took her in his arms and held her. "The moment I saw you, I knew you were my own. The whole world has changed for me this evening. Everything will be fine; don't worry. Just run, dearest, run home to safety." Jonas kissed her tenderly and sent her on her way. "I will come to see you as soon as I safely can. Now go, for the love of God." He got back on the wagon. "You must go quickly, in case they return."

"But where are the books hidden?" Ada whispered.

"In a hidden compartment."

As soon as Ada stepped down, Jonas picked up the reins and began to pull away, the wheels biting into the damp ground.

She picked up her shawl and started to gather the mushrooms.

"Leave them!" he insisted.

"The purse is gone. The captain must have taken it."

"Let the devil take him," Jonas spat.

"Come soon." She started to run down the road but kept turning around to take one last look at Jonas. He waved for her to hurry. Running a bit farther, she stopped at the fork in the road, turning again.

He was watching her, so she waved and rounded the bend toward home.

The moon shone faintly while Ada walked down the road that bristled with shrines, her head spinning from the evening's events. The crickets chirped away and the frogs in the pond were croaking. She was so overwrought that she didn't know whether to laugh or cry. Looking up at the moon, high in the deepening lavender twilight, she saw that the crescent moon was no longer horned. It now seemed to be the same old moon, smiling down at her once more.

-Twenty-eight-

Haymaking was the first and most intense work of the summer. Pacing in front of the farm gate, Viktoras strained his eyes to look down the empty road, fretting and worrying about his grandson, who had promised to return in time for the haying. He cursed the dusty and vacant road, troubled by the delay. It was past time for haying, but Viktoras had already postponed it twice, waiting for Petras.

Ada came to join him. "I told you I met Jonas in the woods," she reminded him, "and he said that Petras was safe. Come have some breakfast and stop worrying."

"What were those cursed gendarmes doing on that road? How did they know?" Viktoras stabbed his finger in the air to make a point. "I tell you I don't like this at all."

"Come eat, Grandfather, dear."

"Ach," he waved her concerns away. "I have no appetite."

"At least come have some tea and then you can return to your pacing."

At the breakfast table, Stasys started in when he saw his father-in-law. "Are we starting the haying or not?"

Viktoras frowned. "No, let's wait for Petras. I've begun to feel superstitious about starting without him."

"The whole village has brought in their hay, but ours is still in the fields uncut," Stasys fumed. "Yet here we sit, with the sun already climbing."

"Calm yourself," Elzbieta told her angry husband.

When Viktoras said nothing, Stasys pointed out the window. "It's a nice, clear day, the sun is shining, and I've already brewed enough beer for the neighbors who will help us bring in the hay." Stasys had helped his neighbors with their haying, and each time they asked him when they should come to help him he had shrugged, not knowing what to say. Each day his unease grew until it became a boiling anger. But in truth, his anger was only masking his worry over his son—a worry so caustic, he could hardly face it.

Elzbieta and Kotryna exchanged uneasy glances. Ada and her sisters said nothing, for it was rare to see their father's temper flare like this.

Throwing his cap on the floor in frustration, Stasys bellowed, "Where is Petras? He said he'd be back for the haying."

Elzbieta bit her lip. "What if something's happened?" She twisted the towel, tears springing. "Pray God, he's all right."

Stasys banged the table and everyone jumped at the unaccustomed gesture. "We can't wait for the haying any longer. Soon the rye will need to be cut, then the potatoes planted and then the clover must be cut. This work won't get done on its own, you know." He looked at his daughters. "I know that you all want to go to the Midsummer's Eve festivities this week, but I warn you, no one in this family will go to that festival without bringing in the hay first."

The girls glanced at each other, alarmed. Midsummer's Eve was a magical night celebrated by all the young people of the district. It would be unthinkable to miss the chance to stay up all night with bonfires, songs and festivities until the sun rose.

Seeing the troubled looks on the girls' faces, Kotryna sympathized. "It'll get done, don't worry, Stasys," she said.

Stasys smiled derisively. "Kotryna, you've been away from the farm too long. You've forgotten how important it is to do the work on time. Look at those white hands of yours. They're no good for real work."

Offended, she snapped back, "You just cut that hay and I'll show you what these hands can do."

It was now Viktoras's turn to pound the table with his fist. "All right then, let's start tomorrow morning. A farmer's work starts with the morning star and ends with the evening star. We'll start without Petras."

Relieved, Stasys left to tell the neighbors.

Ada sat at the table half-heartedly finishing breakfast and wondering what could be keeping her brother and Jonas. It worried her terribly and seemed to be all she could think about.

She went to the granary where the painted dowry chests were kept. When she opened her chest, the smell of dried mint wafted up. She had placed dried herbs in a cheesecloth bag at the bottom to scent the linens—the flax-colored linen towels that she had woven winter after winter, in a pattern of tulips, and her crowning glory, the bedspread woven in the traditional geometric pattern of light and dark linen. Two pillowcases that she had embroidered with delicate violets felt soft in her hands. What heaven it would be to put her head next to Jonas's each night, to have his eyes look into hers, his lips touch hers.

After carefully returning the linens to her dowry chest, she went to the window, fear gnawing, wondering what was keeping them. Perhaps the gendarmes had returned or they were wounded. She covered her face with her hands, unable to bear her own thoughts.

The next day, before the sun fully rose, the neighbors began gathering for the haying.

All day long the mowers could be heard hammering the blades of their scythes or sharpening them. The work started enthusiastically as Jurgis broke out into a lusty song, and everyone joined in for the chorus, singing in harmony. Work continued with songs throughout the morning while the air was still cool, but as the sun rose in the sky, the workers began to slow with the heat. Stasys stopped to sharpen his scythe and saw the storks tiptoeing tentatively at the edge of the field, waiting for the mowers to advance so they could devour the frogs and snakes exposed in the wake of the mowers.

St. George's Church rang the Angelus bells at noon, and the workers knelt in the field, crossing themselves for prayers. Afterward, Elzbieta and Julija brought baskets of black bread and sausage, cucumbers, cheese, beer and *kvass*. Dora hitched her skirt a bit to step over the stubbled field to sit near Jurgis Bartkus, who couldn't resist furtively glancing at her calves. It took a minute for him to pluck up the courage to move a bit closer.

"It's about time you came near," Dora purred in his ear.

Zigmas Bartkus started a song with a force and volume that could be heard in the neighboring village, his face reddening with the effort. Ada wondered why those who had no ear for music were always the loudest and most enthusiastic singers. Despite Zigmas, everyone joined in. Soon the high jinx started as young men threw frogs under the girls' skirts, causing them to shriek while the young men laughed. But Ada was too worried about Jonas and Petras to join them.

It took a few days for the new mown hay to dry. Kotryna rose early and went out to the fields with the others to turn and rake the dried hay into rows. When Petrike came to help, Ada noticed she was pregnant and looking content.

As the sun rose, the hired hand pitched the hay into the wagon, which creaked and groaned under the load. Kotryna's mouth was dry and parched and she could feel the perspiration under her kerchief. "A soul can't even sit down for a minute or two on a farm," she muttered, mopping her brow with her sleeve. Though tired, she would never admit that to Stasys. Ada could see this work was really hard for her aunt so she assured Kotryna that it would soon be time to take a rest and eat something.

Then Ada heard the call. "Yoo-hoo, oh Carmen!"

Ada flinched at the familiar voice and turned to the road that ran next to the field. She shielded her eyes to get a better look. It was Modestas in a fancy *britzka* with two horses. The three widows—his mother, Neda and Mimi sat inside, waving.

"Yoo-hoo, Carmen," Mimi called again. Both Ciginskas widows were wearing white dresses with sailor collars and wide-brimmed white hats. Only Neda was wearing an ordinary navy skirt and white blouse, holding a delicate white parasol to keep the sun off her face.

"It can't be," Ada muttered through her teeth. Utterly annoyed, she rolled her eyes heavenward. She felt dusty and hot and certainly in no mood for the fancy widows. After her time at the tea shop, she had secretly hoped never to see them again.

Kotryna stopped her work and came over to Ada, enjoying the sight of the three widows. "*Nu*, would you look at that," she teased, leaning on her rake. "The tsarina has come to visit her serfs and she's brought her family with her."

Ada whispered, "The daughter has just buried a rich husband."

Kotryna gave her a wry smile and said, "Lucky woman."

Elzbieta shot them a disapproving look. "Hold your tongues," she scolded.

Kotryna stood with one hand on her hip "Well, I think it's strange, don't you? Look at those town folks all dressed up, their finery on display, coming to watch the peasants toil in the fields."

Ada crossed her arms. "She's right, Mama."

Elzbieta frowned. "Get that smirk off your face. It isn't becoming." She wiped the sweat and grime from her own face with her sleeve and then took Ada by the hand to greet the visitors. Julija ran behind, wanting a better look at the elegantly dressed women. She was impressed by how well Modestas looked in his new beige coat with his crisp white shirt.

The three widows stepped off the *britzka*. "Why, Ada, what a bucolic scene this is," said Mimi. "Right out of a painting by Van Gogh. *N'est-ce pas, maman?*"

Her mother merely raised one eyebrow in answer.

Ada introduced her family. Though sweaty and covered in dust, she was unapologetic, for it was honest work. "Hello Mimi, how nice of you to come to help us with the haying," she said dryly, handing her a rake. "Perhaps I can find a kerchief for your head to save that beautiful bonnet."

Behind Ada, Kotryna bit her lip to keep from laughing.

"Heavens no!" replied Mimi. "Don't joke like that. We're not fit for this kind of work. Mama just thought it might be fun to come see your farm. And then, of course, we thought we'd join in this wonderful *tableau vivant* by bringing some refreshments to share for a picnic."

Mimi turned to Modestas, who was bringing baskets of food from the *britzka*. "Modestas wanted to bring simple fare, but we thought it would be more fun to try something a bit more delightful," she smiled teasingly at him. "We insisted that he take us into town where we could get something special."

"But my mother has already prepared a lunch," said Ada.

Modestas approached and put the baskets down. "I told them that you were all too busy to stop for a picnic, but no one would listen, least of all Mimi, who cannot be stopped once her mind is set on something." He flashed Mimi a smile.

"You make me sound like a shrew," she said, pretending to pout. "I only wanted to see our Aida again. After the other day, when you left so suddenly, we thought we had somehow

240

made a bad first impression and wanted to make it up to you."

Ada looked at the two older women and saw the smiles frozen on their faces.

"We found some wine, hazelnut cookies, and these delightful marzipan bonbons, so we thought we'd surprise you and your family with a treat," Mimi chirped. "I hope you like them."

"How kind of you to go to so much trouble," said Elzbieta. "I'll tell the others."

"*Bonjour*, very kind of you, *Monsieur* Modestas. *Merci,"* said Julija, trying out tidbits of French on these wonderful visitors.

Annoyed beyond words, Ada thought Kotryna was right. Perhaps the gentry enjoyed the sight of peasants working themselves into a lather, while they leisurely watched.

Mimi spread some carpets under the shade of an old oak tree and brought out the contents of her picnic baskets. Modestas brought stools for the two older widows, while Mimi sat on the carpet tucking her skirt in around her. Her mother brought an ivory fan out of her pocketbook. "This reminds me of Smetana's opera, 'The Bartered Bride,' no?"

"*Bien sur, maman*," answered Mimi. "The same rustic charm." At the sight of what they had brought to eat at the haying, Ada almost laughed at how ridiculous it looked. The widows saw this as a picnic, whereas the family saw it simply as a break in their workday to eat and rest.

Introductions were made and food was passed around, but the villagers were reticent to begin eating, feeling self-conscious in their sweat-stained clothing, their sunburned and callused hands next to Neda's white hands, which looked as soft as a pair of white doves. The elegant but casual sailor dresses worn by the widows were studied by more than one woman. It was plain to see that the vivacious younger widow had an eye for Modestas, while he had clearly taken special care to look his best. Ada wondered if this was at his mother's urging?

For their part, the villagers noticed that Ada seemed to take no interest in Modestas, neither flirting with him nor trying to capture his attention. In fact, they observed, she hardly seemed to pay any attention to the group at all. Instead she seemed dreamy and far away, often looking down the empty road. Oh, there would be so much to talk about in the village. The speculation would be delicious and endless.

The young widow offered wine, and Kotryna, now cooled by the shade, tried it but found it too sweet. It only made her thirstier. To her delight, she found the marzipan bonbons delicious. She ate four and would have eaten more but good manners prevented her.

Neda waved a scented handkerchief in front of her face, seemingly a bit faint from the smell of so many sweating bodies, and from the grime-streaked and sunburned faces around her. From afar the scene might have been a bucolic painting, but up close it was beginning to turn her stomach.

After a time, Ada stood, not able to stand this picnic a moment longer. In the distance, she noticed the clouds gathering on the horizon. "There's a storm coming," she said, pointing to the gray clouds. "We'd better hurry to get the hay in before it rains." That was the signal for the three widows to bid farewell and wish the workers ease in their labors.

Modestas took Ada aside. "The ladies would like to buy a poetry book in Lithuanian. Do you know where I could buy such a book? You know how much I adore poetry." Modestas smiled at Ada, but it didn't seem genuine. There was something odd in his look, something she didn't trust.

"No, I already told you I don't know anything about that," she said, hardly able look at him. Her thoughts flew to Jonas and Petras who were bringing the precious books across the border. Where were they? What was keeping them.? Her stomach tightened, yet she kept her eyes lowered while Modestas told her he would look for her at the Midsummer festivities.

"Au revoir," said Julija, as the widows walked away with their parasols.

"Au revoir, mes amis," Mimi called, waving a handkerchief. Modestas collected the baskets and ran to join the widows.

Ada was thankful to see them go. They seemed so unreal, like an illustration from an old book that had come to life for a brief afternoon. But when would she get the chance to tell Modestas that the whole charade between them was over?

Elena stood next to her watching them leave. "How beautifully the widows dressed," she said as Julija came to join them.

"I'm going to beg mama to make me a sailor dress like that. Didn't they look elegant? And I've never seen Modestas look better. I hope I find a man like that someday."

"That was such a ridiculous picnic," said Ada and returned to stacking the hay. Petrike began to sing a sad song about lost love, and soon the other women joined in.

The long, hard day continued. The gnats were biting, the hay stubble was cutting hands, dust covered everyone, and sweat burned eyes and soaked clothes, leaving streaks of grime. At the end of the day, the work had slowed to a crawl. The singing stopped and now only the labor mattered.

The haying was finally coming to an end as streaks of lightning broke through the clouds. Removing her kerchief, Kotryna wet it and wrapped it around her blistered hand, fearing Stasys might have been right in his assessment of her. She had grown soft during the eight years in Smolensk, though, she hoped with time she would get used to the work.

The thunder was getting closer, so Kotryna put the rake over her shoulder and followed the hay wagon back to the barn. When they arrived home, Viktoras shook his head when he saw her wrapped hand. "You better take care of that because Aleksas is coming over for lunch tomorrow."

"He is?" Kotryna was thrilled. "But how do you know?"

"I invited him personally," Viktoras informed her.

-Twenty-nine-

Kotryna spent the morning at the village bath house with Ada, hoping to soothe her sore muscles from the haying. "Aleksas mustn't see how soft I've become," she said, putting salve on her blisters.

"Teta, I'll help you prepare the meal, so you can get ready." This morning Ada had already baked a nut cake and made *kugelis*, because the haying had left Kotryna feeling as ancient and tired as Old Vanda.

"Thank you, Ada dear." Kotryna still felt so exhausted and old that soon a nagging doubt began to creep into her thoughts. Her father had probably been mistaken about Aleksas. He couldn't possibly still be interested in an old maid like her when there were so many prettier, younger women in town likely having their photos taken by him, smiling and flirting, flattering him in his American bowler hat.

A little breeze moved the curtain in the parlor. Kotryna stood, tears pooling. It was hopeless. She would die an old maid. The back door opened and her sister and Ada came in. Not wanting to face them in this dismal mood, Kotryna ran out the front door to the barn, her hiding place since childhood. Quickly, she climbed up the ladder to the hayloft, falling into the hay, overcome by its fresh smell. Tears running down her cheeks, she felt worn to the bone. Life had already passed her by. She gave in to her melancholy, recognizing it from the many times she had succumbed to it while in Smolensk, causing teary evenings in her room. Life was often cruel and heartbreaking. She cried and cried, smothering it in her apron, her heart breaking afresh, realizing her recently rekindled hopes were mere mist and fog. He was done with her.

Suddenly, her head shot up when she heard Margis barking. Was someone actually coming? Her heart began to pound wildly. Could it be Aleksas? No, it was too early. She quickly wiped her eyes with her apron and brushed the straw from her clothes. Shielding her eyes with her hand, she peeked outside to see who was coming. She was sure it couldn't be Aleksas.

But there he was happily walking down the road humming an old tune, and all of her doubts vanished in an instant. Her heart leaped in joy when she saw him approaching their farm wearing his American shirt with the small stripes. Here was her solid man returning to her. What was she doing crying in the hay? She scolded herself for her foggy doubts and fears. And now, because she had given in to those doubts, she no longer had time to change into her good clothes. But there he was looking so handsome and she, so eager to see him that she laughed and the whole gloomy spell of the morning was broken as a giddy joy enveloped her. All at once, she was in high spirits. In her exuberance, she giggled when he entered the farmyard and waved for him to come over to the loft, putting a finger to her mouth for him to be quiet.

When he spotted her, Aleksas waved and ran over, climbing the squeaking ladder in the barn, until he reached her, seeing at once that look in her eyes that he remembered from their days long ago when they would kiss until they were drunk with love. Aleksas took her hands in his. Seeing the love in his eyes, she smiled helplessly. "When I saw you coming down the road to me,

I almost melted with joy." She gently caressed his cheek. "I've missed you so."

He smiled. "I've missed you too."

"Aleksas, remember how we were years ago?" He nodded.

"Fate brought us both back to Lithuania, yet neither one of us knew that the other one was coming."

"Not fate, Kotryna, I came back because of the letter from your father. Once I got that letter, my whole world brightened."

"Letter? Papa sent you a letter?" Kotryna was astonished.

"Yes," said Aleksas smiling broadly. "Didn't you know?" She shook her head. "No, I thought he only wrote to me."

"It seems your father has been busy. He wrote to apologize, and to give his blessing to marry you. When I got that letter, my God, I was on fire to get back home to you."

Kotryna stood open-mouthed with surprise. "What made Papa change his mind?" She looked at Aleksas and wondered what other surprises life had in store for her. It seemed life swept you up and it was useless to try to resist it or make plans of one's own.

Aleksas smiled and lifted her chin. "He blessed us, Kotryna, if you still want me."

For a moment, she was speechless. "Is this a marriage proposal then?" She looked at him in wide-eyed disbelief.

"I think you had that proposal eight years ago, but yes, I'll ask you again," he said softly, taking both her hands in his and kneeling. "Will you have me for a husband?"

She knelt down beside him. "Yes, till the end of my days."

He kissed her gently on the lips. "My Kotryna," he whispered, caressing her auburn hair, tied back by a white linen scarf. She looked again like the young girl of his dreams.

"Oh, don't look at me," she said. "I look awful. I've had no time to dress."

"You look more beautiful than the day I met you." Bending down to ardently kiss her cheek, his eyes had such a look of yearning, such intensity, that she felt pierced. That look was irresistible. They both knew they couldn't wait any longer to kiss, to touch, and to be with one another. Aleksas pulled her to him, kissing her cheek and then his lips slid over to hers.

"Aleksas," she whispered, his name trembling on her lips. "You really love me?" she asked in a tremulous voice, as if pleading for her life. She put her arms around him like she used to on those long-gone summer evenings, her heart racing wildly.

He wrapped her close in an embrace. "Kotryna, I've always loved you," he whispered, pulling her to him blindly, kissing her with passion. Their kiss went on, intoxicated by emotion, while he slowly raised her skirt and caressed her thigh.

She felt confused, both wanting him and yet hesitant. "Wait," she said, holding his arm.

His eyes pleaded. "I've waited for you for eight years. Don't make me wait any longer."

Her cheeks burned as she looked into his eyes. "We've waited long enough," she said, thickly, putting her arms around his neck again. A tiny moan escaped as she kissed him and they fell back into the hay. A swirl of tiny moths flew up out of the straw like a bouquet of white flowers to where the sunlight and dust intermingled in the slits between the roof beams. She fell headlong into kisses and embraces. She couldn't stop herself. They made love eagerly, quickly, without undressing completely, an awkward joining, yet it melded them together. And when it was over, Kotryna marveled at the breathtaking brevity and simplicity of it all.

Afterward, they stayed in each other's arms not speaking, as dust motes and bright bits of hay stirred in the streaks of sunlight coming through the weathered boards. Nearby, swallows were building a nest. From somewhere in the fields, they could hear Stasys singing. They heard Dora and Julija arguing about the Bartkus brothers. All of this seemed far away while they whispered endearments to one another. Listening to the swallows chirping, Kotryna felt as if this hayloft was her nest. For thirty-seven years of her life she had been a virgin, and now she was joined to another body and soul. Snuggled under Aleksas's chin, she delighted in the smell of his skin and his mustache wax and the feel of his warm breath on her cheek.

Outside, they heard Elzbieta calling to Ada. "Where's Kotryna gone to?"

"I haven't seen her," answered Ada.

"See if you can find her. Aleksas will be here soon."

Kotryna stood up, covering her cheeks with her hands, suddenly embarrassed. Why was she behaving like a love-struck girl who didn't know any better than to make love in the hay? She turned to Aleksas and put a finger to her lips to caution him to be quiet. They dusted themselves off, picking bits of hay off each other, and when their eyes met, they suddenly broke into muffled laughter like schoolchildren who had gotten away with mischief.

Aleksas peeked out. "Before I go down, tell me, is it really true that Elzbieta got rid of the *domovoi*? That dreadful imp is gone?"

"Go see for yourself if you don't believe me," she teased.

When they climbed down the ladder, she straightened her skirt and asked him if she looked all right.

"Never better. You look radiant," he said warmly.

They crossed the farmyard, greeting Julija and Dora on their way to the house. Dora poked Julija in the ribs with her elbow and smiled knowingly. Julija frowned and waved her sister away, as if it were ridiculous for such old people to be in love in that way.

Aleksas went into the kitchen to peek in the pantry to make sure it was empty. He walked around the rooms and, to his great relief, everything seemed peaceful and back to normal. Satisfied, he went back to Kotryna to tell her how relieved he was. "Thank God, that beast no longer haunts you."

Though glad the *domovoi* was banished, Kotryna felt as if a residual shame still clung to her like a bad smell.

"Oh, and guess what?" asked Aleksas, smiling.

"What" asked Kotryna.

"Your idea about photographing weddings and funerals and putting the photographs in the window worked wonderfully. So many people have come to look at them, especially on market day, that each morning I have to wipe down the many fingerprints and nose prints on the front windows. Now I try to change the photos every day and more people are coming in to get their portraits taken, thanks to you." He grabbed her in a huge bear hug that left her breathless. "Kotryna, you're simply brilliant. How can I thank you?"

"I'll think of something," she said, smiling wickedly.

"I'm sure you will." Aleksas laughed and cleared his throat. "Well, let me go find your father before I lose my nerve."

"He's in the rye fields today."

Aleksas found Viktoras inspecting his crop. It was time to formally ask for Kotryna's hand.

The old man's eyes moistened, and he had to pull his handkerchief out of his pocket to blow his nose before giving his consent. "Of course, you can have my precious daughter in marriage. I couldn't be happier for you both." He shook Aleksas's hand enthusiastically. "This calls for a big celebration."

When Elzbieta was told of the wedding, she squealed in delight, kissing her sister.

"Let's marry soon," said Kotryna, beaming with joy.

Aleksas looked concerned. "I'd like nothing more, my dear, but let's be practical and wait a bit longer, until I've saved enough to build a house. We can't all live in those two tiny rooms behind the studio," he said, sheepishly looking at Viktoras in apology.

"But we've waited so long." Kotryna was disappointed.

He took her hand. "Yes, we've waited this long. Please be patient a while longer." He kissed her hand and smiled, turning to Viktoras. "I bought some land with the money I made in the photographer's shop. I made a holy vow to my mother before I left for America that I wouldn't return home until I had enough money to buy my own farm."

"Really? You have a farm?" Viktoras beamed.

"Not yet. Only five hectares of land. Not as much as I wanted, but I bought it in the hopes that I could add to it someday."

"I see," said Viktoras, trying not to sound let down.

"And the photography studio, of course. But we'll have to wait until I save enough money to build a house on the land."

Kotryna swallowed her disappointment. "Yes, we'll get married when we can."

Viktoras listened carefully and rubbed his chin, making some plans of his own. "We'll have to talk about Kotryna's dowry before the wedding. Let me think about this and see what we can arrange." The two men shook hands and drank a toast.

After lunch, the girls returned to their chores and Aleksas went back to town to tell his mother, while Viktoras congratulated his daughter and told her how delighted he was for her. "It's what I dreamed and hoped for," he said emotionally. "All is as it should be now. The past is forgotten and you have so much to look forward to." He chuckled into his fist. "Those imps will never bother you again," he teased. "They'll have to find some other old maid to bother since you're betrothed."

Kotryna smiled, shaking her head and picking up her bucket to fetch water for the kitchen garden. Elzbieta stopped her on the way out, reaching over to pull a piece of straw from her hair, raising her eyebrows. "*Nu?*"

Kotryna blushed and turned away, not knowing what to say.

"Go ahead and lie," said Elzbieta smiling. "Tell me nothing happened."

That night Kotryna couldn't fall asleep. The day had been so life-changing, that it left her filled with wonder. She touched her face, her lips, remembering the passion of Aleksas's kisses, hardly able to believe that she was no longer a virgin. The thought filled her with shame for she wasn't yet married. Yet her body felt alive in every pore. Lovemaking was a mystery and a pleasure.

She was thirty-seven years old but until this day she had been as virginal as her nieces who slept nearby. Tonight, she would fall asleep a woman at last. And before long, she would be a wife. She felt a peace that she hadn't known in many years. It was as if life, which had taken a wrong turn eight years ago, had finally corrected itself.

-Thirty-

The rye undulated like waves in the wind while the clouds drifted over the fields. Stasys was putting away the farm tools when he heard Margis bark and turned to see Petras running home.

"Oh, thank God, you're back!"

Petras looked around. "I see you've finished the haying without me," he smiled.

"No thanks to you." His father beamed and clapped him on the back, his relief so palpable that it made Petras laugh.

Once the rest of the family heard the commotion, they ran out into the farmyard one by one to greet him, peppering him with questions. His mother burst into tears at the sight of him, hugging him tightly. "You're safe," she kept repeating through her tears.

Stasys took Julija by the arm, "Run and tell your grandfather that Petras is back."

When Viktoras came, he embraced his grandson fiercely. "My boy, I knew you'd be back safely. I wasn't worried about you for one second," he said, his eyes shining with emotion.

Stasys burst out laughing. "He hasn't stopped staring down the road since you left."

"He's exaggerating," Viktoras said, sheepishly.

Petras beamed with pride. "It took us longer because the border police forced us to take another way."

"How was it?" asked Viktoras. "Tell me every detail."

"It wasn't easy, but Jonas and I outsmarted them all. We crossed separately to avoid suspicion."

"Any trouble with the gendarmes?"

Petras snickered. "They think they're so clever, but they couldn't catch a fly if it sat on their nose."

"Will you be staying home with us now?" Viktoras had so agonized over Petras's absence that he didn't know if he could stand another book smuggling trip. He realized that after all of his years of yearning for someone to take up his battle, he now found that he was afraid for his grandson to take the same risks he had.

"Not for long." Petras shook his head. "Grigas, who teaches in the secret school in the Valinskas manor, wants to take us across the border for school books."

"Grigas, now there's a man like an oak," said his grandfather. "I've often brought him books for his secret school."

"He's full of wonderful stories, just like you, Grandfather."

Viktoras could see how proud Petras was of his first book smuggling experience and how he had grown in self-assurance with this trip.

Ada cleared her throat. "Will Jonas be going?"

"Of course! He's like a brother to me now." Petras smiled.

"Is he all right?" asked Ada quietly.

"Yes, he asked me to tell you he couldn't come to see you, but he'd look for you at the Midsummer Festival."

Ada beamed. "He did?" Her heart swelled with joy. "That's the day after tomorrow."

The Midsummer Festival came during the white nights

of the summer solstice when it never got completely dark. The sun no sooner disappeared over the horizon than it prepared to rise again. The Catholics had long ago usurped the pagan holidays of the solstices. The winter solstice became Christmas, while the summer solstice was given to Saint John the Baptist. But this day also celebrated the life-giving sun on the longest day of the year. For the festival, Ada and her sisters had made wildflower wreaths to wear, and the young men wore wreaths of oak leaves.

The evening began when they entered the forest through the ritual gate, built for the festival. Kotryna came with Aleksas because neither of them had seen a St. John's festival in years.

For Ada, this was the night she had been waiting for, the night Jonas would meet her again on his name day. In a swoon of excitement, she looked everywhere for him, only to spot Modestas walking nearby with Mimi. She blanched and quickly hid behind the trees, for she didn't want to pretend that everything was the same as it had been, nor to break the news of her new beau in front of Mimi.

While Mimi watched the revelers, Modestas found Kotryna and told her that he had taken his guests to the sea. "Even Helenka enjoyed herself. But what a restless crew they are! They must always be amused. I'm worn out, I tell you." He said this with a look of mock seriousness, but Kotryna could see that all of this activity had invigorated him.

Mimi added, "Tonight, Modestas wanted to come alone, but I wouldn't have it. I wanted to see this festival for myself and hear about the old customs." She looked around. "It's like some Wagner opera, my dear. I can't get over how exciting this is."

Kotryna humored Mimi, wondering who this Wagner was.

"Why do the girls wear wreaths on their heads?"

Kotryna shrugged. "We've always done it this way."

"And why are they rolling that wheel?"

Aleksas answered, "When it's lit, it symbolizes the sun."

255

"The sun, of course," Mimi tittered. "Such pagans still."

Aleksas tried to suppress his smile. But in truth, the evening had touched a chord in him, reminding him of his youth. They stood at the edge of a clearing and watched while Petras and the Bartkus brothers hoisted the wooden wheel soaked in tar up a hill with a procession following them yelling encouragement. When they reached the top, the crowd began to chant, "Jonas, Jonas, Jonas." On this night called *Jonines*, only someone named Jonas would be allowed to light the wheel, for this was his name's day.

On the other side of the clearing, hidden from view, Ada heard the call for Jonas and turned her head in every direction to see if her Jonas would show up. Her heart raced as she studied every man on the hilltop. When the crowd parted for someone, her breath stopped momentarily, waiting to see him. Instead a tall, thin boy came to light the wheel. It blazed up immediately, casting a halo of light on the revelers. Soon other bonfires were lit, but Ada couldn't find her Jonas anywhere.

Jurgis Bartkus showed off by jumping over one of the bonfires. "Oh, be careful, don't get burned," Dora squealed in delighted fear. Looking around at the gathered group of young girls, Zigmas was not about to be outdone by his brother. He, too, jumped over the bonfire but singed his pants in the effort. Afterward, he rubbed his stinging, smoke-filled eyes, while his brother teased that he wouldn't have much luck with the ladies that year for having made such a bad jump. Soon a line of young people formed, some couples jumping in pairs, yelping if the flames came too close. Soon, the burning wheel was rolled down the hill into the lake. The games went on all night, but others sat quietly around the bonfires, couples singing songs dreamily and making wishes as they stared into the flames.

In the twilight, Ada stood behind the oak tree, listening to the songs and nursing her disappointment. Jurgis and Dora were sneaking into the woods to look for the elusive fern blossom, which it is said blooms once every nine years. If it was found on Midsummer, the lucky person would become wise, rich and able to understand the language of birds and animals. The blossom opened at midnight, just as the imps and witches came, also in search of it. Ada knew the blossom hunting was merely a ruse for the young men to cuddle up to their girls in the woods, as she longed to do with Jonas.

Nearby, Aleksas sat with Kotryna, their heads together watching the bonfires blaze with tiny sparks shooting up to heaven.

On the other side of the woods, Mimi watched the flirting girls with easy smiles going into the woods. She had heard about the fern blossom and the witches coming to hunt for it at midnight. "How exciting, like *Walpurgisnacht.*" Mimi traipsed through the ferns with Modestas.

"Where is our Carmen?" Mimi wanted to know. "It's not nice of her not to be here to show us around. You don't think she's purposely avoiding us, do you?" she said, hoping to plant a seed of doubt.

"Why would she avoid us?" He was eager to take Mimi home and return later to seduce Ada.

Mimi was beginning to feel exasperated. She had flirted, teased, and chased Modestas for the last month and had become annoyed, having assumed that luring him away from that farm girl would be far easier than it was proving to be. He hadn't even attempted to kiss her in all this time. She couldn't understand how he could seriously prefer that milkmaid to her. But now she was losing patience. Lately she had the feeling there was something haunting Modestas. He often seemed worried or cross. She wanted a man with a spark who could make her laugh and feel giddy with excitement. That didn't seem likely with him. Perhaps her mother was right. If he didn't come around soon, she should look elsewhere for a husband.

When Ada saw Modestas and Mimi making their way into the woods, she ran down to the lake to watch her sisters launch their flower wreaths on the water.

"Ada, there you are." Dora came out of nowhere. "I've been looking everywhere for you." Her sister leaned over and whispered. "Modestas is scouring the woods with the tsarina."

"I know. Please don't tell him that you've seen me."

"My lips are sealed," laughed Dora, dragging her sister to a far edge of the clearing. "I have a surprise," she said, her dimples punctuating her gap-toothed grin.

"What is it?" She looked around.

"Close your eyes." Dora looked pleased with herself.

Ada did as she was told and let her sister pull her by the arm. She tripped over a root and Dora apologized.

"Can I open my eyes yet?" Ada asked.

"No. Stand here with your eyes closed and count to twenty. Then open them."

The smell of wood smoke hung in the air while Ada counted. When she opened her eyes, she was looking right into Jonas's face. She smiled in surprise. "Is it really you?"

"Yes, it's me." Jonas beamed.

Powerless to resist him, she laughed. "I'm so happy you found me." Everything about him pleased her, especially those soulful eyes filled with unexpressed feelings.

"Not as happy as I am." Jonas took her hands. He stood motionless, so helplessly in love already. "Don't say a word, Ada, you're beautiful just now. Like I've never seen you before." He gazed deeply into her eyes while she could only stand there, bewitched, so dizzy with delight that a laugh bubbled up from deep inside. She kissed him quickly on the cheek and then ran to the meadow, her enthusiasm evident in her voice as she called to him. Jonas burst out laughing and ran after her, both of them jumping over fallen branches like children chasing one another.

When Jonas finally caught her, they walked, breathless. The need was upon him to touch her. Not taking his eyes off her face, he held out his hand and she took it, intertwining her fingers in his and pulling him closer. Her eyes, clear as lake water, played over his face.

"Ada, my dearest," he murmured tenderly. "Tell me that you love me just a little, because I confess that I love you with all my heart."

Her eyes shone at his confession. "I do love you, Jonas." For a while, neither of them spoke, staring at each other, drunk with emotion.

"Ada," he whispered, slipping his arms around her waist. They kissed softly and stood gazing at each other. Suddenly from behind, she heard a familiar voice calling her name. She pulled away long enough to see Modestas and Mimi coming toward them. Modestas called out to her from afar. "Ada, is that you?"

"Oh no," she whispered, while Jonas turned to see his rival hurrying across the clearing with Mimi close behind, already out of breath. She tripped, falling over a tree root and called to him to help her up. When Modestas turned, Mimi complained, "Ouch! I've ripped my dress and turned my ankle."

Jonas seized that moment to pull Ada deeper into the woods before Modestas could reach them. They disappeared like wood sprites into the trees.

After Modestas helped Mimi back up, she looked around and found the festival had suddenly lost its charm. Now, everything looked primitive. "My ankle hurts. Take me home," she said petulantly. "I've had enough of these rustic pagans."

Modestas gladly agreed. His mood had also soured. Where the devil had Ada gone? He only hoped that Jonas wasn't going to ruin his plans to seduce her. Mimi had already annoyed him by refusing to stay home on such a night. She held on to him with a vise-like grip while hobbling back toward the carriage.

As soon as the moon reached the gate's gable, the round dance started, first around the bonfire, then, like garlands, the dancers threaded their way around the trees, through the ferns.

Walking alongside Jonas, Ada heard the rhythmic croaking of frogs and felt the percussive beating of her heart in her throat. The woods were cool, smelling of loamy earth and deep moss. The muted twilight was filled with fireflies glinting in the underbrush.

Jonas helped Ada climb over a fallen fir tree, and when they jumped down they almost landed on Elena and Zigmas kissing under the ferns. Elena screamed in fright, and Zigmas shot to his feet ready to fight.

"I'm sorry, I didn't see you," said Jonas, embarrassed.

"Oh, it's you!" Elena began to laugh hysterically. "I thought some horrible demon had descended on us."

Jonas shook Zigmas's hand, apologizing for frightening them. "We'll leave you two alone to find the fern blossom," he teased.

"I see that we're not the only ones looking for it," Zigmas countered.

Holding hands, Ada and Jonas walked deeper into the misty pines, the wind humming through the trees. Never had she been happier. No matter what else happened in life, this was a night she would always remember.

Jonas finally stopped by a giant oak tree and gently touched its rough bark, seeking courage. "Ada," he turned and whispered. "I have a confession. I tortured myself for months thinking of you, wanting to come to you, but I didn't dare. But late one night, when I couldn't stand it any longer, I rode my horse to your village and stood in the cold and starry night, wanting to see you so badly it hurt. For a long time I imagined you sleeping peacefully. Finally, I forced myself to ride back home, feeling lonely."

Ada was amazed to hear this. "I must have been silently calling to you."

"Come closer." Jonas slowly gathered her in his arms, and she smiled, liking the invitation in his voice. He kissed her tenderly on this most magical night of the year, and held her face in his hands, kissing her again and again.

Soon, the twilit night began to melt into day as the sun rose again waking the world. Dew covered all those in the woods quietly murmuring their love like doves, heads together in the morning mist. Ada touched a delicate spiral of a newly sprouted fern, coiled tight, waiting to unfurl for the first time. She was that fragile fern, ready to blossom, to open to love.

With the Midsummer night's festivities over, couples began to stroll home through the fragrant woods. Soon sunlight streamed through the trees, and birds serenaded the tired lovers. Jonas walked Ada home, but he couldn't bear to say goodbye. They walked hand in hand down the sandy path. Now that they had finally declared their love, parting was more difficult than ever, so they lingered, clinging to one another, postponing the pain of separation. From down the road they could already hear the geese in the Varnas farmyard. "Shall I go with you to talk to your parents?" Jonas offered.

"No, better if I tell my mother first," she said. Reluctantly, Ada asked him not to go beyond the crossroads near their farm, for tongues would wag if she was seen coming home with him rather than Modestas.

He kissed her on the cheek. "I'm leaving next week for another trip for books. Your brother's coming with us."

"But those awful gendarmes? Don't go, please."

"I gave my word, Ada." He smiled ruefully.

It frightened Ada, yet she was proud of Jonas, who was like her grandfather in his quiet strength and warm humor. She kissed him gently. "Just go safely and hurry back to me."

They walked a little farther, taking their time, lingering, but stepped aside when they heard a cart approaching. When the cart stopped suddenly, leaving a cloud of dust in its wake, Ada looked up, shocked to see Modestas climbing out.

"Ada, I was looking everywhere for you last night," he spoke quickly, annoyed, without even glancing at Jonas. "Where were you?

Before she could answer, he asked, "Have you been with him?" Modestas grabbed her hand, reclaiming her. "Come, we need to talk—alone," he said.

"No," Ada said curtly, quickly pulling her hand away.

Modestas was stunned by her reaction. He looked at Jonas and then at Ada in disbelief. He grabbed her arm angrily and gripped it tightly while she tried to pull away.

Jonas stepped forward. "Let go of her, now," he said slowly but with such menace that Modestas let go of her arm at once.

"Let me tell him," she said to Jonas in a shaky voice.

He frowned and backed away.

She swallowed hard. "Modestas, I know I should have said something much sooner, but I battled with myself, not knowing how to say it. But now I must tell you simply that I have fallen in love with Jonas. I'm sorry."

Modestas looked at Jonas with complete incredulity and then turned to Ada. "That's ridiculous." He almost laughed, waiting for her to say it was a prank. "You can't be serious."

Ada raised her eyes. "Very serious."

Modestas was suddenly enraged, his jaw working furiously. "With this fellow? With no education or family name? You prefer this peasant to me? You must be joking." He could have gone on, but Jonas stopped him.

"You've said enough."

"But I haven't even begun. You have no idea how restrained I've been."

Ada frowned. "Modestas, you go your way and I'll go mine. There is nothing more to say."

Modestas was speechless for a few uncomfortable moments, the anger visible on his face. Then, his fury spewed out in a rush. "My family said you were too common, and I see they were right. You with your lowborn family with their *domovoi*—what a backward lot! My mother couldn't bear the thought of my being seen with your coarse family, with your silly mother with her pretensions, but I lowered myself to be with you." His anger was directed at her because he realized that his last chance to save his house and land was slipping away.

Ada went white, unable to speak.

Jonas punched Modestas so hard that he fell back against his horse. It whinnied and nervously tramped about.

"Are you crazy?" Modestas asked, touching his bloodied nose. At first he was stunned, but then the two men began to scuffle.

Down the road, Julija came strolling home, returning from the night's festivities with Dora and Jurgis. When they came around the bend, they saw the two men fighting, and Jurgis ran to break them up. "Hold on, men." He grabbed Jonas and pulled him off Modestas.

Julija turned to Ada. "Why is Jonas hurting Modestas?" She turned to see his bloodied face.

"For good reasons," Ada said defiantly.

"What in God's name happened?" Dora asked, but before Ada could answer, Julija demanded, "Ada, how could you treat Modestas this way?"

Ada shot back. "You don't know what happened."

Julija turned away from Ada in disgust and gave Modestas her handkerchief, helping the bloodied suitor back into his cart. Seeing how shaken he was by the sudden violence, she felt sorry for him.

Turning to Jurgis, she said, "You take care of Jonas and I'll take Modestas home."

Julija saw Modestas's expression was dark and dangerous. Climbing into the cart, she urged the horse on. As they turned the bend, Modestas began to moan with pain. "That man is an animal."

"I'm so sorry," Julija sympathized. "To be attacked like that. You don't deserve such treatment."

"I most certainly don't," he agreed in a wave of self-pity.

263

Looking at his bloodied face, Julija shook her head. "Please don't be upset. You'll have nothing to worry about soon enough. Jonas will be leaving next week."

"What do you mean, leaving?" Modestas was suddenly all ears.

"He'll be going to Prussia soon. Then Ada will surely come back to her senses."

"Prussia?" Modestas looked at Julija with new interest. "How do you know this?"

Shrugging, Julija said, "I overheard my brother talking about crossing the border near the marshes." She suddenly stopped, remembering that Petras had asked that no one repeat this information. She frowned, feeling guilty. "Oh, I shouldn't have said that."

"No, I'm glad you did," he said.

"Promise me you won't tell a soul." Julija looked worried.

"Of course, I won't. Don't worry," said Modestas, wiping the blood from his nose with her handkerchief. He was feeling enormous relief. Finally, he would have something concrete to tell Captain Malenkov.

At the crossroads, he thanked Julija for her help, telling her he was fine and would go the rest of the way on his own. After she got out of the cart and started back on the road to Sapnai, he drove straight to town. The sword that had been hanging over his head all these months had finally been lifted.

At the tavern, he sat down at a back table and bellowed for some vodka. Zimmerman took note of Modestas's swollen lip and bloodied nose and brought him a wet towel to wipe the blood from his face. Exhausted from the long night and sore from the fight, Modestas wiped his face and then waited for the captain, with glass after glass of vodka to anesthetize body and soul. Feeling optimistic, he decided to buy the ever-present Duda a drink.

At one point, when Zimmerman came to his table, Modestas

took him by the arm, his words already slurred, "Why are women so difficult to understand, tell me?"

The tavern owner shrugged, trying to pull his arm away. He hadn't seen Modestas drink this way and wondered what had happened to the man to bring him to the tavern in this state. He remembered when Modestas's father drank like that. Zimmerman asked him if he wanted something to eat, since it was still early to get so drunk.

Modestas shook his head and looked around the tavern, spotting two Gypsies who were telling Duda they were on their way to the next market town. Modestas snickered, wanting to ask them how many horses were going to be missing after they left. "Hey," he called to them. "There are some nice horses at the Varnas farm in Sapnai." He laughed so hard that tears came to his eyes. He pulled out the bloody handkerchief Julija had given him.

The Gypsies merely shrugged and turned away.

"Laughter and tears are never far from one another," said the older Gypsy.

The door opened and Nikolai entered the tavern. "Hey Zimmerman, bring us some food," yelled Nikolai. "We're tired and hungry, so be quick about it."

Zimmerman frowned at the loud and uncouth Nikolai, but he swallowed his annoyance. "All right, you don't have to yell." At least Ivan was a good-natured drunk who didn't cause trouble the way Nikolai sometimes did. Captain Malenkov entered behind them. All three men greeted Modestas, joining him at his table. "We haven't seen you lately," they teased. The captain saw at once that Bogdanskis was already drunk, and from the battered appearance of his face, he must have been on the losing end of a brawl. He hadn't thought Modestas was the type to fight.

Filled with drunken bluster and bravado, Modestas leaned back. "My good men, I could tell you a thing or two if I had a mind to." He smiled widely and then winced because it hurt his mouth.

Nikolai and Ivan exchanged a smile. Nikolai waved his hand and decided to ignore him.

"What is it, Bogdanskis?" the captain asked, already annoyed, anticipating more evasions and misdirection.

Modestas raised his chin proudly. "I know a great deal more than anyone in this room. I'm a Bogdanskis. I come from a long and noble line."

Nikolai arched an eyebrow. "There he goes again," he said under his breath. "God save us from these self-pitying penniless noblemen."

"He's drunk," Ivan snickered. "He doesn't know anything."

Modestas chafed at the insult. Who were these boorish men to judge him? Turning to the captain with an arrogant smile, he said, "Captain, you've been hounding me for information for months." He smirked. "Well, now you can stop hounding me."

The captain looked Modestas over. With a sweep of his hand, he gestured for the owner. "Bring this man another drink." Then he turned back to Modestas. "I warn you, this better be good."

"Oh, it's good, Captain. Believe me." Modestas took his time finishing his drink, relishing his important news. "Gentlemen," he said, smiling knowingly. "I guarantee this information will be of great interest to you." The smile on his face slowly turned bitter.

-Thirty-one-

A fter the fight, Jonas lingered with Ada, each too agitated to let go of the other. Jonas's jaw was swelling and his shirt was ripped. They found an old oak tree not far from the road and sat under its wide canopy, still fuming over the insults Modestas had flung in every direction. Ada scolded herself for being so foolishly blind to his intentions. Jonas listened, not saying much, but his distaste for the man was evident.

They spent a long time trying to calm each other until, finally, Ada said she must go home. "My family is probably worrying." As they walked, Jonas again asked if she wanted him to explain things to her family.

"No, please let me take care of this." Then looking down the road and seeing it was empty, she kissed him quickly. "Please be very careful crossing the border."

"Don't worry about me. Nothing in the world could keep me away from you after tonight." Jonas smiled and kissed her again before reluctantly leaving.

When Ada entered the kitchen, her mother put down the wooden spoon she had been using to stir a pot of porridge. "Ada what have you done!" She shook her head, shocked by the news.

Julija, sat nearby, scowling. "I couldn't believe my own eyes. How will Modestas ever forgive you after the way you acted?"

Ada spun around, her eyes flashing with rage. "Forgive me? You don't know what you're talking about, Julija! You've got the question backward. How will I ever forgive him?" Before she had a chance to explain, she found out Julija had already told her own version of how Modestas had caught Ada and Jonas returning home, and how Jonas had punched the poor man in the nose.

Finally losing patience, Ada fumed, "Mama, I don't ever want to see that arrogant man again. If you could have heard the things he said about our family, you'd want no part of him either." She turned to her sister. "Nor you, Julija."

Her mother was taken aback, "Our family? What could he possibly say?"

Ada began in a sharp voice. "To begin with, Mama, he said we were coarse and lowborn."

"What!" This was such a shock to her mother that she had to sit down from the blow.

At the sight of her mother's injured expression, Ada regretted her words, but she couldn't help it. "I should have slapped him, Mama." She sat down next to her mother on the bench and took her hand. "He said so much more."

Her mother turned to her, scowling. "More?"

"They think we're nothing but backward peasants with our *domovoi*."

"Really? He really said that?" She was stunned.

"It can't be true," yelled Julija. "Modestas is a gentleman. He would never say anything so cruel."

"Oh, he said more, much more." Ada stroked her mother's arm to soothe her, but she wouldn't mention what he said about her silly pretensions.

Julija glared at her sister. "I don't believe you."

Ada was stung. "You think I'm lying?"

"He's a nobleman." Julija frowned.

"Tell me why he was pursuing me if he felt he was lowering himself so far? The nerve of the man! Why did he bother?" Ada couldn't fathom his motives. It made her boil with anger.

"Lowering himself?" Elzbieta didn't know whether to be hurt or angry.

"Mama, I'm finished with that whole family."

Elzbieta looked around her kitchen, her beloved little fiefdom, and suddenly it all seemed so common. No matter how much she tidied and cleaned, no matter how finely she wove her linen tablecloths, or how many dresses she wore from Smolensk, it would never redeem her in Bogdanskis's eyes. She was born a farmer's wife and she would die one. There was no climbing out of that hole. But when Modestas began wooing Ada, it had raised her hopes that one of her daughters might better her life, and in turn, raise the status of the family. But that door was now firmly shut. Elzbieta was so disappointed she could hardly speak. Julija came over to comfort her mother, who clutched her hand for solace.

Ada wondered who was more disappointed Julija or her mother. Perhaps it was better to leave them to sort things out. Better not to say anything about Jonas for the time being. Instead, Ada set out to do her chores.

When she went out to the farmyard, she found her grandfather sitting on the granary porch mending a rake and looking more worn than usual. "Ada," he said, and motioned for her to sit. "I heard you telling your mother what Modestas said about our family." He nodded, his lips pressed tightly. "Are you terribly disappointed, my dear?" He put his calloused hand on hers.

"Not disappointed, just furious. The man is an arrogant ass and I'm glad he's out of my life. I hate him."

Her grandfather brightened. "Really?"

"He was so horribly insulting." She hesitated a moment, trying to get control of her feelings, but then she broke down

269

completely, the tears coming hard. The old man embraced her, letting her cry on his shoulder.

When Ada finally wiped her tears, she said, "Grandfather, I'm so in love with Jonas Balandis."

Viktoras smiled. "Why, I knew that the morning after Shrove Tuesday. It was as clear as day even then."

"Really?" Ada blinked in surprise.

"I just couldn't understand why it took you so long to admit it." He laughed. "This was my heart's desire when I asked you to write a letter to the Balandis family last fall. I prayed that after meeting Jonas you'd see him as a proper suitor, not like that puffed up scarecrow who spouts his ten French words whenever he gets a chance. *Bonjour*," he mocked Modestas.

Ada laughed and hugged her grandfather fiercely. "Thank you for making me write that letter. What would I have done without you?" She shook her head. "My matchmaker," she said, kissing him on the cheek.

Viktoras's eyes shone. "You better go milk the cows. I've already heard them complaining."

Walking to the cowshed, Ada's mind quickly returned to Jonas and left her so weak with love that she didn't think she would be able to perform her routine chores. When she went to milk the cows, she looked at Buttercup's eyes, so dark and kind, almost as if it wanted to say something. Positioning the stool, she put the bucket down and began to milk. The cow's tail swung back and forth. Before long, Ada stopped milking, lost in worry about Jonas's dangerous book-running. In her mind, she could once again see the gendarmes riding down the road on their horses, pulling them to the side of the road and searching the hay wagon. This memory was so disturbing that she shook it away.

Breathing deeply, she told herself to wait patiently until Jonas returned, and then he would win everyone's heart the way he won hers. Slowly, deliberately, she continued milking the cow, the rhythmic squirts of milk hitting the bucket soothing her.

Soon she was remembering Midsummer, the most magical night of her life. It all came back to her as she relived Jonas's kisses.

Her thoughts began to float to the ferns and deep woods. She forgot what she was doing and put her head on the warm flank of the cow. Closing her eyes, she sighed deeply and whispered, "Jonas." The cow flinched and moved uneasily, waking her from her romantic reverie.

-Thirty-two-

Kotryna slept right through breakfast, only waking when her sister finally came into her room. "Are you planning to sleep until the sun sets, or are you ill?"

Opening her eyes, Kotryna said, "I'm so tired today, I think I could sleep for a week without waking." A faint breeze carrying the scent of rue wafted in from the open window. Kotryna dressed and joined the others in the kitchen.

"It's been a week and Petras still hasn't returned from Prussia," said Elzbieta. "I'm worried."

Like an invalid, Kotryna shuffled over to a chair to hear about her nephew, but then she started to feel even worse. There it was again, thought Kotryna, the rising sick feeling in the pit of her stomach. She had woken feeling nauseated, thinking it was the heat, but here was the same sick feeling again. Perhaps she should take some valerian drops to soothe her stomach. Suddenly, she scrambled to grab the bucket just in time. When she went to empty it, she noticed her sister watching her.

When Kotryna returned to the kitchen, Elzbieta asked her to come sit with her. "What's ailing you?" she asked. While preparing some chamomile tea for her sister, Elzbieta turned, hands on hips.

"If I didn't know better, I'd say you were pregnant."

"Pregnant?" Kotryna blanched. The thought had not even entered her mind, but now that her sister brought it up, she worked it like a tongue returning to a bad tooth. She couldn't leave it alone.

"Maybe I am pregnant," Kotryna whispered, touching her stomach.

"But how can it be?" asked her astonished sister.

Kotryna looked at her directly. "I think the usual way, Elzbieta," she said bluntly, though, in fact, she was a little stunned by it herself. In Smolensk, she had railed against her fate—no husband or children. It had been difficult to be an old maid, but it had been even harder to take care of the other people's children knowing she would never have any of her own. How many nights had she cried in Smolensk. Yet as the years wore on, she finally made peace with being childless. But now it seemed she might be pregnant at such an advanced age. Could it actually be true? Something bubbled up in her wanting to rejoice. If it was true then she had been given an enormous gift—a child of her own!

Elzbieta's mouth dropped. "But what will people say?" She began to pace in the tiny kitchen. "The Bogdanskis family already thinks we're backward. First the *domovoi* and now this!" Working up a righteous anger, she turned to Kotryna. "What will I tell my girls? Really, what kind of example is this for them? And what will Papa say when he finds out?"

"Papa?" Kotryna was alarmed by her sister's reaction. "Don't say anything yet. Aleksas and I will get married right away."

"But will he marry you now?" Elzbieta looked doubtful. "Once he hears about your condition?"

"Won't he?" asked Kotryna, doubt creeping in as she looked out at the fragrant linden branches gently rocking in the breeze.

Crossing her arms, Elzbieta frowned. "I only hope so for all of our sakes. Otherwise, what shame you'll bring on us, having a child out of wedlock."

"That would be terrible—a child out of wedlock. A bastard," she whispered, flinching. Kotryna returned to her bedside to look for her Book of Dreams. Last night she had dreamt that the pastor was dressed like a woman. She looked the dream up in her book. It meant that gossip and scandal might be headed her way. She shook her head. "Oh no, this won't do," she whispered. "What if Aleksas abandons me?" Kotryna was suddenly gripped with fear. "I have to talk to him."

On the way to Raudonava, Kotryna contemplated the stigma of having a bastard. She remembered other women who had gotten pregnant outside of marriage. There was Terese, a slow-witted girl who was said to lift her skirt for any man who raised an eyebrow suggestively. When she got pregnant, her mother put her out of the house. And there was Karolina, the hired girl seduced by the owner. She ran away rather than face the shame. Oh, that wouldn't be her child's fate. Not while she had breath left in her. Don't they dare call her child a bastard. Her face burned with anger at the thought.

She must tell Aleksas. He needed to know he wasn't just some ordinary photographer; he was about to become a father. She pictured a small boy with a curly mop of auburn hair and large hazel eyes, or a sweet girl with Aleksas's wide smile.

The day was getting hotter. Passing a pond with splashing ducks, Kotryna saw one waddle across the road. Was that a bad omen? There were so many things women mustn't do when pregnant. The old women always warned against climbing fences or crossing a plowed field, for it would cause a miscarriage. If a rabbit crossed your path, the baby would be born with a harelip. And there were many foods that caused birthmarks. Though, it was said, kissing a dead man's hand cured some birthmarks. Eating the heel of a loaf of bread ensured having a boy. And she must pray to Mary's mother, St. Anne, for an easy birth. Oh, and what if she died giving birth the way Agota had! Suddenly there were so many things to worry about besides the question of whether Aleksas would marry her.

By the time she reached the photography studio, Kotryna was in a state of nervous exhaustion. She saw Aleksas taking a photo of Yossel the bagel vendor and his frowning wife and four squirming children—one still in her arms. Kotryna sat down to wait until he finished, but her knee kept bouncing in agitation. Once the Yossel family finished their portrait and left, he turned to greet her. Kotryna's face immediately told him something was wrong. "What is it? What's happened?"

Kotryna hesitated, suddenly fearful of his reaction. Her sister had reacted so strongly. Closing her eyes, too nervous about what she might read on his face, she blurted it out. "I think I'm pregnant."

He was speechless for a long moment. "What did you say?" He simply couldn't take it in, glancing at her stomach as if he would see it huge with child.

Kotryna was devastated by his reaction. "I'm pregnant, I tell you." Her face dissolved into misery. "Don't you want our baby?"

He scratched his head. "Baby? Are you sure? So quickly?"

"You don't believe me?" She looked up, pierced to her core.

"It's not that," he stammered. "I...I just never thought about a baby."

Her hurt shifted into anger. "Why that's just like a man to be so thoughtless. Men only think about the pleasures of love, leaving women to bear the burden." She sniffed loudly. "I'll raise the baby alone if I have to."

Aleksas muttered. "At our age—a baby? I thought we were too old for babies."

That was too much for Kotryna. "You don't have to remind me of my age. I know I'm no longer young!" She turned her back and burst into tears.

"Don't cry, Kotryna." He took her in his arms and held her tenderly. "There, there," he said soothingly. He held her for a long

276

time as she quietly wept. "This is just such a surprise, a shock really, but when I turn the idea over in my mind, it's starting to dawn on me that I'm going to be a father. Imagine me, a father." He looked at her tenderly and smiled. "The more I think about it, the more I like it."

Kotryna sniffed and wiped her eyes. "Really? Are you telling the truth?" Her lips trembled with emotion.

"Yes," he said, kissing her nose. "I'm going to be a father! I thought this day would never come for me." He picked her up and twirled her.

Startled, Kotryna laughed through her tears. "Put me down, you lunatic."

"I'm sorry, did I hurt you? The baby?"

"No, but I'm nauseated enough without your twirling." Kotryna held onto his shoulders until her head stopped spinning. "And don't shout it out for the whole town to hear. We'll have gossip enough when this baby comes."

"But we must get married so there'll be no gossip," he said, looking concerned. "We must get married right away."

"We better talk to Father Jurkus first. He'll have to read the wedding banns for the next three weeks. Then we could get married right after the first rye is cut. And it means we would have to live here, behind your studio. I know you wanted to wait until you had enough money for a house on your land. Do you mind very much?"

"Anything you want, little mother." Aleksas smiled broadly and patted her on the stomach. "Mama will be so surprised."

"Before we tell your mother, I'd like to talk to my father. Can we do this together?"

He took a deep breath and frowned. "Of course, though I don't relish facing your father with this news."

When the shop closed, the couple returned to Sapnai to find Viktoras in the barn, oiling his farm tools. His painted coffin, always close by, was leaning against the wall.

They had agreed she would be the one to tell her father. When they entered the barn and saw the hay, Kotryna turned to Aleksas, pointing to where they had first made love, where their child had been conceived. He smiled, but when he noticed the painted coffin, he stopped, shocked to see such a thing in a barn.

Aleksas nodded ruefully to Viktoras. "May you live a long life. Long enough to see another grandchild come into this world."

Viktoras looked puzzled. "Grandchild?" He looked at Kotryna, who stammered but couldn't spit out a word. "Yours?" he asked her.

She nodded. Her blush started at her mottled neck and spread up to her face.

Aleksas was so nervous, he began to stutter. "W-with your permission, we'll marry s-sooner than we thought."

Viktoras clapped his hands. "Oh ho! The Lord be thanked. What are we standing here for? Let me get my homemade cherry wine out to celebrate."

Kotryna stared at her father, hugely relieved. Eight years ago, he might have disowned her for such news. But something in him had softened in the ensuing years to allow her not only to return home but also to welcome her marriage to Aleksas. And, it seemed, her pregnancy was only one more cause for celebration. What miracles those eight years wrought.

"When shall we have the wedding?" asked Viktoras.

"After the priest finishes reading the banns," said Kotryna.

Viktoras went inside to look for his bottle in the pantry, and for a moment, he smiled, thinking about the blessing of having an orderly and imp-free home.

Back in the parlor, Viktoras poured the wine, and they all drank a celebratory toast. Then he sat down at the table to talk to Aleksas about Kotryna's dowry. "I've saved some money in the hopes that one day I might help my daughter. It might not be enough to finish building a house, but it'll be enough to get a good start."

Kotryna was speechless. She blinked away grateful tears and hugged her father. "Papa, I've always dreamed of my own home."

Aleksas sat quietly for a moment. "Thank you sincerely for the generous dowry. My business has picked up a little, thanks to Kotryna's suggestions. Perhaps it might be enough to finish the house."

"Wonderful. I'll hire Litvin, a fine tradesman with a good eye. They say he doesn't even need to measure a single board and everything fits like a hand in a glove. I'll see him tomorrow if you agree." They both nodded, stunned to imagine a house of their own.

Viktoras smiled. "And once the house is built, I'll give you a calf, some lambs, and chicks the following spring."

"I don't know what to say. Thank you very much." Aleksas was moved by the old man's generosity. He shook his hand emotionally. "It means so much to us both and to my mother. And most of all to your grandchild, who we'll raise in that house."

"Well, I'll arrange everything. Oh, it will be great fun for an old man like me—so much better than staring at my own coffin," he said, wheezing a laugh. "Suddenly there's so much to look forward to." Viktoras shook Aleksas's hand and then kissed his daughter and hugged her warmly.

Outside, beyond the open windows, the whisper of leaves seemed to chatter and prattle.

-Thirty-three-

On a sunny, cobwebbed Sunday in July, Ada and her sisters walked the sandy path, barefoot, holding their good shoes in their hands. A drowsy flight of bees hovered over the yellow-and-blue petunia blossoms in Kreivenas's garden. A light breeze blew through the oak tree, its leaves whispering to one another—*Where is he? Where is he? Where is he?*

Thoughts of Jonas tormented Ada the whole way to St. George's Church. Once they reached the town, they put their shoes back on and went to church. Upon reaching the churchyard, Ada looked for Jonas, hardly able to contain her excitement. She thought he might be back but couldn't see him anywhere. Across the churchyard, she spotted Jonas's parents. "Praised be God," she greeted them.

"Forever and ever," Domicele and Jeronimas answered.

Ada leaned over to whisper, "Has Jonas returned yet?"

"No, and not a word." Jeronimas frowned, taking off his hat. "He's been gone two weeks. We came to talk to Father Jurkus."

Ada informed them that the priest had been called away. "The pastor is saying Mass today."

"You don't suppose something happened?" Domicele was

as tense as a wire pulled tight. "God help us. My nerves aren't strong enough for this. It's time my Jonas settled down and got married and gave me some grandchildren. I need a daughter-in-law to help me on the farm. I've been waiting for him to marry the Mockus girl." She glanced at Ada to see her reaction, her mouth a taut line of disapproval.

Ada's face dropped. Stunned into immobility, she could only whisper, "Mockus," and hated the name at once. She had worried about whether or not her parents would accept Jonas, but now she saw it was Domicele who might not accept her. She simply stared at the woman. Was it possible that Jonas was wooing another woman?

Still reeling, Ada went to join her mother and sisters in their pew, feeling as though all of life had turned to dust. There was some Mockus girl after Jonas. She wanted to tear the girl's hair out. Didn't she know Jonas was hers? Ada scanned the church. Of course, she didn't know. No one knew.

Ada watched Graf Valinskas, the count admired by all in the district, walking down the aisle with his wife and sons to the first and best pew in the church. He was followed by other members of the gentry, who sat in the front near the altar, while the lower classes arranged themselves behind them in descending order—bankers, judges, then clerks, followed by the largest group, the farmers. Each group knew their rank and place.

Soon heads turned to watch Modestas saunter down the aisle in his new coat with Mimi on his arm, carrying himself like the count. His mother followed with Neda, while Helenka and Vincentas came last. Walking proudly to their usual pews at the front of the church, Modestas cast an icy glance at Ada and moved on without a word. When he reached the front, the whole church was filled with whispered gossip, as heads turned to see Ada's reaction. Eyes seemed to bore into her. She looked down, gripping the oak pew like a life raft. This would have been the talk of the entire parish had it not been for the pastor's odd sermon.

When Father Kazlauskas stepped up to the pulpit, he started to read his sermon in Sanskrit. In recent weeks, the pastor had been studying Schleicher's comparative grammar of Indo-European languages showing the similarity of the Lithuanian language to Sanskrit, a 4,000-year-old language of Indian high priests. He was convinced by an old Lithuanian proverb: *Dievas dave dantis, duos ir duonos.* God gave us teeth; He'll give us bread as well. The proverb was almost identical in Sanskrit except for a few letters: *Devas adadat datas; Devas dat dhanas.*

Lithuanian was one of the oldest spoken languages in the world, the pastor had found in his research. On the tree of languages, Lithuanian sat apart from the Latin, Germanic and Slavic languages. It sat out on its own limb with Latvian as one of the two surviving Baltic languages on the Baltic tree. Old Prussian was a Baltic language, extinct by the eighteenth century once the Germans colonized Baltic Prussia, which was still called Lithuania Minor by the locals. At the root of the Baltic language tree was Sanskrit. Father Kazlauskas was convinced that if he went to India and spoke Lithuanian, there might be those who would understand him. But since he couldn't go to India, he decided to prove his latest theory with the local Lithuanians. He had painstakingly translated his sermon into Sanskrit.

The parishioners of St. George were a patient lot, accustomed to the mass being said in Latin. And by now they had become used to their pastor's theories creeping into his sermons. But this sermon was too much for them, though they were polite, pretending nothing was wrong. After all, no one dared embarrass the pastor. At first, everyone thought he was speaking a foreign language, but from time to time they could almost make out a word or two. Stasys looked at Viktoras and a half smile crossed his face. Jeronimas shrugged slightly indicating he too had no idea what this priest was up to on this particular Sunday. The Latin *Dominus Vobiscum* and *Sanctus* were often heard, but this was not the usual incomprehensible fare. Yet the parishioners sat quietly, patiently listening out of respect for their learned pastor. After the sermon, Father Kazlauskas reverted back to Lithuanian to everyone's relief. He read the second wedding banns for the intended marriage of Aleksas Simaitis to Kotryna Kulys and asked if anyone knew of any impediments to their marriage. Kotryna had not said anything to the priest about her pregnancy. She looked around, wondering if anyone had guessed.

After Mass, the pastor headed out the door quickly, not wanting to get caught in the intrigues of the parish gossips any more than he had to. And yet, he took some satisfaction in the morning's sermon, gratified that no one had asked him to explain what he had said. He naturally concluded that his sermon had been easily understood by all, thereby proving his theory. On the way to the rectory, he decided he would write a scholarly article on the subject for some philology journal.

As Modestas exited the church, his face exuded a coldness. He offered Mimi his arm as they regally walked out of the church followed by the others.

Elzbieta, sitting on the other side of Ada, stiffened in her pew, refusing to look their way. Seeing the Bogdanskis family now filled her with bitter anger. She glanced up and caught the mother's arrogant smile. Each woman pointedly turned away, ignoring the other. Elzbieta refused to leave her pew until the Bogdanskis family and their guests had left the church.

Ada kept her head down for she, too, burned with the memory of the terrible things Modestas had said. She had never realized what a sacrifice he was making to woo her or how far beneath him in social status he considered her. After all, his family had fallen from their former position and hardly had a kopek left. So why had they put on such airs? And why had he courted her?

When Elzbieta finally stood to leave, she ignored the women in the back of the church whose heads were together, busily gossiping. She held her head high and walked out of the church. Her family may not have had an old and noble name, but it didn't make them any less worthy than the Bogdanskis family. She walked out into the churchyard with Ada, head held high, like a grand duchess, wearing the dress Kotryna had brought from Smolensk.

In the churchyard there was much talk and speculation about what the priest had said during his sermon and in what language. Balys claimed to have understood the whole sermon, saying the pastor had spoken in an old Samogitian dialect used at the time of the Northern Crusade.

"And who made you such an expert on the Crusades?" asked Kreivenas.

Balys shrugged. "I know what I heard from the learned pastor."

"I think he was speaking Latvian." Kreivenas nodded to make his point. "You know how sometimes it seems like you can understand Latvian but it sounds like Lithuanian with the endings cut off? You have to listen really hard."

Povilaitis, the god-carver, chuckled. "Not Latvian. We've heard Latvian before. This was something else, some church language. These priests have a special language between them and God. Like Latin or Greek or something they used when the church was Byzantine."

Kreivenas laughed. "And what does a farmer like you know about the Byzantine church?"

"I think you're all talking nonsense," said Stasys. He wanted to say the pastor's speech was nonsense but he didn't dare. Had it not been for the pastor's stature, more than one parishioner would have described the sermon by making finger circles at their temple.

Kotryna and Elzbieta walked to Glauberman's for a fitting for Kotryna's wedding dress. Afterward, they went to see how the house her father was building had progressed.

Viktoras had been overseeing construction on the plot of land Aleksas had bought. Litvin, it turned out, was an even better builder than his reputation had led them to believe. He had the house framed and talked about a wooden roof, still a novelty in these parts where thatched roofs prevailed. Aleksas and Kotryna hoped that the outside would be finished before their wedding so they could move in, though the inside would be left unfinished, to be worked on whenever Aleksas could afford it.

These days it was good for Viktoras to stay busy with Kotryna's house, because thoughts of his grandson and Jonas were never far from his mind. At night, he traced their steps in his mind, going over the familiar routes, trying to imagine where they might be on their perilous journey, anxious for their safety. The caustic worry was wearing him out.

-Thirty-four-

All the way to the Prussian border, Jonas had burned to ask Petras about how things had gone the morning after he had punched Modestas yet each time he bit his tongue. How he had hated leaving Ada to put things right with her family, but he couldn't have refused her request to let her talk to her parents first. There would be plenty of time for him to talk to them later.

When he could stand it no longer, he took Petras aside and the two men walked companionably while Jonas asked him what happened after he left.

Petras snickered and shook his head, not saying anything for so long that Jonas began to squirm. Finally, Petras declared, "It was a scandal!"

Jonas's stomach tightened. "Tell me."

"My mother was apoplectic when she heard Modestas and Ada had argued and you had punched him," said Petras, trying to hide his smile.

"I'm sorry to have caused trouble," Jonas said, rubbing his lip with his knuckle.

"I'm not." Petras burst out laughing.

"You're not?" Jonas was surprised.

"Not at all. I know my mother and Julija worshiped the Bogdanskis family, but frankly, I never cared for them, and I never felt at ease with Modestas."

Jonas was grinning widely. "Is that so?"

"And if we're being honest," Petras continued, "I have to say I've dreaded the very thought of having such a prig for a brother-in-law." Petras chuckled.

Jonas laughed along. "Very happy to hear it." These words were a balm for his soul. "How is Ada? Has it upset her?"

"Well, if it has, she's hiding it well." Petras snorted a laugh. "Since Midsummer, she's been walking on air. Her feet haven't touched the ground."

Jonas swelled with feeling. "I hope I make her as happy as she deserves."

"No doubt you will, my friend," said Petras, patting Jonas's shoulder.

In the morning, they neared the German border. The sky was gray and heavy with clouds. Old Grigas, like Tomas, was seasoned in the art of crossing the border and knew every meter of the book runner's route. He had a couple of rubles held tightly in his fist for a bribe for the border guards in case they needed it.

Jonas and Petras, the new recruits, were nervous about every step. Jonas found his fellow book smugglers genial company, but thoughts of Ada were never far from his mind.

They stealthily slipped across the German border at night, during a rainstorm, one by one, carefully timing each crossing once the border guards had passed. Tomas was the first to cross, making sure it was safe. Old Grigas was last to cross without incident. All the men were sopping wet by the time they reached the house of Saulaitis, a Lithuanian who lived near Memel, in East Prussia. Saulaitis got his books in Tilsit from the printing shop of Otto von Mauderode in Tilsit and brought them back to his farm. He knew Grigas from his earlier book-smuggling trips and asked the old teacher to send his best regards to Father Jurkus, even though Saulaitis was Lutheran not Catholic. The two men talked long into the night after the others had gone to sleep.

In the morning, once they had eaten and filled their sacks with books and periodicals, they were eager to begin their trek home. Old Grigas slowed them all down, but they never complained because the elderly teacher was well respected. And, after all, the books were mostly for his secret school.

The next evening, they stopped at another Lithuanian farmer's cottage, more prosperous than any of theirs. After sleeping in the hay, the men were given food. When they thanked their host, the farmer told them that in the old days, his father used to bring the Lithuanian books across the border himself and hide them in a special hollowed tree, until another smuggler came from the Lithuanian side to retrieve and distribute them.

The men waited until evening fell before they took the route Jonas's father had proposed. He told them it was safer because, in his experience, the Russian border police hated those unholy wetlands. It would be easier to cross the border there.

It was a clear and balmy evening and the crickets were beginning their nightly serenade while the men sat in a hidden clearing sharing some bread and cheese. Grigas said they were very close to the marshes and would wait until it got darker. He asked his men what they knew of it.

Tomas said his grandfather claimed that devils lived there.

"True," said the old man, "but those little devils are slippery fellows full of tricks. They make you drop a fork or cause you to step on a frog or forget what you were saying. They make women drop their laundry into a puddle or they sour the milk."

"I think we had one in my pantry," laughed Petras, remembering the *domovoi*. He suddenly felt his skin crawl, telling how his mother had banished it to the marshes.

"Brave woman," said Grigas, slicing a piece of farmer's cheese and handing it to Petras.

Old Grigas took a bite of cheese and leaned back against a mossy pine tree. A west wind blew through the woods, the pines soughing   a mysterious but hushed music that seemed to calm them all. "We'll wait until dark and then we'll split up into twos before   we move on. We'll meet on the other side, at the place Father Jurkus designated. And while we wait I'll tell you a bit of history concerning the marshes." The old teacher couldn't resist an opportunity to impart his knowledge.

"Many years ago, much of Lithuania was covered with impenetrable marshes, which kept our country isolated." The men nodded, chewing on black bread and cheese while they listened.

"In the twelfth century, the Samogitian Lithuanians fought the Golden Horde of Mongolia, a fierce band of warriors on small, shaggy horses who had come up against these marshes." Old Grigas stopped a moment to collect his thoughts.

"Later, there was another threat when the pope granted indulgences to those who would join the Northern Crusade against the pagans of Lithuania. The Teutonic Knights came with the terrible cry of *Gott will es*, but the Lithuanians fought back fiercely. Having learned from the Mongolians, they covered their horse's hooves with sheepskin to hide their tracks. The men would retreat from the knights, who would follow them into the marshes with their heavy armor and huge horses, sinking in the bogs, while the small Samogitian horses escaped."

The men listened, imagining the fierce battles fought there. The old man saw he had captured their imaginations and so continued. "In June of 1812, when Napoleon's Grande Armée of 60,000 troops crossed the Nemunas River into Lithuania, thousands joined his army, for he promised them freedom from the Russian Empire. The Lithuanians warned Napoleon that their French horses would be useless in the marshes, but Napoleon didn't listen and lost many horses. As the French continued to Moscow, the Russians burned the city and their crops, leaving a scorched earth. Six months later the starved and frozen French army left Russia. Less than half the men returned to cross the Nemunas River on their way back home, shattering Lithuania's hopes for independence."

Petras said his grandfather often talked about Napoleon's march through Lithuania.

"I've heard him tell those stories many times." Old Grigas smiled and looked toward the marshes. "Your grandfather helped me bring many books through these very same woods."

"Is that right?" Petras was pleased to hear this.

"I'm glad his grandson is following in his footsteps." He was silent for a few moments, looking away as if remembering those days. "These same marshes were often used by those running from the tsar's conscription, and now we book runners are using it to hide from the Russian border police. Soon the night will hide and protect us."

The quiet evening and the damp smell of loamy earth soothed the men while they waited. Old Grigas gave them his last warning: "Before we start, I want to say that if anything happens and we become separated, I want each of you to make your way to the Valinskas manor. The Graf has promised to hide you safely or get you out of the country if need be. All right men, it's time."

The evening demanded courage and Jonas hoped he was up to it. He looked around warily and joined the others to begin the most perilous part of their trip. Walking ahead of the others, Jonas couldn't wait for this night to be over so he could return to Ada. He saw her sweet face before him as he walked.

The border was just ahead, and Lithuania on the other side. In parts of the border, three lines of guards had to be crossed, but next to the marshes there were fewer border police, and they were spread out at greater distances. First Grigas and Tomas had to make it across to the thicket. Then they'd wait for Tomas to give them the all clear to cross. They crouched down and moved slowly. A few more moments and the first two would be safely across.

Tomas made it into the cover of the thicket first, and then the old man followed. Jonas waited to hear the signal. It seemed to take forever, and he was getting nervous. He turned to look at Petras and whispered, "God keep us safe." He could see Petras was biting his lip, nervously looking in one direction and then the other. "What's keeping them?" he whispered.

They finally heard the signal, and Petras made sure the border guards were nowhere to be seen. He hesitated for a moment and then crossed.

Once he was across, Jonas followed him, but before he could join the others, he heard the border patrol calling in Russian for him to stop, firing a warning shot into the air. Jonas turned and saw four border patrolmen running toward him, while ahead Petras stood frozen like a rabbit, too afraid to move. For a brief moment Jonas was torn—should he try to save himself, or should he try to save Petras and risk both of them getting caught?

"Petras," he shouted to shock him out of his fear. "Run."

His hands up in surrender, Petras stood like a statue, his eyes round with fear.

The border police had stopped running and were aiming their guns. Jonas grabbed Petras by the arm, pulling him as they both burst into motion, dropping their sacks into the brush. Tomas and Grigas had disappeared like a mist. He heard gunfire and a bullet ricocheted off a nearby tree. Jonas made a violent dash for the thick forest up ahead and the wetlands just beyond them, holding onto Petras for dear life, his mind focused on getting to some cover. They ran between the trees, breath ragged, thwarting their pursuers. Jonas ran for all he was worth, though he could hardly see in the dark. Behind him, the border patrol yelled for them to stop or they'd shoot, but he decided to take his chances as they ducked behind each tree and bush.

"Go hide behind those trees," Jonas said, pushing Petras. "I'll try to make them follow me. Stay there until they're gone."

The men separated. With a great whooping, Jonas ran

in the other direction and the gunfire followed him. He turned quickly to look for Petras but could no longer see him. The border policemen were yelling in Russian, but he was so afraid he ran like a man possessed, turning from time to time to see if they were gaining on him. Bullets whizzed by. He kept running like the devil amid the gunfire while the yelling got fainter and fainter. He stopped momentarily to catch his ragged breath, praying they were following him rather than the old man or Petras. Tomas had simply disappeared.

Without warning, gunfire started again and he turned to look but couldn't see anyone. Again, he heard bullets ricocheting off the trees. Afraid of being caught, he ran blindly, sprinting, darting around like a trapped animal, until he could run no more. Trembling with fear, he dropped to his knees, barely able to breathe. When shots rang out, he forced himself up, stumbling forward hoping to find a place to hide.

Suddenly a bullet grazed his shoulder like a hot tong, and. Jonas fell. When he touched the wound, grinding his teeth at the pain, he felt blood on his hand. Winded and in pain, he got up and ran for his life, his every breath now ragged as if torn from his chest, his arm getting bloodier with each step. Fearing the border police would overtake him at any moment, he darted forward until his head spun, his shoulder burning. His knees were weak, and all he wanted was to lie down somewhere and go to sleep.

About to give up, Jonas saw a thin crescent moon shining over wetlands up ahead. If he could make it that far, he hoped the border patrol wouldn't follow. He took heart and plowed ahead into the tall reeds, veiled by a thin fog. He wiped the sweat from his face with his sleeve and tore his way past the cattails and sedges, wading through knee-deep water. Trudging through mud and grasses, he clawed his way up a mossy bank until he could no longer hear any gunfire. Fatigue overtook him so he could barely go on. Dropping down, he waited, crouching between the tall reeds. Exhausted and spent, he was sure they would soon find him. He would be like poor Norkus, thrown in prison or deported to Siberia, never to see his Ada again.

Soon he heard one of the border policemen shouting in Russian, and he shuddered in reaction. Before long others came, cursing as they splashed through the puddles. Jonas pushed down low, worried they might see him in the tangle of overgrown reeds, praying the night was dark enough to hide him. The voices were getting so close, they seemed right over his head as if they would trip over him any moment. Jonas didn't know whether to hold his breath or make a run for his life. Waves of nausea rolled over him, and he gulped hard, trying hard to calm his rising panic. He heard them tramping and splashing all around him, their voices right overhead. He gritted his teeth, preparing for capture.

"Where is the bastard? I know I shot him. How did you let him get away?" The voices overhead shouted.

"Damn them all! He got away, the stupid dog, but he's got to be here somewhere."

"Hey, what's that? I see a flicker of light. Is it him?" Jonas heard the men cursing each other. Then he heard their boots slosh to his left. "Where did he go?" The splashing stopped momentarily and Jonas wondered if they found one of the other men.

"There it is, men, after him. He must have a torch. Don't lose him this time." Again, Jonas heard the frenzied sloshing, only this time it seemed to go to the right.

"Look there's another fire over there." Gunfire rang out. "And there. Hell, they're all around us. *Chort!*" They let out a string of Russian curses, listing the many ways to insult the smugglers' mothers.

Jonas was baffled, wondering what the fires could mean.

"I'm getting out of this hell hole!" yelled one of the men. "To the devil with them all," yelled another.

To Jonas's surprise, he heard the voices retreating. Then it was quiet again. Perhaps they were hiding, just waiting for him to rise from the reeds. Was he trapped?

For a long time, he didn't move, waiting and listening, his legs going numb and his shoulder pulsing with pain. He shuddered to think how close he had come to death. Closing his eyes, he sincerely thanked God for his life. Everything had quieted, but he dared not get up yet, nor look for the others. When he finally had the courage to peek out, he managed to scare two crows out of a stunted bush, loudly protesting the intrusion, scaring his heart into wild pounding again. The border policemen were nowhere in sight.

Quietly, slowly, he crawled through the cattails, stopping to listen. He heard nothing but the wind blowing through the reeds. He had to go forward, though his shoulder was burning with pain and his legs felt like rubber. Hoping for a safe dry place to hide and examine his wound, he trudged on, stumbling through the undergrowth, keeping an ear cocked for the soldiers. Every noise made by the dry brush made him skittish. Like a wounded animal, he needed to find a safe burrow in which to rest. Ahead, he saw a dry hillock. On the far bank, he lifted himself and groaned with pain. He finally collapsed and lay there catching his breath. When he had recovered, he sat up and painfully took off his jacket. His shirt was soaked and his shoulder throbbed. Would he die in this God-forsaken marsh or be captured to die in Siberia? He remembered Viktoras's story about the book that saved his life. If only he had been so lucky!

The night turned cool and Jonas shivered, listening to the murmuring stream, the complaint of some night bird, the hum of the wind through the reeds, and the whispering of the dry brush. Though very tired, he tried to stay alert, worrying about his fellow contrabandists and wondering if anyone else had been shot. Alone and lost, he felt like the last person on earth. There was a dark music at night, sad and lonesome like the darkness. Overhead the heavens were so high above him it seemed as if they had forgotten him.

The only thing that gave him any solace was to think of Ada. Where was she this moment? Was she safely sleeping in her bed? Was she looking out the window at the same sliver of moon and thinking of him, wondering where he was? He could see her face in mind, her pale blue eyes. "Ada, my love, my life," he whispered. "Your name is dearer to me than all others. I say it like a prayer to comfort myself. I tell the water your name, I tell the sky I love you. Every bird I see, I call your name, every wind carries your scent. Ada, my happiness, do you hear me calling to you out here in the wilderness? I can't die like this. I have to get back but which way is home, Ada?"

The only sounds were the rustle of cattails and the endless repetitive croaking of frogs. Jonas looked at the stars and the distant moon. He couldn't move or think anymore. Rest was all his mind could grasp as sleep eventually overtook him.

When he woke in the early morning, mosquitoes had made a meal of him. He couldn't stop scratching. Like a ghost, he wandered the gray and desolate landscape with the empty sky above him. Not a human voice anywhere, only the ducks. He tried to find his way out but was afraid he might be heading further into the marshes where he'd be lost. Yet he had no choice but to go on.

Rats scurried by as he trudged on through sharp sedges in the greenish pools. All day he waded through the duckweed and mud full of mossy stumps, and when he reached a dry spot, he crawled through the tall grass, frightening ducks, which flew away in a panic. When night came, he watched the moon and repeated what his father often said. "Let us pray for those we love." His whispered prayers lulled him to sleep.

He was sleeping hidden in the marsh grasses the next morning when a loud noise woke him. His heart beat furiously, his senses awake and attuned to danger. He hoped it was one of his fellow contrabandists. When no one answered his signal, he feared the border police had returned. He listened carefully but heard nothing more. At the sound of loud honking, Jonas raised his head above the grasses, finding dozens of cranes rising overhead, flying gracefully into the new day. Something in Jonas's heart felt soothed by the sight of the birds gliding over him, filling him with hope, however briefly. He watched them become smaller as they flew toward what looked like woods in the distance. A mist was swirling around the marsh grass.

His shirt stuck to his back and the shoulder pain was harsh and insistent. Where could the others have gone? Were they all captured? With aching, trembling fingers, Jonas raised himself, trying to steady himself before he trudged on. His wet feet had shriveled in his boots, and he was afraid that if he didn't dry them soon, they'd rot right off. He stood slowly and looked around to get a better idea where he was. He saw voles and sparrows but no sign of his comrades. Finding a small, clear stream, he drank the cool water and washed his wound. It restored him to clarity for a moment.

He had lost all track of time. His only food had been some berries from a bush. Feeling sore from head to foot, he sat down to rest. Though the police had only managed to wound him rather than kill him, the marshes were now trying to finish the job. His shoulder was hot and tender, and he was starting to feel feverish. With night coming on, Jonas felt so alone. A strange noise caught his attention. Weak, dizzy, and disoriented, he blinked hard, trying to clear his wavering vision, when from afar he thought he heard the neighing of horses. Perhaps the border patrol had followed him into this marshland after all. He heard two horses approaching and so he crouched down. When they passed, he saw the riders were wearing French uniforms and riding elegant horses more fit for parades than marshes. He was amazed they had not broken a leg yet in this boggy place. One of the men toppled from his horse and disappeared. When Jonas turned to look for him, he spotted a uniform button and picked it up and put it in his pocket.

Stepping back behind the bush, he came upon something hard that made a clanging noise. Jonas reached down and saw it was a rusty shield. He could barely make out the cross of the Teutonic Knights. From the corner of his eye, he thought he saw a brown leathery hand rise from the water. Soon he could hear murmurs in German: *Gott will es*. Sweat beading on his forehead, he tried to crawl away. Horses seemed to be neighing all around him. Up ahead he saw a man dressed in bear furs and a Samogitian pointed helmet riding a small, shaggy horse whose hooves were covered in sheepskin to muffle their sound. The moon peeked out from behind a ragged cloud illuminating the watery places with a silver glow. A Mongolian face with slits for eyes began stalking the Samogitian, pulling an arrow from his quiver. Behind him, imps and demons were snickering, their goat horns gleaming in the moonlight.

"God help me," Jonas mumbled, frightened and confused. He rubbed his eyes, and everything vanished in an instant. He could hear horses running somewhere, or maybe they were wild boars. He must have been dreaming, or maybe it was the fever. When he looked around and saw no one, he found a place to rest, bone tired, wet, and weary. The stars were a familiar comfort to him as he looked up at the night sky, and for the first time in his life, Jonas wondered what it was like to die.

-Thirty-five-

Father Jurkus returned with news of trouble at the border. It quickly spread through the district and soon reached the village of Sapnai. People hid their contraband books and braced themselves for the inevitable searches by the gendarmes. Villagers prayed for the safe return of the book smugglers. It seemed everyone was talking of nothing else, shuddering to imagine their fate.

Ada went to church to talk to Father Jurkus. He could only tell her he had heard there had been trouble, but no news of the book smugglers. When she returned home to tell her grandfather, he paced the farmyard with Ada, each trying to console the other. "Where are they? What's happened?" Ada asked.

Her grandfather held her. "Don't worry, my little sparrow. Wait until we know more."

Ada went to the kitchen, where Kotryna was trying to soothe her sister's fears. Elzbieta sat at the table, her face cracked with emotion, her voice like rags tearing as she twisted her apron in her hands. "My boy has gone off to follow in his grandfather's footsteps and now what?" She looked out the window to the distant fields. "I'm terrified for him." Wiping away a tear with the back of her hand, Elzbieta realized these were things she had forbidden herself to say aloud until now. "I sit here not knowing if my boy was killed or arrested," she said, covering her face with her hands.

"We're all waiting for some news," said Ada, feeling sick at heart, wondering if Jonas was in jail, perhaps wounded. Her mother was right—not knowing was worse than knowing. It left the mind room to imagine the worst. She muffled her own sob and put her hand on her mother's shoulder, too emotional to say any more. She too had a sinking feeling something was terribly wrong.

Suddenly, her father ran into the kitchen with Viktoras close behind, slamming the door. He told the women to be strong and prepare themselves for questioning because the gendarmes were coming down the road toward their house.

"Lord Almighty!" screamed Elzbieta. "What do they want?" She ran to the window. "Is it about Petras?"

In the yard, their dog began to bark. When Stasys went to the window, he saw the small band of uniformed gendarmes riding into their farmyard. "They're here."

"What about the books?" Elzbieta was as pale as milk.

"Don't worry, they're well hidden," said Viktoras. He could start his own library with the number of books that had passed through his hands. They were under floorboards, behind walls in the barn, others in the root cellar—all cleverly hidden from view.

There was a loud knock on the door. "Jesus and Mary, help us!" Elzbieta stifled a sob with her sinewy hands.

"Get a hold of yourself," Viktoras snapped, steeling himself for this performance. His years of practice at lying as well as hiding things from the Russian authorities served him well.

Two men entered the cottage with pistols drawn, announcing their search for contraband, while others searched the farmyard. Ada looked out the window and saw three other men looking through the stable. Another man had stayed on his horse, ordering everyone out of the house. The farm was crawling with the gendarmes. Elzbieta held onto her husband's arm when she went outside. The others followed, and Ada recognized Captain Malenkov. Moving behind her parents, she tried to stay out of sight.

The two men inside the house were upturning furniture, throwing things across the room. In the stables, the horses neighed in fright. Elzbieta stood in the yard trying to comfort Julija, while Viktoras stood behind them quietly seething. Their neighbor stood at the fence nervously eyeing the tsar's men.

Elzbieta went to her husband. "We are finished," she whispered hoarsely, wringing her hands and repeating entreaties to the saints until Stasys told her to keep quiet before they all ended up in Siberia.

The gendarmes were poking bayonets into the hay piles. Pigs were squealing loudly at the intrusion. Margis was barking fiercely at the intruders until one of the irritated gendarmes kicked him in the ribs. "Shut up, you stupid beast," he said, threatening to kick him again. The dog let out a piercing whine and limped away.

Hot and irritated, the captain was hung over from the previous night at the tavern, where he had lost at cards. Today, his tongue felt glued to the roof of his mouth and his eyelids lined with grit. He didn't like this duty in the Northwest Provinces, a godforsaken backwater. Taking his handkerchief out of his pocket, he wiped his brow, asking Ada where he could get a drink of water. She pointed to the well.

The captain tried to place her, then smirked. "Ah yes. The girl with the apples in her apron and the mushrooms in her shawl." He sniffed loudly. "And where is the young man who was courting you that moonlit night, eh?" The captain's smile seemed like a sneer. "Is he here?" he asked, looking around.

"No," she could barely whisper, her throat constricted by fear.

He dismounted and walked to the well, taking a drink from the bucket with the ladle, then took off his hat and splashed the cool water on his face. "It's getting hot today," he said as if this were an ordinary social visit. He took a paper from his uniform pocket. "This report lists a son in your household, is that correct?"

"Yes," Stasys answered calmly.

"And where is he?" The captain scanned the farmyard.

"He's with relatives in Palanga," Stasys said coolly. "My wife's cousin is sick, so he went to bring them home remedies my wife prepared." Viktoras had prepared Stasys in advance.

Captain Malenkov watched him carefully, reading his face. "Was he one of the men at the border? Tell me right now and I might be more lenient with him than the others."

Stasys calmly said. "I already told you where he is, Captain."

From afar Ada saw one of the gendarmes swat a bee as he entered the root cellar and she held her breath, hoping the books were well hidden. Kotryna watched another man enter the granary. Through the open door she saw her wedding dress hanging on a nail. She saw him bend over to look at something as the dress fell to the floor. She watched him step on it and prayed the dress wasn't ruined. Her wedding was a week away.

Nikolai, the older man with drooping eyelids, stopped to smile at Julija. "I've never seen this one before." Julija could smell the alcohol on his breath, so she looked down at her feet trying to ignore him.

One of the gendarmes came over and took his friend by the arm. "Nikolai, leave the poor girl alone."

Nikolai ignored him and lifted Julija's chin. "Hm, how pretty you are." Squirming, Julija pulled away, making him angry. He came closer and was about to take her arm when Viktoras pushed the gendarme away.

"Don't touch her," he snapped, his eyes flashing. The words were barely out of his mouth when Nikolai hit him on the side of the head with his pistol. Julija screamed to see blood stream down her grandfather's temple as he slumped to the ground.

"Grandfather," Ada cried, running to him. She cradled his head in her lap while she tied his forehead with her scarf.

Julija stood frozen with fear as a dark red blossom of blood on the scarf grew.

Stasys was seething with controlled anger. He protested to the captain. "You come looking for God only knows what and you end up hurting an innocent man and frightening my wife and daughters."

The captain raked his beard with his fingers while looking him over. "And what's your name?"

"My name is Stasys Varnas." The effort it took to contain his anger was visible.

"Maybe you're one of these contrabandists, or even worse, some nihilist? If I were you I'd be quiet before we take you in for questioning," the captain said with menace.

Four gendarmes came out of the granary looking hot and irritated. "Nothing to report in any of the outbuildings, Captain." Ivan scratched his ear.

The irritated captain mounted his horse and looked once again at his paper. "All right men, mount up. We have other places to go. Let's get this over with. But make no mistake," he paused glaring at Stasys, "we will be back." The gendarmes mounted their horses and rode away, leaving the farm in shambles.

Once they were out of sight, Viktoras, ashen and hushed, held his injured head and muttered a litany of curses through clenched teeth.

Standing next to her father, Elzbieta collapsed in a heap.

-Thirty-six-

There were three days left until Kotryna's wedding, yet there was still much to do. Elzbieta was a whirlwind of preparations with her daughters pitching in. While happy for Kotryna, her thoughts were often elsewhere, plagued by worry for Petras as she waited for any shred of news. Ada helped but could not stop worrying about Jonas and the others.

Friends and relatives were invited to the wedding, as was the whole village. Stasys had made beer, the girls had decorated the tables with flowers, and Elzbieta busied herself with cooking and baking, while Kotryna went to town to pick up her mended and washed wedding dress. Glauberman, having noticed she had put on weight, had to let out the seams considerably.

The day of the wedding Kotryna proudly wore her white dress and a simple veil. Viktoras blessed her, saying how happy he was to see her a bride at last.

Two white butterflies danced around her head while Kotryna walked to the farm gate. "A person's soul often returns as a white butterfly," Viktoras said, wondering if it was the soul of his late wife returned to see her daughter's wedding. "Butterflies, birds, and souls come back to the place they were happy," he said almost to himself. "Bless you, my child. May your marriage be as happy as mine was to your mother, may she rest in peace." His voice choked. "How happy she would have been to see this day."

Viktoras was so worried about Petras and Jonas he could hardly concentrate on the wedding. Stasys joined him, but kept glancing out the window in expectation of seeing his son return. "What could be keeping Petras?" he finally blurted.

Viktoras shook his still-bandaged head. "It's been too long. Even Father Jurkus is worried."

"Let the damned Russians go back to their own country."

"You know the old curse," said Viktoras, frowning. "So far from God and so close to Russia."

In church, Kotryna and Aleksas exchanged their vows. It seemed as if they had never been apart, all those years of loneliness and heartbreak forgotten. Now they were joined in marriage and would walk through life together.

Viktoras smiled when he saw his daughter's face, so happy to be wed to Aleksas. After all of his meddling to keep them apart, he had finally rectified his mistakes and made her happy.

Father Jurkus said a few words after the ceremony. "This is truly a miracle for Sapnai to have two of its own return from foreign lands and find each other again, still in love as before. It warms the heart to see such abiding love."

In the back of the church, old gossips buzzed like a hive of agitated bees. "Why did Kotryna need to get married so quickly?" Vanda asked. "It must be because she's pregnant." Stasia said Kotryna was too old to have a child.

Weddings were a social affair for everyone to attend and comment on the size of the dowry and the handiwork of the bride, and to speculate on how the match would fare. They felt a sorrowful envy that one of their tribe was actually getting married at such an advanced age.

"It'll come to no good," said Vanda, scrutinizing the couple.

The resentful women wished the couple good fortune, but as the bride walked out of church, they craned their necks to see if her waist was expanding.

Afterward, when the family and a few friends returned to the farm to celebrate, Viktoras met the couple with the traditional blessing of bread and salt. The musicians played a waltz, and Elzbieta and her daughters brought out food while her husband set up a keg of beer on the long table outside.

Viktoras celebrated as best as he could, but his bandaged head ached, and his heart was filled with a bitter worry for his grandson and the other book smugglers. He saw that Elzbieta and Stasys were also weighed down by their concern for Petras, and Ada looked haunted by her fears.

Nevertheless, they carried on for Kotryna's sake, for Viktoras knew they couldn't postpone the wedding. There was a child coming to join the family.

Although Stasys thought he'd be relieved to finally be getting rid of Kotryna, he found himself feeling a bit sad, in spite of her imp and her constant hysteria that had driven him mad. He observed Aleksas with sympathy. The poor man may have been through a lot in the coal mines of Pennsylvania, but it was nothing compared to what was waiting for him with Kotryna. But when he looked at the happy couple, he had to admit Kotryna had settled down considerably once she and Aleksas became engaged. Shrugging, he smiled at the mystery of women.

As everyone gathered at the table, Viktoras toasted the couple. "I've been praying for this, and now my prayers have finally been answered." He raised his glass, his eyes filled with tears. Kotryna was so touched by her father's words that her own eyes filled, but Elzbieta begged her not to cry on her wedding day for it augured ill for the marriage.

Aleksas stood, raising his glass. "To my father-in-law who made this marriage possible for us. To his good heart and generosity. Long may he live." The toasts continued.

Viktoras toasted Aleksas's mother, who raised her glass, smiling, for she would soon be joining the newlyweds at their new house.

When the festivities were over, the wedding party moved to the newlyweds' home in order for the priest to bless it. Afterward, Viktoras proudly showed each unfinished room, with the smell of freshly sawed wood still hanging in the air. Their wedding bed had been carefully prepared and decorated with flowers. Kotryna's dowry chest stood by the window, her handiwork on display.

The soft, tender light of a late summer evening infused everything. Kotryna and Aleksas finally went to sleep on the wedding night they thought would never happen. The guests continued their merrymaking, declaring they never expected to see either Aleksas Simaitis or Kotryna Kulys back in their village, never mind married.

Jone Kreivenas raised a toast. "It's like Father Jurkus said. Miracles do still happen. Not just in the Bible but right here in our little village of Sapnai."

-Thirty-seven-

The gendarmes continued to search farms in the district. The following week, the Bartkus brothers were brought to town and interrogated, as were several other young men from the village. Despite the troubles, families needed to return to their farm work, but the villagers hung their heads low, trying to stay out of trouble. Speculation flew about with everyone wondering what really happened at the border. No one dared mention a name because tension and suspicion hung in the air.

It was the busy time of summer on the farm; the wheat had to be cut and potatoes planted, clover cut. Viktoras couldn't help with the work. Instead, he lay in bed with a terrible headache, worrying without cease for his grandson and Jonas.

Ada's head also swam with worry. Whatever she attempted, it was as if her hands didn't belong to her. "God help them," she mumbled prayers, tears always at the ready. She could hardly eat a mouthful at any meal, and her eyes were haunted.

At night, she quietly cried herself to sleep, only to be woken by terrible nightmares filled with gendarmes, prisons, and crashing furniture. One night, her mother heard her scream and came to sit with her the way she had when Ada was little.

She hugged her mother tightly. "Mama, I don't think I could bear it if something happened to them." Her mother tried to calm her, but she too was harrowed with worry.

After her mother left, Ada sat up in her bed and looked at the moon outside her window. "Where are you, Jonas?" she whispered. "Watch over him." As the moon slowly rose over the linden tree, she finally fell asleep.

In the morning, Ada's eyes popped open, and she was surprised to see the sun shining and her sisters' beds already empty. How could she have slept so long and soundly that she didn't hear anything this morning? It seemed she was just talking to the moon but a few moments ago.

Dressing quickly, she went out into the yard, where Julija was feeding the chickens and geese. "Mama said to let you sleep because you were up with nightmares." A white goose stretched its neck hissing at the dog, which barked fiercely in retaliation.

Ada went to the well, pulling the sweep that brought up the bucket, she drank the cold water and splashed her face.

On a bench nearby, her mother peeled apples into a pan and sliced them for apple pancakes. "I'm making these for you, Ada. I haven't seen you eat more than a bite or two lately, and I know how powerless you are to resist them."

Later that day, as the sun's last rays shone through the window. Ada stiffened when the dog barked and she ran to the window. "Thank God, it's the priest." Everyone breathed a sigh of relief when Ada opened the door. "May He be praised."

"Forever," mumbled the priest. The minute he was in the door, they rushed to question him about the young men and Grigas. "Where are they? What have you heard, Father?" Viktoras came out of his room to hear the news, his head still bandaged.

The priest looked worried. "We've tried to go to the border, but the patrols were everywhere searching for the escaped smugglers. My thinking is that if they're still searching, then it's good news. I only pray they don't find them."

Elzbieta ran to the priest. "What have you heard about Petras?" she asked, her face a mask of worry.

"Tomas has returned. He thinks Petras got away."

Elzbieta collapsed with relief. "Oh, thank God."

"But why hasn't he come home?" asked Stasys.

"Tomas said he got away, that's all I know," he said. The weary priest looked up. "It seems the Russians have decided to increase their vigilance. You know very well what that means. We have to be even more careful. I've suspended all book-running for now." Ada went to the priest, holding her breath. "What about Jonas, Father?" Her face twisted with apprehension, exchanging an anxious glance with her grandfather.

For a few moments, Father Jurkus said nothing, his anguished emotions obvious. Then he took her hand and quietly, slowly, told her what he knew. "Ada, my dear, I don't know how to tell you." He rubbed his tired eyes so as not to have to look at her. Then he took a long breath and said it softly, "I'm so sorry to be the bearer of such terrible news. Tomas said he saw Jonas running from the border police. He saw them shoot Jonas. I'm so sorry."

Ada blinked, but made no move, so shocked by the priest's words that she was unable to take them in.

Father Jurkus lowered his head, his face creased in concern. "Let us pray for Jonas and the others." He began and the family joined in.

Ada's eyes blurred until the room shrank around her as everything stopped. Blood roared in her ears, and a gray fog seemed to enter her, making a terrible trembling deep in her stomach, rising until she shuddered from head to foot. Shutting her eyes tight, she tried not to let this news sink in. *Jonas was shot.* The thought speared her like a lightning bolt. She felt as if she would shatter into a million pieces if she acknowledged his death. No, she simply couldn't face it.

311

Turning away, she shook her head, desperate to deny it. "No, no," she whispered, "I won't believe it until I see him." Burrowing deep inside herself, she could hardly speak, stunned by an ache so deep, it felt like an illness. She sat quietly in the corner, trembling from head to toe. When the priest took her hand, expressing his sorrow, Ada hardly heard him.

Viktoras looked at his granddaughter, his heart breaking to see how the news had shocked her to the core. He felt a bottomless guilt for having sent Petras and Jonas out to follow in his footsteps and face such danger. It was his fault those good young men were there in the first place. He felt his own culpability keenly.

"Listen to an old man, my dear Ada. He's probably hiding somewhere. Take it from an old book smuggler who's been in his shoes." She nodded, only half listening.

Suddenly, Ada felt as if she couldn't breathe in the room. Running outside, she gulped air, holding herself to keep from flying to pieces. She ran toward the fields until she was forced to stop, emptying her stomach on the bare earth. And then she ran farther until her breath was ragged, until she collapsed like an empty sack, calling his name. "Jonas, don't leave me," she whispered from her very soul to his. "Where are you?" she yelled to the empty sky like an accusation, a terrible fear rising at the thought he might be lying somewhere cold as the earth, forever silent and gone from her.

Dora came looking for her, afraid of what Ada might do in such a state. When she finally found her, she sat there, holding her sister silently until the two could return home. "Why, Dora?" Ada protested. "Wasn't it enough that I mourned all those years for Henrikas? Why does every man I love die?"

Dora shook her head and hugged her tightly.

Her mother met them at the door and gave Ada tea with brandy. "Ada, drink this, my dear, and go to bed."

But Ada heard her grandfather in the parlor asking the priest how the gendarmes knew that the men were crossing at that particular place. She went to hear the rest of the conversation.

Her grandfather was so angry he could hardly spit the words out. "Judge for yourself; there's a traitor among us. You know the gendarmes keep a large network of informers and agents. Someone must have known about Grigas's secret route, but how?"

Julija, who had not said a word the whole evening, now stepped out of the shadows of the room, her face a mask of pain and sorrow. Solemnly, she began to speak, "It was me, Grandfather." She stood stone still and pale. "This is all my fault." Her voice was so soft, he could hardly hear her.

"What are you saying?" asked her mother.

Julija couldn't look anyone in the eyes, her hands shielding her mouth, afraid of the words she was about to utter. She finally began to speak quietly, almost in a whisper. "I heard Petras talking about crossing the border at the marshes."

The priest frowned. "Did you tell anyone?" She nodded slightly, biting her lip.

"Who was it?" Viktoras shouted.

Taking a deep breath, she said, "Modestas Bogdanskis." Tears rolled down her cheeks at the mention of his name. "I'm so very sorry."

"How could you?" Ada gasped.

"Modestas? Would he betray us?" asked Stasys. "A crow won't take another crow's eyes out."

"We now see what kind of bird he is," Viktoras added angrily. "This crow is a filthy vulture."

Julija shook with shuddering sobs. "I'm so, so sorry," she repeated, falling into a heap of tears in her mother's lap.

Ada stared across the room at her sister, her heart dropping like a stone.

Too upset to speak, Viktoras went to his room. When he heard Jonas had been shot, it was almost the end of him.

Opening his old prayer book, he prayed fervently for Jonas and the others, unable to forgive himself. It broke his heart to see

Ada walking around as forlorn as an empty doll. She would never get over this.

Later that night, when Ada heard the night owl calling to her, a messenger from the other side of death, she put her pillow over her head to block its mournful cry. Had she finally found the love of her life, only to have him snatched away? And for what? To die for books. Suddenly, she hated every word that had ever been printed in those cursed books, and she hated every Russian gendarme with a passion that frightened her.

When the pitiless moon peeked in her window, she turned to the wall and bit her lip until she tasted blood—anything not to conjure Jonas's face or imagine his end. But it didn't prevent the grief from seeping into her bones. Yet if something had truly happened to Jonas, wouldn't she feel it in her very soul? She hung on to that irrational hope with every fiber of her being.

Unable to sleep, she put a shawl around her shoulders and went to the orchard to sit on the bench. Looking up at the night sky, she watched the vast Milky Way floating above her. It was then she saw a shooting star streaking across the sky. She knew it was a sign, but she wondered if that star was dying or being born.

-Thirty-eight-

Since the day Ada was told Jonas had been shot, she had not allowed herself to face it for then the pain became searing. She went about her daily chores, striving to keep busy so as not to think or feel, going through her days lost in a dark cloud. At night, in her dreams, she searched for Jonas in the woods. In the morning, though she didn't want to believe he was gone, it began to seep into her heart the way water seeps into rocky soil—little by little. But if it were true, then she was lost. What was life if she couldn't share it with Jonas? Then she would once again become what she had been a year ago—a sad, heartbroken old maid. Then the heartbreak had been Henrikas, now it was Jonas. Between fatigue, fear, and worry, Ada had reduced herself to such a state of misery, she was hardly able to eat or sleep. She roamed around the house, her sadness like a cape tucked around her.

Often, Julija would come to sit beside her, bringing a glass of milk or asking her if she could stay and help. Ada noticed how in this short time her sister had become so quiet and sober for such a young girl. Since the careless day when she had told Modestas of the border crossing, Julija had been crushed by guilt and remorse. Now, desperate for atonement, she worked tirelessly, doing many of Ada's chores along with her own. "Forgive me, please," she whispered. "It was all my fault."

"Hush, Julija," she said, stroking her sister's hand.

"I feel wretched, Ada." Julija looked up at her sister, her eyes spilling over with tears. "It's still hard to believe Modestas would betray them." Julija shook her head. "How could he, Ada?"

"I don't know," she said, feeling a bitter taste in her mouth at the mere mention of his name.

The next morning, Viktoras paced, smoking his pipe, absentmindedly rubbing his elbow. When he heard the dog bark, he ran to the window and was relieved to see Father Jurkus.

Ada was bringing water to the kitchen when she saw the priest. Dropping the buckets, she ran to meet him, hoping to see her brother returning. She was disappointed to see the priest was alone and steeled herself against any more bad news.

"I had to come again, for I have some important news. Gather your family, Ada." The priest looked so serious that her stomach dropped. Had Petras also been shot?

The family nervously gathered in the parlor. Viktoras came last, feeling wary. At once, the priest told them Petras was safe and unharmed. "Safely hidden in the care of Graf Valinskas, along with Tomas, so I came to ease your worries."

"Thank you, Lord," said Elzbieta, fanning her face with her apron. Viktoras was so relieved, he couldn't even speak. He had been wound tight like a ball of twine, worrying he had sent his only grandson to jail or worse. Now it felt like a huge boulder had rolled off his chest, but it left him so emotional that he held his fist to his mouth to keep from sobbing.

"Tomas showed up at the manor first, then Petras came," the priest explained. "I'm sorry to say they will have to stay at the manor because the gendarmes are still looking for the smugglers."

"Did Petras say any more about Jonas?" Ada asked hesitantly, hanging on the priest's every word.

He put his arm around her shoulder and said quietly, "Petras said that Jonas was a true hero who risked his own life to save him."

Ada blanched. "How?"

"Jonas diverted attention from Petras by running toward the swamp, where he was shot."

Upon hearing these details of her beloved's death, Ada felt ill. Sitting down at the table, her thin shoulders shook as she laid her head on her arms. Finally, she went to lie down.

The room was silent. Then Stasys asked, "When will they be able to come home?"

"I'm not sure. If the gendarmes know who was at the border, then we have to be careful. We can't let the men leave the manor for the foreseeable future." When he saw the shocked looks on the family's face, he added, "I know this is not what you wanted, but we can't risk them being jailed or worse. It may turn out we will have to smuggle them into Prussia with the other exiles."

"Life in exile!" Viktoras exclaimed, lowering his head into his hands. "I should have never sent them. This is my fault."

"Now not a word of this to anyone, please." The priest looked at Julija pointedly.

Sitting at the other end of the table, Julija burned with shame, knowing she would carry this shame to the end of her days.

Father Jurkus pulled a newspaper out. "Somehow the exile press obtained a copy of a letter to the tsar from Prince Sviatopolk-Mirski, the governor-general of Vilnius. He urges the tsar to repeal the Press ban." He looked at Viktoras's astonished face and then began to read aloud,

> *Prince Sviatopolk-Mirski reported to St. Petersburg that the Cyrillic script has not established itself among the Lithuanians and that, despite the government's efforts, illegal publications were spreading throughout the Northwest Territory.*
>
> *"The number of such publications kept increasing*

despite strict sanctions and persecution of the activists. The ban created a well-defined and organized opposition to Russian rule and culture—the opposite of its original intent."

"What do you make of this?" The priest asked. "Those in exile have asked us to distribute this widely."

Viktoras listened and nodded, his pipe between his teeth. "We've brought them to their knees, haven't we? Imagine thousands of book runners, and the Russians can't seem to stop them."

The priest added, "This book smuggling business has grown so that for every distributor or smuggler they catch, six more rise up to take their place." Father Jurkus turned to Viktoras. "Soon they'll have to give in completely."

The old man nodded. "We've waited such a long time for this."

Father Jurkus looked up from his newspaper. "But we've moved beyond book smuggling, my friends. A great many plans have been made while in exile. The best minds of our country have been forced to flee, but they have plans for a country free from Russia, for independence. We've organized a petition of the local government and a meeting of the local district to present a resolution to end the restrictions on language and press, demanding Lithuanian instruction in our schools, and books in the Latin alphabet. It was passed by our district and the petition was given to the local officials."

"Would Petras be able to come home then?" asked Stasys.

"We can only hope and pray." The priest said he had some other news to report. Their neighbor Duda recently stopped at Zimmerman's tavern and was happy to report it was filled with the tsar's men, and vodka was flowing like water.

Stasys bristled. "That's nothing new for Duda or the tsar's men."

"He said it was so crowded that Zimmerman had hired a

Gypsy band to play Russian songs. Many gendarmes were there singing along, telling stories of the fires and swarms of demons they saw in the marshes and how they wouldn't return there even if the tsar himself commanded them. Duda heard them say the smugglers could rot in the marshes as far as they were concerned because the men were sick and tired of this duty and wanted a few drinks at Zimmerman's tavern. Captain Malenkov has gone to St. Petersburg. Word has it he might be promoted."

"A tavern full of drunken Russians. A hell all its own, if you ask me," said Stasys.

The priest continued, "But Duda also reported that Captain Malenkov and Bogdanskis used to play cards at Zimmerman's, talking like old friends. Bogdanskis often lost at cards and owed the captain a small fortune that he couldn't possibly pay back. Duda overheard a conversation that Bogdanskis had been compromised. He became an informer for the gendarmes, sniffing around suspected book smugglers as a way to repay the debt."

"Why the scoundrel!" Stasys exclaimed.

"I knew it," said Viktoras.

"The traitor!" Julija spat the word out without blinking.

"Shouldn't he be punished?" asked Stasys.

"You know the proverb: 'A person with a bad name is already half-hanged,' said Father Jurkus. "Once word gets out about this, no one will have anything to do with the collaborator."

"But what of Old Grigas? Has no one heard anything?" Viktoras asked.

At the mention of the elderly teacher's name, everyone stopped talking. No one had said a word about the man, fearing the worst. Viktoras saw at once the priest was hiding something.

"Do you know what happened to him?"

The priest hesitated, looking down at his hands, clearly upset. "I'm afraid it's bad news," he finally said.

"What?" Viktoras braced himself.

"Grigas was captured at the border. He's in prison. I'm afraid Siberia is next."

Viktoras turned ashen. "He'll never survive there."

Father Jurkus blessed himself, saying a prayer aloud for the old teacher and the other men. For a long time after, the room was quiet. Thoughts of the old teacher filled everyone with sadness.

The following day, as news of Old Grigas spread, eight young men approached Father Jurkus asking to take the old man's place as book smugglers. Already many were on fire to follow his example. Instead of quashing the loyalty and pride in their country that was growing in Lithuania, his arrest only served to harden the resolve of those who dreamed of a free country—free to read in one's own language.

-Thirty-nine-

E
ventually, though Modestas's debt had been forgiven by the captain, he was still drawn back to the card tables. Unable to control his need, he left Mimi alone again and again. He dreamed of winning enough at cards to be able to live like the old days, but if that failed, he still had an ace in his pocket. He would propose to Mimi, who had been chasing him all summer. After a few more card games in which he lost once again, he decided he would ask for her hand that very night when he returned home.

He drank one shot and then another. It was then he noticed people still seemed to turn away whenever he came near. It galled him that when he tried to greet old family friends, they now shunned him. It seemed that word of his betrayal had gotten out even among the gentry.

Modestas overheard a conversation in which Zimmerman mentioned that Captain Malenkov was soon to return from Saint Petersburg, and he thought bitterly that at least the captain was someone who wouldn't turn his back to him. And then he smiled, relief washing over him remembering that his debt to the captain had been paid. At least he didn't lose their summer home to that man. And perhaps his luck would change at the card table.

Tonight, when his luck proved to be as bad as all the other nights, he went home drunk and could hardly walk, never mind make any attempt to propose to the young widow. Only this time Mimi didn't seem to mind as much as before.

With the end of August, the widows decided it was time to go home, thanking Neda Bogdanskis for her gracious hospitality and assuring her that, after all, the purpose of their trip was to help Vincentas regain his health. Now that he had fully recovered, it was time to return home. In private, the widows had decided they had had enough of the provinces—meaning also enough of Modestas. They chose to return to Vilnius and, more importantly, invited Helenka to join them for the season, a nugget of good news to placate the mother's old friend. Perhaps Helenka might be introduced to a man who could provide for them.

While Neda Bogdanskis, was pleased at the invitation offered to Helenka, she was devastated by Mimi's departure without an engagement to her son. She mourned the loss of her last hope for bettering her family's situation. With the rich widows' departure, she sensed a disaster in the making. Her son seemed to be more interested in card games than in saving the family from further ruin. Her anger boiled, wondering why Modestas had waited so long to capture Mimi's heart. He could have proposed to her months ago, but he was distracted by that Varnas farm girl for some reason. "He's just like his father," she murmured through clenched teeth.

The next evening, Captain Malenkov, who had returned from Saint Petersburg, met Modestas at the tavern. "How is that charming young widow who is so besotted with you?" the captain inquired.

322

"Fine," said Modestas. Not mentioning a word about the young widow's recent departure, he raised his glass of vodka and drank it down quickly, feeling the burn of it in his throat. With the summer ending, he dreaded the cold season to come, for there was no longer any way to escape to the city for the season. Modestas's new debts threatened his family, yet he was powerless to keep away from the card games, always chasing the illusive dream of winning. What else was there to do in such a backwater in the provinces? He simply couldn't stop himself.

-Forty-

I t was steaming hot in August, making Ada more irritable, as she waited for a good storm to clear the heavy air. Once the last rye was cut and the threshing finished, Ada didn't know what to do with herself anymore.

The cows were lowing, returning from pasture. Ada watched with sadness as the storks began their yearly long flight to the Nile Delta in Africa, leaving their giant empty nests. It was amazing to see those large birds flying with such grace over the rooftops of Sapnai. She wished she could fly away with them.

On this particular Sunday she had no heart to go to town and talk to neighbors after church. They would ask questions that would only upset her. Instead, she decided to stay home to care for the animals, something her grandfather often did. Today she volunteered to stay home, allowing him to go to church in Raudonava.

At church, Viktoras stood at the door, wiping his brow as he complained to Father Jurkus. "The heat is blistering today."

The priest pointed to the dark clouds gathering on the horizon. "But it looks like there's a good storm brewing and heading this way."

"Thank goodness," Viktoras said, going inside.

After Mass, as the neighbors gathered in the churchyard, the talk turned to Modestas, who seemed to be the topic of every conversation. "The Bogdanskis name is ruined," said Kreivenas. "The viper."

"Swine," Viktoras muttered, choking with rage. "To think we let him into our house to court Ada." Modestas's reputation was now firmly sealed, as people purposefully shunned the man and his family.

Graf Valinskas pulled Viktoras aside after church to ask if he could have a private word. "This weather is impossible," said the count, his face red from the heat. He knew Viktoras well from the days he used to smuggle books for him. The two men had much to talk about. The count took off his hat and mopped his brow with his handkerchief.

"How is Petras doing at the manor?" asked Viktoras.

"The men spend their days reading smuggled books and talking, playing cards, but they're young men, so they're bored and restless in that basement and very anxious to go home."

"I'm sure they are." Viktoras nodded, sadly, wondering when that day would come.

The count leaned over to say, "I've been waiting impatiently to tell you that I have some important news."

"What is it?"

Graf Valinskas took a deep breath and smiled. "Two days ago, Jonas Balandis showed up at my door."

Viktoras was stunned. "Alive?"

The count nodded, putting his handkerchief back in his pocket. "Yes, but severely injured by a gunshot wound. It only grazed him, but he's weak and completely exhausted by the ordeal."

"Thank God! But where has he been all this time?" Viktoras was both astonished and hugely relieved by this news.

"Apparently, he barely made it out of the marshes. It was by considerable luck that a local farmer found him semi-conscious in the woods and brought him home, but Jonas wanted to reach the safety of the manor. The good people there nursed him until he was strong enough to make the trip to the manor house. By the time he reached us, he looked half dead. I've had our doctor out to treat him, and he said the lad is strong. And certainly, the good company of your grandson and Tomas will help him recover."

"But what happened to him? Tell me everything." Viktoras wanted to know every detail. "Will he recover?"

"I'm sure with time and rest and good food," the count assured him. "You know how the young heal so much quicker than men our age."

"It's true," Viktoras said, thinking about how slowly the wound to his head had healed, leaving a scar. His head now often pounded, forcing him to lie down with a cold towel on his forehead.

The count added, "As for the rest of Jonas's story, you'll have to wait until he tells you himself."

"I'm so very happy and relieved," said Viktoras grinning widely as the good news began to seep in. "You see, my granddaughter is in love with Jonas, and it's my fondest wish that they marry one day."

"She couldn't find a better man than the son of Jeronimas Balandis, another hero like you."

Viktoras smiled at the compliment. "Jonas is a good man indeed." he concurred. "She was being wooed by Bogdanskis for a while, and it turned out the cad was circling around her in order to report back to Captain Malenkov about any book-smuggling activities he might find in Sapnai."

"The traitor," Graf Valinskas bristled. "I heard all about it." The count looked around the churchyard.

Viktoras heard the roll of distant thunder. The wind was picking up, and leaves swirled in the churchyard.

"We need a good storm to clear this terrible heat, and we could certainly use the rain," said Viktoras. He heartily thanked the count for the wonderful news. "Please give Jonas our heartfelt wishes for a quick recovery and tell my grandson we miss him dearly."

"I will be happy to pass on your good wishes."

"Thank you again for sheltering these good men. Now I must go home to tell my granddaughter the good news."

The two men shook hands and parted.

The lightning was streaking through the bank of dark clouds that followed Viktoras home. He quickly set about looking for Ada and found her in the kitchen mashing a pot of boiled potatoes. A pan of pork cracklings sizzled nearby.

"Smells good," he said. "But please, put that down for a minute. I have such extraordinary news for you and it can't wait another second." He tried to suppress his glee but couldn't.

Ada turned to look at her grandfather, who was grinning. She put the pot on the table and wiped her hands on her apron, still watching his face, which seemed to light up the room. "What is it?" she asked, wary of any more news, since it had been so catastrophically bad of late.

Viktoras took her hands in his and laughed a quiet and infectious laugh. She smiled wondering what he was up to. "It's Jonas, my dear. It's Jonas," he repeated, smiling widely. "I came to tell you that, by God, it's a miracle—he's alive."

"What?" She felt faint like a bit of dandelion fluff about to blow away. She grabbed the table to steady herself.

"He's alive!" Viktoras beamed. "I just heard the news from Graf Valinskas himself. He's at the manor with Petras and Tomas." He laughed again.

Ada was stunned. "Alive? Is it true?"

"Yes, my dear," he nodded and cleared his throat. "I'm

afraid he's injured, but don't worry because the doctor tending him says he'll heal."

Ada closed her eyes, so grateful for this stunning news that she stumbled to her grandfather, burying her face in his chest.

Now all the uncried tears, the tears she had held at bay for so long, poured out of her, relief washing over her like a new baptism—reborn to life—a life with Jonas in it. Her grandfather held her, his own tears running down the furrows of his cheeks.

When she recovered, Ada had so many questions about Jonas. Viktoras told her what little he had learned from the count. Then she asked if she could see Jonas.

"Absolutely not!" said Viktoras. "The count was adamant that we are not to visit or even send a letter. "You'd only lead the gendarmes right to our men."

Shaken, Ada couldn't stand still. There was such happiness boiling in her. She needed to be alone. The wind was billowing the curtains. The air was charged and the sky was getting darker.

"I need to go to the woods, Grandfather."

"Go, my dear, but be careful. There's a storm brewing outside."

Ada didn't care. She loved a good storm and always ran to meet it. She took off her apron and took the cracklings off the stove. Grabbing her woolen shawl, she ran out the door. The wind whipped around wildly, stirring the earth and all that grew on it.

It filled her with fierce energy to see the dark clouds gathering while she ran to the woods, the only place that soothed her.

"Jonas is alive!" she yelled into the howling winds, hardly able to believe it. "He's at the manor with Petras!" she told the pine trees above her.

Running to her favorite clearing, she lay down on the grass and covered her eyes with her arms, overflowing with joy, hardly knowing how to contain it. She remembered being in this same clearing where she had mourned Henrikas and later for Jonas. Closing her eyes, she listened to the wind sough through the trees above her. "Jonas, you're alive," she whispered, as if he could hear her. When pine needles dropped on her face, she opened her eyes and saw high above two old pine trees, their branches wildly dancing above her.

She thanked God, the saints and the sky and trees above her for this miracle of bringing Jonas to safety. And then she prayed for his recovery and continued safety.

After a while, Ada brushed herself off and started back home, flooded with relief. All was made right again—Modestas was gone from her life forever, she was not going to be a spinster like her Teta Kotryna, haunted by a *domovoi*, and Jonas Balandis, whom she loved with all her heart, was safely recovering at the manor.

A blinding streak of lightning blazed through the sky and thunder rolled in as a rainstorm finally broke over Sapnai, heavy drops falling while Ada walked back home, soaked to the bone, but happier than she could ever remember, wondering how long before she could see her beloved again.

That night Viktoras was filled with gratitude, humming a remembered song from childhood, humming quietly so that Death wouldn't hear him and stop his song for all time. When he finished one song, he softly began to hum another. Lithuanians were a singing people, but what was the song that would keep Death away, he wondered. Turning over in his bed, he began to hum the lullaby his mother used to sing to him. It soothed him and finally put him to sleep with a smile.

-Forty-one-

Christmas came and went for the Varnas family, but it
seemed strange to celebrate without Petras. It pained them
not to be able to see him or even write him a letter.
Ada yearned to see Jonas, but she had steeled herself, knowing it
wasn't possible. The only news they got was the occasional word
by way of the count, who would pass the information to the priest.

Before the New Year, word came from the neighbors that
Petrike had given birth to a daughter. Ada decided to bake some
raisin buns to take to her. She walked down the snow-packed
road holding a bowl covered with a clean towel. Her felt boots
slipped on the packed snow, until she reached Gadeikis's cottage.
Surprised, Petrike welcomed her, grateful for the buns, making tea
to go with them. They talked amiably, and Ada asked to see the
baby. Petrike brought her to see her tiny daughter, pink-cheeked
with large blue eyes, swaddled in her wooden cradle.

"My little beauty looks just like her mother, doesn't she?"
asked Gadeikis, kissing his wife. Both parents were proudly
smiling, as they leaned over the child.

Ada saw how happy the baby had made them both. Glancing
around the parlor, she noticed the many changes Petrike had

made. The parlor was clean and well ordered, with everything in its place, comfortable and homey. Ada was happy for them. She remembered feeling sorry for Petrike when she had gotten engaged to a widower, expecting her friend to be miserable in this arranged marriage. But now she realized how wrong she had been. They were happy together, but even more so with the birth of their daughter. Perhaps one day, Ada would have a home like this with Jonas. But when would he be able to leave the manor? Perhaps Jonas would be forced to go to America since he could face prison or Siberia if he remained in Lithuania. And her brother would probably have to join him.

The wind whistled over the snow while Ada gazed at the frost flowers glazing the window, sighing heavily and feeling sad. It was such a heavy price to pay for books.

In February of 1904, as if anyone needed any more bad news, word reached Sapnai of a surprise Japanese attack on Port Arthur. War had broken out between Russia and Japan. The villagers gathered in Viktoras's parlor to discuss the war, each household worried about their young men. By the end of the month, both Bartkus brothers had been conscripted into the Russian army.

Viktoras was so angry he took off his cap and threw it down on the floor. "Why do our young men have to fight Russia's war? What do we care about Japan? Now they're being sent to the other side of the world to fight for the tsar. For what? This isn't Lithuania's war."

"The only good part is that the Russians will turn their attention to the Far East instead of smuggled books," said Stasys. Balys added, "At least the conscription isn't as bad as the old days, when young men were conscripted for twenty-five years. It was like a life sentence."

Kreivenas shook his head. "Don't worry, the Russians will

win this war before another month passes. Tsar Nicholas called the Japanese *makaki*, little monkeys, saying this attack was like a flea bite on the back of the Russian bear." He laughed. "He's expecting a quick victory. After all, how can the small island of Japan possibly win against the mighty Russian Empire?"

"Oh, I hope so," said Dora. But nothing could ease her anxiety for her beloved Jurgis, already fighting the Japanese.

"They say the Japanese army has new guns that shoot continuously without stopping," Stasys said, frowning.

Balys waved his arm dismissively. "What can they do against the tsar's whole Pacific fleet?"

"I heard that the Japanese used submarines with torpedoes to attack the Russian ships in Port Arthur," said Stasys. "They've badly damaged the Tsesarevich and the Retvizan, Russia's heaviest battleships."

"Well, they didn't sink them, did they?" protested Balys.

Stasys sighed in exasperation. "Everything is changing, including warfare. Didn't you hear the pastor last Sunday? Father Kazlauskas spoke of progress and industry. Soon machines will do our work for us."

Set in his ways, Balys wasn't convinced. "You still have to milk a cow and plow a field. I'll believe those miracles of progress when I see them with my own eyes."

Kreivenas laughed and added, "The only progress I've seen is at Zimmerman's tavern. He finally put up a new sign in front and added a pretty new Gypsy singer, who, I might add, was sitting on Bogdanskis's lap the last time I was there, may his tongue rot in his traitor's mouth."

"Did you hear Bogdanskis is losing at the card table again?" Balys asked. "The family will be beggared soon. His mother is rarely seen since the Ciginskas family left."

Kreivenas raised his eyebrows. "I imagine that once the rich widow got wind of Bogdanskis's gambling, she decided to leave, not wanting to risk her own fortune with a gambler."

"Where does it leave Modestas?" asked Balys.

"A penniless drunk," said Julija. "And a villain to everyone in the district. The widow probably couldn't wait to get away from that Judas," she said, a hot core of anger rising. "I will hate that snake for as long as I live."

Two weeks later, Kotryna, stood at the mirror combing her auburn hair when the baby kicked her in the ribs. Rubbing her huge stomach, she smiled, whispering, "Soon, little one, soon."

Restless and impatient, she waddled slowly, wanting to bake, or clean the house. She didn't know herself what she wanted. Their newly built home was still unfinished, but the kitchen was completed and the beds were in the rooms. They had added a room for Aleksas's mother. Kotryna took pride in having her own place.

When Kotryna went to her father's farm to collect the eggs her sister had promised her, Elzbieta's eyes widened at the sight of her sister's enormous stomach. Elzbieta gathered the eggs instead and then sat down for a visit. Since Kotryna moved into her new house, her sister found she had missed her.

Their father came into the kitchen with a dripping honeycomb, giving Kotryna a piece to taste.

"Your honey is the best, Papa. You take care of those bees like they're your own children." When Kotryna stood to wash her hands, a sharp stab of pain took her breath away. Her stomach tightened so that she had to hold onto a chair to catch her breath.

"What is it?" asked Elzbieta, coming to her sister's aid.

"Is it time?" asked her concerned father.

The pain slowly subsided until Kotryna's breath came easily again. "I'm not sure." She waited a moment until it passed and then went to look for her egg basket. She took no more than four steps when she doubled over in pain again, grabbing her sister's arm. "Help me," she croaked.

Her sister helped her to the bed just as another contraction overtook her. Elzbieta called Ada to go tell Aleksas that the baby was coming. Then she summoned Julija to get Vanda, the midwife. "Quickly!" Elzbieta continued to bark out orders in every direction—to boil water and get clean sheets. By the time Ada returned with Aleksas and his mother, Kotryna's yelps had turned into howls and her water had broken.

"Oh my God, is she going to live?" Aleksas was terrified.

"Don't worry, I've sent for the midwife," said Elzbieta.

While Ada stood at the door with her grandfather, waiting for Vanda to arrive, she reminded him of the stories he used to tell of *laumes*, the fates. According to her grandfather, the *laumes* were fairies with bird's feet who came to every birth, whispering to one another at the window: "Hundreds are born, hundreds die. What will this one's fate be?" Another *laume* would ask, "Is the birth at morning, noon or night?"

"Yes, I remember," he said. "Those children born in the morning would be hard working, diligent, and productive, and those born at noon would be happy, full of life and wealthy, while those born at night would be lazy, poor, and good for nothing." He paced nervously. "I wonder when my grandchild will arrive. The day is quickly passing."

By the time the midwife arrived, Kotryna was in hard labor. Vanda ushered the villagers through the two most important doors in their lives—the door of birth and the door of death. She came inside like the high priestess of birthing, ceremoniously washing her hands. Once she donned her special apron and rolled up her sleeves, she examined Kotryna, declaring, "You're very lucky, because tonight is the new moon."

Bathed in sweat, Kotryna rolled her eyes at the mention of the moon, wondering what this daft woman was blathering about. The midwife noticed her doubt and admonished her. "The moon is a most important influence on childbirth. Everything starts well in the young face of the moon. A child born tonight will be beautiful, while one born in a full moon will be ugly but strong and healthy."

Kotryna hardly listened as a new wave of pain overtook her, making her howl, her face red with strain. The labor continued long into the night. Finally, Vanda saw the head crown, and a tiny boy slipped into the world. Cutting the cord, she washed and swaddled him and brought him to his mother.

"He has Aleksas's nose and Papa's eyes," said Kotryna, thoroughly exhausted.

Aleksas ran into the room. When he saw his wife holding his precious son, he was overwhelmed with relief and love, kissing them both, gulping down his rising tears. After all his years away, working like a mole in the black tunnels of the earth, when he thought he would never see his home or Kotryna again, this was another true miracle.

Aleksas sat next to Kotryna while she put the child to her breast. They were like the holy family as they sat with their heads together, watching the sleepy child.

Soon the rest of the family was invited to see the newborn. "What will you name him?" her father asked.

"There's only one name for this child." She smiled. "He'll be christened Viktoras, of course. After you, Papa." She kissed the baby's head and blessed him.

The next day, the women in the village came like a flock of *laumes* to see the child, cooing and fussing over the handsome baby. As was customary, no one told the mother how beautiful the child was, because no one wanted to tempt fate. They smiled and patted the child, clucking like hens, giving Kotryna advice on child rearing, especially since he had been born at night. Even though he was a beautiful child, Kotryna would have to make sure not to spoil him, or he was sure to be lazy.

Vanda elbowed Stasia. The old maids counted the months since Kotryna's wedding on their fingers to see if they added up to nine. Stasia's eyebrows rose when she only counted to eight.

-Forty-two-

By late May, the lilacs were again blooming profusely, perfuming the air, enchanting the villagers walking to church to take in the warm day to admire the pink peonies growing along the fences. It was wonderful to have the sun warm one's skin after a long winter spent indoors.

At the end of Mass, Father Jurkus asked his parishioners not to leave yet as he had a few important announcements. First, he confirmed their worst fears. "The Russo-Japanese war is not going well. The humiliating setbacks of the war last year shocked the Russian Empire, and now there is tremendous unrest with people clamoring for change."

Father Jurkus had the congregation's full attention. "And there's been some other momentous news that has reached me recently, something remarkable and totally unexpected."

Everyone was sitting on the edge of their pews waiting for the news. Whispers were starting as people began to speculate what this momentous news might be. The priest raised his hands, trying to quell the speculation. He cleared his throat and his smile widened.

"I received a letter from Tilsit from our compatriots across the border informing me that what we've been praying for and fighting for, waiting forty years for, finally happened. Though due to the war or the fact that the Russians didn't announce this change, few have received the news as yet." Father Jurkus, now grinning widely, stopped for dramatic effect, waiting until his parishioners were impatiently leaning forward.

"It took a long time, but we've finally won our battle!" declared the priest with satisfaction. "After forty dark years, a long black night for us all, we have regained the blessed light at last." Father Jurkus raised his arms. "This is a great day for Lithuania—the press ban has finally been revoked by Tsar Nicholas II." He shook his head and laughed, as if he could hardly believe it himself.

At first the parishioners were shocked, but when the news sunk in, they cheered, wild with surprise and joy.

Then he pulled out the letter, no longer afraid of gendarmes listening nearby. "Press is allowed!" he shouted with a note of triumph, holding up a letter. The congregation stood, clapping and shouting their praise enthusiastically, having forgotten they were in church.

"This was translated from the Russian," shouted the priest. as he read:

> *The Press Ban and the resistance it aroused among the people mobilized and developed Lithuanian forces. It created a tremendous feeling of national injustice and the sense of being singled out for especially harsh treatment.*
>
> *Eventually, the complete failure of Cyrillic reform, the inability to contain contraband in illegal Lithuanian publications, and the rising tide of public protest, showed that the Press ban was unworkable. Russia's Council of Ministers concluded that there was no practical way to halt the flow of the illegal press into Lithuania. The Ministry of*

Education concluded the Cyrillic reform was a failure and that the Press ban should be repealed.

The priest looked up at his parishioners, overcome with delight.

"Take your books out of their hiding places. We've lost enough books to mold and mildew." He laughed from the pulpit. "Enough books have been confiscated and burned. Now it's time to build bookshelves so your children and their children can read their language without fear. It's time to plan starting schools in our language again, and newspapers we can read."

Father Jurkus pulled out a banner he had made. It read: "Lithuania's battle for a free press is won!" And best of all it was written in the ordinary Lithuanian alphabet, not the hated Cyrillic one that no one understood. The priest went to nail it to the door of the church. The parishioners crowded out of the church as they followed him.

A cheer went up again. The jubilation among his parishioners was overwhelming. Some women dabbed their eyes as they left the church, while other women hugged and kissed the cheeks of men they hardly knew, out of sheer delight. Outside, girls started a circle dance, and even some older folks joined in. Songs and hoots echoed through the churchyard. Balys played his concertina while the parishioners sang along.

It was truly a momentous day for the little corner of the world known as the Northwest Territory in Russia but called Lithuania by those who lived there. Father Jurkus was carried on the shoulders of the young men who had worked as book smugglers. When they spotted Viktoras Kulys, they lifted him as well, cheering and laughing from the sheer joy and relief. Viktoras was so jubilant he thought his heart would burst. He told the young book smugglers how grateful he was to have lived long enough to have seen such a day. "I'm so relieved you young men no longer have to face death, prison, or Siberia, and for that, I rejoice."

339

Finally, when he could break away, Father Jurkus walked over to Viktoras. "This means we'll be able to get Old Grigas out of prison, and we'll try to get Norkus released from Siberia."

Viktoras added, "Grigas is dancing a jig in prison today." Father Jurkus was elated. "This Press ban has strengthened our national pride. Like the biblical battle of David against Goliath, we may not have toppled the giant yet, but we will keep throwing rocks until we do." There was a note of triumph in his voice.

Ada came over to congratulate her grandfather, "I can hardly believe it," she said, hugging him fiercely, her eyes brimming with happy tears.

"God bless us all, such happy news!" Viktoras crowed. "This was something I was beginning to think would never happen in my lifetime."

The Graf's carriage pulled up to the church and out jumped Jonas, Tomas, and Petras. Jonas ran to Ada from behind, pulling at her sleeve so that she when she turned quickly to see who it was, her mouth dropped open. Seeing Jonas alive and well, she laughed in delight as he grabbed her and swung her around.

"We just heard the news from the Graf's friends and couldn't wait another moment to come here and share in the celebration," Jonas said breathlessly. "Oh, Ada, my love, how I've missed you." He kissed her tenderly.

"Oh, Jonas, the day when Father Jurkus came to tell us you were shot was the worst day of my life." Tears sprung up.

"Shh, my Ada," he whispered holding her close, unable to say anything but her name.

Ada wiped her tears. "I never want to let you go again."

He held her close and whispered in her ear. "Ada, would you do me the honor of becoming my wife?"

Her tears flowed. "Yes, my love, yes."

"First, I must ask your father's permission and talk to my parents. But Ada, I can't wait any longer to be with you always."

Petras ran over to join the couple and his sister hugged him warmly. "Ada, you better marry this poor fellow. He's been talking about nothing but you since the day we left for Prussia. In fact, you were the first person he asked for when he came to the manor." He smiled happily. "I'm afraid there's no cure."

Ada was so overcome with feeling, she couldn't utter a sensible word.

Soon, Viktoras came over, so happy to see the young men back among those who loved them. "Congratulations, my heroes!" He embraced each one warmly, too choked with emotion to say more.

Jonas turned to Viktoras, putting his hand on his heart and bowing his head in respect. "This is all the work of giants like you and my father."

"Oh no, this took the courage of countless men and women. And don't forget you almost gave your life to this cause," said Viktoras gravely.

Petras added, "Imagine, newspapers in our own language!"

"And proper Lithuanian schools!" Ada smiled. "We won't have to hide anymore."

"I'm so grateful you men prevailed." Viktoras put his arm around his grandson. Petras looked at his grandfather and then at Jonas. "Well, what shall we former book runners do now with our free time?"

Jonas laughed and pressed Ada closer. "I'm sure we'll think of something."

Over his grandfather's shoulder, Petras spotted the gendarmes spilling out of Zimmerman's tavern across the square. They came out to check on the commotion in the churchyard. It was unusual to see such a display of merriment after Mass. Usually, small groups of people greeted relatives and neighbors, quietly talking until they went home.

When Viktoras turned to see the gendarmes, he cursed, "May the devil take them all and keep them in a warm place."

341

Then Jonas saw Modestas Bogdanskis follow the gendarmes out of the tavern, and he bristled. Jonas had not seen the man since the morning of their fight after the Midsummer festival. But here he was, the traitor, standing next to the occupying forces—a perfect tableau for all that was wrong with this country.

Julija came to her brother's side. "Look at the Judas, so pleased with himself," she hissed. "Strutting like some Polish count with his friends in the gendarmerie."

Turning, Ada caught Modestas's eye as he watched them. She quickly looked away, feeling sick to her stomach, angry that she had ever said a civil word to such a man. It was because of him that Jonas had almost died.

Julija shuddered. "I can hardly look at him without shame at how I foolishly trusted him." The two girls quickened their steps to get away, while Jonas stood still, his jaw muscles tensing. Without consulting each other, both Jonas and Petras set out across the square, heading for the tavern.

When Modestas saw the men heading his way, he quickly turned and slithered away behind Zimmerman's door. Jonas and Petras started to run in pursuit. They leaped over the steps, past the gathered gendarmes, into the tavern. When they couldn't find Modestas, they asked the owner where he went.

"I don't know," said Zimmerman, loudly, but he tipped his head in the direction of the back door. Jonas and Petras found Modestas crouched behind some empty beer barrels.

Jonas faced the cowering man. "Testing out the beer, Bogdanskis? We meet again. Only this time we are no longer rivals for Ada's hand."

Raising his trembling hand, Modestas protested. "I n-never wanted to marry her," he said, stuttering.

"Oh, so you were just playing with her affections. Like a true gentleman." Jonas's face twisted into a sneer.

"No, no, I didn't mean it like that!" Modestas protested loudly.

"God help her, who knows what might have happened to her in your hands." Jonas came closer.

"Don't hurt me," Modestas cowered. "I didn't do anything."

"This is not so much for me but for Old Grigas, one of the best men I've ever known!" Jonas pulled him up roughly by his new jacket and punched him in the face so hard that a fine spray of blood spattered his white shirt. "And this one is for Ada." Modestas shielded his face in a vain attempt to protect himself, but Jonas punched him in the stomach. Modestas fell against the barrels, knocking two over.

Then Petras came over and a laid into him. "For the good men you hurt." Afterward, he shook his sore fist. "Don't ever let me see you near our farm again, do you hear me?"

Modestas nodded, cringing on the ground, curled up like a bloody caterpillar.

-Forty-three-

The war with Japan continued to rage, but to Viktoras, it seemed far away. All morning he had busied himself with measuring and sawing boards. When Ada asked him what he was doing, he answered, "What Father Jurkus told us to do. I'm making a bookcase so I can proudly display the books I've brought across the border. It's time my favorite books came out of the root cellar and the granary, don't you think?" He returned to hammering nails into the boards.

"What a wonderful idea," said Ada. "It'll be strange to have them out for everyone to see after all the years of hiding them. But how wonderful to pick one up whenever we like."

Shortly past four, when he had finished the bookcase, he and Ada carried the books out of the granary. They carefully placed each precious book on the shelves, then went to get the ones out of the root cellar, the barn, and even in one of the beehives, which held no bees or honey.

When the books were put away on their shelves, the whole family came to admire them, looking over the many titles and remarking which ones were their favorites. There was Donelaitis, Baranauskas, Valancius, Maironis, Žemaite and others. To Ada it seemed that the books were all singing soundlessly in their bookcase.

"A proud moment," said Petras, moved by the collection. "It's still hard to believe we won't be arrested for doing this."

"May God bless those who died or were sent to Siberia for their books." Viktoras crossed himself. "May this be a testament to their hard work and sacrifice."

In the village of Kelmai, Jonas had returned home to his parents, who cried from relief and later celebrated with the whole village, gathered in the parlor for his homecoming. The next morning, Jonas asked for his parent's blessing to marry Ada.

"But what about the Mockus girl I had chosen for you?" his mother asked, looking slightly aggrieved.

"Mama, I was never going to marry her."

"But you should listen to your mother," she complained. Domicele liked to think she ruled her little roost.

Jeronimas stepped in. "Domicele, not another word, you hear me?" He said it slowly but with a force that made his wife take notice. "Our Jonas has returned to us, by the grace of God, and I'll be damned if anything gets in the way of our only son marrying the girl he loves." He faced his wife, his bushy eyebrows knitted together in anger. "You agree, don't you?"

Domicele pursed her lips in a show of petulance, but knew she was outweighed by her husband, who often deferred to her in the small everyday affairs, but never in the things that really mattered.

The next day, Jonas came to Sapnai wearing his best clothes, having bathed in the sauna until he shone and whipped himself with birch branches until his skin tingled. It was time to ask for Ada's hand. Nervous and tongue-tied, he could barely utter a greeting. He stood at the door smiling until Stasys asked him in.

Jonas entered and asked if they could speak privately. "I've come to ask for Ada's hand in marriage." Stasys had always thought Jonas was a man after his own heart. He knew how much his daughter loved him, for she had talked of nothing else.

Looking into Jonas's eager eyes, he said, "Yes, I entrust my daughter to you." He shook Jonas's hand warmly. "Be a good husband to her."

"I will do my best." Jonas hadn't realized he had been holding his breath. Now he breathed freely, full of grateful relief. They went back inside, and Jonas glanced over at Ada, who smiled. She wanted to hug him, to be alone with him, but she waited patiently. Across the room, they kissed each other with their eyes.

Her father continued, "Shall we plan the wedding for October, after all the busy work of summer is finished and the harvest is behind us, so there's time to celebrate?" Jonas nodded, though October seemed like a hundred years from May. Shaking his hand, Stasys said, "Well, it's settled then."

Beaming, Viktoras announced to his family that Ada and Jonas were officially engaged. Ada couldn't stop smiling at Jonas, beaming with love. Jonas finally relaxed, relieved the ordeal went well. Everyone congratulated the new couple.

The celebration went on with neighbors stopping by to congratulate the couple. Even Petrike came with her baby on her hip, her husband wishing them many happy years together. Ada recalled the day she learned Petrike was getting married and how, at the time, it seemed as if she was the last old maid in the village. Now here she was about to marry her true love. When Elena came to congratulate her, Ada's heart broke for her friend who was now truly the last old maid in the village.

That evening, before Jonas left, Ada walked him to his cart. He kissed her over and over, looking into her eyes. "My dearest, soon you'll be my very own, my wife." He said it with such emotion, that Ada felt a tremble run through her. "I can hardly stand to leave you even for a short time." He kissed her again.

Five months later, in the first week of October, two weeks before Ada's wedding, the banns had been read and the food was being prepared. Stasys had been making beer throughout the autumn. But he often stopped and thought how the house would seem so empty without his eldest daughter.

The war was still raging on the other side of the world. The Japanese had proved to be a much stronger enemy than the tsar had expected. After four battleships and two cruisers of the Pacific Fleet were sunk in August, the tsar had ordered the Baltic fleet to assist. It turned out the Russian bear was feeble compared to the mighty Japanese flea.

Zigmas Bartkus returned from the war after being wounded by shrapnel. He now limped, using a cane for support, but he came back changed in other ways, as well. The carefree, amusing young man who had left for war no longer resembled the angry, sullen one who returned from it. Once Dora saw Zigmas, she was distressed for him and more troubled than ever about his brother, Jurgis, wondering what horrors he was facing in Japan. Whenever his sporadic, hurriedly written letters arrived, she suspected he scrupulously left out any bad news.

Dora felt such a stab of pity for his invalided brother that she began to visit Zigmas to talk to him about the war. It had taken a bad turn for Russia and the casualties were high. Making matters worse, Petras had been called up and would be leaving after Christmas. Viktoras was sick at heart over the prospect of his grandson fighting Russia's war. Word had it the cities were restive, and one could feel dissent and revolution in the air.

Zigmas came over to sit with Petras, talking seriously about the latest news from the front. He lit a cigarette and frowned. "Our tsar's revered Trans-Siberian Railway is a nightmare for supplying our troops. Whose bright idea was it to build a railroad with only a single track so that you have to wait until it crosses half the world and back before the troops get their supplies?" He shook his head.

"Now there's progress for you," snickered Petras. "How will they manage?"

"They obviously won't," said Zigmas with a scornful huff. He put his hand on his friend's shoulder. "Take care of yourself, Petras. None of us understands more than a smattering of Russian, and that makes it harder. Remember Admiral Togo is a fearsome opponent. Be careful, this is not our war, so keep your head low and come back to us, and bring my brother with you."

Julija, who had noticed the two men huddled in conversation, said to Elena, "What a shame so many young men have been taken to war."

When Petras stood, Elena called him over. "When will you be going to war?"

"I leave right after Christmas," said Petras.

Elena smiled her most encouraging smile. "I'll miss you when you go."

"I'll miss you too, Elena," Petras replied, smiling. "Will you write to me?"

"Of course." Elena nodded.

Julija raised her eyebrows, surprised to see her brother flirting with Elena Kreivenas. This was a new development she hadn't seen coming. Elena had practically been a fourth sister to him. She glanced at Ada to see if she noticed the new couple, but Ada was lost in a cloud of love anytime Jonas was near. The two had their heads together, holding hands and smiling foolishly, whispering in each other's ears. Julija smiled, hoping she would someday fall in love in that same way.

The next day, the household boiled with preparations for Ada's wedding. It would start the third week of October and continue for three days, the last day at the groom's farm in Kelmai. Kotryna gave Ada her wedding dress and had Glauberman alter it to fit her, adding lace at the bodice and sleeves. When Ada tried it on, she was speechless to see herself a bride in the full-length mirror.

Kotryna put her veil on Ada, pronouncing her the most beautiful bride in Sapnai.

A week later, Aleksas and Kotryna waited until the rain stopped and then walked from their new home to help with the wedding preparations. Kotryna had already made the wedding cake at her house, but now there was other food to prepare. She bustled into the house, her son balanced on her hip. Her son, started to cry and fuss. Screeching and straining to get out of his mother's grip, the child wanted to crawl around on the floor to join the others. He was strong-willed and had his grandfather's smile. Elzbieta picked the boy up and bounced him on her knee. "Our little Viktoras is beginning to look a little like Petras."

"And our Petras has become quite a handsome man. Young women seem to follow him with their eyes," Kotryna teased. "But I see Elena has her eye on him."

Ada turned to her grandfather. "Where would Teta Kotryna and I be if you hadn't written your letters?"

Kotryna laughed. "It turns out Papa is the best matchmaker in the district."

Ada took her grandfather's hand and pressed it to her cheek. "If I thank you each day until I die, it would never be enough."

Viktoras nodded, touched by her gesture. "I'm so very happy for you both."

-Forty-four-

The weather got colder with each passing October day. One evening, Viktoras sat at the kitchen table playing cards with Stasys. He moved his chair closer to the warm stove, slapping at the discard pile, getting close to accumulating all the cards in the deck. Across the table, Stasys hummed an old tune.

Petras came in to tell his grandfather about the threshing machine he had seen in another village. He warmed his hands by the stove, explaining the infernal new machine. Viktoras listened, nodding along, simply happy to be in his company. When Petras finished, Stasys asked his son to help him fix the cowshed door.

Left alone, Viktoras lit his pipe and spent a quiet hour smoking. He was at peace, knowing he had kept Death away long enough to see Kotryna back home and not only reunited with Aleksas but married with a child named after him. And preparations for Ada's wedding were being enthusiastically organized by the overworked Elzbieta. Not only had his dearest wishes come true, he had received far more than he could have imagined. His grandson and Jonas had returned from their perilous smuggling trip, and the press ban had been lifted. And who knew, perhaps he would live long enough to see a great grandson from

Ada. Crossing himself, he gave thanks for such abundant gifts.

But it is often said, don't praise the day until you've seen the night. In the evening, when the family was getting ready for bed, a fierce wind began to blow. He thought he heard an owl hooting in the old linden tree. Uneasy about the omen, he looked outside but saw nothing.

When night fell, he went to bed, his head aching, as it now often did, and it seemed so cold tonight that even his thick eiderdown couldn't keep him warm. As the frigid wind blew outside his window, he felt a great longing for his past. He found he couldn't sleep, thinking more about his wife, who would have loved to have seen Kotryna's child. Tonight, he yearned for her. With her by his side, life had been full and happy, and tonight, though he had counted his blessings all evening, he still felt her absence like a terrible ache.

There was the ordinary world of the living and there was the mysterious world of the dead, those ancestor spirits who were said to watch over their progeny. One day he would join them to watch over his daughters and grandchildren. He sighed again, for it seemed suddenly that life was so short and there was much less of it to look forward to than to look back on.

He stared out the window at the sliver of moon that curved into the clouds. Tonight, for some reason, he also thought of his father's rich baritone when he used to sing the national anthem with emotion, so long forbidden by the Russians.

Long into the night, after he had finally drifted off to sleep, he woke when he heard Death approach him again. Like an old soldier, he had resisted and struggled against her for so long, it was wearing him out. Bone-weary, he finally fell asleep again. He soon slipped back into his favorite dream. It was harvest time, and the sun was the color of butter, the shocks of rye were piled high, and his young daughters were romping nearby. Balys was playing his concertina. He took his wife's hand and pulled her close.

She was soft and yielding and smelled like bread. They would dance and kick up some dust.

"Viktoras," he heard Death whisper intimately in his ear. Not wholly awake, it sounded like his beloved wife was calling to him.

"Come, dearest, let's have another dance," Death said in the voice of his wife.

Viktoras smiled in his sleep.

She asked softly, "Do you hear the music playing? Here is my hand. It's time," she insisted.

Viktoras lifted his hand to hers. "I'm coming, sweetheart." In his half-dream, he saw her, young, beautiful, and full of love for him. "Wait for me," he whispered, and only then did he realize with such sorrow and regret that it was not his wife but Death who was calling him, and this time he had answered her call. His heart raced wildly, pounding in his temples. He opened his eyes and looked out the small window at the crescent moon smiling down on him, so benevolent in the dark night, while Death plucked his soul like a flower. Viktoras sighed and closed his eyes for the last time, giving up his spirit after a long and hard-fought battle with Death, who, as everyone knows, was bound to win, sooner or later.

Viktoras's soul rose from his body and went outside in search of his favorite whittling knife, lost three days ago. His soul hadn't yet realized he was dead. There was a rosy glow rising behind the pine forest; a new day was beginning. He stooped to look under his bench in the orchard where the bees in his beehives still slumbered inside. He looked here and there but didn't find it. He watched the sky fill with glorious color, and suddenly he stood there feeling odd, a bit disoriented, and weightless. He held onto the apple tree and sat down on the weathered bench, feeling unutterably sad. He sat there for a long time until he saw a woman coming through the orchard wearing a clean apron and a white scarf. She was young and beautiful, and it lifted his spirits to watch her as she walked toward him.

When she came closer, she called his name, "Viktoras," she whispered intimately. "I've been waiting for you. Come, my husband." She held her soft hands out to him, and he reached up and took them in his own strong young hands.

"Emilija, my beloved," he whispered. "I've missed you so."

She smiled warmly. "I've been with you all along."

"You have?" He was elated to hear this.

"Of course, my love."

He put his arm around her waist as they walked together through the orchard, watching as the bees came out to greet them.

-Forty-five-

In the frigid morning, Ada entered the kitchen with a heavy heart, wondering what was wrong with her. Why did she wake feeling sad?

"How did you sleep?" her father asked.

"Not well," said Ada, realizing she felt like crying for no reason.

Her mother stirred a pot of gruel. "Is your grandfather up yet?" she asked.

"I haven't seen him," said Ada. "Maybe he's feeling too cold to get up this morning. I'll bring him some hot tea." When the kettle was ready, Ada stirred honey into the cup of tea and went to wake her grandfather. She knocked softly and then entered his room to find him still sleeping. The floorboards creaked a bit when Ada crept in, gently shaking his shoulder.

"Good morning, Grandfather," she said. "I have some tea to warm you," The moment she saw her grandfather's face, she could hardly breathe. In shock, she dropped the cup when she saw his eyes were open, gazing at something eternal, something no longer of this earth.

"Oh no...dear God, no." She fell to her knees, burying her

head in his bedding. Sobbing, she called to him, "Oh Grandfather," she moaned, realizing she had woken half-expecting this.

Viktoras Kulys of Sapnai was dead. Though he had been seriously ill with the grippe and had painted his own coffin and made amends to his friends in the village, in the end, no one was really prepared for his death. He had lived so long and so well, outliving two wives and most of his friends, that it seemed he would surely live forever. And even though Viktoras had been dutifully preparing for his demise, when Death finally plucked his gentle soul from his body, his family, and indeed the whole village of Sapnai, were stunned and bereft.

Before long, Old Vanda arrived, chasing the family out of the bedroom while she prepared Viktoras. At sixty-three, she liked best to prepare the men who might have been her suitors in the villages around Sapnai. Since they hadn't married her, she was glad to bury them. No grudge, however, was borne against Viktoras Kulys because he was too old to have been her suitor. Respectfully, she washed and carefully anointed him with rosewater and dressed him in his best brown wool suit.

In the kitchen, Ada shined her grandfather's Sunday shoes, tears mixing with polish, but she couldn't stop herself. It broke her heart to look at her grandfather's good shoes that he would now wear only to his grave.

"Don't cry, Ada," said Vanda. "The soul might not leave with so much crying." She nodded in her all-knowing way. "The dead don't go far, you know. Why, the very air we breathe is full of spirits, both good and evil." She blew her nose gravely as if emphasizing an important point.

"*Na*, Vanda, aren't you exaggerating?" Stasys asked.

Vanda didn't like to be questioned in these matters. "Don't believe me, but Elzbieta knows I'm telling the truth. Look how she's covered the mirrors so we wouldn't see any dead souls."

Ada looked around the room. The mirror was covered with a tablecloth and the clock had been stopped, as was the custom.

When Vanda was finished, she pointed the foot of the painted coffin toward the door so Viktoras's soul would know the way out when the time came. "The poor soul is lost for three days after it dies. It stays around, close to those he loved, trying to understand what happened."

"We watched him paint that coffin and now he lies in it," said Elzbieta, wiping her tears.

"Death is hard," the old maid continued, "like birth is hard. Both are a struggle. If you look at the face of a newborn, you see he doesn't know where on earth he's landed. It's just as confusing to die. That's why we don't leave them alone for three days. We sit with the deceased, we sing, eat and drink with him, and someone keeps him company at night so he won't be lonely. After a while, the poor soul slowly realizes what has happened. When he hears the church bells tolling for his funeral, he says good-bye to his family and home and then he can rest in peace."

Vanda put four large candles around the coffin, and the family invited their neighbors to come pay their respects.

Balys was the first to come. He stood and toasted his dead friend as was the custom, by pouring a drop of beer off the porch, toasting the earth as well. "Sweet earth, you made us, you fed us, you carried us, and, in the end, you will hide us."

Soon, the rest of the village came when they heard the news. One by one, they came with books and laid them in his painted coffin, thanking him. Gadeikis came with Petrike who paid her respects and then sat down with her toddler on her lap,while her husband stood to put his prayer book in the coffin. "He risked his life so the rest of us could read in our own language and teach it to our children."

The next day, Jonas and his family came to pay their respects despite the light snow flurries. Jeronimas was deeply moved to see his old friend in his coffin. "My sincerest condolences to the Varnas family." He took off his hat and bowed deeply to Elzbieta. Then, he stood at the painted coffin a long time, his trembling lips moving in silent conversation with his old friend and fellow book runner. Jonas slipped Viktoras's favorite poetry book—the one with the bullet—into the coffin. "So you can tell a good story about it in heaven," he whispered.

Father Jurkus toasted his old friend with great feeling: "I always told Viktoras Kulys, may he rest in peace, he would be the last book smuggler in Lithuania, and it turns out I was right. He was one of the unsung heroes of Lithuania who kept our literature and history alive, quietly and humbly." The priest shook his head sadly. "You meet a man like Viktoras only once in a lifetime."

Zigmas came last and went straight to Dora, handing her the official letter he received. She could see his face was tense with held emotion. Immediately, she blanched, afraid to open it. She could already read the bad news on Zigmas's face, and tears ran down her face as she opened it. The letter informed the Bartkus family that their son Jurgis had been killed in action and was buried in Manchuria.

Dora broke down completely. Zigmas held her tenderly. "Buried so far from home—on the other side of the world," she said. "I can't bear to think of him there."

He frowned. "I shouldn't have left him alone," he said solemnly. "We should have gone to America instead of the war."

Dora listened, weeping softly, her heart broken. She had loved Jurgis for so long. All of her hopes for a future seemed to have died with him.

Now the family and all of Sapnai had two deaths to mourn, but only one to bury.

On each of the three nights of the wake, different members of the family took turns keeping a vigil through the night, making sure the four candles were always lit while they kept the old man's soul company in the loneliness of his death. On the third night, it was Ada's turn. She sat by the window, watching the trembling candles cast moving shadows over the room, while her beloved grandfather lay in his coffin.

The parlor was drafty, so she pulled her woolen shawls tightly around her while the flickering light of the candles played over the features of her grandfather, making it look as if his face was moving, as if he wanted to say something. As if he were about to wake from a restful sleep to tell her a dream.

The night was getting colder so she put another log on the fire, and it squealed the way logs sometimes do. "Saints preserve us," she whispered. There was something her grandfather used to say—that no matter how dark the night, the cock still crowed, and the sun always returned.

A tear ran down her cheek when she went to sit by the window etched in frost ferns. Everything was quiet now, all the voices still, and the animals sleeping. The dark night hid everything until the light returned. The night came so that people, birds, and animals could sleep, and even the dead rested after a long life just the way each living thing rested after a long day. Then the souls of the departed whispered in your ear to guide you.

For a long time, she stared at the starry night, awed by the mysteries of life and death. Where was her grandfather now? The house already seemed empty without him. It soothed her to think he watched over her. After all, he was still a part of the family, only he was with the dead members of the family while she was with the living.

At last the black night gave up its darkness to the light. Beyond the birch woods, a rosy glow was visible. Morning was here. Soon the whole family would be up preparing for grandfather's funeral and burial. Across the room sat the bookshelves he had built, filled with books they had all read over and over, now proudly displayed in the light of day.

At breakfast, Ada's mother informed her that her wedding to Jonas would have to be postponed for the customary year of mourning. "We'll have to wait until next year, my dear."

Ada sighed. "Of course." It broke her heart to wait a whole

long year before she could be Jonas's wife. She had already waited so long.

The church bells rang, and soon the neighbors gathered to take Viktoras on his last journey to St. George's church. A solemn procession walked behind the coffin, singing the somber hymns as white puffs of breath escaped every open mouth. Povilaitis carried his wooden statue of the Worrier with the roof that Viktoras had requested, to be placed at his grave. The fields were lonely and lifeless, dusted with snow. Only Viktoras's coffin bloomed with color, a vivid tableau of his life as he and his bride stood at the altar, Napoleon marched through Vilnius, and the serfs were freed. His whole life was laid out for his family and friends to contemplate.

The wind was picking up, and a few snowflakes slanted toward the east. This was the season when the world had no colors, when everything was gray, thought Ada. Animals slept in their lairs, the stork's nest was empty, the flowers were waiting to be reborn, and the river was a long ribbon of ice. Even the fish were sleeping, quietly dreaming of dragonflies hovering over gurgling water. Summer was when birds and fish and flies all danced their wild dances for a short season. For those few months they lived vividly, reproduced, and then were stilled once again—like all who lived.

At the church, Jonas joined the pallbearers when they carried the painted coffin inside. The stained-glass windows cast a weak glow in the winter light. At the Requiem Mass, Father Jurkus was visibly moved to eulogize his fellow book smuggler, speaking of him in mythic terms. "Today we accompanied my good friend, Viktoras Kulys, to his final resting place. We'll see him off to the next world. And I'll say this—we won't find another as dedicated as he was, nor as brave or honest. He gave his whole life to our country."

Afterward, a grim procession of mourners followed Viktoras in his brightly painted coffin to his final resting place. Father

Jurkus said the prayers, his cassock flapping in the wind, as they finally began to lower it into the ground.

"The 'Owl' is gone. Little earth, cradle him gently," said Jeronimas Balandis, tossing a handful of earth.

"Dear Earth, you won't find a braver heart than this one in your bosom," said Jonas.

"Sleep well, dear grandfather," Ada said. She went to Jonas, finding comfort in the circle of his arms. He held her close without speaking while each mourner bid their farewells to Viktoras Kulys, the only man in Sapnai to have a painted coffin so beautiful that it seemed a shame to cover it with dirt. The coffin was buried, but the legend of it continued to live on the tongues of the locals who often told the story of how Viktoras vividly painted his own coffin.

In the evening, the whole village celebrated Viktoras's life, drinking, telling tales, remembering his jokes, and drinking his cherry wine. In years to come, Viktoras's name would be mentioned with reverence and respect. And both his and Jonas's heroic escape from the border police into the wetlands would often be retold to the next generation as they sat at the hearth.

Later, everyone went home but Balys who had had one too many toasts. Lately, he reflected, too many of his old friends had died and while he would miss each one dearly, there was something about a funeral that made him want to celebrate the fact that it was not his time yet, that he was, by some miracle, still alive! He curled up on the bench by the stove where it was warm, and no one disturbed him.

Outside, the snow-dusted yard gleamed silver. Ada left the overheated room to look up at the velvet night, where winking stars danced quietly in their orbits. The spill of stars above her seemed endless. She scanned the mysterious night sky above her, wondering if one of those winking stars was the soul of her dear grandfather. How she missed him already. Silent tears rolled down her cheeks. She felt so alone without her protector, her hero,

361

her friend. How was she going to live without him? Her sadness had seeped into her very bones.

"Thank you for all your gifts—the many books, the work of smuggling them and teaching with them. All of those things shaped me. And thank you for bringing Teta Kotryna home. Suddenly our family has grown. But most of all thank you for sending me Jonas."

The starry night blanketed everything on the farm. Only the cottage was lit.

Before long, Jonas came out to look for her. "There you are, my love." He held her face while a tear ran down her cheek. He wiped it with his finger and then wrapped his arms around her. "Why, you're shivering. Come inside to warm up, my little sparrow," he said tenderly.

She nodded, smiling at the endearment her grandfather had always used for her.

Above the rooftops, the quiet stars kept the gentle night company. Ada gazed at the twinkling sky above and saw the rising moon climbing over the treetops.

"Look," she said to Jonas, pointing to the crescent moon. They craned their necks to see the moon standing guard over the sleeping earth, full of secrets. "It's Grandfather's smiling moon." She so missed that good man. He was up there somewhere, and that thought made her smile for the first time in days.

"His work is done," she said softly, putting her head on Jonas's shoulder. Together they gazed at the genial moon so far above them in the cold and clear night, smiling down at the never-ending antics of the humans below, watching with gentle amusement as one night followed another in a quiet and forgotten corner of the world called Sapnai.

-Afterword-

On December 23, 1904, the first issue of *Vilnius News* appeared in Lithuanian. Other newspapers and books soon followed. After the ban was lifted, all proceedings against the book smugglers were dropped.

The intellectuals finally returned from exile, urging radical reform, the boycott of Russian schools and the return of Lithuanian schools. In January 1905, on "Bloody Sunday," revolution broke out in the Russian Empire. In May Admiral Togo sank 22 Russian vessels. Not a single Japanese warship was lost. By September, the Treaty of Portsmouth was signed, ending the Russo-Japanese War. In December 1905, the Grand Assembly in Vilnius was attended by 2,000 delegates from all corners of Lithuania. The Assembly demanded Home Rule with a capital in Vilnius and schools in their own language.

Lithuania went on to fight for Russia in World War I, and in 1918 declared its independence, forming a volunteer army to fight the Russians, the German Bermontians, and, finally, the Polish Army. My father, Feliksas Putrius, was one of those brave volunteers. He was captured by the Poles, escaped prison of war camp, and walked back home from Poland.

After a few decades of independence, World War II broke out, and Lithuania suffered under three murderous occupations—first the Soviets, then the Nazis. Lithuania's Jewish population faced genocide and was tragically decimated under the Nazi regime. It was followed by another crushing takeover by the Soviets. Many thousands were deported to Siberia. It was during this last occupation that my parents fled to escape genocide at the hands of the Soviets.

Even after the war ended, Lithuanian partisans continued their valiant resistance to Soviet oppression for years.

After fifty years of calamitous Soviet occupation, cut off from the rest of the world, Lithuania once again declared its independence on March 11, 1990. The government declared that all former book smugglers would receive a pension. March 16th is now celebrated as a day to commemorate book smugglers.

In 2004, on the 100-year anniversary of the press ban's end, UNESCO declared it would be considered "The Year of the Lithuanian Language and Book," noting that book smuggling was a unique cultural phenomenon not found elsewhere in the world.

Today, in Kaunas there is a statue dedicated to "The Unknown Book Smuggler."

-Acknowledgments-

This book was born in the stories my father told of his father, a book smuggler. I owe so much to my entire family for reading drafts of this novel and weighing in with advice and support. And a huge thanks to my writing groups who have been meeting faithfully every two weeks, as they sat in a circle listening to stories. There is something in that ritual that feels ancient and sacred to me.

I will be forever grateful to Jonas Balys for sending me his books on Lithuanian folklore and customs, written in Germany and America. In the late 1980's as I began this novel, information on Lithuania was not easily available online. Instead I read many Lithuanian history books, including, "Forty Years of Darkness" by Juozas Vaišnora.

Deepest thanks to Violeta Kelertas, who read and reread offering valuable suggestions. Special thanks to Aušra Kubilius, Maria Ercilla and Kristina Boving, for their generous and valuable imput. Many thanks to Lois Smith, my editor, and to Odeta Braženienė for her beautiful paper cut art which graces the cover, and to Anna Serota for the map and Max Serota for copy editing.

There were many others who helped and for anyone I may have inadvertently overlooked, I humbly apologize.

And finally, I'm grateful to my late husband, Algis Keblinskas, who read every version of this book but the last.